IF WISHES WERE EARLS

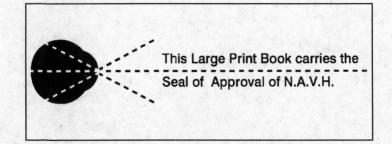

This Large Print Book carries the
Seal of Approval of N.A.V.H.

IF WISHES WERE EARLS

ELIZABETH BOYLE

THORNDIKE PRESS
A part of Gale, Cengage Learning

GALE
CENGAGE Learning·

Farmington Hills, Mich • San Francisco • New York • Waterville, Maine
Meriden, Conn • Mason, Ohio • Chicago

GALE
CENGAGE Learning·

LIBRARY OF CONGRESS CATALOGING-IN-PUBLICATION DATA

Boyle, Elizabeth.
    If wishes were Earls / by Elizabeth Boyle. — Large print edition.
        pages ; cm. — (Rhymes with love) (Thorndike Press large print romance)
    ISBN 978-1-4104-6998-4 (hardcover) — ISBN 1-4104-6998-0 (hardcover)
    1. Aristocracy (Social class)—England—Fiction. 2. Large type books. I. Title.
    PS3552.O923I35 2014
    813'.54—dc23   2014008399

Published in 2014 by arrangement with Avon, an imprint of HarperCollins Publishers

Printed in the United States of America
1 2 3 4 5 6 7 18 17 16 15 14

To Tiffani A. Storck,
and all the young women like her who
dream of jobs in writing and publishing.
Believe me: work hard, study, and
never stop daydreaming.
This one can come true. I know.

PROLOGUE

It is but one night, my truest, my dearest, Miss Darby, but it is all I need to carry you into the starry heavens of pleasure. I promise you this, come with me and from this evening forth you shall reign forever as the Queen of my Heart.

Prince Sanjit to Miss Darby
from Miss Darby's Reckless Bargain

The Masquerade Ball, Owle Park
August 1810
"Oh, there you are, Harry. I'm almost afraid to ask what the devil you are doing —"

Miss Harriet Hathaway looked up from her quiet spot on the patio to find the Earl of Roxley standing in the open doorway.

Some hero! Oh, he might look like Lancelot, what with his elbow-length chain mail glittering in the light, his dark blue surcote and the leather breastplate trimmed with gold that seemed to accent both his height and breadth, but he'd taken his bloody time showing up to rescue her. It had been hard enough slipping out so that only he noticed.

And even then it had taken him a good half hour to come find her.

"Oh, Roxley is that you?" she feigned. "I hardly recognized you."

"Wish I could say the same about you," he said, his brow furrowed as he examined her from head to toe. "I've been sent by my aunt, oh, Queen of the Nile, to determine if you are awaiting Caesar or Marc Antony."

She'd spent most of the night dancing with rogues and unsuitable *partis,* waiting for him to intervene, and now he had, only he hadn't really . . . it had been by his aunt's bidding that he'd come to claim her.

Yet Harriet wasn't one to wallow in the details. For here he was, and this was her chance.

"Caesar or Marc Antony, you ask? Neither," she told him. "I find both quite boring."

"They wouldn't find you so," he said, stepping down onto the patio and looking over her shoulder at the gardens beyond. "You've caused quite a stir in that rag, minx."

Harriet turned around, and grinned. "Have I?" Of course, she'd known that the moment she donned the costume. And had very nearly taken it right off and sought refuge in some milkmaid's garb. But once Pansy, her dear friend Daphne's maid, had done Harriet's dark tresses up into an elaborate maze of braids, crowned them with a golden coronet of entwined asps and painted her eyes with dark lines of kohl, Harriet had known there was no turning back.

Roxley had come to stand beside her at the edge of the patio. Here, away from the stifling air of the ballroom, the soft summer breezes, tinged as they were with the hint of roses, invited one to inhale deeply.

It was magical. Well, nearly so, she discovered.

The earl glanced over at her again and frowned. "You shouldn't be out here alone."

"I'm not," she pointed out. "You're here. But I had thought to take a turn in the gardens." Then she looked over at him again, standing there with a moody glower worthy of Lancelot. "Whatever is the matter?" she asked, hands fisting to her hips.

"It's that . . . that . . . costume you've got on," he complained, his hands wavering in front of her.

"It was supposed to be Daphne's."

That did not seem to appease him. "I cannot believe my aunt allowed you out in that shameful rag."

So much for magic.

"There is nothing wrong with this gown," she told him. "It is as historical as yours."

Good heavens, I'm wearing more than I was when you kissed me in Sir Mauris's garden, she wanted to remind him.

Then again, perhaps the kiss hadn't been as memorable to Roxley as it had been to her . . . Her gaze flew up, only to find his face a glower.

"Historical, indeed! Mine covers me," he replied. "No wonder Marc Antony lost his honor."

Harriet brazened her way forward. Better that than consider that Roxley had no interest in kissing her again. "Perhaps I should go find him and see if he will walk with me in the gardens." Since the only Marc Anthony inside the ballroom was Lord Fieldgate, this managed to darken Roxley's scowl. For most of the evening, the resplendent and rakish viscount had done his utmost to commandeer Harriet's time, declaring her his "perfect Cleopatra."

Roxley, as it turned out, wasn't done complaining. "How convenient for Fieldgate that Miss Dale's untimely departure —"

"Elopement," Harriet corrected.

"That is still left to be seen," Roxley commented. "It is only an elopement *if* they marry."

"*When* they marry."

"So you insist," he demurred.

"I do," Harriet said firmly. Daphne would never have run off so if she hadn't been utterly positive that she was about to be wed. She just wouldn't. "Besides, Preston will see them married."

"The duke will do his level best. He just has to find Lord Henry and Miss Dale before her cousin interferes."

Viscount Dale. Harriet hoped his carriage tumbled off the road. He was a rather bothersome prig, and could very well put a wrench into Daphne's plans.

"True love can overcome all odds," she said most confidently. At least it always did in her Miss Darby novels. Besides, she had to look no further than Tabitha and Preston, or Lord Henry and Daphne, for her proof.

True love always won the day.

And now she and Roxley would have their chance . . . Harriet glanced over at him, searching for confirmation.

"True love?" he scoffed. "Harry, you astound me. Now, here I've always thought you the most sensible, practical girl I've ever

11

known, but —"

The earl continued on, though Harriet had stopped listening at that one wretched word.

Girl. Though *sensible* was nearly as bad.

Would he ever stop thinking of her as a child? He certainly hadn't thought her merely a girl when he'd kissed her back in London.

Had he changed his mind since then? He couldn't have. He'd kissed her, for heaven's sakes. He wouldn't have done that unless . . .

She shook her head at the doubts that assailed her.

The ones that had plagued her since their arrival here at the Duke of Preston's house party.

What if Roxley didn't think her worthy of being his countess. It was easy to think so when she compared herself to the rest of the company. Then it was all too easy to see she had faults aplenty.

A decided lack of a Bath education. Like a proper lady.

Not one provided by her brothers' tutor.

She laughed too loud.

Her embroidery was nonexistent. Much like her skills at the pianoforte and watercolors.

In short, she wasn't refined enough to be a countess.

Even Roxley's.

But perhaps those things didn't matter to him, she told herself for about the thousandth time.

And certainly there was one way to find out.

Harriet straightened slowly, and then tipped one shoulder slightly, letting the clasp at her shoulder — the one which held up the sheer silken over-gown — slide dangerously close to coming off her. The entire gown was like that — illusion after illusion that it was barely on, wasn't truly concealing the lady beneath. For under the first layer of sheer silk was another one in a shimmering hue of gold and beneath that, another sheer layer. The wisps of fabric, one atop the other, kept the gown from being completely see-through, though when she'd first donned it, she had to admit, she'd felt utterly naked.

Now she wanted to see if Roxley thought the same.

She tilted her head just slightly and glanced up at him.

"Yes, well," he managed, his gaze fixed on her shoulder. He looked as if he couldn't quite make up his mind or not to intervene

13

— because to save her modesty he would have to touch her.

So she nudged him along, dipping her shoulder just a bit more. Perhaps this was exactly how Cleopatra had gained her Antony — for even now, Roxley appeared transfixed, leaving Harriet with a dizzy, heady sort of feeling.

But just before her gown fell from her shoulder, the earl groaned, then reached out and caught hold of the brooch at her shoulder and pushed it back up where it belonged, his fingers sliding along her collarbone, her bare skin. His hand was warm, hard, steady atop her shoulder, and suddenly Harriet could imagine him just as easily plucking the brooch away . . .

And then he looked at her, and Harriet saw all too clearly the light of desire in his eyes. Could feel it as his hand continued to linger on her shoulder and knew it would be nothing for him to gather her in his arms and . . . and . . .

"Demmit, Harry —" he muttered, snatching back his hand and stepping off the patio.

More like bolting.

"Whatever is the matter?" She hoped she sounded slightly innocent, for she certainly didn't feel it. His touch had left her shivering, longing for something altogether different.

"I . . . that is . . . I need some air. Yes, that's it. I came out here to get some air."

"I thought you came out to find me." She let her statement drift over him like a subtle reminder. "Yes, well, if you just came out for air, that's most excellent. I was of the same mind." And with that, she followed him.

For she couldn't help herself.

He looked over his shoulder at her. "Harry—"

"Yes, Roxley?" she tried to appear as nonchalant as possible.

"You cannot come out here with me," he said, pointing the way back to the well-lit patio.

"Whyever not?" she asked, as if she hadn't the slightest notion what he was saying.

And he didn't look like he wanted to discuss the subject either. But he did anyway. "It wouldn't be proper."

"Proper?" She laughed as if he were making a joke. "Oh, bother propriety. How long have we known each other?"

"Forever," he grumbled.

"And have we ever indulged ourselves in anything scandalous?" She strolled toward him and then circled him like a cat.

Other than that kiss . . .

"Not entirely," he managed, sounding a bit strangled, as he gaped at her, at her bare shoulder, and then just as quickly looked away.

Well, that was something of an admission. At least she hoped it was.

"So whatever is wrong with you escorting me into the garden for a bit of air, especially since you've promised my brothers to keep an eye on me — which you have, haven't you?"

"Well, yes —"

"Do you think they would prefer I go for a walk in the gardens with Lord Fieldgate?"

More to the point, Roxley, she wanted to say, *do you want me out there with that bounder?*

"Bother you to hell, Harry. No, they wouldn't like it."

Neither would she. "So?"

His jaw worked back and forth, so much so, he did look like Lancelot caught between his loyalty to his liege and something less honorable.

Harriet hoped the less honorable part would win.

And to her delight it did. For the most part.

Roxley muttered something under his

16

breath, and then caught her by the elbow and tugged her down the path. "Come along. Just don't do that thing with your lashes again." He frowned at her. "If your mother could see you —"

"She's in Kempton."

"As should you be," Roxley said, more as a threat. "I blame my aunt. She should never have brought you to London." He glanced at her again. "It's changed you." Then he added, "And not for the better."

"I see nothing scandalous about taking a walk in the gardens. I did this earlier with Lord Kipps and there was nothing so very wrong there. Why, your aunt encouraged it."

"She did?" he said, sounding none too pleased.

They rounded the first corner and came to a complete stop, for there before them was a couple — a water nymph and her Neptune — entwined together beneath an arbor, kissing passionately, between murmured endearments and confessions.

My dearest, my darling —
Oh, however did you know it was me?
How could I not?

"You see," Roxley was saying once they were well past the scandalous pair. "You are far better off out here with me than with

17

Fieldgate."

"Yes, I suppose." She let every word fall with abject disappointment.

This brought the earl to a halt. "You suppose? Do you know what the rogue would do out here? Alone with you?"

Harriet shrugged. Truly, he had to ask? She had five brothers. She knew exactly what Fieldgate would do given the opportunity.

Wasn't it much the same as what Roxley had done back in London? Granted he'd been a bit foxed that night.

Oh, good heavens. She'd nearly forgotten that. He had been foxed.

What if he didn't remember kissing her? Or worse, he didn't want to recall the evening. Harriet drew in a deep breath, knowing full well the only way to get Roxley to admit anything was to provoke him.

Just a bit . . .

"I suppose, being the horrible rake that he is, he would have tried to take advantage of me —" Harriet sighed as if it were the most delicious notion she'd ever considered.

"Most decidedly," Roxley said with a disapproving *tsk, tsk* and a shake of his head, as if that made him the hero.

"You truly think so?"

He huffed a sigh. "Of course he would.

18

You wouldn't have made it past the patio before he'd have tried."

"Oh, that is excellent news," she said, catching up the hem of her gown, turning on one heel, and starting to march back toward the ballroom.

Roxley caught up with her about where the couple was still locked in each other's embrace. Discreetly — well, as much as one could — he tugged her back down the path. "Where were you going?" he whispered as he dragged her away.

"I would think my plan was obvious. At least to a rogue like you. I was going to find the viscount."

"Fieldgate?" Roxley couldn't have sounded more shocked.

"Yes. Is there another lascivious viscount by the name of Fieldgate that I've missed?"

Roxley's jaw set as he marched her farther down the path, through the long column of plane trees that lined the way.

Harriet could only hope this was the path to ruin, much as the other young lady had found.

A very unladylike tremor of envy sprang up inside her.

"Why would you want that clod to take advantage of you?" Rowley was asking. No, demanding.

"Because I've merely been kissed — and that lady" — she said with nod over her shoulder — "who I believe is Miss Nashe —"

Now the earl's head swiveled. "I highly doubt that's —"

But then he must have realized that just as Harriet's costume was so very memorable, so was the one Miss Nashe was wearing — of course minus the feathered hem that had caused her so much trouble earlier in the week.

"Told you," Harriet said triumphantly once they were well out of earshot. "That is Miss Nashe and Lord Kipps."

She held back an indignant *harrumph*. Lord Kipps had walked her down this very path and hadn't tried to kiss her.

Then again, Harriet wasn't an infamous heiress like Miss Nashe. Just plain old Harriet Hathaway. A spinster from Kempton. With barely enough pin money for just that. Pins.

Oh, why couldn't she have been born fair and petite like Daphne, or inherited a fortune like Tabitha?

Roxley was still glancing back at the entangled couple. "Then I suppose we can expect an announcement at midnight. Lucky Kipps. He's gone and borrowed my family motto."

"*Ad usque fidelis?*" Harriet said, thinking that "Unto fidelity" was hardly the translation for what was transpiring in the arbor.

"No, minx, our other motto. The one we Marshoms find more apropos."

"Which is?"

"Marry well and cheat often," he teased.

This took Harriet aback. "The Marshoms advocate cheating on their spouses?"

"No." He laughed. "Unfortunately, we tend to love thoroughly and for life. We're an overly romantic lot — we just make sure to fall in love with a bride with a fat purse. And when that runs out, then there is nothing left but living by one's wits. My parents were a perfect example."

"You mean your parents lived by cheating at cards?"

"Of course. If only to stay ahead of their debts."

"Then it's a terrible shame," Harriet said, looking back at Miss Nashe and realizing how convenient it was that she'd found her countess's coronet with that earl, and not Harriet's.

"What is?" her earl asked.

"Kipps catching Miss Nashe's eye before you could cast your spell on her . . . and her fat purse."

21

Roxley shrugged. They had come to a stop by one of the larger trees. "Actually, I'm quite distraught about her choice."

"You wanted to marry her?" Harriet reached out and steadied herself against the white trunk of the tree.

He laughed. "No, Kitten. I had no designs on the lady. But I wagered she'd corner Lord Henry."

Kitten. Harriet nearly sighed at the familiar endearment. It held so much promise. Like a daisy being plucked of its petals.

He loves me . . .

Harriet laughed, at him and her hopes. "You should stick to cheating at cards." She put her back to the trunk, leaning against it, and letting the solid strength of the tree support her.

"You still haven't answered my question." Roxley dug the toe of his boot into the sod.

Harriet glanced up. "Which was?"

He looked up at her. "Why the devil would you want to come out into the gardens with Fieldgate?"

"For the very simple reason that I want to be kissed. Properly, that is. By a man of some skill." Harriet let her gaze drift back once again toward the house, her insinuation landing precisely as she'd intended.

Spectacularly.

"Kissed properly? Of all the insulting . . ." he blustered.

Harriet laughed again, and realizing he'd been lured into a trap, Roxley laughed as well.

"Good God, Harry!" He pushed away from the tree. "You're going to be the death of me."

"Well, if you were to kiss me . . . *again* . . ."

"Which I won't," he shot back.

"If you insist." Harriet did her best to appear indifferent, as if his quick retort was the least of her concerns.

"I do."

Truly, did he have to sound so adamant? "But if you did —"

He paused. "Harry, you can stop right there. Kiss you? Once was enough."

Harriet whirled around on him. "Aha! So you do admit to kissing me."

His voice ran low, rumbled up from his chest, his words filled with longing. "How could I forget?"

She shivered, for it was longing she shared, one that resided in her heart, restless and tempting.

"But you are being ridiculous," he continued. "If I were to ruin you, your brothers would shoot me."

"If they were in a good humor," she

conceded. Actually, all five of them would most likely insist on taking a shot.

Unfortunately, Roxley knew this as well, for he echoed her thoughts exactly. "And since I don't favor an untimely death by firing squad, I fear for tonight your desire to be kissed again is going to have to remain on the shelf."

Like her life. Like her chances of ever being loved.

Passionately. Her gaze slid back in the direction of the arbor.

Oh, it all seemed so patently unfair. And yet, a few months ago, she would never have considered such things possible. She had lived her entire life content in the knowledge that as a spinster of Kempton she would never marry, never be kissed, never . . .

And then, on that fateful day when Preston's carriage had broken down in Kempton and she'd seen Roxley after all that time apart, she hadn't been able to help herself, she'd begun to dream of the impossible.

So, after coming to London with Tabitha and Daphne, and seeing her two dearest friends find happiness in such unexpected ways — not just happiness, but *love* — she'd begun to hope.

And here she was, with the only man she'd ever desired, in this garden, under this moon, and why shouldn't she want to be kissed?

Again. And again . . .

"No one would have to know," she whispered. "No one would ever find out."

"Someone always does, Kitten," Roxley told her. He'd circled round the tree and now stood much as she did, leaning against the great trunk but on the opposite side, so the wide breadth separated them.

How she longed to cut it down, to make it so that nothing could keep them apart.

"There are no secrets in the *ton*," he added.

Well, she didn't care if the entire population of England, Ireland and Scotland knew. It wasn't like she was an heiress with prospects, or anyone else was going to come along and claim her.

But the real question was, would he?

"Roxley?"

"Yes, Harry?"

She pressed her lips together every time he called her that. Did he have to use that horrid name? But taking a deep breath, she dove in. "What do you see when you look at me?"

"Not much," he said. "If you haven't noticed it is rather dark out here."

She rolled around the tree, her fingers

tracing over the rough bark as if seeking a clear path, until she was right beside him. "Oh, do stop being *him*. I deplore *him*."

"Him? Who?"

"You know very well who I mean." Harriet was losing patience with him. If he pushed her much further she would go find Fieldgate. "Stop being the fool all London takes you for."

"But he's quite a handy fellow, that fool."

"He's an annoying jinglebrains."

"That's the point, minx."

"I know *who* you are."

"Do you?" He'd turned a bit and whispered the question into her ear.

Her breath caught in her throat, so that she was only able to answer with one word. *"Yes."*

Oh, yes, she knew who he was. The only man who had ever made her heart beat like this.

And then he moved closer, brushing against the hem of her gown, and Harriet clung to the tree to steady herself. "No one would believe you, Kitten."

Kitten. Not Harry, but Kitten. His Kitten.

Harriet looked up at the bit of the night sky peeking through the thick canopy of leaves overhead and spied a single star. A lone, twinkling light. And so she wished.

"You don't have to hide from me," she whispered.

It was an invitation, one she knew he desired. She'd seen his struggle for months now — this game he played, this role he lived. This capering fool. Society's ridiculous gadfly.

But that wasn't the man she knew. The man she'd kissed in Sir Mauris's garden in London. The earl she'd known since they were children.

No, the one she loved, adored, desired, was the one with his gaze fixed on hers, his jaw set as if he were determined to do the right thing.

Oh, he'd chosen the right costume for the night. Lancelot. A man conflicted by duty and passion.

And he told her as much, his words almost desperate. "Why did you have to grow up, Harry? Why couldn't you have stayed in Kempton — stayed my impossible imp?"

"I still am."

"Oh, you are, but in an entirely new and utterly impossible way."

"Why is it impossible, Roxley?" *It certainly wouldn't be if you would but kiss me.*

"I promised your brothers I'd keep an eye on you."

Harriet moved closer, caught hold of his

lapels and did the impossible, even as she whispered, "Then close your eyes."

CHAPTER 1

I have seen one night be the ruin of many
a good man.
Lt. Throckmorten to Miss Darby
from *Miss Darby's Reckless Bargain*

London, April 1811
Eight months later
Every gambler knows the moment when his
luck changes.

And not for the good. Luck is too fickle of
a lover to whisper in a gamester's ear to
encourage him to double down.

No, when she turns her back on a fellow,
he knows it. As sure as all the air in the
room has rushed out.

Like a fish out of water, he suddenly finds
himself grasping at anything that might
return her bright favor to his dark and
empty pockets.

So it was with Tiberius Maximus Marshom, the 7th Earl of Roxley.

Roxley, who took wagers that no one else would, and won . . . The earl who always had pockets of vowels that only needed collecting was now dodging friends and ducking out of White's to avoid the embarrassment of his current dire financial straits.

And his shocking turn of luck was what had brought him here. To the City. To the offices of one Aloysius Murray.

"So you see, my lord," the merchant was saying, his hands folded atop a pile of notes, "you have no choice but to make my daughter your wife."

The earl looked across the wide expanse of the man's desk at a fellow he hadn't even known existed until two days ago when he'd received Mr. Murray's summons. Still, despite the gravity before him, Roxley could not resist smiling.

It was all he could do. A Marshom through and through, he knew he was trapped, but he was certainly not going to let this mushroom, this Mr. Murray with his most likely equally uncouth daughter, know that he had Roxley in a corner.

Mr. Murray pushed the papers across the top of the desk. "I've managed to buy out all your vowels, all your debts. You're solvent, for the time being. I think a kindly given 'thank you' would be in order." He

30

paused for a moment and then added belatedly, "My lord."

Roxley looked at the pile of notes and scribbled promises and realized that his hopes of reclaiming all that he'd managed to lose over the past eight months — his money, his position with the Home Office, his standing (what there had been of it) — was for naught.

His legendary luck was gone.

If he were inclined to be honest — which he rarely was — he could point to the exact moment when Fair Fortune had abandoned him.

Eight months ago. The third of August, 1810, to be exact. The night he'd kissed Miss Harriet Hathaway.

And since we've established that the Earl of Roxley possessed very little honesty, kissing had been the least of his sins that night with the aforementioned Miss Hathaway.

He'd demmed well ruined her.

But enough of contemplating an evening of madness — it wasn't his insatiable desire for Harriet that had gotten him into this mess.

Oh, Harry what have I done? he thought as he looked at his all his wrongdoings piled up atop this *cit*'s desk and knowing that no matter how much he . . .

Well, admitting how he felt for Harriet Hathaway was just too much honesty for one day. Especially this one.

When he was having to face his ruin. A reckoning of sorts.

If it was only the money, only his own ill-choices, that would be one thing. But there was more to this than just a gambler's reversal. His every instinct clamored that this was all a greater trap, a snare, but why and how, he couldn't say.

More to the point, he couldn't let this calamity touch anyone else.

As it had Mr. Ludwick, his man of business. Roxley's gut clenched every time he thought of the fellow — disappearing in the middle of the night with a good portion of Roxley's money.

Yet Ludwick wasn't the sort. And that was the problem. There was no explanation for his abrupt departure. None.

Further, the man's vanishing act had been followed by the revelation of a string of soured investments. Wagers began going bad. Files for the Home Office stolen from his house. None of it truly connected, yet he couldn't help feeling that there was a thread that tied it all together, winding its evil around his life.

But who was pulling it, and why, escaped

Roxley entirely.

Sensing the earl's hesitancy, Mr. Murray pressed his case, pulling out a now familiar document.

The mortgage on Foxgrove.

The one property of his that wasn't entailed. The one with all the income that kept the Marshoms afloat. Without Foxgrove . . .

Mr. Murray ran a stubby, ink-stained finger over the deed. "I've always fancied a house in the country. How is this village? This Kempton?"

"Kempton, you ask?" Roxley replied, wrenching his gaze up from the man's covetous reach on his property. "Oh, you won't like it. Cursed, it is."

Mr. Murray stilled at this, then burst out in a loud, braying laugh. "I was told to expect you to be a bit of a cut-up, but that! Cursed, he says." He laughed again, more like brayed.

Good God, Roxley could only hope Murray's daughter didn't laugh like that. But to keep Foxgrove . . . to keep his family out of debtor's prison, Roxley knew he could bear almost anything.

And if he did his utmost to make this mushroom's daughter miserable for the next forty years, he'd never have to hear that sound again.

That was, if anything, a small condolence.

"I have a mind to drive down next week," Mr. Murray was saying. "Probably needs renovations like the rest of the piles of stones you gentry keep."

Roxley ruffled at this. For his residences were his pride and joy. As had been his infamous luck that had kept them in good order. "Yes, well, currently my Aunt Essex lives at Foxgrove and she would be most put out to have strangers arrive at her residence."

"Isn't really hers, now is it?" Mr. Murray pointed out, once again running his ugly fingers along the edge of the deed.

He didn't even want to think about it. Aunt Essex forcibly removed from the house she'd lived in most of her life. She'd have no choice but to move permanently to London.

Into the earl's house. And without the income from Foxgrove, Aunt Eleanor in Bath, and Aunts Ophelia and Oriel at the Cottage would soon be forced to follow. All of the Marshom spinsters together. In one house. His house.

Worse than that, he'd have failed them. When they had once rescued him in his darkest hours.

He must have twitched as Mr. Murray

chuckled. "Got your attention now."

"Mr. Murray, you had my full attention when you sent me the list of my debts you were holding. But what I don't understand is, why have you chosen to invest in me?"

Now it was Mr. Murray's turn to still, as if he wasn't too sure which direction to turn. But he had an answer at the ready soon enough. "Always fancied my daughter a lady, and a countess seems the right place to start."

Roxley nearly asked if the merchant was planning on sending him to an early grave, if only to climb the noble ladder again and gain a duke for his daughter the next time around.

"And," Murray added, as if suddenly finding the rest of his answer, "your situation is not unknown."

Roxley sighed. That was the truest thing the man had said since the earl had entered his study.

His fall from grace and rapid descent into debt had every tongue in London wagging. Hadn't he once told Harry as much?

There are no secrets in the ton.

So the word had spread quickly that the Earl of Roxley was up the River Tick.

Worse, to those who'd lost to him over the years, it was a just reward to watch. And since that was most everyone, the entire *ton* seemed delighted by his plummet.

"It's my daughter or the poorhouse with your aunts, my lord." Murray smiled as he folded his hands atop what was the ruin of Roxley's fortunes. "The choice is yours."

After the earl departed Mr. Murray's study, a door concealed by a bookcase opened, and a tall, darkly clad figure stepped out.

"I did as you instructed," Mr. Murray hurried to say. "But he won't agree to the marriage, my lord, until he meets my daughter."

"He'll agree," the man said with his usual supreme confidence.

A confidence that made Murray anxious. He didn't like being part of all this. Blackmailing a member of the House of Lords. It was bad business all around.

But so was the man before him.

"I did as you said —" Mr. Murray repeated.

The man arched a dark brow and studied him. "Yes, you did. Perfectly."

"Now the matter of that other issue . . ." The one that had brought Murray to the attention of this very dangerous stranger.

The man shook his head with a negligent toss of dismissal. "No. Not yet."

"But I —" Then Murray stopped as the

man's brow arched upward.

Roxley's last man of business, Ludwick, had gone missing. Never been found. Nor had Roxley's money. Murray had known the man personally. Ludwick had always seemed an honest sort and certainly not the kind willing to embezzle a fortune and leave his wife and three children behind.

Murray looked up and met the other man's gaze. A cold shiver ran down his spine, as if this fellow could read his thoughts, the questions behind his silence.

"Yes, you have done all I've asked," the man assured him ever so smoothly. Like a knife in the dark sliding between one's ribs. "You bought up all of Roxley's debts and you've cornered him into this marriage" — he paused for a second — "to your delightful daughter. But our agreement will be concluded when he, and those accursed relations of his, are driven to ground and give me what is *mine.*"

The malice in that one single word left Murray with the uncomfortable feeling that he was about to soil his own drawers. He chose his next words carefully.

Very carefully.

"You must despise the earl quite a bit to go to all this trouble." He waved a hand at the pile of notes on his desk — debts and misfortunes, Murray had no doubt, orchestrated by this deadly foe. "You must truly hate him, my lord."

"Hate Roxley?" the man laughed. "How droll. In truth, I count him a friend."

Eight long months. Harriet tapped her slipper impatiently. Eight months since that unforgettable night at Owle Park and the even more memorable day which followed.

When she'd discovered Roxley had fled.

Deserted the house party.

Abandoned her.

She could continue to list his failings, but that, she'd discovered over the fall and winter that had followed with not a single word from him, hardly served.

It only reopened the wound that had torn her heart in half.

She did her best to hold the broken parts together, yet it was as if the wound was still fresh and new, filled with festering doubts.

Oh, why had she agreed to come to London?

As much as she wanted to know why Roxley had abandoned her — oh, bother, she *must* know — she wasn't too sure she wanted to hear the truth.

But there had been Lady Essex, arriving at the Pottage and insisting that Harriet travel with her to London and Harriet's mother happy to oblige.

The two of them had packed her traveling trunks and shoved her aboard the Marshom barouche before she'd had a chance to rally a decent objection.

Certainly the truth wasn't an option.

Maman, Lady Essex, I have no desire to go to London and face the man who ruined me. Oh, yes, that would have been well received.

So here she was, about to do just that — see Roxley — and whatever would she say to him?

Perhaps she could ask this Madame Sybille everyone was fawning over — a mentalist or some such nonsense. All Harriet knew was that the lady had all the matrons buzzing when she'd arrived tonight. Perhaps this mystic could read her future and reassure her that Roxley's desertion was naught but a misunderstanding.

Harriet made an inelegant snort that drew a few censoring looks. Well, honestly, she didn't need some charlatan's advice, she needed help.

Glancing around, she pursed her lips. Where the devil was Tabitha? Or even Daphne, for that matter. They would know what to do.

Of course, that would also mean telling

them . . . Harriet didn't know if she could bear the shame of it.

And then, as if on cue, there was a ruffle of whispers through the crush of guests.

Harriet had to guess that not only was Tabitha here, but her infamous husband as well.

She glanced at the steps leading down into the ballroom to find the happily married Duchess of Preston standing with her arm linked in the crook of her husband's elbow. Tabitha had defied all conventions and won the heart of the most unlikely of rakes.

Speaking of rakes, the duke and duchess had not arrived alone. Preston stepped aside and was joined at the entrance by his uncle, Lord Henry Seldon, who grinned at the matrons who regarded him and his bride with abject horror.

Daphne's happiness rather defied the oft-repeated admonitions to young ladies all over proper society that nothing good ever came of a runaway marriage.

The former Miss Daphne Dale, now Lady Henry, flaunted evidence quite to the contrary. For not only was she gowned in a most fetching silk, her slightly wicked smile said her runaway union was very satisfying . . .

Harriet sighed with relief, feeling as if part

of her burden was lifted. She had missed her dear friends ever so much. With Tabitha and Daphne married and living in London and at their husbands' various estates, Harriet had found herself alone in Kempton, the distant village where the three of them had grown up.

Of course, not even Kempton was the same. It had been decades since a Kempton spinster had even dared to marry, let alone the centuries that had passed since one had made a marriage that hadn't ended with the bridegroom meeting a horrific and untimely ending.

Usually on his wedding night.

And for several months after Tabitha and Daphne had married, it seemed every miss in the village had held her breath waiting for some disaster to befall Lord Henry or the Duke of Preston, or, heaven forbid, their brides.

But when neither Tabitha nor Daphne had gone mad and dashed their husbands over the head with a fire poker, there had been an emergency meeting of the Society for the Temperance and Improvement of Kempton.

Rising to her feet, the most esteemed of all the spinsters, Lady Essex, declared the curse broken.

"However can that be?" Miss Theodosia Walding asked, pushing her spectacles back up onto her nose. A bluestocking through and through, Theodosia liked her facts.

"Love," Lady Essex announced.

"True love," Lavinia Tempest corrected, her twin sister, Louisa, nodding in agreement.

The rest of the spinsters, who of course had heard Lavinia — one always heard Lavinia before one saw her — sighed with delight, while Theodosia frowned. She found such a fickle emotion as love or as ethereal as "true love" rather impossible to believe.

Yet, wasn't the proof before them? Tabitha and Daphne happily married. The curse must be ended and now it was time for all the spinsters, daughters and misses of Kempton to do what had been unthinkable before: prepare a glory box and make a match.

The rush at Mrs. Welling's dress shop had been akin to a stampede.

Not that Harriet had gotten caught up in the furor.

No, Harriet Hathaway's heart had been lost months earlier and all the evidence suggested he'd forsaken her.

42

No, he couldn't have. Not Roxley, she told herself.

It was an endless refrain she couldn't get out of her head.

He loves me. He loves me not.

She rose up on her tiptoes to look over Preston's tall shoulders to see if his party included one more.

Roxley.

But to her chagrin, there was no sign of the earl. No hint of his devil-may-care smile, his perfectly cut Weston jacket, or that sly look of his that said he was working on the perfect quip to leave her laughing.

Bother! Where the devil was he? Harriet's slipper tapped anew.

"Harriet!" Tabitha called out, rushing toward her and wrapping her into a big hug. They had been best friends since childhood, and had never been separated for so long. "How I have missed you."

"And I you," Harriet confessed. Unfolding herself from Tabitha's warm embrace, she smiled at Daphne. "And you as well."

"Truly, Harriet?" Daphne said, waving her off. "I doubt very much you've missed me chiding you about the mud on your hem."

Harriet pressed her lips together to keep from laughing. Truly, she hadn't missed Daphne's exacting fashion standards. Still, she hugged her anyway, and to her surprise, Daphne hugged her back.

"I've missed you," her friend confessed. "You and your horrible Miss Darby novels."

Harriet dashed at the hot sting of tears that seemed to come out of nowhere. It wasn't until this moment that she realized just how lonely Kempton had become without Tabitha at the vicarage and Daphne down the lane at Dale House.

How much she wanted to tell them . . . and yet couldn't.

"The Miss Darby novels are not horrible," she shot back, more out of habit than not. "I just got the latest one. *Miss Darby's Reckless Bargain.* You *must* read it. Both of you. She's been captured by a Barbary sultan, a prince actually, and he's about to —" Harriet came to a stop as she found her friends pressing their lips together to keep from laughing over her earnest enthusiasm for her beloved Miss Darby.

Preston and Lord Henry, after exchanging a pair of befuddled glances, begged off and went to find where Lord Knolles kept something stronger than lemonade.

"Oh, don't look now, Tabitha, but Lady Timmons is here," Daphne said, nudging the duchess in the ribs.

"My aunt won't come over here as long as

you are beside me, Daphne," Tabitha replied, and rather gleefully so.

"Whyever not?" Harriet asked, glancing over at Lady Timmons, who stood across the ballroom encircled by her three unmarried daughters. With a duchess for a niece, it made no sense that the lady wouldn't be cultivating Tabitha for introductions.

"She considers Daphne a bad example," the duchess confided. "She wrote me that it was imperative I sever my friendship with Lady Henry or else she couldn't, in good conscience, acknowledge me."

"Then I suggest you stay close at hand for Tabitha's sake," Harriet told Lady Henry. They all laughed again, for Lady Timmons had done her best to prevent Tabitha from marrying Preston, then had conveniently forgotten her objections to the match once she could claim a connection to a duchess.

As Tabitha and Daphne begged Harriet for news of Kempton — the most recent antics of the Tempest twins, Theodosia's newest scholarly pursuits, Lady Essex's latest complaints — Harriet noticed something else.

She looked from Tabitha to Daphne. "Why didn't you tell me?" she nearly burst out, looking at the swell of their stomachs, Tabitha's far more advanced than Daphne's.

45

"You know these things are not spoken of," Tabitha whispered, once again the vicar's daughter.

"Pish," Daphne said. "Men talk of breeding dogs and horses all the time! We mention a single thing about being in the family way and you would think we were asking them to walk down Bond Street without their breeches on!" She huffed a grand sigh. "Henry has gone so far as to forbid me from dancing — he won't have me exerting myself in any way." Her hands folded over the bulge. "He's become as fussy as Aunt Damaris, but I don't dare tell him that."

"Speaking of your Dale relations," Harriet said, "your mother actually mentioned your name the other day."

Daphne's parents had refused to acknowledge their daughter after she'd gone and eloped with a Seldon. Harriet never understood the point of it all, but to the Dales, the Seldon clan was akin to the devil. And vice versa. That their daughter had married one . . . well . . .

"Our happy news has helped, but I believe I have Cousin Crispin's recent match to thank for their changing opinion about my husband and his family."

"Then it's true," Harriet said. "Lord Dale has married her?"

46

Daphne covered her mouth to keep from bursting out with laughter. "Oh, he did. Mr. Muggins saw to that."

Tabitha, mortified over the part her dog had played in making Lord Dale's proposal of marriage — having locked the viscount and his unlikely choice in a wine cellar — changed the subject. "Is it true the Tempest twins are coming to London for the rest of the Season?"

Harriet nodded. "Yes. They'll be here in a fortnight. Their godmother, Lady Charleton, is sponsoring them."

"Lady Charleton?" an old matron who was standing nearby blurted out. "Did you say Lady Charleton?"

"Aye, ma'am," Harriet replied.

"Can't be right. Lady Charleton died . . . What is it now?" She turned to the even more ancient crone beside her. "When was it that Lady Charleton died?"

"Two years now. So sudden it was," the other woman said, shaking her head, leaving the yellow plumes in her turban all atwitter. "Dreadful situation still."

"Lady Charleton is dead?" Harriet shook her head. "I must have the name wrong."

"You must." The old lady turned back to her cronies and began clucking about yet another misfortune.

"Speaking of sponsors, where is Lady Essex?" Tabitha asked, glancing around them as if to gauge who else was eavesdropping on their conversation.

"Have you missed her as well?" Harriet teased.

Daphne and Tabitha both laughed. The spinster was a bit of a holy terror, not that Harriet minded.

"Some old roué swept her off her feet the moment we arrived," Harriet said. "Called her 'Essie.' "

"No!" Tabitha gasped.

"Yes!" Harriet nodded. "A Lord Whenby, I think his name is."

The three of them looked over at the eavesdropping old lady, but the name didn't elicit a response.

Daphne leaned closer. "Who is he?"

Harriet shrugged. She'd never heard Lady Essex mention the man. "I don't know. Perhaps that's why she's been at sixes and sevens for weeks now."

At this, Tabitha and Daphne exchanged a wary glance, one that suggested they might have quite a different explanation.

Harriet kept going, for now her interest was piqued. "I didn't think she was even going to come up to London this Season, but she arrived a few days ago at the Pottage and insisted my mother pack my bags."

There was yet another silent exchange between Daphne and Tabitha, but before Harriet could dig deeper into whatever *on dit* they were hiding, they were joined by a less than welcome guest.

"Miss Hathaway? Is that you?"

Harriet cringed at the familiar masculine voice.

"Do my eyes, nay, my heart, deceive me?" An elegantly dressed man in a dashing coat and well-glossed boots stopped before them.

She pasted a quick smile on her lips. "Lord Fieldgate," she acknowledged before dipping into a curtsy.

When she rose, he immediately caught hold of her hand and brought it to his lips. "My long-lost Hippolyta."

Daphne leaned over to Tabitha. "Hippolyta?"

"Queen of the Amazons," the duchess whispered back.

Daphne snorted.

"Roughly translated it means 'an unbridled mare.' " Tabitha's education by her vicar father always came in handy in situations like this.

Daphne pressed her lips together to keep from laughing.

"Yes, exactly," Tabitha remarked. "If only

49

the viscount knew how close to the mark his title for Harriet is."

Harriet shot them both a sharp glance. *It isn't as if I can't hear you.*

"I must beg a dance of you," Fieldgate continued. Nor had he let go of Harriet's hand. "No, make that two." Oh, no one could say the viscount lacked charm, for his smile smoldered with promise, a sort of smoky glance that could make a lady go weak in the knees.

"Two?" Harriet shook her head at her ardent suitor who had pursued her so steadily the previous Season. Apparently absence had not dimmed Fieldgate's ardor.

"The supper dance, at the very least," he pleaded.

The supper dance? Harriet's pique returned. Roxley would deplore that. He had hated it every time she'd danced with the viscount last Season.

Then again, it would serve the earl right to have to partner some leftover debutante to supper, especially after all these months of silence on his part.

Her heart gave a familiar leap into that horrible abyss over which she'd been teetering for months.

He loves me, he loves me not.

Well, tonight, she'd discover the truth. If

she had to carve it out of the cursed man with one of the ancient broadswords mounted on the wall. Manacle him to a sideboard and . . . why, she'd . . .

And then Harriet stopped. For indeed the entire world seemed to stop all around her. For across the room, off to one side, she saw him.

Roxley.

He *was* here. Had been here for some time, for there he was holding court in the far corner.

He loves you, he loves you not, her heart prodded.

"Can I take your silence to mean you're granting me the supper dance . . ." Fieldgate's words were both encouraging and full of confidence.

Harriet barely heard him, her heart hammering wildly. Roxley. With the crush of guests, she'd nearly missed him, but the crowd had parted for a moment and in that magical instant she'd spotted him. The cut of his jaw, the wry smile she loved.

Her breath stopped, as it had when his lips had teased across the nape of her neck. His hands had caressed her, *all of her,* and she'd trembled then as she was trembling now.

"A mistake, Kitten. This is ever so wrong,"

*he'd whispered that night at Owle Park even
as his head had dipped lower, his lips leaving
a trail of desire down her limbs.*

*Oh, please don't let it all have been a mis-
take,* she told herself yet again. Harriet took
a step toward the earl without even thinking, pulled by the very desire he'd ignited
that night, forgetting even that the viscount
still held her hand.

Roxley loves me.

Or loves you not, that dangerous voice of
doubt whispered back.

"You cannot refuse me, my queen, my
Hippolyta," Fieldgate continued, all gallant
manners, though he might as well have been
grasping at straws.

"Yes, yes," she said absently, glancing
quickly back at him before plucking her
hand free. Meaning, *Yes, I can refuse you.*
But the viscount took her words for assent
and grinned in triumph.

"Harriet, there is something we need to
tell you —" Tabitha began, reaching out to
stop her, but Harriet sidestepped her grasp.

"Yes, dear, you must listen," Daphne
continued like a chorus.

If they were going to warn her off from
spending too much time in the roguish
viscount's company, they needn't bother.
She had no intention of spending another

52

second with Fieldgate.

Not with Roxley so close at hand. She'd have her answers, he'd apologize profusely, sweep her off her feet and marry her as soon as a Special License could be procured.

That was how it always happened.

In fiction, her sensibilities reminded her.

"Harriet, please," Daphne called after her.

She ignored her. Truly, whatever they had to say could hardly matter, but just in case, Harriet hurried a bit, only to find her path blocked by her brother Chaunce.

Oh, pish! Was there ever a girl more overly blessed with bothersome and meddlesome brothers than she?

And Chaunce, her second oldest sibling, had that look of unrelenting determination about him.

All the Hathaways were determined, but Chaunce's tenacity came with all the solid warmth of a brick wall.

In December.

"Harry," he said, bussing her warmly on the cheek. "There you are. Mother wrote that she thought you would arrive in time to attend tonight."

Harriet was not deceived. He hardly looked thrilled to be attending Lady Knolles's soirée, rather more like the bearer of bad tidings.

Couldn't Chaunce, just once, leave well enough alone and just enjoy the world?

Just as Harriet meant to once she was reunited with her beloved Roxley.

"And so I have," she told her brother. "But I must —"

Chaunce glanced over his shoulder and spied the direction of her determination. If anything, his grim smile now turned into a hard line. "That won't do, Harry. You can't just run after him. Not now —"

Freeing herself from him, she patted her brother on the arm and circled around him, dodging his grasp. "You've become as stodgy as George," she chided. "Roxley is our dear friend. I am merely greeting him. He'll be delighted to see me."

He'd better be . . .

"Harry —" Chaunce continued as she slipped again into the crowd before he could stop her.

"No, Harriet! Don't. Not just yet," Tabitha called after her, having finally caught up.

But there was no stopping Harriet now.

Mr. Chauncy Hathaway turned around and frowned at his sister's friends. "You didn't tell her?"

"We hadn't the time," Daphne replied.

Chaunce groaned, raking a hand through

his dark, tousled hair. "How long does it take to tell someone that the man she loves is marrying another?"

CHAPTER 2

. . . and woman.
Miss Darby in reply to Lt. Throckmorten
from Miss Darby's Reckless Bargain

It had been a fortnight since his meeting with Mr. Murray and in that time, and much to his chagrin, Roxley had managed to make the man's daughter society's newest Original.

All over the *ton,* from drawing rooms to ballrooms, the same refrain was heard.

Whoever is this Miss Murray? For if Roxley was courting her — poor dear Roxley, so down on his luck — she must be *someone.*

And so, they all rushed to claim an acquaintance with her.

For his part, Roxley had high hopes some bounder would come along and sweep her off her feet, stealing his march, but unfortunately, the gel came with a grim-faced chaperone in tow, Miss Watson, a dragon of a spinster, whose beady gaze was enough to turn away even the most determined fortune hunter.

Worse, Miss Murray's schoolmate from Mrs. Plumley's in Bath, the former Miss Edith Nashe, who had used her heiress status to move up the social ladder and was now the Countess of Kipps, had latched on to her "dearest friend" to ensure that as long as the girl was in the spotlight of society's notice, she was right there to "help."

As the countess was this evening, having dispatched Miss Watson to the wallflower section and taken up the role of Miss Murray's dutiful chaperone.

At least Lady Kipps took some of the burden off his shoulders, leaving him a moment or two to ponder his investigations. So far he'd managed to stave off Mr. Murray's demands for the last fortnight, but his time was nearly up. He'd spent every waking moment he could salvage to determine who was behind this meticulously plotted ruin.

And yet every time he thought he'd discovered something, every time he pressed a lead or a hint at some deception, the answer eluded him like a whiff of smoke.

One moment it was there for him to grasp and the next it was gone.

But what wasn't gone was the never-ending sense of foreboding, a madness of sorts that haunted him wherever he went.

Why? The question hammered his every thought. Why?

The old Roxley would have made a ribald quip about the entire situation and suggested a séance with Madame Sybille to solve the problem.

He was getting to the point where even that might be in order.

So for the hundredth time this night, he made yet another sweep of the crowded room. And this time as the press of people shifted, his gaze fell on a tall, dark-headed figure on the opposite side of the room.

Harry? His heart wrenched.

He shook his head and looked again, but whoever he'd spied had once again been swallowed up in the crowd.

Harriet Hathaway, indeed! He was going mad.

"You were telling Miss Murray about your parents, my lord," Lady Kipps said, nudging him out of his reverie. "I must say I find their story ever so tragic." She smiled at Miss Murray. "His dear parents . . . so very young, so very much in love. Coming home from the Continent . . . when their carriage overturned." Her handkerchief rose to her dry eyes, though it was a touching attempt at sympathy. "Isn't that so, my lord?"

"Yes, they died in the accident," he replied, still distracted by that brief moment when he'd thought he'd seen Harry.

"They were killed?" Miss Murray gasped, her white-gloved fingers coming to rest on his sleeve. "How terrible for you, my lord!"

Once again she looked up into his eyes as if expecting something from him.

As if he didn't know what she expected. Her father had made it abundantly clear in the note he'd sent around this evening.

Make your proposal tonight, my lord, or else.

And yet as Roxley forced himself to look down at the lady by his side, his heart prodded him to scan the room one more time.

No, that was the last thing he needed. Harry connected in any fashion to this mystery.

"My lord?" Miss Murray prodded.

"Oh, yes, my parents. I was ever so young to have lost them. Both of them. Gone." Roxley did his best to appear brokenhearted and in need of comforting.

"Terrible," she agreed.

"It brings to mind my family motto," he said a bit wistfully. He leaned back and looked off into the distance, across the expanse of Lady Knolles's crowded ballroom, as if he was seeing something lost in time.

And not as if he was looking for Harriet.

Which was impossible, he reminded himself. She was safely ensconced back in Kempton. Where she belonged. Far from his ruin.

"Your family motto?" Miss Murray repeated.

"Ad usque fidelis," he confided.

Miss Murray blinked and tried to look like she understood every word.

"Ad usque fidelis," a lady off to one side repeated, her Latin impeccable. "Unto fidelity. And here I'd always been led to believe, Roxley, your motto meant 'Marry well and cheat often.' "

Trying to breathe and not look, Roxley stilled his quaking heart — for he knew exactly what he'd see once he did look — a tall, willowy wisp of a lady, with her coal black hair, and those eyes — those demmed green eyes that could look right through a fellow. Grab his heart and never let go.

Harry!

Roxley, who had flinched the moment he'd heard her dulcet tones, recovered enough composure to turn to his right, where his great-aunt's always meddlesome prodigy stood, picking absently at the blades of her fan, the toe of her slipper digging at the dance floor as if seeking out a stone to kick.

She looked up, her expression a mirror of surprise, as if she'd just noticed him there.

As. If.

It struck the earl that Harriet Hathaway's sole purpose in life was to drive him mad. Had been since the first day they'd met all those years ago.

And speaking of driving him mad — he glanced around the room, and yes, there she was. Aunt Essex.

Of course.

In the meantime, Lady Kipps, taking to heart her self-appointed role as the guardian of Miss Murray, eyed Harriet with all the feral delight of a cat who'd just discovered a pack of lame mice at her dish.

Oh, Lady Kipps, Roxley mused, sensing an impending disaster, *when will you learn?*

Roxley knew all too well it would take more than Lady Kipps's haughty and murderous disdain to dent Harriet's pluck.

He straightened, knowing what must be done and hating himself all the more for having to do it. "Harry, my aunt appears to be looking for you." He nodded in the lady's direction — well across the ballroom.

Her wrinkled nose said she hardly appreciated his use of her family nickname, the one she always shed the moment she set foot in London. Well, she'd always be Harry to him, no matter how hard she tried to appear the perfect miss. "No, she isn't," she replied without looking, and continued on. "As we were discussing, isn't that how the Marshoms translate their family motto, 'Marry well and cheat often'?" She smiled. "I did get that right, didn't I, Roxley?"

"What is this about cheating and marriage?" Lady Kipps demanded, first of Roxley and then of Harriet, whom she had never liked. "Better still, what do you know of these things, Miss Hathaway?" The sneer in her address held every doubt of Harriet's place in good society.

Roxley flinched again, for heaven help him, he couldn't imagine what Harry was going to say next.

And if he'd known, he would have wisely sought refuge behind the punch bowl.

"Of cheating and marriage, you ask? Enough, I suppose," Harriet replied with all the aplomb of a woman with a noble bloodline that ran back for ages. Oh, her father might be only a knight, but the Hathaways had been raised up by Henry V. She tapped her fan onto the palm of her hand, as one might have brandished a halberd, and she turned to face down her adversary as her forebear had most likely faced the French at Agincourt, with a slight smile on her lips and bloody resolve in her heart — the same resolve that had caught the king's eye and gratitude. "Though from what I hear, not as much as you, Lady Kipps."

Gratitude was not the word Roxley would use at this moment. *She hadn't just said —*

Oh, yes, she had. If this were Gentleman Jim's boxing ring instead of Lady Knolles's annual soirée, round one — bloody hell, the entire match — would be awarded to Harriet.

Which, Roxley had to imagine, was the direct result of the minx spending way too much time in his great-aunt's company. She had managed to capture Lady Essex's interfering tones and insulting turn of phrase precisely.

He shook his head. As if Harriet needed any help with perfecting her skills of butting her nose into matters that were none of her business.

But you made your business hers when you ruined her . . . all but promised her . . .

Yes, well, there was that.

For her part, Lady Kipps looked as if she'd swallowed a bucket of coals. The countess drew in a deep, furious breath, which did nothing to cool the fire in her belly, rather it made her brows knit together in indignation, and her eyes narrowed.

"Lord Roxley, do you know this *person*?" Miss Murray asked, her hands fluttering in Harriet's direction like one might ask a footman to take away a plate of kippers that had gone off.

Harriet's gaze narrowed, looking from him to Miss Murray — more specifically, Miss Murray's gloved hand atop his sleeve — and then back at him. Her eyes widened as she obviously came to the conclusion that he'd been too cowardly to tell her.

Written to her. Gone to her and begged her forgiveness. If he thought he'd done the right thing, hoping to spare her from having to watch his fall and then his marriage to another, he was wrong.

The hurt and anger in her eyes was enough to cut him in two.

"Roxley?" Miss Murray's jaw set with a determined line. "Do you know her?"

"Of course he does," Harriet supplied, before she leaned in and explained, "We were betrothed for a night."

"Harriet!" Roxley shot back, before he turned to the lady at his side. "Miss Murray, let me explain —"

Lady Kipps stepped in to do it for him. "I

fear Lord Roxley's previous inclinations toward these country sorts is showing. How you once preferred a lady who is not a fair blossom, but more like a common cornstalk, I cannot see, my lord."

True enough. Miss Murray was a petite June bell compared to Harriet's lofty reach.

"Perhaps my father was misinformed about your intentions —" Miss Murray began.

"No, no, no!" he rushed to assure her. "I fear Miss Hathaway is a bit of a . . ."

All three of the ladies glared at him as they awaited his answer.

Oh, how the devil had he ended up in this spot?

He caught Miss Murray by the arm and turned her so her back was toward Harriet. "I fear Miss Hathaway is a matter of honor —"

The lady's brows arched slightly.

Damn, that had hardly come out right.

"Not that sort of honor," he corrected. "It has to do with her brother —"

The brows rose higher.

Now that had *definitely* not come out correctly.

"No, no," he raced to explain. "The Hathaways are old friends. Nearly family. She is rather like a sister to me. I promised her brothers —"

Harriet leaned between them. "I've never known a brother to kiss me like you did, Roxley."

The earl held his ground. As he should have done that reckless night last summer instead of . . .

Oh, demmit! Now was not the time for recriminations or regrets. Besides, he reminded himself, strangling her in public would only cause a scandal.

Just as ruining her that night should have.

He notched up his chin and ignored Harry, focusing what was left of his tattered charms and grasp on the heiress's attentions. And mostly reminding himself what he must do — if only to keep Harriet safe. "She's a trifling, really. A bothersome little —"

"A trifling?" Harriet interjected, this time wedging herself between Roxley and his soon-to-be-or-else bride.

A petite specimen, Miss Murray was now completely overshadowed by Harriet's height. A hollyhock rising grandly over the faded spring blossoms which preceded it.

"Harry, don't you need to rejoin my aunt?" Roxley glanced over her shoulder at the crowd beyond. "Help Miss Manx with some errand or other?"

Wasn't someone going to come fetch her away? Even the Duchess of Preston or Lady Henry would do nicely about now.

Of course, so would Bow Street.

"Your aunt? Would you like to introduce her to Miss Murray?" Harriet's nose wrinkled and she leaned in close. "I don't think she would approve. But now that you mention her, it was about Lady Essex that I sought you out."

About his aunt? Roxley ground his teeth together. Of all the flimsy, unlikely excuses. He leaned in close and whispered at her, "Leave me be, Harry. Please. I'll explain everything later."

"No," she replied, standing her ground.

She would.

"I came over so you could attend to your aunt immediately. The situation is desperate."

Desperate? "Is she ill?" the earl asked.

"No, but —"

"In league with French agents?"

"Well, of all the foolish —"

"Is her life in imminent danger?"

"Why of course not." Harriet appeared as annoyed with him as he was with her. "It is her heart, my lord. It is in danger."

"I thought you said she wasn't ill."

"She isn't. Rather the ailment is a Lord

Whenby."

"When — what?"

"Whenby," she corrected. "Lord Whenby. Oh, botheration, Roxley, the man is trifling with your aunt and you need to do something."

"You came over here to tell me that some aging Lothario is dangling after my aunt?" Roxley didn't know whether to laugh or throw up his hands in despair.

Of all the ridiculous notions . . .

Harriet took him by the elbow and turned him toward his Aunt Essex. "This is a matter of grave import."

Now she was near enough that he could smell her perfume. It wasn't violets or roses or lavender water for Harry, but something wild and indescribable that assailed his senses.

Drove him mad. Chipped at his resolve.

Keep her well out of this, Roxley. Well away from you.

All he needed was someone, anyone thinking Harriet was important to him.

Ludwick's fate prodded him to do what needed to be done.

"Harry, you demmed well know that is a lie!" Roxley stepped back, away from her, away from her perfume. Any minute now she'd flutter her dark lashes and then he'd be in knots. But his words had done the trick, and now the lady was indignant.

"I would never lie, not about this!"

But she wasn't talking about Aunt Essex anymore. She was talking about them.

He ignored the pleading look in her eyes and said instead, feeling like a complete heel, "Oh, now look what you've done!"

Harry spared a glance over her shoulder at the empty spot Miss Murray and Lady Kipps had occupied. Then to his dismay, the chit moved closer.

Again.

"Whatever has you in such a fettle tonight? Were that mousy chit and that wretched Lady Kipps bothering you? They certainly appeared to have been overstaying their welcome."

"No, hardly," he told her, setting her aside and trying to catch a glimpse of the heiress. "But you've gone and pushed her away. And tonight of all nights."

"Me?" Harriet's lips pursed together for a moment as she considered his accusation. "Wasn't much of a push if my arrival was all it took to get the lady to abandon you."

"Your arrival, if only! And carrying tales, Harry. That's beneath even you. My aunt being romanced by some dilapidated roué. You wretched, impossible child —"

"*Tsk, tsk, tsk.* I'm hardly a child." She tipped her head and gazed up at him. Suddenly she wasn't just the simple country miss Lady Kipps had claimed, but something altogether more forbidden.

And certainly no child. That jinni had fled her bottle sometime ago. Outgrown it, as it were.

In all the right places, he recalled, unable to resist taking a glance at her familiar curves, the rise of her breasts, the long, coltish legs hidden beneath her skirts.

"Don't remind me," he said, more for his benefit.

Please, don't remind me.

Of course she did.

"You didn't think I was a child last summer at the Duke of Preston's house party when you —"

"Harry —" This time his warning tones worked.

"Oh, if you insist."

"I do."

"Whoever is she?" she asked. "I can't see why you would want to spend time with any friend of Miss Edith Nashe —"

"Lady Kipps now," he reminded her.

Harriet's gaze rolled, her lip curling at the notion of that upstart merchant's daughter holding an old and esteemed title. "You can dress up a sow —"

"Harry —"

She appeared unimpressed by the warning in his voice. "And what, pray tell, did you intend to do with that mousy miss *Lady Kipps* is dragging about?"

He'd been lucky so far that his actions at Owle Park hadn't gotten him shot; explaining the particulars of his plans for Miss Murray would certainly qualify him for a full display of the infamous Hathaway wrath.

Deciding cowardice was the better part of valor in this instance, he caught Harry by the elbow and started dragging her through the crowd, not that such a plan was any better. This close, her perfume left him wavering again.

Resolve, my good man. Courage, he told himself. *You can't drag Harry into this mire.*

This is for her sake. Her very life.

"Well, I doubt you plan on marrying *her*," she protested. How like Harriet to get right to the heart of a matter. No dancing on the head of a pin for her.

Rather she stuck the sharp end right where it needed to be.

Which was exactly the reason he'd wanted his courtship of Miss Murray all tied up and buttoned down before Harriet got wind of it.

He'd never thought she'd just turn up in London, where she would do her utmost to remind him of what he should be doing.

Marrying her . . .

His gut twisted and he pulled to a stop. Because he knew without a doubt there was no way to explain this other than being blunt and hateful.

And lying through his teeth.

"And why wouldn't I marry her?"

If he hoped she'd turn and leave, he should have known better.

She laughed. "Her? Your countess?" She continued to laugh until she was holding her stomach. "Please, Roxley, don't tease so."

"You don't think I'd marry Miss Murray?"

Her reply was another fit of guffaws.

"I am, you know," he declared.

She snorted a bit. That is until his staunchly stated words appeared to sink in. All her nonchalance, her confidence melted away, as if the truth was driving a wedge into her heart. Tearing it in two. "You aren't," she said. More like stated as a fact.

"I am."

Her chin notched up a bit. "You haven't asked her, have you?"

No, he hadn't. He'd been putting the matter off for more than a fortnight now. And he knew why.

Well, he did now.

Because part of him — well, most of him — didn't want to succumb to Mr. Murray's blackmail, or settle for the man's daughter. He had wanted to get to the bottom of all this chicanery — his unfathomable string of bad luck, Mr. Ludwick's inexplicable disappearance, and then Mr. Murray's perfectly timed arrival into his life.

Roxley was a gambler at heart, and coincidences left him suspicious.

Yet suspicions alone were all he had, and could no longer hold sway. He needed facts, evidence. Proof. Before someone else "disappeared."

He glanced over at Harriet, so bright and alive, like a freshly lit candle.

No, he vowed. No matter what, he wouldn't let anything extinguish her brilliant light.

So perhaps Harriet's untimely arrival was just the push he needed. A reminder of what must be done.

"I was just about to." Roxley rose up a little, squaring his shoulders. "And she'll accept, Miss Hathaway. Mark my words."

Harriet shook her head, ringlets dancing

about. "She's not your type."

Of course she isn't, his heart clamored. *She isn't you.*

Roxley screwed up his courage and charged in. "I'll go ask her right this very moment —" He chucked his chin in the opposite direction, toward the punch bowl. He had no idea which way Miss Murray had gone but right now it hardly mattered.

Besides, he had Harry's full attention. He'd break her heart and send her on her way. Keep her far from this mire.

"No?" He shrugged. "You know me, Harry. I never wager where I'm not sure of the outcome. I'll go ask her to be my bride this very moment. See that I won't."

Harriet's mouth opened, her lips moving, but the words failed her.

Not that it was any problem for his Aunt Essex.

"Who the devil do you mean to marry, Roxley? Tell me now!"

Harriet's heart hammered an unthinkable refrain. *I'll ask her to be my bride.*

She'd heard him wrong, certainly she had.

"Roxley, do stop gaping and answer my question," Lady Essex repeated. "Who is this you intend to marry?"

Harriet didn't know if she wanted him to answer.

And nor did Roxley, apparently. "My dearest and most favorite aunt," he replied, leaning over and bussing her on both cheeks, thus avoiding the subject altogether.

As well as stretching the truth a bit.

Harriet knew for a fact his Aunt Oriel was his favorite. A fact she doubted this Miss Murray knew.

Lady Essex had ignored her nephew's subterfuge and continued pressing the point. "I came to Town the moment I heard the most distressing bit of gossip about you — though I give it little credence."

Harriet swiveled at this. Lady Essex had known? Known that Roxley was entertaining the thought of marrying someone, and still had insisted Harriet accompany her?

Whatever for?

"Distressing?" Roxley looked around as if he hadn't the slightest idea what his aunt could mean. "Aunt Essex, if you toddled up to London every time you heard a distressing bit of gossip about me, you'd have worn your barouche out years ago."

Lady Essex huffed, and then turned her failed chiding on Harriet. "Miss Hathaway, whatever is wrong with you? You look pale." The old girl nudged her in the ribs to stand

75

up straight.

Harriet did her best to straighten even when it felt as if the floor beneath her feet was spinning out of control.

I'll ask her to be my bride.

"I fear I might have a megrim coming on," she said.

No one who knew Harriet would ever believe such a lie. Harriet Hathaway gave megrims, she was never on the receiving end.

"Pish!" Lady Essex declared. "You are made of sterner stuff. Why, we just got here. And here are Miss Timmons and Miss Dale." The lady grinned from ear to ear at the sight of her former protégées — at least she claimed them as such since their spectacular marriages.

Of course, when both had been embroiled in scandal, the lady wouldn't have been caught dead uttering their names.

"Miss Timmons, how you have blossomed! Oh, dear, I mean, Your Grace. And Lady Henry!" Lady Essex beamed. "Perfect timing. Perhaps the two of you can help cure whatever it is that ails Miss Hathaway."

The Duke of Preston and Lord Henry had returned as well, and they all shook hands, making their usual greetings, but there was an uneasiness about all this, and Harriet re-

76

alized why.

They all knew. About Roxley. And hadn't wanted her to learn the truth.

No wonder they hadn't invited her to Town for the Season as they'd once promised. And why their letters had become more and more scarce.

But whyever wouldn't they have told her *this*?

Probably because they knew you would have jumped aboard the first mail coach to London and caused a fine scandal.

Yes, well, perhaps, Harriet would concede.

Meanwhile, Lady Essex was once again off and running. "Oh, goodness! Whatever is she doing here? I would have thought society would have grown tired of her by now."

"Whoever has you in such a fettle, Lady Essex?" Tabitha asked, looking in that direction.

"That loathsome Miss Nashe," Lady Essex said, her nose wrinkling.

"Lady Kipps," Daphne corrected. "Miss Nashe is now Lady Kipps."

"Yes, yes," Lady Essex said, waving her hand at Daphne. "So the *cit* has gotten her coronet, but now it seems she is bringing her friends along." The lady sniffed. " 'Tis akin to feeding squirrels. Feed one and the next thing you know you are feeding them all." She peered in that direction again, and turned to her nephew. "Who is that dreadfully thin lady with her? She looks French."

This was apparently not a characteristic in the lady's favor.

And before anyone could reply — not that anyone was rushing to supply Her Ladyship an answer — Lady Kipps and her companion were before them.

"Lady Essex!" Lady Kipps said loudly, so all could hear her. "How delightful to see you again." The countess curtsied perfectly, and they had no choice but to make theirs to her. "I am in alt that I have the privilege of introducing you to my dearest friend, Miss Murray."

Again, there was a round of strained but polite nods and curtsies.

"Miss Murray," Lady Essex mused, tapping her fan to her lips. "Do I know you?"

"Oh, you will," Lady Kipps rushed in. "Miss Murray was my particular friend at Mrs. Plumley's School in Bath."

"I thought your particular friend at Mrs. Plumley's was Lady Alicia." Daphne glanced around. "By the way, where is Lady Alicia? You seem to have lost her this Season."

It was well-known that once she'd gained her marriage, Lady Kipps had dropped the poor but well-connected spinster, setting her sights for higher connections.

"Lady Alicia? Poor darling girl. I believe she is taking the waters in Buxton. The rigors of the city and all," Lady Kipps said with a breezy and dismissive wave.

Harriet had spent her time taking Miss Murray's measure, and found there wasn't anything in particular she could dislike. Miss Murray, for her part, smiled slightly, and stood with perfect Bath posture in a proper, yet well-appointed gown.

If anything, she seemed a bit mousy.

But Harriet's study of the other girl had not gone unnoticed.

"Oh, Miss Hathaway!" Lady Kipps exclaimed. "Here you are. Yet again. How you do pop up."

Like a bad penny, her tone implied.

"We just arrived," Lady Essex said, edging closer to Harriet.

"Has your mother come this time?" Lady Kipps asked, looking around.

Harriet shook her head slightly. "No. I came to London with Lady Essex." She had the distinct feeling she was being drawn into a trap.

Of course she was. This was Lady Kipps. And she probably hadn't forgotten Harriet's part in the Mr. Muggins debacle.

Harriet certainly hadn't, doing her best to tamp down the memory and the wicked grin that threatened to give way.

"And did you bring a companion this time?" Lady Kipps pressed, brows furrowed, all proper concern and care.

And then Harriet heard the metal snap of the jaws.

Of course she hadn't, and Lady Kipps knew that. Harriet had limited means, and hired companions and expensive gowns were luxuries she couldn't afford.

"I could recommend an agency," Miss Murray offered kindly. "I would be lost without my Miss Watson." She turned to Lady Kipps. "A lady should never be without the steady grace of a proper lady's companion."

Both ladies laughed, and when no one else did, Lady Kipps explained. "It was one of Miss Plumley's most oft-repeated admonitions. No? No one else has heard it? But of course not. It is only at such a dignified and discerning establishment that one learns the true graces of society."

Harriet heard Daphne groan behind her fan. Lady Kipps had spent the entire house party last summer going on and on about her incomparable education at Mrs. Plumley's and using her lofty and expensive education to compare herself to the other ladies in the company.

Miss Murray turned to Tabitha. "Your Grace, I don't recall seeing you about Bath. Which establishment did you attend? Miss Emery's, perhaps?"

The Duke of Preston snorted and looked about to double over at the suggestion that his wife was the product of a Bath education.

Nothing could be further from the truth.

"I was educated at home," Tabitha replied.

"How remarkable!" Miss Murray declared, as if anyone of any consequence could have married a duke without the requisite pedigree of a Bath education.

Harriet noted that the girl didn't bother to ask her or Daphne where they went to school. She probably assumed there was no need to bother.

Their answer was self-evident and unimpressive.

"Lord Roxley," Miss Murray said, having edged herself over to the earl's side, as if that was her rightful place. "I cannot believe this is your Aunt Essex. You described her so differently and yet here she is, and so utterly delightful." The girl smiled as if her words both were both a scold and a compliment.

"Indeed," Lady Essex remarked with a bit of a sniff. "How odd that he hasn't mentioned you. Not a single word."

There was no mistaking that her words *were* a scold.

"I am certain, in the future, Lord Roxley will be mentioning Miss Murray most often," Lady Kipps said, smiling at her dear friend.

"How long have you known the earl, Miss Murray?" Harriet asked, trying to sound sincere.

"Oh, my, what is it now? A fortnight," she said, blushing slightly. "Why, I feel as if I have known dear Roxley forever."

Of all the smug and presumptuous statements. Harriet's hands fisted at her sides, that is until she spied Tabitha giving her a nearly imperceptible shake of her head.

Not here. Not now.

Bother, Tabitha! But she was right. Harriet did her best to paste a smile on her face, but it probably looked more like a snarl.

Which it was.

"Only a fortnight, and already . . . Well, we'll leave that for another time," Lady Kipps cooed. "And how long is it that you've known the earl, Miss Hathaway? Ages, isn't it? Aren't you *old* acquaintances?"

To Harriet's surprise, it was Roxley who answered. "Miss Hathaway and I have known each other since we were children — her and her brothers," he replied, his eyes never straying over toward Harriet.

Look at me, she wanted to demand. *Look at me and tell me that you could marry her after a fortnight and abandon . . . everything we . . .*

Harriet couldn't even bring herself to finish the thought.

"So long?" Miss Murray replied. "You don't truly look *that* old, Miss Hathaway."

Her hands fisted once again, and Harriet did not dare look at Tabitha. Or Daphne. Or Lady Essex.

But the old girl had her own way of helping. "Ah, yes," she said, her lips twitching, "I remember well when Roxley and Miss Hathaway first met. So very memorable."

And because everyone else knew the story, they laughed.

Save Miss Murray. And Roxley. And most of all, Harriet.

"Oh, you must tell!" Miss Murray declared. "I know so little of my —" She stopped herself as if she had said too much.

"Yes, do tell," Lady Kipps urged. The woman had the instincts of a shark. The story hinted at a bloodletting and she certainly wanted to have her portion of all the gory details.

"Yes, do tell, Roxley," Lady Essex urged, closing her fan and smiling at her nephew.

"I don't really remember —" he demurred. "It was long ago and is not worth repeating."

Harriet was going to rush to agree, for she hardly needed her childhood transgressions being repeated in front of the likes of Lady Kipps.

But it wasn't Lady Essex who dove in. No, to Harriet's horror, her brother Chaunce paved the way. He'd come up upon them in that barely noticeable way of his that made him such an asset to the Home Office. "I hardly think, Miss Murray, you want to learn how Roxley was floored by a little girl."

Harriet whirled around. Did everyone know about Miss Murray except her?

Apparently so.

"I was only ten," the earl was protesting. "And I hardly expected a little girl to —"

Then everyone had to add their own version of the story.

Wasn't that the first time you ever visited Foxgrove?

. . . summoned up for inspection and . . .

Harry's temper . . .

Our mother was horrified.

"Whatever happened?" Miss Murray asked, stopping the flow of chatter and catching everyone by surprise with the authoritative tone in her voice.

"Nothing," Roxley and Harriet said at once.

Miss Murray turned her smile toward Chaunce. "Will you tell me, Mr. Hathaway?"

Harriet hoped her dark glance at her brother told him all too clearly that Roxley's long ago fate would soon be his if he dared open his mouth.

But being a Hathaway, Chaunce dared.

And while he did, Roxley remembered.

Kempton, Surrey
1792

"Lady Hathaway and her offspring, ma'am," the butler at Foxgrove intoned in ominous tones. "All of them."

"All of them?" Lady Essex muttered under her breath with a mixture of horror and indignation as she glanced around her perfectly ordered salon and then at the bustling mother hen — all ribbons and bows — who was shooing her brood into the room.

The mistress of Foxgrove was not happy,

and her brows arched imperiously as she sent a withering stare down at her nephew, the Earl of Roxley.

He might be only eleven, well, nearly eleven, but Roxley knew the necessity of this visit was going to be counted against him.

Aunt Essex was most likely worried about her collection of china figurines or the chinoiserie vase she held in such high esteem.

Not that Roxley cared about a few painted shepherdesses or that ugly dragon of a pot. He was rather more dismayed by the horde of children lining up in front of him.

Six of them. All tall and rather strapping.

So this was what the doctor had meant when he'd told Aunt Eleanor that a summer in the country would help him catch up with the other boys his age.

Roxley gulped. What did he know of boys his own age? He'd lived with his various maiden aunts most of his life.

The aforementioned Lady Hathaway bobbed a curtsy to Lady Essex and launched into the long process of introducing the children, the names whirling off her tongue. "George, Chauncy, Benedict, Benjamin, Quinton, and my dearest, darling daughter, Harriet."

The boys all chortled a bit, and then

remembering themselves — that is, after a quelling glance from their mother — they straightened in unison.

Roxley looked down the line of Hathaways searching for which of them might be the girl.

He'd seen girls in the park and they were frilly affairs with fluffy petticoats and ringlets. From what he could see, the one at the end was wearing breeches and a patched coat. Certainly there was no sign of tidy ringlets in the dark strands of hair that stuck out at all angles. "You're a girl?"

"I'm Harry," she corrected. "My name is Harry." A replica of her brothers, right down to the coal black hair and startling green eyes, she stepped forward, arms crossed over her narrow chest, her nose crinkled up as she looked him up and down. She sniffed and turned her gaze toward the suit of armor standing in the corner.

Roxley shifted. What the devil did he care if he'd been all but dismissed by a little girl?

But for some reason, what this little girl thought mattered.

He'd worry about the *why* later.

"You don't look like a girl," he told her, a statement which brought a hearty round of guffaws and laughter from her brothers.

"Well, I am a girl. And one day, Mama

87

says you'll want to marry me. With any luck, that is."

A stunned silence filled the large parlor. Had this wretched little imp just said what he thought she'd said? She must have, because the heat of mortification rushed to his cheeks.

And he wasn't alone — Lady Hathaway was also sporting a rather bright shade of pink.

Marriage? To a country ragamuffin? He'd rather marry Aunt Ophelia's mangy cat.

Standing a little taller, which still left him infinitely shorter than the rest of the Hathaways, he said in his most noble of tones, "I hardly think so." Then he looked down his nose at her and added, "No, decidedly not."

After another uncomfortable moment of silence, the Hathaway brothers burst out laughing, as if they couldn't contain themselves any longer.

As for Harry, she shot one vengeful glance over her shoulder at the lot of them — traitors all — and then turned to Roxley and unleashed her wrath. She launched into him like a cannonball and tackled him to the floor, small fists flying and her knee gouging toward his private parts.

Roxley had no idea what to do, other than howl in dismay. His fencing master had made it abundantly clear: a gentleman never harmed a lady.

Then again, he doubted Monsieur Coquard had ever encountered the likes of Harriet Hathaway.

"You take that back!" she cursed. "You'll marry me one day or so help me —"

"Owww —" the young earl wailed as the little vixen atop him continued to mercilessly pummel him. "Get off me!"

"Oh, gracious heavens!" Lady Hathaway sputtered, losing all her poise and flutter. With the air of a woman who could herd cats, she reached into the fray and hauled the two up to their feet. There was a clunk of heads and a good shake before they were set on their feet.

Having already inherited, Roxley was used to being deferred to, to being advised, to being told what and how a gentleman did. Now here he stood, humiliated, ruffled, and his head ringing from the little girl's blows as much as it was from being knocked into Harriet's thick skull by Lady Hathaway.

He straightened his coat and waited for the apology that he knew was his due.

Lady Hathaway did none of that. "Now, there, the two of you stop this, or grant me patience, I will knock your heads together yet again."

Again? What had he done? He was about to protest the matter, when he noticed that Harriet just shrugged and wiped her nose on her sleeve, before settling back into line.

Apparently this was how such matters were decided among the Hathaways, so Roxley followed suit, but he still felt as if there was a cloud of humiliation over his head. But when he glanced down the line of children, one of the boys — Chaunce, he thought — winked at him.

As for Lady Hathaway, with the mayhem managed, she was once again all gracious smiles and elegant manners, as if her daughter hadn't just knocked a future member of the House of Lords to the floor.

"Children, this is the Earl of Roxley," she said, nodding at them to make their greetings.

They all did, giving him varying degrees of bows, including Harriet.

Yet it was Lady Hathaway who held his attention, giving Roxley a once-over from head to toe and then dipping into a curtsy for his benefit.

Roxley glanced over at his aunt, who was watching the proceedings with her jaw set and her gaze hooded. Then he looked back at Lady Hathaway, and in her eyes was something so poignant, so sad.

It wasn't pity — that he'd seen enough of in his young life. Orphaned at four, and having spent the last six years being shuffled between his aunts, pity he knew in spades.

It would take years for Roxley to decipher that memorable glance, and when he did, he came to the unshakeable realization that in that moment, probably a little before that, Lady Hathaway had added him to her brood without a second thought.

That she'd seen what had been missing from his life and knew exactly what needed to be done.

Even if it was the occasional sharp rap to his head. Earl or not.

"Lady Hathaway," he said, just as he'd been taught, and made a perfect bow in return.

Which garnered another raft of guffaws and coughs from the gallery of groundlings known as the Hathaway children.

"Yes, well," his aunt said, still giving a wary eye to this horde in her salon. "Perhaps the children would like to walk in the gardens."

This was not a question, but a suggestion. Nay, an order.

"A walk," Lady Hathaway echoed. "Yes, *a walk* sounds like the perfect activity."

"Can we take that?" little Harriet asked,

pointing at the suit of armor.

Aunt Essex gaped in horror. "Certainly not!"

"Maybe just the breastplate so he doesn't get hurt?" she asked, nodding at Roxley.

So he didn't get hurt? Roxley's gaze went in a frantic sweep to his aunt.

"You may walk in the park," Lady Essex told them. "Armor will not be necessary."

Again, this was answered with duly nodding heads, which were followed by carefully hidden chortles and guffaws.

Roxley knew right there and then, his demise was imminent. And that armor might be the only thing standing between him and some gory end.

Which should have been evident to his great-aunt when, without any further urging, the Hathaway children went surging toward the French doors that led to the gardens as if thrilled to make their escape.

"A walk, boys, nothing more," Lady Hathaway repeated.

More? Roxley, who, having been nudged by Aunt Essex, fell into line behind the Hathaways, glanced back at his aunt in real alarm. He'd never played with other children, never been outside in the country, and certainly had no idea what "more" might mean.

Though having seen how this Harry Hathaway managed herself, "more" would certainly be the death of him. Which ran rather counter to what Aunt Eleanor had ordered when she'd sent him to Foxgrove.

More like banished.

Roxley was of half a mind to remind Aunt Essex that he was the sole remaining Marshom capable of holding the earldom, but his aunt was already ensconced on the settee, having launched into an avid discussion with Lady Hathaway about the upcoming Midsummer Ball and the need for new buntings.

And then something happened.

Harriet Hathaway looked over her shoulder at him, and smiled. Her grin, which it turned out was missing a few teeth, did something rather odd to his heart. It erased all his enmity from earlier and left no doubt in his mind that this Hathaway was indeed a girl.

Her eyes sort of sparkled a bit when she smiled like that, and without another word, she reached back and caught hold of his hand.

Warm, round fingers wound around his, and she tugged him out the doors and into the bright sunshine. "I won't let them hurt you. I promise." This was followed by her spitting on the ground, as if that bound her words around him in some sacred childhood ritual he knew nothing of.

Still, he took it as a good sign. For having witnessed her scrappy nature, up close as it were, it also implied — just as he suspected — that his life was in imminent danger.

He was about to smile back when he found himself in the middle of yet another valuable lesson that had eluded his solitary childhood.

The pecking order.

"Look, Harry's got a suitor," one of boys mocked. It was either Benjamin or Benedict.

It was impossible to tell the pair apart. But those words were enough to send a raucous volley of laughter through all the boys.

Roxley tugged his hand free, and scowled at them. "How dare you laugh at me," he said, doing his best to imitate Aunt Eleanor, who had quelled a group of lads in the street with much the same statement. "I am the Earl of Roxley."

His imperious stance and words only made the Hathaways laugh harder.

Even, to his embarrassment, little Harriet.

"Well, I am!" he repeated, knowing even as he said the words, they were not helping his cause.

"Yes, well, prove it," the one named Chaunce declared, slapping him on the back so hard he stumbled forward. "Race you to the trees."

And that was all. The lad pointed at a stand in the distance and took off like an eager colt, galloping across the lawn.

The rest of the Hathaways whooped and yelled complaints about a "head start" and "cheater" and then followed their sibling with the same exuberance, racing across the lawn in anything but a walk.

Only Harriet stayed put.

Yet it was obvious from the way she quivered with excitement that her veins hummed with the same valiant blood. "Well?" she said, elbows jutting out at sharp angles as she stuck her fists to her hips. "You know how to run, don't you?"

Then she took off like a fleet little doe, quickly catching up with her brothers. Roxley followed and was winded and humiliated by the time he reached the trees — well after the Hathaways.

All the Hathaways.

If he expected to be mocked and taunted yet again, the Hathaways had their own way of doing things. That he was game to try won them over. And in the true world of children, they claimed him with all their hearts.

Especially one Hathaway in particular.

"You won't flatten him now, will you, Miss Hathaway?" Lady Kipps remarked, and there was a round of laughter all around.

"I'm rather undecided on the point," Harriet replied, looking not at the earl but her brother. Oh, the Kempton curse might be lifted, but Harriet would remain cursed for the remainder of her days.

Cursed with five ruinous, horrible brothers. Glancing over at this one, she changed that tally to four. Four brothers. She was positively certain, if the opportunity presented itself, she'd murder Chaunce before the night was over.

Couldn't he see how Lady Kipps would be telling one and all what a hoyden Harriet Hathaway was — once a hoyden, always one, she'd imply to each and every audience she could find. Not a lady . . . hardly proper.

Though, sadly, Harriet realized, bludgeoning her brother might just prove that point. How utterly unfair!

"I'm certain Miss Hathaway has learned her lesson now," Miss Murray was saying, in a way that suggested that it was her certain belief that Harriet probably hadn't improved much in the ensuing years.

"What lesson might that be?" she couldn't resist asking, trying to sound demure and innocent.

"That a lady never strikes a gentleman," the heiress informed her, as if Harriet needed the benefit of Miss Murray's superior education.

"One can hope," Roxley remarked to no one in particular.

CHAPTER 3

It is my only wish, Miss Darby, that we hadn't met, so that this day would never come to pass — where I must take up an honorable course and do what is right for my regiment, my country, my king. I know you shall not forgive me — why should you when I cannot forgive myself.

Lt. Throckmorten to Miss Darby
from Miss Darby's Reckless Bargain

Much to Roxley's dismay, Fieldgate arrived just then and claimed Harriet for the next dance. Kipps offered to dance with Miss Murray, and Lady Kipps wandered off seeking more interesting gossip.

Roxley used the opportunity to escape his aunt's notice and slipped away.

"Harriet Bloody Hathaway," he muttered under his breath, as he watched the viscount squire her to the dance floor. The minx had a way of leaving him all tangled up. Always had. And especially when he saw her with that bounder Fieldgate.

Not that you've been much better . . .

No, he hadn't been.

And the moment she got off the dance floor, he'd do his demmed best to explain everything.

That is if she didn't box his ears first.

Apparently, Harriet would have to get in line for the privilege. "Roxley! Is that you?" called out a short lady in a large plumed turban, who plopped into his path like a wayward garden toad.

"No, I fear not, Lady Gudgeon," he said politely.

She laughed. "Oh, you are as droll as ever, my lord — even if you are all but rolled up."

He wished he could be rude and just depart, but that would hardly do. His aunt thought Lady Gudgeon quite discerning so it would never do to snub the woman — not when he'd already antagonized Lady Essex once this evening.

The baroness, not waiting for any further pleasantries, launched right into the object of her desire. "I have been in Bath of late —"

How unfortunate you chose to return, he mused, though with a polite smile on his face.

"And I am overwrought with worry regarding your aunt, Lady Eleanor."

Aunt Eleanor? Whatever could she have done now? One would think that a lady of her age would be past shocking society, but leave it to Essex's twin to continue her lifelong pursuit of infamy.

"And I came back to London straightaway —"

Of course you did. If only to be the first to report my aunt's latest peccadillo. If there was ever a wager being placed on who was faster, Lady Gudgeon or the Royal Mail, Roxley knew exactly where he'd place his blunt.

"Only to discover that my dearest friend has fallen prey to the same dire situation. Dear Roxley, I implore you to do your duty."

Between her jabbering and her wavering feathers, Roxley was starting to feel slightly dizzy. "My duty?"

He hadn't the least notion what she meant.

Lady Gudgeon was happy to indulge him. Roxley couldn't say he shared in her joy.

"Yes, of course, your duty," she said, her thick brows waggling as if that made this all clear.

There was only one duty that he knew — having been reminded often enough by his aunts — that he had yet to fulfill. "You mean marriage?" he exclaimed. "Why, my dear Lady Gudgeon, are you proposing?" He leaned over and with a most serious tone said, "Whatever will Lord Gudgeon say?"

The old girl blinked, then let out an exasperated sigh. "Roxley! Oh, heavens, you are a wicked fellow. Not me! I am only here to remind you that you are the head of your family."

"So they tell me," he agreed with a solemn nod.

"And your dear aunt, my particular friend, Lady Essex, is in need of your wisdom."

Now it was Roxley's turn to blink. Since most society thought him a fool, it was a rarity, no, this was perhaps the first time anyone had ever called upon him for that particular talent. "Heaven help her on that score," he told the matron. "My wisdom?" He looked around. "Are you certain you have the correct Roxley?"

Lady Gudgeon was not only blunt, she did not suffer fools. She rapped him sharply on the sleeve with her fan. "Mind what I am saying. Your aunt is in dire straits and needs your guidance."

He rubbed his arm as he looked up and across the room where his Aunt Essex was holding court.

"Can you not see what I do?" Lady Gudgeon whispered as she squinted in the same direction. "She is in grave danger."

The only danger Roxley could imagine this night that was in store for any of them was the disagreeable supper Lady Knolles was known to set down before her guests.

"Lady Gudgeon, I am certain there is no harm about to befall my —"

Rap. "You must save her, my boy! Everyone is talking about it tonight. They all see what poor, dear Lady Essex does not." This was followed by another significant, squinty glance across the room to where his aunt stood.

Roxley did his best to come up with an answer. "How that turban hardly works with that gown?"

Thwack. "No, you fool. Look!" She nodded again.

"The Duchess of Preston? I assure you, her dog was not invited."

Lady Gudgeon colored at the reminder, for the duchess's dog had chased the lady across Hyde Park one infamous afternoon . . . a memory the lady preferred to forget.

"Oh, good heavens, Roxley! Not that duchess. *Lord Whenby.* There at her elbow. How could you not notice?"

Whenby? Whatever had Lady Knolles put in the punch bowl? First Harriet, and now Lady Gudgeon.

"I try not to notice my aunt if I can help it," he confessed, even as he was trying to place Whenby. But he couldn't. Not from his clubs. Not at the races. Not at boxing matches. Roxley hadn't the least notion who this aging gallant was.

But apparently the female half of the *ton* did.

"Must I remind you, she is your responsibility."

"I think my aunt would disagree." *Vehemently.*

Lady Gudgeon leaned closer, holding up her fan to hide what she was saying. "Whenby is out to fleece your aunt."

Roxley pressed his lips together. The old fool could try. After all, it was usually the Marshoms who were doing the fleecing. But he knew he needed to mollify Lady Gudgeon or he'd never be rid of her. "I hardly think —"

"Of course you don't," she snapped, clearly having run out of patience with him. "You never do! But you must try, Roxley. Now more than ever. Whenby is a ruinous, scandalous roué —"

Lady Gudgeon was worried about Lady

Essex's reputation? Finally something amusing about this entire conversation.

Had the dear old matron ever really met his aunt?

He endeavored to keep a serious expression. "You think Lord Whenby is going to seduce my aunt?"

"I don't know what he is about, but it can't be good." Again the fan came up. "Whenby is barely received."

"Probably because he is barely known," Roxley pointed out. Then he remembered why the name was vaguely familiar. "Then again, my lady, I do believe he was part of the Duke of Preston's house party last summer. Lady Juniper would hardly have included this fellow on her guest list if —"

"Lady Juniper? Whatever would she know of men? Married what, three, nay, now four times — and willingly. Bah! Whenby's poor *ton,* clearly evidenced by the fact that he's lived on the Continent for ages. Everyone knows what *that* means. Don't let it be said that I didn't warn you. When Lord Whenby leaves your aunt ruined and penniless you will have no one to blame but yourself."

Roxley crossed his arms over his chest and took another look at this fellow. "You must own, Lady Gudgeon, that if all of that were to befall my aunt, Lord Whenby would bear some responsibility in the matter."

"Bah! You'll see! When it all tumbles down around your ears, you'll see that I was right." With that, Lady Gudgeon stormed off.

Wasn't his life already tumbling down atop his ears, as Lady Gudgeon so eloquently put it?

Straightening his coat and shaking off the remaining ill-will the lady left in her wake, Roxley took a quick glance around the room, searching for Harriet — and found her still dancing with Fieldgate.

Would this demmed set never end?

In the meantime, he took another look around the room and spied his old friend Poggs, probably the only remaining man in Town who still owed him money — and had been like a fox to ground in paying up.

Roxley crossed the room and clapped his hand on the baron's shoulder before the wily fellow could give him the slip. "Poggs!"

"Roxley!" the baron said, smiling widely. "Just the man I've been looking for."

Looking for him? This was rather out of character for Poggs. Roxley had quite expected the fellow to bolt once he'd caught wind of the earl's approach.

"And here I thought you were avoiding me —"

"Never, never, my good man!" Poggs said, looking overly affable. "Should I be?"

"Well, now that you mention it, there is that matter of that wager from last spring —"

"Oh, yes, well, you'll be utterly diverted when I tell you the most interesting *on dit*. Why, I daresay you'll forget that trifling vowel entirely when you hear what I have to tell you —"

Roxley doubted he'd forget such a large debt or dismiss it as trifling. His Marshom forebears would rise up from their graves and haunt him for such a thing.

Forgiving a debt, indeed!

Poggs, meanwhile, continued nattering on. "— for you see I've had a letter from my mother —"

"Your mother, you say?" Roxley scratched his chin. "No, I can't say I am diverted. Not in the least."

"No, no, Roxley! You miss the matter entirely. My mother wrote me with instructions to seek you out."

"Your mother wants to pay your debts?"

The man's brow furrowed and he leaned in. "No. And I prefer that she doesn't hear of them either. She can be rather difficult over such things."

Roxley pasted a sincere expression of

concern on his face and nodded his agreement. There were times like these when it was rather convenient to have been orphaned at a young age. No parents to fuss and worry over one's indiscretions.

Though he did have his aunts . . .

Speaking of which . . . Poggs's next words couldn't have surprised him more. "I must warn you, Roxley. It is a personal matter." The man lowered his voice and leaned closer still. "About your aunt."

Roxley reeled back. What the devil? More tales of Essex and her swain? He'd put an end to this affair if only so he wouldn't have to be bedeviled by the gossip. "Yes, yes, I know all about that."

"You do?"

"Yes. Lady Gudgeon was just filling my ear with dire tales of —"

"Lady Oriel," Poggs said, nodding in agreement. "Then again, it might be Lady Ophelia. Devilishly tricky to tell the two of them apart."

"Lady Oriel?" Roxley shook his head. "No, you must mean Lady Essex. My God, this Whenby fellow gets around if he's romancing Aunt Essex and Aunt Oriel."

"Whenby?" Poggs squinted. "Never heard of him. But you will want to hear this. My mother wrote that she was *seen.*" The baron's bushy brows rose noticeably.

"Seen? Whatever the devil does that mean? I don't think she's ever been invisible, so I would assume she's always been 'seen.' "

"No, no. You don't understand," Poggs hurried to say. "She was *seen*." Then he nudged Roxley with his elbow as if that made the entire puddle of mud crystal-clear.

The earl threw up his hands. "Poggs, do get to the point."

"I thought I was. My dear Roxley, my mother wrote to me that I must carry word to you that your Aunt Oriel was seen in a rather high flyer of a phaeton, not even a sennight ago." Poggs's toady chest puffed out until it appeared that his buttons would pop.

"Lady Oriel, you say?"

"Yes, that's right."

"And this was cause for alarm? Scandal enough for your mother to put pen to paper?"

"Of course. Now I hope you don't think ill of me for carrying such a tale —"

"My dear Poggs, once you've repaid me what you owe me, I shall most likely forget your very existence."

"That would be overly kind of you, my lord," the fellow agreed rather too hastily.

That is until the words slowly sank in. "No, no, Roxley. You haven't got the entirety of it. Your aunt was *seen.*" When Roxley continued to gape at him, the man took another deep breath and continued, "Your aunt was seen in a phaeton. A rather fast one. If you know what I mean."

"Yes, Poggs, I know what a phaeton is. I've seen one. Hell, I own two." Owned, rather.

The man nodded happily. "Then we are in agreement that this is a most disagreeable business."

"You mean disagreeable in the fact that I am having a devil of a time getting my hundred pounds?"

"No longer, sir," Poggs replied, for some unfathomable reason appearing quite indignant over the mention of his debt. "You must see that! I've done the honorable thing and warned you."

"Warned me? About what?"

"About your aunt."

"Yes, yes. In a phaeton.

"Yes, exactly," Poggs replied happily.

If only Roxley could share his elation. "What the devil do I care about my Aunt Oriel riding about in a phaeton?"

"Care? Why, you should be outraged! I would be if my dear aunt was lingering in the company of Sir Bartholomew Keswick!"

"Sir Bartholomew?" Roxley huffed. "Him?"

He was most assured now that Poggs had been drinking. He hated to tell the man but Sir Bartholomew Keswick was a figment of his aunt's overly wrought imagination.

Poggs grew even more exasperated by Roxley's lack of dismay. "My lord! Your aunt's treasured reputation — those were my mother's exact words, 'treasured reputation' —"

"Good heavens, I should hope they weren't yours," Roxley told him.

The barb was lost on the baron, intent on delivering the rest of his message. "My mother says there won't be a bit of plate left at Marshom Court with Sir Bartholomew about —"

Roxley didn't want to let poor Poggs know there hadn't been real plate about the house in three generations.

And while he was at it, perhaps he ought to check on Poggs's mother's brandy bottle. She must be imbibing if she was seeing Sir Bartholomew as well.

"— and that he is the worst sort of bounder, roué who ever lived."

Certainly, Poggs had the right of it — the man was a bounder.

But he also was merely another of his Aunt Oriel's delusions. There was no Sir Bartholomew, save in his aunt's fertile imagination.

Yet this news tugged at him, like a noose tightening around his neck. It all had a rather Machiavellian familiarity to it. First Essex, then Eleanor, now Oriel. Could this all be related?

What with his own pending ruin, and now his aunts, who were just as much a part of his inheritance, as they were his duty, as Lady Gudgeon had so eloquently reminded him.

And not for every coin in the realm, or even just enough to dig him out of his current mire, would he admit they were also his heart and soul. His dearest girls. He loved them so completely that to think that any harm might befall them because of something he'd done —

Or failed to stop . . .

At this point, Poggs drew a deep, shuddering breath, but before he could launch into the rest of his promised lecture, Roxley stopped him.

"What does your mother propose? Is she willing to chase off Sir Bartholomew? For if she is, then by all means, I'll forgive your debt — for it will save me a trip out to the

Cottage."

Poggs took great offense to the earl's suggestion. "My mother! My mother, indeed! Sir, this is *your* responsibility."

And there it was. His responsibility. As if he didn't demmed well know that.

"I rather detest that word, Poggs. And I don't like it flung about. So off with you. Or I'll ask my old friend Mr. Hathaway to come over and help me turn you upside down and we'll shake the coppers you owe me out of your pockets." Roxley jerked his head toward Chaunce, who stood lounging against one of the walls.

The baron glanced in that direction and his face went beet red. For two very good reasons. Certainly because Roxley wasn't above making good his threat. Nor would Poggs stand a chance of escaping such a humiliation.

That didn't mean he still wasn't going to get the last word in before he hopped away like an indignant toad. "I've done you a favor, Roxley! I have indeed! I was only trying to help."

Roxley glanced up and flicked his hand, summoning his friend, but Poggs was already on the run.

Yet his final word hung in the air around the earl. *Help.*

The notion prodded him. *Help.*

He had tried for months now to determine what the devil was going on — whether this singular plan to ruin him was an old grudge, a leftover case from the Home Office, the tattered remnants of a dalliance that had ended badly — but none of those offered even an inkling of understanding.

No, he needed help.

And when he looked up, his gaze landed once again on his oldest friend. Chaunce nodded in reply, as if the fellow understood exactly what the earl needed.

No one could say more with a flick of a glance and a nod than Chaunce. Then again, that was probably why he was the Home Office's most effective agent.

"What the devil are you doing out here?"

The nondescript woman in the plain black gown winced at the bite of hard, solid fingers into her elbow as the man pulled her off the garden path and into the shadows of an archway covered in roses.

"Keep your voice down," Madame Sybille scolded, yanking her arm free and glaring at him. She found it best to keep this man unsure of how much she feared him.

Not that she couldn't be dangerous when needed. "We've run into a complication."

"I doubt it. I have everything in order, madame. Now get back in there before someone sees you out here with me." He gave her another rattle.

"Everything in order!" she scoffed. "Did you know Roxley's aunt Lady Essex has arrived from the country?"

This took him aback, as she knew it would. "Lady Essex?"

"Yes," she told him. "And she isn't pleased about Miss Murray."

Her partner wasn't really listening. "That's excellent news," he was saying more to himself. He looked up. "She's precisely who we need. Perhaps he's even summoned her —"

"No, no, it isn't like that. He was shocked to see her."

"Hmm. Still, this might be perfect timing. Perhaps she came bearing an engagement gift." He glanced at the open doors and then back at Sybille. "Has he made his proposal to Miss Murray?"

"No, he hesitates," she confessed. "But he's a fool to delay. He'll be ruined before the end of the week."

"Don't let that capering facade deceive you." There was an edge to his words, sharp and dangerous. "Lord Roxley is no idiot. He's a Marshom through and through.

Nothing escapes those cheating culls. He's biding his time."

"He hasn't much left, *mon cher,*" she told him. "When he proposes, we shall have what we've been waiting for."

"No. No more waiting. I will have my due now," he said, that familiar edge of madness that had always worried her lacing his every word. He brushed past her roughly and moved deeper into the shadows.

"Where are you going?" she called after him, picking up her dark skirts and taking a few steps toward him. But she wasn't so foolish to follow him completely into the shadows.

"To take advantage of an opportunity." Nor were his words of any comfort. Cold and foreboding like the man himself.

Sybille shivered as a garden gate, hidden in the darkness, creaked open. There was no sound from his boots. He was as silent as a cat. That was exactly how he had snuck up on her and entangled her in this dangerous game to begin with.

But one she intended to win. Eventually.

No matter who else had to meet an untimely end.

"Superb dancing, don't you agree, Miss Hathaway?"

"Pardon?" Harriet replied. For she hadn't really heard a word that Lord Fieldgate had uttered since he'd claimed her hand for the supper dance. In fact the entire evening had become a bit of a blur.

Roxley to marry Miss Murray?

It couldn't be true. Not when . . .

She blinked back the tears that threatened to spill over. She never cried. And yet, suddenly she was as much a watering pot as that silly Miss Fidgeon from the Miss Darby novels.

Harriet took a steadying breath, for up ahead was Roxley escorting Miss Murray into the supper. This should have inspired a bit of the Hathaway temper, wrath, a few cutting words, but how could she when all she could hear was Roxley's voice from that night at Owle Park.

I love you, Kitten. You hold my heart.

He loved her. He did. He couldn't have been lying. And yet . . .

Here he was squiring an heiress, the perfect sort of lady earls married.

Not the daughters of impoverished baronets who wore made-over gowns and hadn't the dash and polish that came with a proper Bath education.

"The dancing, most excellent," Fieldgate was saying, slanting a glance at her. "Are

116

you well, Miss Hathaway?"

She glanced up at the viscount and found him studying her most intently. That he'd actually noticed her distress rather surprised her. Here Harriet hadn't thought Fieldgate much more astute than a loose carriage wheel.

"Just a bit fatigued," she told him. "From the travel. Lady Essex and I only just arrived today from Kempton."

"Today? And you are already out in company? My, my. Dare I hope, Miss Hathaway, you have done this because you were anxious to rekindle an acquaintance?"

I was, she thought, glancing once again at the back of Roxley's dark head.

"I will take your silence as the reticence of a lady to admit her heart," Fieldgate said, sounding far too smug.

This got Harriet's attention, for when she looked up at the viscount, she realized he meant himself. As in she had been pining away in the country for him.

Oh, good heavens. However could she tell the man her preference wasn't so much for him but his unsavory reputation. Where other ladies would politely decline such a nefarious fellow, Harriet had waded in with a flirtatious smile on her lips.

Honestly, she'd never understood why the

viscount returned her attentions. She wasn't his usual pursuit — at least so she knew from having overheard Lady Essex with one of her more gossipy friends. Apparently the viscount preferred widows and other sorts of ladies . . . the kind with a Mrs. before their name and no husband to speak of.

But suddenly last Season he'd become enamored of her, and his pursuit had been a bit of a mystery.

Not that she'd minded — Fieldgate, it turned out, was rather handy.

For the man had a way of putting Roxley out of sorts. Brought him to her side in no time, if only to scold her. And then remembering his manners, he'd dance with her, leaving her dizzy with joy.

But not tonight. She'd danced with Fieldgate twice and Roxley still hadn't appeared to scold her. Not even to wag a finger. He hadn't even sent her a level glare from across the room.

Of course, glancing ahead to where he stood beside Miss Murray, she understood why, for her heart was echoing only half of the familiar refrain.

He loves me not.

"Whatever happened?" she said aloud without thinking.

As it was, Fieldgate answered her quite

unwittingly. "Ah, yes, Roxley," he said, his gaze following the direction of hers. "And Miss Murray. Quite stole the march on any number of us. How he discovered her is a mystery. Demmed fine luck, that."

"A mystery?" Harriet asked, her gaze still fixed on the woman who was now the bane of her existence.

"Oh, yes," Fieldgate told her. "The earl went too deep last fall. Pockets to let, so I hear. All but rolled up. Worse off than Kipps was last Season. Then like some conjuring fellow at a country fair, he appears with Miss Murray. She'll save his hide, she will. Well, her dowry will."

But all Harriet heard was that Roxley was in trouble. She glanced around the crowded room and knew without a doubt that such news wasn't a secret. So why hadn't anyone told her?

Why hadn't he? Her heart did a double thump, but then a very practical part of her smoldered white hot.

He should have told her.

The viscount led her through the packed room, where the tables had been set up nearly on top of each other to accommodate all the guests. Across the way, Tabitha and Daphne shot her apologetic glances that said very clearly they had tried to save her a seat, but it appeared the duchess's Timmons relations had come and made themselves welcome to the empty chairs, despite her aunt's misgivings over associating with the likes of Lady Henry.

Across the room, Chaunce had spotted her, and then spied her companion. She glanced away to avoid the dour expression of protest that was sure to follow.

So Harriet searched for another place — one far from her brother — and realized the only seats Fieldgate could manage were at the table directly adjacent to Roxley's.

And Miss Murray.

Harriet's nose wrinkled. Oh, bother! The dainty heiress made Harriet feel like an unseemly country bumpkin.

As the viscount pulled out a chair for her, it smacked directly into the earl's.

"My apologies," Fieldgate said, with sly twist to his brows as Roxley spied Harriet about to take her place so close at hand.

For a moment, as Harriet sat down, she swore she'd seen that old flicker in Roxley's eyes, the one that warned her off from keeping such company and the spark that said the earl knew all too well that her heart was his.

Anytime he wanted to claim it.

But now, that spark barely had a chance

to flicker before he extinguished it. "No worries, my good man," Roxley told the viscount. "A bit of a crush tonight." Once again all glib manners and foppish cares.

Harriet wanted to dash him over the head — she glanced around for something well and good for dashing — but spying nothing of weight or value, had to make do with the hope that someone would wander by with a rather large vase.

"Probably hoping to catch another infamous scene," Fieldgate was replying. "Willing to provide one, Roxley?"

"No, not I," he demurred. "My scandalous days are over."

His words rang with a warning, as if he knew exactly what she was thinking, or rather planning.

She bristled a bit. He thought she meant to ruin his plans? How could he? Her indignation gave way to the realization he had every right to think thusly, especially given that she'd been having a rather delightful fantasy of seeing a chinoiserie vase crack over his thick skull.

Then there had been her behavior earlier. When she'd interrupted him and Miss Murray.

Well, in her defense, how could she have known that he was about to pledge his future to such a whey-faced *cit*?

Harriet straightened, her indignation returning. She'd show Roxley she wasn't some bothersome little scamp who followed him about. She, Miss Harriet Hathaway, the daughter of a gentleman, could spend the evening as the epitome of good manners and ladylike demeanor, who is utterly and completely above reproach.

Even if she was being partnered by the rather scandalous Lord Fieldgate.

On cue, the viscount leaned over and said, "Miss Hathaway, I had forgotten how devilishly pretty you are."

Behind her, Roxley shifted in his seat, and usually she'd use such a perfect moment to say something equally shocking, some quip that would have the earl out of his seat and protesting, demanding satisfaction, but . . .

Oh, bother! This was going to be harder than she'd realized.

Composing herself, Harriet smiled blandly at the viscount's compliment, sitting with all the precision that Lady Essex had drilled into the Kempton Society members.

Posture, Lady Essex liked to say, *is what marks one a lady even when a situation is most dire.*

She supposed this evening counted as "most" something.

Aggravating, perhaps? *No.*

Horrible? *Getting there.*

Heartbreaking? *Decidedly so.*

She pressed her lips together. Roxley just couldn't marry this Miss Murray.

She stole a glance over her shoulder where her adversary sat, all excellent posture and precise manners, the markers of a miss with a superior education.

And an heiress to boot. Harriet glanced down at her own gown, remade from one of her mother's, and sighed. She might not have even noticed such a thing once, but it came with being friends with Daphne. Eventually the difference between a made-over gown and one sewn of fine silk by a London modiste became evident even to Harriet.

And much to her chagrin, Miss Murray wore what could only be described as a perfect gown. Harriet grimaced as she glanced again at the fine point lace and the little brilliants sewn into the sleeves.

Make that *very* well off.

Harriet shifted in her seat as jealousy wiggled down her spine like a worm. *An heiress.* Bath educated. All the requisites of a future countess.

Of course, he loves you not, that horrible voice of doubt whispered at her.

Yet when she stole one more look at her adversary, something about this perfect nonpareil seemed wrong. Not that Harriet could put her finger on anything precisely, but everything about Miss Murray was too right.

Harriet shook off such a musing, for it was nothing more than her envy talking. Leaning toward the viscount, she whispered, "My lord, tell me more of Roxley's misfortunes. I had no idea —"

The man brightened, because apparently sharing another's misfortune was his favorite diversion.

Better than admitting to his own failings.

The viscount lowered his voice to a conspiratorial whisper. "Roxley's always been a lucky devil. Pockets of vowels on the most unlikely of wagers. Luckiest demmed fellow who ever lived."

Harriet nodded. Roxley, for all his capering ways, always landed solidly on his feet. But then again, he wasn't the fool he pretended to be. Something only his closest friends understood.

"But when he came back from Preston's last summer, it seems he left Lady Luck at Owle Park."

"Last summer?" she echoed. "After the duke's house party?"

"Yes. You might not have noticed, but he made a rather abrupt departure after the masquerade ball." The viscount waggled his brows at her. "You recall the night?"

She remembered. Even now she could recall the press of Roxley's body against hers, the eager claiming of his lips, his hands caressing her, exploring her. She might have started the kiss — yes, she'd been that brazen — but oh, how the earl had carried off the night.

Even now, with the earl just behind her, their chairs nearly touching, she could smell a hint of his cologne, that subtle combination of rosemary and lemon and something very masculine, so unique that it could only be described as *Roxley*. How she'd inhaled deeply as he'd held her that night, the very scent of him intoxicating.

Fieldgate, meanwhile, had continued pattering on about the earl's bad luck. A mortgage to cover debts, bad investments, some unsavory rumor about his man of business, and now he was being dunned at every turn. "His title is all he has left."

Which would fit neatly into the plans of an upstart heiress with her sights set on a countess's coronet. What else did an heiress of sketchy connections wish for but an earl down on his luck?

Look how Miss Edith Nashe had fared last Season. And that conniving minx was as low as they came.

"Yes, well, shall I fetch us something to eat?" the viscount asked. "If I don't hurry, all the beef will be gone."

"A most excellent idea," Harriet said, favoring him with a smile. "Oh, and a glass of champagne, if you can manage?" This would delay his return, and leave her with more time to consider all the viscount had revealed.

Fieldgate rose and bowed and then moved toward the supper line.

Roxley done for? She shook her head. Had he truly mortgaged Foxgrove — the house that had been Lady Essex's home since birth? She took a steadying breath, not so much for the earl but for his dear great-aunt.

That the Marshom family with all their freewheeling ways hadn't gambled away the estate generations ago was a bit of a miracle.

Now it might be lost? Harriet didn't know what to think. However would the earl continue to support Lady Essex, not to mention his other aunts — the ones he complained of frequently, but she knew he loved dearly — if he was so deeply encumbered?

The answer struck her squarely between the eyes: by making a quick and hasty marriage of convenience.

If she didn't like Miss Murray for her stunning gown and distinctive education, she quite despised her now for the fortune she held. The one that would rescue Roxley.

No less helpful in the other lady's favor was her apparent friendship with Lady Kipps. The countess and her husband had joined Roxley's party. After a few moments of levity, the countess had taken Miss Murray off to visit the retiring room.

When Harriet was certain that Miss Murray and Lady Kipps were well out of earshot, she leaned back in her seat.

"Roxley," she whispered. When he didn't respond, she tried a little louder. *"Roxley!"*

She hated that it sounded like a plea, as if she were begging, but in truth, she was. Her heart was breaking — to be this close to him and unable to turn around and clasp his face in her hands and press her lips to his as she had in the garden at Owle Park.

Convince him that no matter the circumstances he didn't have to do this . . . this terrible thing.

"Oh, Roxley," she said once more.

"Aye, Harry," he said, the resignation in his voice tearing at her heart.

Harriet was never one to beat around the bush. She was a Hathaway after all. "Why didn't you tell me? Why didn't you write?"

"You know I'm terrible about those things. Just ask my aunts."

He could quip at a moment like this? She didn't know whether she wanted to dash him over the head with the nearest plate or overturn his chair.

But she'd promised, vowed, to be a lady tonight.

And ladies did not cause scenes.

Drawing a deep breath, she stuck to her course. "Last summer . . . I thought . . ."

She just had to know.

"Thought what, Kitten?"

Not Harriet. Not Harry. But Kitten. *His Kitten.*

Goose bumps ran down her arms even as tears stung at her eyes. For nothing could have told her more than that precious endearment.

He loved her still. She just knew it.

"Is it because I have no fortune?"

He laughed. "I'd rather have you without one."

"Without?" Practical in the ways of money and fortunes, she couldn't imagine why he would want her as she was . . . penniless.

"Of course. If you came to me with a

fortune in hand you'd lord it over me until the day I died."

"I would not," she protested, but they both knew that was a lie.

And Roxley made a rather inelegant snort to put an exclamation point on his opinion.

Yes, well, he had her there.

"Better me than her," Harriet told him, arms crossing over her chest.

Definitely better.

"Kitten, can we forget last summer? Can you set aside that night and forget?"

Harriet shook her head. Forget?

Forget Roxley kissing her, his lips teasing hers to open up to him. His hands exploring her, slowly sliding her costume from her until she was naked, his skin against hers. Her fingers curling into his shoulders, clinging to him as he brought her . . .

"Go back to Kempton," he continued. "Tomorrow if you can. Then forget me."

"How can you ask such a thing?" she said, exhaling the words in a rush.

"Because I must," he told her.

Harriet turned around. Oh, damn her vow, she'd make a scene if she must, she couldn't let Roxley do this.

And when she turned, she found Miss Murray and Lady Kipps coming up toward them.

Miss Murray's gaze seemed fixed on Roxley, a calculating look that rang with the clarity of a shop's bell.

And then the girl turned her astute eyes on Harriet and the look that followed was one of pure calculation and then in a blink of an eye, dismissal.

Just like that. She was dismissed as unworthy of Miss Murray's concern. But there was something else, something worrisome in the girl's measured glance that sent a chill down Harriet's spine.

Something is very wrong, a chorus rang out, and Harriet began to push her chair out, some wild, nonsensical plan forming in her head, when she realized that not far behind Miss Murray stood Lady Essex.

Lady Essex, who would lose her beloved home, her place in society if Roxley was ruined. And Harriet owed the dear old girl so much. Not for all the dratted lessons in how to curtsy or dance a quadrille or pour tea, but Lady Essex was her friend. Her dear and beloved mentor.

For her, Harriet would do anything.

Even sit down and silence her heart.

Which she did.

And in that moment of silence, she swore she heard Roxley whisper one more thing.

I'm so sorry, Kitten. Ever so sorry.

CHAPTER 4

If I were to kiss you, Miss Darby, it would be the most dishonorable thing I have ever done.

Lt. Throckmorten to Miss Darby
from Miss Darby's Daring Dilemma

Roxley steeled his heart as he heard Harriet settle dejectedly into her chair.

Perhaps there was still a chance, he mused. And then it was an opportunity lost, for here came Miss Murray.

"My lord," she said as she sat down beside him. "You had mentioned earlier that you had something you wanted to discuss with me."

Roxley looked over at the girl and knew what he was supposed to do. Propose. Charm her into accepting him. To save his aunts. To save his estates.

But out of the corner of his eye, he saw Harriet, or rather her riotous ebony curls cascading over her shoulders and falling nearly to the middle of her back, and something inside him shifted. He saw that hair as he'd seen it once before, loose and long. So very inviting. He knew what it felt like sliding like silk through his fingers.

And he heard her.

You'd come after a lady, if you ruined her. You'd never abandon her.

In an instant, he remembered that night, how her faith in him had been unshakeable.

It had all begun that very night, this madness in his heart. It had begun with naught but a kiss.

Harriet's kiss. Binding him to her.

Then. And still.

Roxley glanced over at Miss Murray. "Discuss? Hmm. I fear I've forgotten what that might have been."

For his thoughts were far too full of visions of a moonlit London garden. A night so very unlike this one.

Half foxed, he'd stumbled into Sir Mauris Timmons's garden with nothing but a dodgy plan to cast up stones at windows, searching for what he knew not, but discovering everything he'd ever desired in a kiss.

London, one year earlier

It had been the most scandalous night of

the Season, and one would think that the Duke of Preston's example of getting himself entangled with Miss Timmons and ruining the gel in the middle of Lord Grately's ball would be enough to warn Roxley off from his current course of action.

Actually, it was because of the quagmire from this evening that he was here — in the garden behind Sir Mauris Timmons's London house — tossing stones at the windows hoping to find Harriet, or at the very least, Miss Timmons, to see how the poor lady fared.

Oh, bother, if he was being honest, he'd readily admit he was looking for Harriet. And Harriet alone.

What with her long dark locks and emerald eyes . . .

No! No! No! That wasn't going to do. She was Harry. He chided himself to remember that.

Roxley shook the lingering vision of a lithesome, utterly desirable woman from his memory and reminded himself why he was really here. Given how furious Sir Mauris and Lady Timmons had been when they'd left the ball with their disgraced niece and her friends in tow, Roxley wouldn't have put it past the rather furious baronet to have locked them all in the attics or worse.

Yes, that was it. He wanted to ensure that Harriet was safe and sound. His moonlight and most scandalous visit was not the least bit motivated by how her dark lashes fluttered so demmed invitingly. Or the way she'd looked tonight in that new gown — lush and tempting.

He shook his head and picked up another small stone. Lush and tempting, indeed! This was Harry. Harry Hathaway. That wretched little minx who always tagged along after her brothers, all scrawny elbows and knees and always demanding her fair share of whatever trouble her brothers and Roxley had managed.

And then, just before he was about to cast up yet another hope-filled stone, like a wish into a pond, the door from the kitchen down below opened and out she stepped.

Still trouble, yet now ever so tempting. He blinked and looked again. More so.

Like a nymph she came up the steps, wearing a pink wrapper over a white muslin night-rail that peeked out at the hem. Her hair was simply bound in a long braid that fell over her shoulder down nearly to her waist.

Squeezing past came Miss Timmons's wretched brute of a dog, the infamous Mr. Muggins.

"Roxley, what the devil are you doing here? Do you mean to get me in more trouble than I already am?"

He grinned. He couldn't help himself. When she scolded him like that, it warmed his heart in ways he didn't understand. "That's why I'm here. Wanted to make sure Sir Mauris hadn't drowned the lot of you in the Thames like a litter of unwanted mongrels."

Mr. Muggins walked him past him and slanted a glance at the earl that said all too clearly there would be no talk of mongrels. Not in his hearing.

Roxley was still watching the dog amble deeper into the garden when Harriet came alongside him and caught him by the hand, saying, "Drowned us, indeed! Truly, Roxley, it is nothing like that." She pulled him through the narrow garden to an alcove in the back, where they could stand in the shadows and not be seen from the house. "But he and Lady Timmons are furious."

"Is that regret I hear in your voice?" he asked.

"For helping Tabitha?" Harriet shook her head most adamantly. Of course she didn't regret her part in the scandal.

Any more than he regretted coming here.

At least not yet. Then he realized she was

still holding his hand, her warm fingers wound with his. This wasn't the first time they had stood so — with their hands entwined, bound together — but why, how had everything changed? The heat from her hand moved through his limbs, and with it came this sense of belonging.

For someone who always held society and life at arm's length, the sense of coming home left him a bit breathless.

"We are all to return to Kempton tomorrow," she was saying.

That caught his attention. "Tomorrow? Whatever for?"

Harriet let out a breathy sigh. "Because Tabitha is ruined."

That hardly made any sense. "Isn't Sir Mauris planning on calling on Preston first thing on the morrow? Though I wouldn't recommend it, for when I last saw the duke, he was headed in the direction of White's — he'll still be half-seas over at dawn. Not that it will matter either way. He won't marry her."

She scoffed at this. "He will indeed. The duke loves Tabitha. Any nobcock can see that. Besides, it is how it is done — she's ruined, after all — he'll ask her to marry him, even if he must follow her to Kempton to do so."

"Oh, Harry —" Roxley began, not knowing how to tell her that not all men were so honorable. And a man of Preston's reputation . . .

Harriet scoffed at this. "You'd come after a lady, if you ruined her. You'd never abandon her —"

Roxley shifted uneasily at this, for all she had to do was change that sentence a bit.

You'd come after me, if you ruined me. You'd never abandon me.

For it wasn't her confidence in him — that unwavering faith that he wouldn't disavow her — but his desire to test her theory that left him shaken.

Kiss her, Roxley, and find out.

What the devil was he thinking? Ruin Harry? Good God, no.

He straightened and tried to look impervious to her prodding. "Since I have no intention of ruining anyone in the immediate future —"

"You'd follow," she said as if she knew him better than she knew herself.

And it struck him that perhaps Harriet Hathaway was the only woman in all of England who knew him just that way. Always had.

She glanced over her shoulder at the house. "However did you know which

137

window was mine?"

"I didn't," he told her. "I just kept tossing up stones until you arrived."

Harriet swatted him on the shoulder playfully. "You're lucky it is me out here and not one of Tabitha's loathsome cousins. I doubt you'd want to be found in the gardens with one of them."

Roxley shuddered. "No, not in the least." Especially given Sir Mauris's infamous temper, and Lady Timmons's well-known desire to see her daughters rise up in society. He'd be in the parson's trap before dawn.

"Remember when you thought my window was Chaunce's and you sent that rock right through it?" Harriet was saying. "I don't know how you mistook the matter —"

"Yes, perhaps I was a bit squiffy," he murmured, caught by the way the moonlight cast her dark hair with an almost bluish hint. And it hadn't been a mistake — he had come over from Foxgrove that night looking for Harriet. He'd hoped then . . . Well, never mind what he'd thought. Not that he'd tell her. It would only give her ideas.

As if Harry needed the help — good heavens, she was out here in her night-rail, which was giving him terrible ideas. Devious notions. Ridiculous temptations.

Couldn't she have tossed on some old cloak over this gossamer bit that clung to her willowy form and left a man with no doubt what his hands, his lips, his body would find beneath.

He glanced up and realized she was looking at him — an amused little smile playing on her lips, pursed as they were and so ready for . . .

Don't look at her lips.

So Roxley did his best to change the subject. "Actually Chaunce is why I'm here. He was busy, so I offered to come by and check on you."

Her brow furrowed almost immediately. "How kind of you to do a favor for my brother. Now that you've checked, I suppose I should go back inside." She turned to leave.

But he didn't want her to go just yet. Demmit, this was ridiculous. This was Harry Hathaway, and yet . . .

"At least you look like yourself again," he said aloud without thinking.

Harriet stilled. "Myself?" she asked, glancing over her shoulder. "Whatever does that mean?"

Roxley moved to block her escape. "Not all done up," he told her, waving his hands at her hair and the length of her lithe, willowy form that was so perfectly outlined by her wispy night-rail and wrapper.

The rise of her breasts. The curve of her hips. The line of her collarbone that was so temptingly kissable . . .

Good God, man! Don't look at her that way. This is Harry.

Oh, but Harry had changed. Ever so much.

And while he was gazing at her, doing his best to ignore the way her night-rail dipped down to reveal the rising tops of her breasts, she was gaping at him. "Are you bosky?" she asked, hands now fisting to those tempting hips.

"What a terrible thing to ask a fellow, Harry," he admonished. Because, yes, he was. Slightly.

Pot valiant, one might say. That, or stark raving mad.

He had to be mad because he was seeing Harriet in an entirely new light. A tempting one. A ruinous one.

Gads, this was the same sort of foolish thinking that had gotten Preston all tangled up with Miss Timmons . . . and here he'd ridiculed the duke for haunting the park in search of the vicar's daughter and following her about at balls and soirées, and now he was making the very same mistake.

Harriet, unaware of his inner turmoil, had continued on unabashed. "My mother always says if you have to ask a man if he's drunk, you probably already know the answer." She leaned in and sniffed, and immediately had her evidence.

"Your mother is a wise woman," Roxley agreed, not willing to admit it had taken a good half a bottle of brandy to get his courage up and come over here.

Not when he knew that one false move, one wayward kiss and the entire Hathaway clan would be hunting for him. Including Lady Hathaway, a veritable Amazon when it came to her children. She might count him an honorary Hathaway, but if she discovered he'd been dallying with Harriet, he wouldn't put it past her to flay him alive.

"Wise?" Harriet shook her head. "Maman is determined, you mean. When I left, she was measuring my room for repapering. She said once I went to Town, I'd never come home again. And now . . . it will be all roses and gilt and she'll have invited Cousin Verbena to come stay indefinitely. I'll be sleeping over the stables."

"She couldn't have meant it," Roxley told her.

"I do believe she was counting on me falling in love and running away like she and Papa did."

Roxley had to stop himself from turning and looking at her right then. For if he did, he didn't know if the suggestion behind her words — *run away* — would become reality.

Instead, he saved himself with a light-hearted quip. "Would save your father the expense of a wedding."

Not that Harriet was about to let him off the hook. She moved closer to him. "Are you offering, Roxley?" she whispered softly, the way a woman did when she wanted to touch you but hadn't quite the nerve. Yet her softly spoken words were like a lure; they drew a man closer.

Tempted him to do the reaching.

Where the devil did these chits learn how to do these things?

He could hardly blame her wiles on some Bath school. Then again, her mother had been a bit of scandal herself if all the old gossips were to be believed.

Indeed, Harriet Hathaway came by her siren manners naturally — though luckily for him she had yet to discover them — completely.

The earl held his ground and kept up with the lighthearted banter. "Offering what? To pay for your wedding, Kitten?"

Her gaze flew up at that. Not Miss Hathaway. Not Harriet. Not even Harry. *Kitten.*

A smoky, intimate light ignited in her eyes.

Now, what had he done? Kitten? He was mad. Or too foxed. Or well in over his head.

No, not Kitten. Minx, perhaps. Bothersome, troublesome minx. Yes, that was better.

And yet when he glanced at her, with her loosely woven braid and those tempting green eyes, she was all kitten. His Kitten. Ready to wind him around her finger with soft glances and even softer curves.

"No, my lord," she told him, taking another step closer. "Are you offering to carry me away?"

He took back his conviction that she had yet to grow into her wiles. Oh, they were all there. And fully engaged.

As was he, he realized, shifting uncomfortably in his suddenly too tight breeches.

"There you are again, Harry," he told her, edging away from her, trying to catch his breath. "Asking me to marry you again."

It was the perfect jibe, for she was all indignation now. "I was not," she replied hotly.

"I beg to differ. You quite plainly are trying to tempt me into running away with you."

But her ire didn't last long. "Is it tempting, Roxley?" She glanced over her shoulder at him and, damn her, fluttered her lashes.

He stilled and in an instant saw the entire plan unfold before him. Whisking her away. Riding for the border. Carrying her into his bed . . .

But even in that moment, he came to his senses. "Run away with you? Are you mad?" He wasn't too sure if that was for his benefit or hers. "Your brothers would take turns murdering me."

Even as he said the words, he realized he hadn't outright denied the notion, just thrown up the real obstacle to such a plan.

"Roxley, don't be foolish. They can only murder you once."

How kind and practical of her to point that out.

"I would never underestimate your brothers' ingenuity," he told her. "They'd find a way so they could each have a turn."

She moved slightly, coming closer. To him, Harriet was always such a tumbling ball of energy, but now, she'd found a woman's grace and could move . . . oh, how she moved, slowly, seductively. It left him off balance and at the same time trying to keep up with her.

More like one step ahead.

"They wouldn't dare. I wouldn't allow it," she whispered.

There it was. They could run away — free from her brothers' wrath. And again, he saw the end of that long road to Scotland, with this ethereal, willful creature in his bed. In his life. In his heart.

He could nearly feel the Fates nudging him in the back. *Steal her away. Whatever are you waiting for?*

Roxley shook that brandy-muddled thought away. Just how foxed was he?

"This a foolish discussion, for I'm not carrying you off," he told her, hoping his words sounded final.

"At least not tonight," she shot back.

Well, she needn't sound so confident.

"Not ever, minx. Never."

"Never is a long time, Roxley."

"Not long enough," he told her. "You should go back in before we are discovered and you are stuck with me."

"Ruined because I was out here with you? How ridiculous," Harriet scoffed. "You haven't even kissed me."

Kiss her? Oh, no, there wasn't anything scandalous in that.

Save everything.

Yet here he was, eyeing her and halfway considering the notion. How could he not?

She had the most kissable pair of lips he'd ever seen. Lips meant to be teased, explored, opened . . .

Roxley closed his eyes, well aware that if he kissed her there would be no going back. If he even kept considering such thoughts he'd find himself entwined with her . . . his hands exploring those delectable curves, his lips . . .

Taking a deep breath, he clung to his last shred of honor. "I am most decidedly not going to kiss you."

He sounded convincing, didn't he?

Perhaps a bit, for Harriet glanced up at the moon and shook her head. "Then for heaven's sakes, whyever did you come here?"

"Like I said, to make sure Sir Mauris hadn't tossed you and those reckless jades you call friends out on the street."

"Would you have been inclined to kiss me then?"

One could never fault Harriet for her determination.

"Harriet, there isn't going to be any kissing."

She came right up to him and Roxley backed up, only to find himself trapped by the garden wall. With all her twisting and turning, she'd managed to herd him into a corner. Literally.

He glanced around and found Mr. Muggins at his flank. The large Irish terrier sent him a baleful glance as if utterly disappointed in his purported reputation as a rake.

Truly, how long is this going to take?

Roxley ignored the dog. If only he could dismiss Harry as easily.

Practical to a fault, Harriet pressed him for answers. "Then why did you drag me out of bed in the middle of the night into the shadows of the gardens if you didn't want to kiss me? That is how these things are done." Her hand came up to rest over his heart. "Good heavens, given how your aunt goes on and on about your reputation, you wouldn't think you would need to be shown how."

He got over that moment of panic that she was going to show him — for there she was, reaching out to him, and her hand was ever so warm against his chest. The moment her fingers had fanned out, his heart had taken off in a gallop.

Yes. Oh, yes. Ooooh, yes, it thudded.

With only the heat of her touch, Harriet stole her way into his heart.

Because that was how these things were done. With only a look, a touch.

And it might have, if he hadn't been distracted by something very important. He let her hand fall away, and then crossed his arms over his chest — and not because he was trying to ward her off — which he wasn't. He was made of sterner stuff. He was.

Especially when he was faced with this . . . this . . . minx of a woman. "How the hell do you know how these things are done?"

She mimicked his outraged stance. "I just do."

Roxley shifted and went over the various times he'd seen Harriet over that last fortnight. And had a moment of panic. "Not that bloody ass Fieldgate. Has he been —" He couldn't even say it. "Because if he has —"

Now it was Harriet's turn to be outraged. "Fieldgate? Oh, really Roxley! Why would I want to kiss him?"

Well that was a relief. And crossed off the only item on the hastily made list he'd just imagined for the first thing in the morning.

Murder Viscount Fieldgate.

"Then who?" he demanded.

"No one," she said, her lips pursing slightly and a bit of blush rising on her cheeks.

Well, she needn't sound so disappointed.

She wasn't supposed to be kissing just any bounder who came along.

Himself included.

"Then what do you know of these things?" he asked, this time a little more kindly.

"How any lady learns of these things — I read about them —"

Good heavens, she hadn't broken into his Aunt Essex's stash of French novels? Not only were they scandalously detailed, but also how he'd managed an early education in these matters.

Then again, if Harriet had been reading from Aunt Essex's top shelf collection, they'd probably be halfway to Gretna by now . . .

To his relief, her explanation was slightly more tame. "Why, in the last Miss Darby novel, Lt. Throckmorten took Miss Darby out into the gardens and after he proposed, he kissed her." Harriet glanced up at him, all starry-eyed wonder as she recalled the moment with such innocent enthusiasm. "At least I think that was what he did. Something about 'heavenly rapture in his arms.' " She moved right up into his reach. "Is it heavenly, Roxley?"

And then from his flank came Harriet's reinforcement.

Mr. Muggins used his large, bushy shoulder to give Roxley a nudge. *Good God, man! Do I need to draw a map?*

There was a terrible moment as Harriet stood in front of Roxley — watching the conflict of desire and restraint war in his expression — that she thought he was actually going to set her aside.

So she helped matters along — gave aid to the enemy as it were.

She slid her hands up his arms — oh, heavens, how could a man have such muscled limbs? Only momentarily distracted, she continued her exploration upward until her fingers curled around his shoulders and she could pull him closer.

Men! Sometimes the honorable ones just need a nudge in the wrong direction.

Roxley moved slowly, tentatively tipping his head down until his lips were just a whisper from hers. They brushed against hers, tentatively, hesitantly.

Harriet didn't know what was expected of her, but being bold by nature, she rose up on her tiptoes and closed the distance.

If Roxley meant to kiss her, she was going to get kissed.

And he indulged her, by hauling her up against him, one hand on her hip, the other at the small of her back. And with the most inconspicuous of movements, she was up against him, intimately so and his lips teased over hers, calling to her to open up to him, brushing against hers and then his tongue teased an opening and began to explore her.

Harriet nearly gasped. *Oh, my goodness. Yes, this is heavenly.*

She'd never been so close to him before — to any man, for that matter — but there was no doubting his desire for her — especially considering she was wearing only her night-rail beneath her wrapper and could feel everything about him.

Everything.

Harriet shifted and edged closer. She'd done this? To him? Left him hard and trembling where she felt only this tight, dizzy desire to be even closer to him, to feel him. And with just two slight layers of muslin covering her, wherever he touched, the heat of his fingers left a trail of answering desire in their wake.

Oh, yes. Touch me, Roxley. Kiss me.

"Are you cold?" he whispered as she shivered.

"No," she told him, pulling him closer. Not. In. The. Least.

He made a satisfied sort of sound and he began to kiss her right behind her ear, down the nape of her neck, and Harriet could only lean against him, cling to him as his kiss awakened her further, left her heated right down to that point between her legs.

Fire poured through her limbs, left her breasts taut, her knees wavering. Raced, really. Thundered through her veins, bringing a breathless delirium. For more. *Please, more.*

"Don't stop," she managed to whisper. And Roxley obliged her, catching hold of her and turning her so now she was the one trapped, the one with her back to the garden wall, the one totally under his control. Not that she cared, for he was kissing her neck, along her jawline, and then catching her lips anew, this time in a kiss that was hot and demanding. He was over her, around her, and inside her as his tongue slid over hers, tangled against hers, rough and tantalizing all at once.

There was nothing tentative between them now.

She trembled, for if the wall behind her was cool with the night air, Roxley was igniting a bonfire within her, one she'd only wondered at, his lips continuing to add to her torment, stealing over hers, his tongue sliding across hers, teasing hers to explore him.

And it wasn't just his kiss . . .

However did Roxley know she would love having him stroke her back? His other hand — dear heavens, the other one had risen from her hip to cradle her breast, and when his fingers ran over the nipple and then rolled back over it again and again, leaving it hard and budded, she nearly cried out.

With it tight and anxious beneath his fingers, Harriet couldn't imagine that there was more, but then she felt the cool nip of the night air, for somehow, someway he'd loosened the tie at her throat and opened her night-rail — how seemed to be a pointless concern — for he slipped her breast free and even now, bent down to take the hard nipple in his mouth.

The pad of his tongue had bedeviled her lips and now it was rough as it laved over her nipple, leaving her gasping. He suckled her deeply into his mouth, and let his other hand roam farther down until it reached the apex of her thighs, that place that was even now clamoring for attention.

Yes, there, oh, yes, please . . . she wanted to tell him as he slowly pulled her gown up, and his hand roamed freely over the curls there, brushing against her, sliding closer.

Oh, yes, this is what I need.

The very thought, the certainty that it brought, startled her slightly. How could she know such things? She'd never been kissed, never been touched, but some part of her, a very delicious part of her, knew, nay, remembered as if this was an awakening, a gift to every woman.

To remember.

As his fingers teased her, exploring, moving intently deeper into her most private place, she opened up for him, her back pressed to the wall. It was wanton, and perfect, and so very needed.

"Oh, yes," she said as she exhaled in surprise. "Yes." He grinned at her and then caught her lips in a deep kiss, as his fingers teased her, while his fingers worked such a similar, such a more dangerous magic.

Then his fingers found their treasure, and just as his tongue had teased her nipple into a hard point, his touch, sure and confident, found yet another taut nub. His exploration was tentative, just a brush over her, but it was enough to leave her gasping. "Oh, my. Roxley, what is this?" For suddenly she was breathless and trembling, as if he'd pushed her from an abyss.

"Wait, Kitten, just wait," he promised, and sealed his vow with a deep, searing kiss.

His tongue lashing over hers, his finger dove deeper, finding her wet, heated core, and he slid it over her, over and over again, leaving her gasping, shaking and trembling.

Oh, this was heaven. And yet . . .

Harriet reached for something to hold on to, something to touch, her hands sliding from his shoulders where she'd been clinging to him, until she came to the solid, hard ridge beneath his breeches.

He shuddered as she ran her hand down his length, but even as she did so, his finger delved deep, deep into her cleft and *into* her. He was inside her, and Harriet rose up on her tiptoes and it was her turn to shiver, to tremble. His fingers continued to stroke her, tease her, surge inside her, only to subside and tease over her.

Again. And again.

Harriet looked up, the London sky clear enough so she could see a smattering of stars peeking through the haze. She was rising toward them, about to climb upward with them, Roxley carrying her along with his kisses and his touch.

And then it was heaven, breaking over her, inside her, all around her. Roxley pulled her close, kissed her deeply and continued to tease her through wave after wave of rapture.

Yes, indeed, once again, Miss Darby was ever so right.

CHAPTER 5

I'll be the judge of that.
Miss Darby in response to Lt. Throckmorten
from Miss Darby's Daring Dilemma

London, 1811
That night, over a year ago, in Sir Mauris's garden had ended as quickly as it had begun. Once Harriet had sighed with such utter happiness, the back door had swung open and Sir Mauris himself had come out into the garden, blunderbuss in hand.

Even as foxed as he was, Roxley knew this wasn't a time to overstay his welcome. He'd slipped into the night, while Harriet had managed some hastily crafted excuse about Mr. Muggins needing a trip outside.

Sir Mauris's loud complaint, "I thought I'd locked you all in," had made Roxley grin.

As if there was any lock that could hold back Harriet.

His determined minx.

Then the baronet had turned his ire toward Mr. Muggins, complaining that the "wretched beast was digging at his roses again" and to get inside. And thus, their scandalous interlude ended, with Harriet and Mr. Muggins being hustled into the house and Roxley wandering through Mayfair in a state of wonder, a newly ignited spark burning his chest.

Nay, he'd be honest this time. Inside his heart.

Even now, that kiss, which was naught but a memory, refused to do anything other than spark and smoulder inside his heart, reminding him of what he was missing, what he desired more than anything.

Harriet. Always Harriet.

It had pushed him forward the night at Owle Park, teased him into believing that having Harriet was just the beginning of a lifetime. And now it left him with the certainty that having her close would only endanger her life.

His enemy — whoever he was — seemed determined to take and ruin everything Roxley held dear.

And there was no one more dear to him than Harry.

He glanced around Lady Knolles's ballroom, for with the supper ended and the dancing resumed, the room had returned to the sort of crush that made a hostess beam with pride. He'd have to find her before he decamped to White's to meet up with her brother Chaunce, but then he heard his name being called.

"Lord Roxley? Pardon my interruption, my lord."

The earl turned around and found Lady Knolles's butler awaiting him, an expression of long-suffering dismay pasted on the solemn man's face. "Yes?"

"There is a person at the door who is demanding to see you."

Roxley winced. Another bill collector. Or one of the less reputable characters he owed money. A determined lot if they were willing to wait until the wee hours of a soirée to make their presence known. "What sort of someone?"

"He claims to be your valet." The stuffy fellow's words rang with disbelief and a hefty measure of disdain. "He insisted."

Ah, yes. Such disdain could only be inspired by Mingo. Still, Roxley probed a little further just to make sure. "Unsavory sort of fellow with a crooked nose and one eye?"

The butler's brow furrowed. Probably because the earl had described the man to the letter. "Yes, my lord."

"Lead on, my good man," Roxley told him. "Mingo is a bit of a shock at first, but he's a demmed fine valet."

"Yes, my lord. If you say so," the butler agreed in tones that suggested he was merely being polite because he must.

Sure enough, there was Mingo standing in the front foyer, looking as out of place as a blacksmith in a milliner's shop. Shifting from one foot to another while he cracked his knuckles, he looked more like a house-breaker than a nobleman's valet.

That, in Roxley's estimations, was one of Mingo's more endearing traits.

"Ah, it is you, my good man. You have poor Lady Knolles's butler in a stew," Roxley said, stopping in front of his employee. "Coming to call at the front door. Badly done."

"They turned me away at the back," Mingo complained, chucking up his chin at the haughty butler, followed by a glare that would probably be considered a deadly challenge in the rough streets of Seven Dials where Mingo hailed from. "So came around front. Had to see you, I did. Right smart."

"If you are here to warn me that my Aunt Essex has descended upon us, I have already had the pleasure of discovering that little *on dit.*"

Since his Aunt Essex rarely if ever gave him advance notice of her arrival, it was up to Mingo to come up with His Lordship's excuses even as he packed Roxley's valise and snuck it out the back for an extended stay at the earl's club or, if his friend Preston was in an obliging mood, a hasty move to Harley Street.

"Didn't come about that," Mingo said. "But if you must know, your aunt is here. And she brought that smart bit o' muslin with her." Which translated into Miss Manx. Mingo held the gel in high esteem because it was rumored about the house that she had beaten the crafty valet at *vingt et un.* "Oh, and that tall, dark-haired mort you fancy," he added with a bit of a sniff.

Mingo held highborn spinsters in the same category as teats on a bull. Unexplainable and entirely useless.

"Miss Hathaway," Roxley corrected. "And thank you very much for the warning, but I've already had the pleasure of running into Aunt Essex and Harry tonight."

"No trouble, guv'ner," Mingo said, sending him a sly wink. "But that isn't what I come about." He slid closer and nodded for the earl to lean in. "Some rumdrubbers done broke in." When Roxley just blinked and looked at him, the man continued. "A cracksman — more than one — done got in the house. Slipped past me and Fiske and rummaged about above. Made a bit of a mess of things. Did a real number on Her Ladyship's trunks . . . Fiske is fetching Bow Street and I came to get you."

Roxley stepped back, taking it all in. His house had been robbed? Again? What the devil?

And here he thought everyone in London knew he was rolled up. They might have bothered to tell these thieves, so they needn't waste their time in another fruitless search for anything of value.

Then again, it struck him that this wasn't just some random break-in.

"Got the carriage outside —" Mingo was saying.

"I'll go get my aunt and Miss Hathaway," Roxley told him, steeling himself for the moment when Lady Essex had to be told that her belongings had been rifled through by a pack of ruffians.

He only hoped Miss Manx had her over-sized reticule of smelling salts and miracles close at hand.

Mingo shook. "Won't be necessary, guv'ner —"

161

"Why not?" Roxley asked, looking around for his aunt. Come to think of it, he hadn't seen much of her or Harriet since the supper dance.

"It was herself that discovered the blokes," Mingo told him. "Near screeched down the roof when she found 'em in her bedroom."

As his carriage turned right onto Hill Street, leaving behind the calm of Berkley Square, the anger that had been filling Roxley all evening boiled over.

He hopped out of the carriage before the driver even stopped and strode up the steps, the servants and strangers alike parting without a word for him. He crossed the threshold to find most of his household assembled there — his butler Fiske, the housekeeper, even the cook, while the maids and footman hurried and up and down the steps, lighting every candle in the house.

Just out of the chaos, Harriet stood halfway up the stairs, her expression flat, guarded. When she spied him, her expression shifted slowly and deliberately to that dangerous glower he remembered from their childhood.

It was a warning no one ever forgot.

So he made a note to avoid the stairs at all costs, no matter that his heart tugged at him to gather her close, to reassure himself that she was safe.

Not that his aunt was about to let him go anywhere.

"Roxley! Good heavens! There you are!" These exclamations exploded out of Lady Essex and she was a flurry of feathers and ribbons as she bustled to his side. "Where have you been?"

"At Lady Knolles's, as you well know," he told her. "Whatever mischief is all this?"

"This? This? Why we've been robbed! Violated! In my very house."

His house, he would remind her, but it hardly seemed the time.

As Aunt Essex continued to wail and rant, he had no choice but to turn to Harry. "Can you explain this?"

She straightened and related the facts much as her brother Chaunce might. "It is as your aunt says, my lord. We came home and when we went upstairs we found a trio of rough fellows in Lady Essex's room."

"Imagine the horror!" Lady Essex said. "They were in my room!" She shuddered, and for the first time in his life, he saw his aunt as others probably saw her, an aging relic of another time.

He didn't know what came over him, but he began to fold the old girl into his arms, much as she used to do to him. He glanced up at Harriet, but she had looked away, a shimmer of tears at the corner of her eye.

Drawing his aunt closer, he was stopped by a hard, cold object in her grasp. "Whatever is that, Aunt Essex?" he asked, holding her out arm's length and examining the treasure she held.

"Why, Pug, of course," she told him, the large china figure there in her arms, cradled like a baby. "What if those foul villains had taken Pug?"

If only they had, he mused, looking at the hideously ugly and battered china figurine that his aunts held so dear. The eccentricities of the Marshoms knew no bounds, and Pug was one of them. Chipped and faded though it was, the old girls fought over Pug as if it were the most valuable possession the Marshoms held.

Sadly, it probably was.

"Dear Pug," Lady Essex was explaining to no one in particular. "He's been in the family for ages. So beloved, and it would have been a tragic loss. My sisters would never have forgiven me. Why, I just left him out on the mantel where he could have been . . . might have been . . ."

Smashed. Stolen. Dashed into the street. All of those were perfectly satisfactory fates for the demmed thing, for it would have meant Roxley would no longer have to receive complaining letters from Eleanor or Oriel or Ophelia that Essex was once again keeping Pug all to herself.

Before he could find an appropriate reply for Pug's spared fate, out of the shadows stepped Lord Whenby.

Roxley took a second glance, unsure how he'd missed the fellow. But here he was soothing Aunt Essex as if they were old and familiar friends.

"There, there, Essie, you are a brave lady in the face of such circumstances," he was saying.

Essie? Roxley looked to Harriet to see if he had heard the other man correctly.

I told you so, the rise of her brows, the turn of her lip told him.

"My own *maman* had a dear figurine she was quite fond of —" Whenby was saying. "It is a sign of elegance and distinction when one favors such craftsmanship."

At this, Lady Essex shot an arched expression at her nephew as if to say, *See! Someone understands.*

Roxley was more taken aback by the realization that Lord Whenby was here. In his house. With his arm around Aunt Essex. This mousy, cozening nobleman obviously had a way of blending into the walls.

And, the earl decided, he was blind as a bat. For anyone looking at Pug would never call it elegant or notable for craftsmanship. When not even a thief will take something . . .

Rather than spend any more time debating Lord Whenby's inexplicable presence, the earl turned to his butler and valet. "What the devil happened here? Where was everyone?"

"The servants' night off. Me and Mr. Fiske were going over the accounts." Mingo coughed a bit and then added a belated "my lord."

The earl translated this explanation into the more likely scenario that the pair of them — Fiske and Mingo — had been playing cards and drinking whatever decent vintage Fiske had stashed well out of his aunt's notice.

Not that he blamed Fiske in the least. With Aunt Essex under the same roof, he'd be tipping the bottle as well.

Before Roxley could probe further, the Runner from Bow Street arrived and he took over, asking one and all to relate what had happened.

Lady Essex chose this moment to be overcome by the "shock of it all," so it was up to Mingo to provide the facts.

"All we heard was herself, er, I mean, Her Ladyship hollering enough to wake the dead, and by the time Fiske and me got upstairs, there was a trio of cracksmen running out the front door, bold as brass. Then here comes the mort there chasing 'em with a candlestick in 'er hands and herself not far behind." He sent an approving nod toward Harriet, who just shrugged away her part. "Once they were out the door, I seen that they had a diver out front. No lot of Fidlam Bens these, for they had the niftiest set of glyms I've ever seen — dropped one of them on the way out." He nodded toward a small battered lamp sitting on the receiving table. "Then they were off afore Fiske and I could stop them, not that they got anything. Dead cargo is all they made off with, from what we can find."

Roxley shook his head and turned to the Runner. "Can you translate any of that pedlar's French?"

"You've been robbed," the man told him blandly.

"That's what I said," Mingo complained, and then turned on Roxley. "And don't you go making a show like you can't patter flash." He frowned and then belatedly added, "My lord."

"Housebreakers," Lord Whenby said mournfully. "A sad tale. They make London a dangerous place for delicate ladies of quality."

Good God, he hoped the man wasn't counting Lady Essex in that lot — had he missed the part about Harry and Aunt Essex chasing the fellows out of the house like a pair of furious Valkryies?

But Aunt Essex was taking up the man's words like warm cat-lap. "Indeed, Lord Whenby. I feel most overwrought by all this."

Having had enough of Aunt Essex's dramatics and Whenby's fawning, Roxley turned his back to both of them. "What was taken?" he asked Fiske.

His butler was a model of discretion. He leaned closer and said in a voice that would not carry, at least not to the audience in the foyer, "Nothing much that we can discern, my lord. I believe they were caught early in their venture."

"Early? Why, my things were mauled!" Lady Essex looked around the foyer until she found her hired companion. "Miss Manx, make a note: I want all my belongings removed immediately. Burned! Then I'll need an entirely new wardrobe."

"Aunt Essex —" Roxley began, then gave

168

up, for his aunt was making a long and detailed list of all the items she would need to replace.

When she got to her unmentionables, the fellow from Bow Street nearly choked, and immediately and as diplomatically as he could began to question Harriet. "Did you lose anything, miss?"

"I have nothing worth stealing that wasn't lost before," she told him, chin chucked up with determination, the infamous Hathaway pride.

Roxley did his best not to flinch at her double entendre. Yes. Guilty as charged.

Mingo nudged the earl. "Oh, and we searched the house to make sure there's no snudges about."

Roxley looked to the Runner for a translation.

"Thieves hiding under the beds," he supplied.

Roxley shuddered, wondering who in London would be foolhardy enough to come out from under Aunt Essex's bed. The thief's ears would never stop ringing.

Speaking of Aunt Essex, she'd gotten to the end of her list and was proceeding on a new tack. "Of course, you are correct. Returning to Foxgrove as quickly as arrangements can be made is the wisest course. You will see to it, won't you, dear Whenby?"

"I would carry you myself if it would give you comfort in this time of trial," the old gallant declared.

"Return to Kempton?" Harriet and Roxley said at the same time.

They glanced at the other, Harry glowering.

Moving out? And with the Season only half finished? If Roxley had known his aunt could be so easily persuaded to leave London, he would have hired a pack of cracksmen years ago, if only to make an annual appearance which coincided with Aunt Essex's yearly migration.

"So soon?" he added, trying to sound a bit distraught by the idea.

"Ah, a return to the comforts of home will endow your nerves with just the right amount of balm," Whenby replied.

Roxley wished he could return Whenby from wherever he'd come and said as much. "My lord, you've been overly attentive tonight, but I know my aunt, and in her current state, she may not realize how we are imposing on you."

"Never!" the man declared, planting himself squarely at Aunt Essex's side. "I am merely honored to be here so I can be of assistance in this time of trial."

"If that's all, my lord?" the Runner was saying, beating a none-too-hasty retreat.

Roxley followed him. "Sir, may I ask you something?" he said quietly when they got to the bottom of the front steps.

"Certainly, my lord —"

"Have you ever heard of a trio of thieves breaking into a house to tramp through an elderly lady's possessions?"

The man shrugged. "You wouldn't believe the half of what I see and what gets nicked. But it does seem a rather odd one all the way around."

"Odd? How?" Roxley suddenly needed confirmation that his instincts weren't entirely gone awry.

"If you pardon me for saying it, my lord," the man began, "it seems as if they had something in mind they were looking for. And they had a good notion where it might be."

Roxley arrived at White's with trepidation in his heart. He was broke. In debt. About to be ruined. And now, the danger he'd sensed dogging his every move the past few months had come directly to his doorstep.

Worst of all, now there was Harry to consider.

Not for anything would he have her in the middle of this. What he truly needed was Chaunce's help to ensure Harriet was in that carriage tomorrow with his Aunt Essex, headed back to Kempton.

He took a deep breath and went into the private room the waiter had directed him toward, only to find that Chaunce hadn't come alone.

Seated in the various chairs were the friends he trusted the most: Chaunce. Mr. Hotchkin, Chaunce's assistant at the Home Office. The Duke of Preston. The duke's uncle, Lord Henry Seldon. Lord Howers, the head of the Home Office — the same man who tossed him out of the service not a month earlier stating he was unfit for duty, what with all his troubles hanging around his neck.

Howers deplored the least bit of indiscretion and had been more than willing to cut off Roxley at the first hint of trouble.

Old Iron Drawers, Chaunce liked to call him.

Behind his back, of course.

Still it was a bit of a shock to see them all assembled. To have to confess to them all that he'd failed.

"Ah," he drawled as he entered the room and took center stage. "How kind of you all to remember my birthday."

Preston snorted at this. "Do you always make a joke of everything?"

"Better than wrenching off my cravat and wailing," he replied. He glanced down at the disheveled mess of lace. "Though I will have to talk to Mingo about using more starch."

Lord Henry was a more practical sort. He got to the point. "About time you asked for help."

The earl raked his hand through his hair. "You all know I'm not good about asking for assistance."

"Might have kept your house from being ransacked . . ." Chaunce pointed out. But his dark glance added more. *And putting my sister in danger.*

"Which is exactly why Howers pulled you from service," Preston told him.

At this Roxley gaped. He had never told his old friend about his work for the Home Office. The only people who had ever known of his connection were Chaunce, Howers, Hotchkin, and the man who recruited him, Lord Mereworth.

Or at least, so he'd thought.

"Didn't think I knew, did you?" Preston said, smiling slightly. "You were far too clever last spring in helping me win Tabby."

"And I with winning Daphne." Lord Henry smiled. "Got that Special License and the business with the archbishop settled rather too fast for such a heathen and a gadabout. And why someone as intelligent and perceptive as Mr. Hathaway would put up with you only added to our suspicions."

"So you have found me out," Roxley said, nodding to them. He might have minded a year ago, but right now, having fallen to the very bottom, he realized the only way out of all this was to ask for help. "It's just that I've gone it alone for most of my life."

"No more," Preston told him. "Now let's get on with this." He nodded for Mr. Hotchkin to begin.

But before Chaunce's assistant did, he glanced at his true superior, Lord Howers, who also nodded his assent. The young man swallowed, his Adam's apple bobbing nervously as he launched into his report, meticulous to a fault. "I started by compiling a list of your previous work, connections you might have had. Then moved on to your gambling associations. Large wagers. Peers you might have offended —"

"Which turned out to be an entire bloody volume of *Debrett's,*" Preston added. "Demmit, Roxley, you aren't very popular."

Roxley ignored this and turned to

Chaunce. "You've been investigating me?"

Never mind that he'd dug into the private lives of others in his work, having his own life turned inside out and examined by his friends had him suddenly furious.

Chaunce bristled with indignation. "What else was I supposed to do? I thought you intended to marry —"

Marry my sister.

There it was. Harriet. This was about Harriet.

Here was another secret he'd thought was all his own, and now even that — his true weakness, his only love, his heart — was laid bare for all to see.

"Someone has it out for you, Roxley," Lord Henry said out, quietly, firmly. "We couldn't stand by any longer. You've helped all of us with —" Well, it was too devilishly personal to admit, so the duke's uncle continued on with his previous course. "We are merely repaying the debt."

Roxley turned from one man to the other, not wanting to admit how much he needed their assistance. How much tonight had brought home how close he was to losing everything he loved — and not just Harriet. There were his aunts to consider as well.

"Besides, when you turned up with Miss Murray," Preston said, "we knew this was something more than just a string of bad luck."

"Whatever is wrong with Miss Murray?" Roxley said. "She's a pretty thing. Immense dowry. Whatever would be suspicious about that?"

"It's blackmail, isn't it?" Chaunce asked. Then he looked up and directly at Roxley. "This potential betrothal — her father has some leverage on you, doesn't he?"

Roxley shifted. Demmit. Then he thought of Harriet standing on the stairs, glowering at him.

To see forgiveness in her gaze, well, he'd do anything. Even this.

"He bought out all my vowels," Roxley admitted. "Told me he'd take everything that wasn't entailed and leave me in debtor's prison if I didn't marry the chit."

"Oh, good God!" Preston managed. "The man should be horsewhipped!"

"Hardly seems the fatherly thing to do," Roxley admitted. "But he's one of those newly minted fellows. Thinks he can buy the world."

"Appears he might be right," Lord Henry muttered.

Meanwhile, Hotchkin was busily taking notes. "Haven't gotten far with Mr. Murray, but will continue my inquiries."

Preston rose to his feet. "Who the devil hates you so much?" he asked. "Surely you've got some idea?"

Then the door opened. "Am I late?" a deep, familiar voice inquired. "Demmed difficult to get a carriage this time of night."

"Mereworth," Roxley exclaimed. He hadn't seen his mentor in months. Not since last summer. And here he thought the man had gone off on assignment to the Continent.

"Came as soon as I heard," the man said, nodding to the others. "Now what is all this about some devil ruining your life?"

"We were just going over that," Lord Howers said. While he and Mereworth had joined the Home Office at the same time, it had been Howers who had advanced through the ranks and finally taken command.

But no one could deny that Mereworth's talents lay in the field, and Roxley was demmed glad to have him here.

Roxley shook his head. "I've been going over and over in my head who it might be."

He could hardly tell them his string of bad luck had begun the moment he'd taken Harriet Hathaway into his heart. Stolen those kisses from her lips, taken her to his . . .

Well, this was neither the time nor the place to admit that.

Especially with her brother seated just across the room.

Had he mentioned what a good shot Chaunce was?

Then, out of nowhere, Lord Howers spoke up. His deep voice commandeered everyone's attention. "Perhaps this has to do with the diamonds, my good man."

All eyes turned toward Roxley with the same question: *What diamonds?*

"Do you know what he's talking about?" Chaunce asked him.

The earl nodded. "Foolish rumors. That my father won half the stones from Marie Antoinette's doomed necklace in a card game."

"The Queen's Necklace," Hotchkin enthused, flipping through the pages tucked into a well-used portfolio.

Roxley shook his head. Here he'd always thought Hotchkin a sensible sort. But the Queen's Necklace? Ridiculous.

Not that it was the first time he'd heard of his father's sketchy connection to those cursed stones. While at Oxford, a run-down old gambler at an inn, having heard someone call him by his title, had caught hold of

178

Roxley and begged to know if the story was true.

That his father had played in the most infamous card game ever.

From the corner of the room came another note of skepticism. "The Queen's Necklace?" Mereworth shook his head. "Utter rot." He turned to his contemporary. "Howers, you know it as well as I."

"I agree," Roxley said. For after the incident in Oxford, he'd nosed around a bit, searched what was left of his parents' possessions and found . . . well, found nothing — nothing but a story that was legend among the gambling set but had little in the way of evidence . . .

"Not rot. Not in the least, my lord," Hotchkin asserted. "Your father did indeed win half the diamonds from that necklace." And though he was speaking out of turn, and before Chaunce or Lord Howers could give him a quelling glance, he dove into the story he'd obviously spent so much time researching.

But to Roxley, it was more than just a recitation of facts and half truths. It was the story of his family. His parents. His inheritance.

And like seeing Harriet again today, he wondered what might have been if his father hadn't sat down to that tempting game.

Calais, 1785
The Rocaberti was, even for Calais, a shady sort of inn.

Certainly not an establishment for one of the more affluent travelers who swanned back and forth between the glittering worlds of Paris and London.

Yes, the patrons of Berti's, as it was known, moved between those cities, and quite often, but their means . . . well, they weren't always so predictable that one could count on having a roof over one's head the next day or the coins to pay for a good meal.

Or even a bad one.

So it was one dark and dreary night that an odd collection of travelers found themselves in the common room, and of course, someone had a deck of cards. The seas and tides had been against anyone seeking to cross the Channel that day — at least that was what this motley assortment had agreed among themselves.

Better that than confessing the true reason they were stuck in Berti's on this wretched night: they hadn't the blunt for the passage.

Yet they knew one lucky hand of cards could change all that, so it was inevitable that most of them ended up at the table by the window.

The first four players were Englishmen. There was no doubt each and every one of them had tried his luck at the Continental tables and now, for whatever reasons, were ready for the greener pastures of home, including Tristan Marshom, the 6th Earl of Roxley.

The last player was a Frenchman, the Comte de la Motte, Tristan thought he'd said, though the fellow hardly had the look of a nobleman to him. Then again, the French often gave themselves titles to raise their own stakes.

Not that English noblemen were much better, he mused. Oh, his title was real, but sadly he had pockets to let. He glanced over at his dear wife, Davinia, who watched the other players with the eyes of a sharpster. In her hand, she played with a coin, the silver bit weaving between her fingers like magic, a trick she'd picked up in Italy.

A sorry lot, her wan smile said.

Perhaps this will be the one, my darling, he silently encouraged, as the tall, thin man to his right gathered up the cards. *This is the game that will restore us.*

She smiled slightly — a wistful look full of hope — blew him a kiss and made her way upstairs. This was his game tonight and she left him to do what he did best.

Then came that sound, that *ffft* of the boards as they brushed against each other as the man shuffled the deck. That purr always reminded Tristan of the wiles of a cat, rubbing against one's leg.

"Come now, Batty," the man to the right of the dealer said, "our new friend has a look of impatience to him." He nodded toward the Frenchman, who looked neither impatient nor impressed by his companions.

The aforementioned Batty waved aside his friend's request to start the game. "Corney, I'll not deal until the cards tell me so."

"I would spend the remainder of my days in Calais if I were to wait for the cards to talk," complained the other of Batty's companions.

"Ah, Moss," Batty replied, "you'll die from this wine before that."

They all laughed, save the comte, who smiled blandly, and the innkeeper behind his bar, wearing an expression of Gallic forbearance . . . or perhaps disdain. It was hard to tell the difference.

And when Batty finally did deal out the cards, they all recognized the telltale signs in each other — they were all professional and this was no game for novices.

Nor would tonight offer any of them the

favor of picking a ripe purse. Or so it seemed. This was going to be all about skill.

Or that fickle bitch, Luck.

Another man, English by the look of him, dozed by the fire.

Tristan kept a wary eye on the fellow. He could be an accomplice, a card spotter perhaps, partnered to one of these fellows. Davinia, on the other hand, would insist the man was a smuggler or a spy.

But she had rather romantic notions of those professions.

"Sir, do you play?" Corney asked the fellow by the fire.

The mysterious enigma shook his head. "I am no gambler."

"If you drink the wine in this place, I would argue that you are," Batty advised him, nodding at the half-filled glass at his side.

The innkeeper muttered under his breath, a string of French that no one bothered to translate.

"Are you certain, sir?" Moss prodded. For it was obvious to each of them that they were all too well-matched to gain what they wanted.

A fat purse. And this stranger might be the only one likely to possess such a rare commodity.

"No, thank you," the man said, shifting in his seat so his long legs were closer to the fire. "But good luck to you all."

Moss shrugged and they went back to playing.

"Then what happened?" Lord Henry asked.

"Nothing," Roxley told him. "The diamonds came to London with de la Motte and were pawned." He paced away from them and stared moodily into the fire.

Demmed, bloody diamonds. How he hated those wretched stones. Wasn't it bad enough that his parents had abandoned him to the care of his great-aunts so they could chase after their gambling dreams on the Continent? That they'd died coming home, as broke as when they'd left.

Probably more in debt.

And all for what?

To restore the Marshom name.

Those were the only words he could remember his father ever saying. He'd been half asleep when his parents had come into the nursery at the Cottage.

We must go, my dear boy, his father had said. *To restore the Marshom name.*

Roxley couldn't even remember the sound of his mother's voice, but had never forgotten the cold tears on her cheeks as she'd bent down to kiss his forehead.

To restore the Marshom honor. Bah! Every Marshom had sought to do just that. Gambling. Failed business ventures. Loveless marriages.

Marry well and cheat often.

"Your father won that night. Half the diamonds from the Queen's Necklace — at least by all estimates," Hotchkin insisted with his usual frank assurance.

"My father died penniless. Most likely as will I," Roxley corrected him.

"But he won that night," Hotchkin continued to argue like a terrier after a rat. "Perhaps your mother hid them."

Roxley was growing impatient with the entire conversation. "Mr. Hotchkin, for once you are wrong."

The young man looked ready to belabor the point, but a shake of Chaunce's head stopped him from continuing.

"Are you so certain, Roxley?" Lord Howers asked.

They all turned and looked at the man who was considered the mastermind of the Home Office.

"I actually read young Hotchkin's report and it stands to reason . . ." Howers paused as he was wont to do when he wanted his agents to listen. He studied the rich amber

185

liquid in his glass before he looked up and continued, "There were five men there that night —"

"Six," Mereworth corrected.

"Pardon?" Howers blustered. The man never liked being corrected.

"If you were listening," Mereworth dared, for he liked to tweak Howers at any opportunity, "there were six men there that night. Five at the table, and our agent. He was the one who made the report. The one I imagine Mr. Hotchkin discovered misfiled."

Hotchkin blushed, for he was well-known for digging things out of the files and archives that most had thought could never be unearthed.

"Which agent?" Chaunce asked, getting back to the point.

Hotchkin shook his head. "The report is unsigned and I don't recognize the hand."

Howers shrugged as well. "Those demmed stones. Hated them back then, and detest them still. Wasted months back in '85 searching for them." He let out an exasperated breath. "So in the interest of expediting this matter, we will agree that there were six men. Though we can only count five of them, since Lord Roxley is dead."

At this, Mereworth conceded, though

when Howers turned his head, he made a cheeky wink at Roxley.

One only Mereworth would dare.

"These men know exactly who left Calais with those diamonds," Howers said, pointing out the obvious.

"But sir," Roxley said, leaping into this fray. "Over the years, whoever won them could have broken them up, pawned them carefully not to draw attention to themselves. They could have been gambled away long since." He just couldn't believe they were even discussing this. It was utterly ridiculous.

Howers showed exactly why he was in charge of their division, and why one day Hotchkin would probably take his place. His dogged determination was unmatched. "Perhaps. But eventually those stones would have passed through London. And when diamonds are moved in London —"

"They go through Mr. Eliason," Chaunce said, breaking in.

Howers nodded. "And Eliason owes me a few favors, so when stones get pawned, unusual ones, he lets me know. Besides, he was de la Motte's original broker for only half of that necklace, so he knows exactly the cut and shape of those stones. And in all these years, he's never seen the missing half."

"How do you know so much about all this, my lord?" Roxley asked, the overly familiar sense of dread returning to niggle down his spine.

So close, so very close, it taunted.

In the corner of the room, the candles on the sideboard flickered, having finally run their course.

"When the Queen's Necklace first came to London, there was some discussion — at higher levels — of seeing it returned to the French court. Though when it was discovered the stones had been conned from the Paris jewelers by de la Motte's wife and that Marie Antoinette had never possessed the necklace, the talks ended. And then of course the revolution truly finished the matter. Or so I thought."

Mereworth snorted. "Had us running around like fools trying to get our hands on them to appease the Frenchies, eh Howers?"

"Silence for all these years, and now suddenly, it seems someone wants what they believe is rightfully theirs," Lord Henry observed.

Lord Howers, always on the lookout for likely gentlemen to help, glanced over at the duke's uncle and took his measure.

"One of the other gamblers?" Hotchkin suggested.

"There is someone else: the agent," Chaunce added. He looked around at their shocked expressions. "We cannot discount the man because he is one of ours."

Howers sputtered a bit. He didn't like that notion, not one bit. "There is also the possibility that this was arranged by someone in France. The Comte de la Motte returned to France after his wife died — he had no choice — for they'd run through their ill-gotten gains and her infamy was all they'd been living on."

"Perhaps de la Motte offered up the other half — or at least the notion of where they might be — to gain his return," Preston posed. "Those diamonds were, after all, made for a queen. A *French* queen."

It wasn't too hard to figure out who might have engineered such a wild plot if such a theory were true.

Napoleon. Hadn't he just last year installed his new empress, Marie-Louise, and she'd only in the last month borne him a son. Such a cache of diamonds would be only fitting.

And Boney was known to covet anything royal.

"I won't have those diamonds going back to France to adorn some self-proclaimed empress," Howers sputtered.

After a few moments of uncomfortable silence, Hotchkin coughed a bit.

"Something the matter, Mr. Hotchkin?" Roxley asked.

"It's just that, well . . ." He glanced over at Lord Howers and then plunged on in. "I don't think the comte's wife just 'died.' I would suggest she was murdered. That whoever is after these diamonds has been searching and waiting all this time for them."

Roxley was only half listening as the theories abounded. It was all too farfetched, too unbelievable. His parents had come home from the Continent broke. Died in a carriage accident and had never had more than two guineas between them. That was the end of it, as far as he was concerned.

Yet something about the catch in Mr. Hotchkin's voice caught his attention.

I would suggest she was murdered . . .

Murdered. He shook his head as a long-lost memory floated free, dislodged from its hidey-hole by that odd note in the younger man's eager words.

Murdered.

Roxley felt his entire world shift. Everything he believed fell away as this tiny fragment, this recollection, unfurled inside him. The shadows in the room swallowed him up and carried him back all those years.

He was just a child again, sound asleep in his room at the Cottage. That is until the cozy familiar silence of the night had been interrupted by crying. Deep cries of grief being torn from someone. More than one person. He'd come downstairs to investigate and found the large front doors of the Cottage flung open.

The memory drew him further into the past until it was as if he were even now standing outside in the cool night air.

Beyond, in the yard, his aunts stood gathered around a wagon. The one, he knew, that had been sent to fetch his parents' belongings from Dover. Yet instead of trunks and valises, the wagon carried only a matching pair of coffins.

"They were *murdered,* my lady. It was no accident," the driver was saying.

And then Aunt Oriel had spotted him in the doorway and rushed forward, gathering him into her arms and carrying him back up to bed.

"Poor lamb, poor lamb," she'd whispered the entire way up the stairs. "Don't you worry over any of this."

And he hadn't, in all these years. Never

again had he heard any one of his aunts utter that word. It had always been "their grave accident" or "those tragic circumstances," but never the truth of it. Never that word.

Murdered.

"My parents," he gasped. Wrenched out of the memory, Roxley tried to breathe as a new truth dawned around him.

"What about them?" Mereworth asked, quietly and firmly.

"They didn't just die in a carriage accident. They were murdered. Shot. Both of them."

Then Lady Gudgeon's words collided with the image of those coffins. *Your aunt is in dire straits.*

"My aunts," he exclaimed, getting to his feet, while in his heart another name rang out. *Harriet!* Dear God, she was in the middle of this now. "My aunts are in danger."

"Your aunts?" Chaunce looked at the empty glass beside him as if that might be the cause for this unfathomable outburst.

"Yes, precisely." Roxley stilled his beating heart and rushed to explain. "Lady Gudgeon —"

There were groans about the room at the mention of the matron's name.

"Yes, yes," Roxley asserted. "Lady Gudgeon. She claims this Lord Whenby, the one lingering after my Aunt Essex, is a bounder. And then Poggs —"

"Poggs?" Howers exclaimed. "That pup?"

"Yes, well, I agree he's hardly the smartest whip," Roxley conceded, "but he claims my Aunt Oriel is being courted by some ne'er-do-well. I thought before it was naught but too many trips to Lady Knolles's punch bowl, but now . . ."

Lord Howers sat back. "Whenby, you say? Never heard of him."

"Neither had I," Roxley said, while Hotchkin once again reached for his ever-present pen and ink.

"We need to get to the bottom of this and quickly," Howers said, frowning at this development. "Hotchkin — a dossier on the man. On my desk by tomorrow."

Chaunce's assistant grinned with delight. Impossible assignments made the young man wiggle like an excited puppy

This wasn't the end of Howers's orders. He turned to Roxley. "I suggest you get Lady Essex out of London and away from this Whenby. Immediately. At least until we know his motives."

Roxley nodded. "That shouldn't be a problem. She's ready to return to Foxgrove after —"

Now suddenly the break-in at his house held a different and startling implication. What had the fellow from Bow Street said?

It seems as if they had something in mind they were looking for.

He turned toward the low embers in the grate. And if they were willing to come break into his house . . . If whoever was responsible for this was willing to kill — again he was assailed by the image of those narrow coffins, lying side by side in the back of the wagon — it wasn't just his life at risk, but the lives of his aunts, and anyone close to him.

Which meant it was imperative that Harriet be as far away from all this as he could send her. China, perhaps. If he failed in that, she'd be in that carriage with his aunt on the morrow if he had to personally stuff her in a trunk and tie it shut.

No doubt Mingo would be delighted to help.

Meanwhile, Howers was still issuing orders. "Roxley, you need to question your aunts. In person. This isn't a fit subject for a letter."

The earl nodded in agreement. A letter could be intercepted, as could a reply. And while he began to make preparations for the trip — a list of things he'd need done — he remembered one point of order.

"I cannot go," he blurted out.

"Whyever not?" Lord Howers blustered, looking up from the instructions he was giving Hotchkin. "If it is this marriage nonsense, I'll call on this Murray person in the morning and set him straight. Blackmailing nobility, indeed! I won't have it."

Roxley hadn't even gotten to the problem of Murray's demands yet. He had a more pressing problem. His aunts. Glancing around the room, he knew he'd have to confess one last matter.

That while he might be the Earl of Roxley, head of his family and heir to all, in most matters his aunts still looked upon him as their orphaned nephew in short pants.

Especially one.

But there was no leaving off now, not when his friends were willing to help.

Even if it meant the worst sort of humiliation. The sort they'd cast up in the years to come.

Well, at least Preston would.

"My Aunt Eleanor and Aunt Oriel have refused me entrance the last two times I've come to call. Say they won't allow me in until I bring them a bride."

"Then get yourself engaged to this Miss

Murray," Howers pressed. "Without delay."

Roxley had been afraid the man would say that.

CHAPTER 6

Meddling is never wrong when it is put to
good purpose.

> Miss Darby to her best friend,
> Miss Cecilia Overton
> *from Miss Darby's Reckless Bargain*

Harriet came downstairs the next morning
to find Lady Essex already arisen and in a
conquering mood.

Her panic from the night before had been
replaced with the steely resolve of Nelson
shaking off a minor setback. Nor had she
any interest in departing for Kempton.

"Return? Whatever for?" she'd asked when
Harriet had broached the subject. "Miss
Hathaway, we just arrived." She paused and
slanted a challenging glance directly at Harriet. "I would think you of all people would
want to stay."

Stay? And watch Roxley marry another?
No, thank you, she wanted to tell the lady.

197

Of course then she would have to venture into the other unmentionable subject: Roxley's financial straits.

Or worse, the state of her broken heart.

So they had spent the morning hours visiting Lady Essex's favorite milliner, her modiste, and a warehouse that a friend had recommended. No Town hours for the old girl.

As she kept saying, "There is much to do."

Apparently so.

With Lady Essex's shopping completed, they had returned to the house on Hill Street and she'd immediately begun ordering Harriet and Miss Manx about, in order to have everything ready for her "afternoon in."

Throughout this mad scramble, every time the bell jangled, the front door was opened, Harriet braced herself for the sight of Roxley — his long-legged stride, his rakish smile, that wry twinkle in his eyes as if he always found the world around him utterly amusing.

Pausing before a bowl of flowers that Lady Essex had asked her to rearrange, Harriet realized something.

Not once during the previous night had Roxley smiled.

Oh, he'd made a show of gallantry, his

lips upturned, but he hadn't smiled — not like he usually did.

Like he did for her. Like he had that first night he'd kissed her in the Timmonses' garden. Or as he had at Owle Parke when they'd . . .

She turned and glanced across the salon, where Lady Essex was rearranging the teacups on the sideboard, only to find the old girl watching her. That wry glance that was a Marshom characteristic. In that moment, she swore she could hear Lady Essex's battle cry, *There is much to be done.*

Harriet shivered and went back to the rebellious peonies in front of her, their grand blossoms falling this way and that.

Did the old girl mean for her, Harriet, to save Roxley? Had that been the reason for this hasty and utterly unplanned trip to London?

Harriet wouldn't put it past Lady Essex to put her oar in where it wasn't wanted. Then again, Harriet rather subscribed to the same philosophy.

Sometimes, one just had to butt in.

And Harriet couldn't think of a situation that cried out more for some sort of intervention. If only to see Roxley smile yet again.

But however could she manage such a feat?

You could entice him to kiss you, a wry voice offered.

Oh, it was a ruinous task, but Harriet was rather up for the challenge, especially when Fiske came in and announced their first callers.

"Lady Kipps and Miss Murray, my lady."

"Right on schedule," Lady Essex muttered under her breath, as she glanced over at Harriet and gave her a slight nod that seemed to say, *Do what you do best.*

So Harriet did.

The salon at No. 10, Hill Street filled quickly, for the news of the burglary had spread through the *ton* as if on wings.

From the servants' halls, through the mews and to every breakfast table in London, or so it seemed.

The tidbit had run the gamut: from the truth, that Roxley's house had been broken into and the ruffians chased off; to wild tales that the entire residence had been ransacked; armed marauders had invaded, injuring one of the footman and making off with one of the maids, who was presumed . . . well, it was too terrible to say what was presumed of the poor girl.

Harriet's favorite tale, brought courtesy of Lady Knolles, was that a grand cache of diamonds had been stolen — a bouncer of a story that had Lady Essex barking with laughter.

"My dear baroness," Lady Essex managed between guffaws, "if Roxley had diamonds in this house, my sisters and I would not be gadding about merely in pearls."

"I still think it is ever so alarming," Lady Kipps told one and all. "I demanded just this morning that Kipps hire extra footmen. I would be inconsolable if I were to lose my emeralds."

"As I am sure, Lord Kipps would be just as inconsolable," Roxley added from the doorway.

Harriet caught hold of the arms of her chair to keep from bounding up at the sight of him — everything about him so very familiar — the crinkle in his brow, the way he always leaned against the door jamb, all jaunty mischief.

Roxley, you're here, she wanted to cry out, as she'd done many a time at the Pottage when he'd come to visit.

And yet she couldn't. For he wasn't her Roxley anymore.

At least for the time being.

Lady Gudgeon, who had made her entrance right behind Lady Kipps and Miss Murray, brightened noticeably. She'd been a bit put out to be the second party to arrive — not getting the first account of the dire news — but Roxley's appearance assured her a delicious and irresistible *on dit* to drop at the rest of her visits. "Oh, Lord Roxley," she scolded. "A husband must be sympathetic to our delicate natures, yet when I asked the baron the very same thing this morning — to hire more footmen — he was unmoved."

Roxley strolled into the room and bowed slightly to his aunt before he turned back to Lady Gudgeon. "He should be chastened for such a callous disregard, my dear lady. For you are a jewel to be protected."

The old girl blushed, the silk flowers in her hat swaying this way and that, like the peonies in the bowl behind her.

"Aunt Essex, I'm surprised to find you still here," Roxley said. "You had said last night —"

"So now you've taken to listening to me, have you Roxley?" she shot back. "I simply changed my mind. Besides, I could hardly drag Miss Hathaway away from Town — not when she has so much to accomplish." The lady smiled at Harriet and then back at Roxley. "But I am so glad you've come to call. Do take a seat. There is one right there next to Harriet."

Harriet watched this exchange with some delight. No one could get under Roxley's skin the way his Aunt Essex could.

Nor could he protest her change of plans — not right here in front of every gossip in London — so he had no choice but to sit.

Right next to Harriet.

"Miss Hathaway," he murmured as he took his seat, his leg brushing against her skirt. It was all very innocent, yet his touch sent shockwaves of memories through her.

Their limbs entwined, his bare skin against hers. Lips dancing together and then blazing new paths of exploration.

And yet, now they must be ever so proper. Ever so distant.

"My lord," she replied, hoping she wasn't blushing with the same heat uncoiling inside her, clamoring for him to ignite the fire once again.

Across the room, Miss Damaris Dale, who had made a rare appearance, spared Roxley a quizzing glance and then another at Miss Murray, as if she appeared to be weighing the validity of such a match, a subject she wasn't afraid to bring up.

"I would say that this matter of burglaries and ruffians is hardly fit for some of us," she said, well, more like decreed. "Might we discuss something more interesting." Again, it wasn't a request. With that she turned her calculated gaze back on Roxley. "I have heard that felicitations will soon be in order."

Harriet stiffened. This was the last subject she wanted to discuss, but apparently she was the only one who held such an opinion, for immediately the gathered ladies burst into a cacophony of hints, and veiled congratulations lofted toward Miss Murray and the earl.

"Is it true there is to be an imminent announcement?" Lady Gudgeon pressed, her eyes glittering like those of a hawk.

Harriet pursed her lips. Of course the old busybody would ask such an impertinent question.

For her part, Miss Murray blushed prettily, keeping her gaze modestly fixed on her hands, which were folded in her lap — while she let her friend convey a hint of what was to come.

"I do believe, it will be very soon indeed that I won't be the newest countess about Town," Lady Kipps said, preening a bit as if the entire match was of her making.

Here was one oar that Harriet would like to happily dump in the Thames.

After she snapped it in half.

But it was Lady Essex who stormed into the fray with her own sort of oar. "An announcement? Why, of all the foolish notions," she said, shaking the skirt of her gown as if it was suddenly covered in scone crumbs. When her verdict was met with nothing but stunned silence and more than one gaping mouth, she sighed as if she had never met such a score of nitwits.

Including her nephew.

She directed her gaze at Roxley. "There can be no announcements before there has been a mustering."

What the devil that was, Harriet hadn't the least notion, but Roxley's wide-eyed shock said all too clearly he knew exactly what his aunt meant. Indeed, he looked as if his aunt had just asked him to take off his jacket and his boots and prop his stocking-clad feet up on the low table before one and all.

"Marshoms and their musterings," Damaris Dale muttered with some animosity, but no one other than Harriet seemed to hear her, for everyone was focused on Lady Essex, who smiled slightly now that she had the attention of everyone in the room.

Lady Gudgeon — who could scent gossip through the stench of the Southwark stews

— rushed to ask, "Whatever is a mustering?"

Looking around at her bewildered guests, Lady Essex explained. "A mustering is a long-held Marshom family tradition. When the heir or holder of the earldom decides to . . ." She glanced over at Miss Murray and seemingly got stuck on the words *take a bride.* Instead said more vaguely, ". . . continue our lineage, the family is given the opportunity to meet and consider his potential countess to ensure she meets our high standards —"

Over to the right, old Damaris Dale was off and running yet again, muttering, "For card cheats and gadabouts."

If she heard, Lady Essex ignored her by finishing with "— for demeanor and nobility."

"Why, how positively medieval!" Lady Gudgeon declared with a little too much delight.

"I hardly think that will be necessary," Lady Kipps said, smiling over at Miss Murray, "when it is obvious the earl is about to take a most advantageous step."

"A mustering." Roxley said the words as if testing them for himself, and then a sly smile turned at his lips.

Harriet's eyes narrowed. Whyever was he

being so agreeable over this?

Suddenly she wished herself seven again and back at Foxgrove. She wouldn't pull her punches this time.

"I will not see our family traditions tossed to the wayside, Roxley," Lady Essex told him, her voice rising. "Mustering it is. Or there will be no more talk of announcements." This statement was aimed squarely at Miss Murray, and then at Lady Kipps.

"Dearest Aunt Essex," Roxley said, all roguish charm. "I must thank you for reminding me of my duty and obligation to my family. You are correct, a mustering is the only proper thing to be done."

"It is?" Harriet and Miss Murray both demanded at the same moment.

The two of them exchanged wary glances, but having the upper hand — a dowry that would make a princess weep with envy — Miss Murray continued in a more gracious manner. "Whatever does this mustering require?"

Of course, being a *cit*'s daughter, she'd want to get to the point of the transaction.

As for Harriet, whatever this mustering was, she hoped it involved musket fire, and long, tiring marches through Seven Dials.

Lady Essex happily supplied the particulars. "It requires the lady to meet the various members of the immediate family so they can form an opinion as to her merits, likely character, and advantages."

Again there was a snort from Damaris Dale that made it clear she found the entire notion of the Marshoms being overly picky about a likely bride — especially one of Miss Murray's pedigree and purse — quite amusing.

Everyone chose to politely ignore the old girl.

Not that they weren't thinking exactly the same thing.

Including Miss Murray. But she wasn't about to naysay Lady Essex on the issue. "Why, it seems quite reasonable. Perhaps my companion — once she has recovered from her recent accident — can send round invitations —"

"Oh, no, no, Miss Murray," Lady Essex told her. "This isn't something accomplished over a single meal. A mustering is far more complicated."

Harriet perked up. Complicated? Her hopes for a mention of muskets, mayhap a bit of dueling, were renewed . . .

"Now let me see," Lady Essex said, pursing her lips. "I suppose you have it quite easy — for there is only myself and my sisters left."

Miss Murray blinked, but the pasted smile on her face never wavered. "And do you have many sisters, Lady Essex?"

"Two, well, three," she said. "Eleanor, who resides in Bath. Of course, she cannot leave Bath, because of the stipulation in our lease on the house. Lovely residence. On Brock Street — such an advantageous address. You'll love it there this time of year. And of course then —"

"Excuse me?" Lady Kipps interjected. "Bath? Miss Murray would need to go to Bath?"

"Whoever Roxley intends to marry will need to travel to Bath, and then on to Plymouth. Well, not Plymouth precisely, but the family seat isn't too far from Plymouth. We call it the Cottage. It has some fancy name attached to it —" She raised her fan and tapped it to her lips as if the name truly escaped her.

"Marshom Court," Roxley supplied.

"Yes, yes, but whoever calls it that? It is just the Cottage to us." Lady Essex smiled. "And then of course, the lady in question would need to come to my house, Foxgrove, in Kempton."

Miss Murray's smile was reaching its limits. "Whyever would one need to go to Kilton —"

"Kempton," Harriet corrected, and was rewarded with a pair of murderous glances from Lady Kipps and Miss Murray. She wondered if those were looks they'd learned on their own or were a staple of Bath-educated misses.

Recovering quickly, for indeed there was a coronet at stake here, Miss Murray's expression softened. "Thank you, Miss Hathaway," she said, drawing a deep breath as if clearing the bile from her throat. "But again, Lady Essex, you are here in London, there would be no need for me — well, not me precisely — but a young lady to travel so far afield."

Lady Essex gave her a puzzled glance as if her words made no sense. "Of course it can't be done in London." She glanced up at Roxley and shook her head slightly as if she couldn't believe he was choosing such a dull gel.

"Dear me, but all that is quite impossible," Lady Kipps declared. "Miss Murray's hired companion has had a terrible accident."

"An accident?" Lady Gudgeon interjected with a gleeful pounce. "How horrible?"

And yes, it was a question, not an expression of condolence.

"She twisted her ankles last night while

leaving Lady Knolles's," Miss Murray supplied.

"*Both* her ankles," Lady Kipps added, shaking her head woefully.

"One is unfortunate," Miss Dale declared. "But two is just foolish."

"Yes, exactly, Miss Dale. And most inconvenient for me," Miss Murray declared. "So you see, Lady Essex, without a suitable companion, I could not undergo this mustering."

Lady Essex sighed. "Then I suppose any sort of announcement will be similarly impossible. Perhaps something can be managed next Season."

And there it was, the spot for Harriet's oar. She knew exactly how to wedge herself between Miss Murray and Roxley.

"Would I do, Miss Murray?" she asked. "As your companion, that is?"

"Are you mad?"

Harriet had no idea if Roxley's question was directed at her or at his aunt. He had waited out the most persistent of Lady Essex's afternoon callers and then closed the door on the pair of them, having sent Miss Manx packing a moment earlier with one very dark and threatening glower.

Miss Manx was a resourceful, steady

companion — she had to be to last as she had in Lady Essex's employment — but she also knew who ultimately paid the bills.

Harriet almost envied Miss Manx her escape, because she didn't think she'd ever seen Roxley so furious.

Well, save the other night at Lady Knolles's when she'd interrupted his flirtatious interlude with Miss Murray. She'd banished her rival then, and she'd stand her ground now so she could do the same again.

And from the determined set of Lady Essex's jaw, one might hope, even believe, that she was of the same mind.

"Whatever are you going on about, Roxley?" Lady Essex was in the process of straightening the tea tray in front of her. She continued by replacing the cover on the sugar bowl and taking a glance inside the creamer before she looked up at her nephew. "Well, what is it?"

"What is it?" He clenched his teeth and pointed at Harriet. "Her, that's what's it."

"Me?"

"Harriet?"

The two ladies looked at each as if they hadn't the least notion what he was going on about.

"What do you mean by offering to go along with this mustering? To act as Miss

Murray's companion?"

Harriet put her hand to her mouth, as if she was quite taken aback. "I only meant to help."

He snorted. "Help? Help by staying well away from Miss Murray." *From me.*

He didn't say the words, but they were there in his glower.

But Harriet had put her oar in and she wasn't about to stop rowing just yet. Besides, whatever was Roxley doing — going along with this ridiculous mustering, as it was? Why, he'd practically jumped at the idea.

So she turned to Lady Essex and then back to Roxley. "Why would I want to do that? I find Miss Murray ever so enchanting. I think we will become fast friends." She smiled as sweetly as she could.

It fooled Roxley about as well as it would have fooled one of her brothers. The earl hadn't known her all these years not to know when she was plotting.

"You little minx — you are not going along on this mustering. That is the end of it."

Lady Essex sighed and sat back into the settee. "Then I suppose you will have to wait until Miss Murray can hire a suitable companion. How long that will take, heaven

213

knows! She'll have to post an advertisement
—"

"— or contact an agency," Harriet added.

The old girl nodded at Harriet for her excellent point. "Yes, yes, exactly. But it won't do any good."

"Whyever not?" Roxley demanded as he stood between the two of them.

His aunt shook her head as if she were instructing a lad right out of the country. "You foolish man, what do you know of these things? Truly, Roxley, the timing is all wrong. All the respectable candidates have already been snapped up for the Season. Miss Murray won't be able to find someone for at least a month. Why, I had a horrible time finding my Miss Manx. It could be autumn before an appropriate candidate is unearthed."

"If not longer," Harriet added, hoping she sounded most helpful.

Roxley's gaze narrowed as he looked at both of them. No matter that they spoke the truth, he was having none of it and so returned to his earlier refrain. "You are not going, Harry, that is all there is to it." Then, as if struck by inspiration, he smiled like a cat. "Miss Manx can go in Harriet's place. She's respectable and capable and perfect for the position. In the meantime, Harriet can stay with you, Aunt Essex, in her place." He smiled smugly at the pair of them, with a look that said, *Check*.

Harriet shot a wild glance over her shoulder at Lady Essex, for she had hardly expected such a suggestion. Send Miss Manx instead? Oh, that would never do.

But Lady Essex was cool and calm in the face of this possible routing. She replied with her own version of checkmate. "I fear that won't be possible. Miss Manx had a letter only this morning from her . . . her . . . sister. Yes, her sister. The dear girl is expecting and asked to have Maria come and lend a hand. I would be remiss not to let her go. As such, she is unavailable to help Miss Murray."

Roxley glared at both of them.

Harriet didn't see why he blamed her. It wasn't as if she had a sister about to go into labor.

Nor did Miss Manx, but that was hardly the point.

"You are not going!" he told Harriet, setting his heels and his jaw.

"Whyever are you harping on Harriet?" Lady Essex tipped up her nose. "I can't see why you'd object to traveling with her. The Hathaways are practically family and it was overly generous of her to offer." Then she paused and looked him squarely in the eye. "Unless you have a good reason why you cannot travel with Miss Hathaway? Some objection to her character that I am not aware of?"

Harriet stilled. Good heavens! Did the lady realize how close to the truth she was dabbling? She didn't even dare look at Lady Essex for fear the lady would see the truth in her eyes.

Nor could she look at Roxley. To look at him might show everything in her heart.

And her determination to set this all to rights.

But even in her meddling, Harriet wondered if she was right. What if Roxley truly didn't love her? What if he preferred Miss Murray and her bountiful dowry?

You should just leave well enough alone, Harriet, her practical side rallied, if only to keep her heart from being hurt yet again. *Find someone else.*

Harriet did pride herself on being a practical sort. And yet . . . when it came to Roxley, her well-regarded common sense took flight.

Harriet knew right down to the soles of her best slippers, she had to stop Roxley from marrying Miss Murray. No matter the consequences. It was selfish and awful and ruinous of her, but she just couldn't shake the notion that this was exactly what needed to be done.

What Miss Darby would do.

Hadn't Miss Darby saved Lt. Throckmorten from marrying Miss Everton when she'd proven that the marriage contract Miss Everton claimed had been agreed upon was counterfeit? *Miss Darby and the Counterfeit Bride* was one of Harriet's favorite books.

And this was no different.

Well, without the fake marriage contract . . . or the horde of angry Hottentots . . . or the poisoned soup.

Poisoned soup. She paused, biting one lip as she considered the notion. No, that was probably going a bit too far. Then again . . .

Harriet realized she was smiling when she found Roxley staring at her. Immediately, she focused on the problem at hand: dogging his every step until he admitted that he loved her.

Not that poisoned soup was entirely off the table . . .

"You are not going! Do you hear me?" Roxley told her. "Over my dead body."

"Roxley," Lady Essex said, "don't give the girl ideas."

"Are you mad?" Tabitha said as she came unannounced into Harriet's room the next day. "We hurried over as soon as we heard the news."

Much to Harriet's chagrin, her best friend had brought reinforcements. Daphne. She braced herself for the lecture that was certain to follow.

And true to form, Daphne did not disappoint. "Harriet Hathaway! You cannot go chasing after Roxley in the company of his betrothed!" she complained. Then she came to a stop in the middle of the room and looked Harriet up and down. "At least not wearing that gown." She glanced over at Tabitha and winked, and then Tabitha moved away from the door.

Almost immediately, a haughty woman trailed by not one, but three assistants, all lugging large baskets and armloads of gowns, entered Harriet's room.

Daphne tipped her head and smiled. "The right dress is wanted for a situation such as this. Or perhaps two." She took another look at the gowns Harriet had laid out to pack and shuddered. "No, make that six." And then she nodded at the modiste, and the woman set to work.

Certainly his aunt's demand for a mustering had been a brilliant stroke of luck — Roxley's first in months — but Harriet's offer to come along was an unmitigated disaster.

What if something happened to her? His heart nearly stopped each time he thought of her . . . lost, harmed.

Caught in the middle of all this. Roxley shuddered.

No. The only solution was to see Harriet sent as far from harm as possible. Since his appeal and outright order for her to remain behind had been ignored by his aunt and the lady herself — he should have known Harriet would be an impossibly obstinate opponent — he chose to strike in a new direction.

Leaning over during a break in Lady Papworth's musicale evening, Roxley used every bit of charm he possessed and said, "Miss Murray, I don't mean to offend, but are you mad?" He'd often found in his work for the Home Office that the right amount of charm, coupled with a direct assault, could defuse an explosive subject efficiently. "Certainly you can find someone other than Miss Hathaway to accompany us on this wretched mustering my aunt is insisting upon?"

"Whatever is wrong with Miss Hathaway?" Miss Murray asked. "This is a wonderful opportunity for her. Will give her references for her future employment."

That stopped Roxley cold. "Future employment? Who do you think she is?"

"A poor man's daughter with little prospects of ever finding a husband," Miss Murray replied succinctly.

Roxley bristled because to him Harriet was so much more, but before he could defend her, the lady at his side — the one he would remind himself he was supposed to be courting — continued on. "Isn't she from that dreary little village where no lady ever gets married? Kilton? Kefton?"

"Kempton," he corrected. "She is from Kempton. Where my Aunt Essex lives."

"Yes, that's Foxgrove, isn't it?" Miss Murray asked. "Built during King Charles's reign, wasn't it?"

So the chit had been reading up on his family holdings. Or whatever reports her merchant father and his team of lawyers had dug up.

"Yes, it is in the rococo style. Lots of gilt and cherubs. A bit fussy, but Lady Essex won't change one brick."

"Oh, even your aunt can change with the times," Miss Murray said, confident in her own wishes and ways. "Besides, it sounds so much nicer than this Cottage of yours. Why would one call their home a cottage?" She made a *tsk, tsk* and shook her head.

You call it a "cottage" when you don't want your creditors to know you have a demmed castle, Roxley mused and then realized he would have to cool his heels for a few more minutes while another simpering miss went up to the stage to play a painful piece of dreary music.

Instead of covering his ears, like he would have preferred, he set his face in an appreciative smile and found his thoughts wandering toward the green gardens of Foxgrove where he'd played as a child, to the vast landscape around the Cottage and all the nooks and crannies of a house that had started as a Norman keep and had been added on to over and over again. The Cottage reminded him in so many ways of the Hathaways' beloved Pottage. Save without the family that made the Pottage a home.

Family. Roxley had no idea what that meant, and when he glanced over at Miss Murray, he cringed inwardly. This was not what he had planned when he'd returned to London last summer, with his heart on his sleeve, and ready to turn his own world upside down.

Marry Harry. Throw his aunts into a panic over a bride who didn't come with a fat dowry. A breach of Marshom tradition if ever there was one.

Oh, but they'd love her. Just as he did. Certainly Aunt Essex was already inordinately fond of Harriet.

As for him? He told her the truth that night at Owle Park — she held his heart. And somehow, someway, he'd find a way to make good that promise.

Yet that meant ensuring that Harriet didn't become embroiled in any of this. Keeping her from catching the eye of whoever was behind all this, especially when they had shown how willing they were to do anything to retrieve those demmed diamonds.

Even murder.

"I don't want Miss Hathaway to come along with us," he whispered to Miss Murray.

The girl eyed him with a calculating gaze. "If I were a jealous sort, I might suspect you carry a *tendré* for her." This was followed by an aggrieved sniff.

"For Harry?" he shook his head, arms

crossing over his chest. "She's naught but a scamp."

"Then I shall be a good influence over her," Miss Murray avowed, settling deeper into her seat, and unfortunately, her resolve to have her way.

"No, Miss Murray, I must put my foot down," he told her. "She cannot come with us. You will have to find another companion."

And so, one would think that was the end of the matter.

Much as it had been with his Aunt Essex.

CHAPTER 7

Now that we have planned, organized and
gathered our wits, a mustering is in order.
Colonel Darby to Lt. Throckmorten
from Miss Darby's Perilous Journey

Not three days later there was, much to
Roxley's chagrin, a festive crowd gathered
around the large coach Miss Murray's
father had provided so his daughter could
travel in a style befitting a future countess.
The merchant might have objected to the
entire notion of mustering, but ever so
quickly, like his daughter, he wrote it off as
one of the many quirks of the aristocracy.

As for the earl, he felt that a funereal black
would have been more appropriate.

Try as he might, he could not — without
outright forbidding the matter, which would
have required a rather detailed and lengthy
explanation, something he was determined
to avoid — prevent Harriet from traveling

with the party.

So there she was standing with her friends, the Duchess of Preston and Lady Henry, done up in the latest fashion.

He suspected Lady Henry's hand in the new clothes — for they were a bit daring as well as perfectly cut to capture Harriet's tall, willowy figure to advantage.

Harry, oh, Harry, you shouldn't be tangled up in this, he wanted to warn her, but didn't dare. Knowing Harriet, she'd hear that as a call to action.

Even her brother Chaunce hadn't been able to dissuade her, having come away from his audience with her with what he called a "Moffett flea in his ear." Apparently Harriet had inherited a double dose of obstinacy — from both her Hathaway and her maternal forebears.

Nor had Roxley been able to gain an audience with Aunt Essex. In a last act of desperation, he had decided to confide in her, but she'd been notably absent the last three days — as if she were avoiding him.

Of course, now that it was too late, what with the last trunk being loaded, Lady Essex suddenly hurried down the steps with a small hatbox in her grasp. "Oh, dear, I feared I missed you all. Such a happy day!" she exclaimed as she came to a flurried stop beside Harriet. "Dearest girl, could you see this returned to my sister? Tell Lady Eleanor it is her turn to decide." The spinster patted Harriet's arm affectionately as she handed off her parcel. "Now all is well."

"Aunt Essex, a moment of your time," Roxley said, before his aunt got out her handkerchief. He always suspected that she cried when guests left with a bit of joy in her heart that her life would now go back to its perfectly ordered routine.

"Oh, yes, Roxley, what is it?" she asked, patting at her pocket to see if she had a square of linen handy.

He offered her his.

"Yes, well, thank you, now off with you," she said, nodding toward his horse.

Not for all the gold in England would he ride in that carriage — not when the only seats were either beside Harriet or facing Harriet.

"I'll catch up," he told her. "Why do I have the distinct feeling you have been avoiding me these last three days?"

"Avoiding you? What nonsense," she said, waving her handkerchief at him. "Are you bosky?" She sniffed at his breath.

"I am not drunk. And I know well enough that you have been avoiding me —" When she looked a bit alarmed at being caught out, he gently took hold of her arm.

"Truly, Roxley, your imagination is getting the better of you —" She pulled at his grasp.

"Aunt Essex, I must ask you something," he continued, taking a glance down the street where the carriage was about to turn the corner. "It is about my parents' effects."

"Your parents?"

He hated doing this, because his father and mother had been Aunt Essex's light and joy, and bringing up their deaths always took the spark out of her eyes. Yet, he pressed on. "Yes, when they came back from the Continent — was there anything unusual in the wagon with —"

Their bodies.

He didn't say it, but saw a nervous flutter in her eyes, before she waved the handkerchief at him, dismissing whatever memory had flickered to life.

"Unusual?" she asked, parroting his question. "Whatever do you mean? Good heavens, Roxley, that was years ago. I don't want to think about those horrible days. So tragic. *Ever so tragic,*" she emphasized.

He leaned over and looked her directly in the eye. Marshoms were a cagey lot, gamblers at heart and liars always, so it took a master interrogator or another Marshom to ferret the truth out of them. With her cornered, he took the direct approach, hoping to startle a confession free. "Was there a cache of diamonds with them?"

She stared at him for another moment and then blinked. "Diamonds?"

"Yes, a great number of them —"

Lady Essex continued to gape at him, then she laughed and pushed him away, swatting at his hand as if it were a fly. "You are bosky! Diamonds indeed!" She stole a glance down the street where there was no longer any sign of Miss Murray's extravagant carriage. "There were those horrible statues from Italy. I'm sure they're counterfeit and not worth a ha'penny, but Eleanor has them all. You are welcome to them, but I doubt Miss Murray will approve. Upstarts and mushrooms never do appreciate the natural, classical form."

"No, no, there must have been something unusual about their —"

She didn't let him finish. "Honestly Roxley, as I told Lady Knolles the other day, do you think I would be wearing pearls if there were diamonds about?" She leaned closer and held the strand around her neck closer for him to examine. "These aren't even real. There hasn't been anything in this family but paste for three generations." She shooed him back toward his horse. "Diamonds indeed! And do stop tippling so early in the day! It did in the fourth earl. Well, that and the harridan he married. I won't have the same mistake ruin you." She once again slanted a glance in the direction of the carriage, a sly smile on her lips, the wicked spark back in her eyes. "Now follow your heart."

As Roxley rode away, he had to wonder if his aunt knew how close she was to the truth.

Once Roxley had turned the corner, Lord Whenby came down the front steps, and put his arm around Lady Essex. "It is time, my dear," he told her.

"Yes, yes, I know," she said, blowing her nose into Roxley's handkerchief. "I just worry so about him."

Whenby glanced in the direction the earl had gone. "He is not his father."

Lady Essex nodded in agreement. "No, he is not. But he is all we have." Then she sighed and rallied. "However, Harriet is with him, and she will guard him well."

"Does she know?" he asked, as the two of them went back into the house, where Lady Essex's trunks were now being brought down for their journey to Foxgrove.

"Harriet?" Lady Essex shook her head. "No."

"You have great faith in this Miss Hathaway," Lord Whenby mused as he picked up his own traveling case.

"She loves him. And he her." Lady Essex dabbed her eyes again. "And if anyone can save that dear boy, it is Harriet, even if he doesn't realize it yet."

"As you saved me, my sweetest, darling Essie," he told her, putting a kiss on her wrinkled forehead.

For two days Harriet tried her best to catch Roxley's eye or get a private word with him, but to no avail. Even now, she stood in the yard of the inn as the trunks and bags were sorted out and he had his back to her.

It was as if she truly was just the hired companion, a necessary ornament for Miss Murray's all-important respectability.

Worse, Roxley seemed determined to carry on with this mustering as if he were seriously considering marrying a woman he clearly did not love.

Of this, Harriet was certain: Roxley did not love Miss Murray.

Oh, he was respectful and kind, and even thoughtful toward the heiress — asking after her comfort, obliging her with extra time in the morning over breakfast and seeing that she had the best rooms each night.

But his eyes had never held that passionate fire that Harriet had basked within.

Found her heart in its deep-seated glow.

No, he didn't love Miss Murray.

Yet perhaps Chaunce had been right the other day when he'd told her that love wasn't the issue when it came to Miss Murray — that Roxley as a Marshom wouldn't marry merely for that blithe emotion when a fortune was so very necessary.

So even if he must marry, and marry well, there was one piece to all this that made absolutely no sense to Harriet — the inclusion of Mr. Hotchkin with their party.

Whatever was her brother's assistant from the Home Office doing tagging along with them on Roxley's mustering? Him and his endless correspondence, reports he spent every night scouring over, well away from everyone else — well, more to the point, her prying eyes — she had to imagine.

When she'd asked him just that, why he'd come along, Hotchkin had stammered something about an ailing uncle in Bath and then made some flimsy excuse about checking on the horses and fled her company.

Ailing uncle, indeed. The whole thing sounded as fictional as Miss Manx's pregnant sister.

Harriet puzzled it over once again as she watched the young man conferring with Roxley across the yard. There was more to all this than met the eye, but however was she to discover the truth?

Then opportunity came tumbling into her lap.

"What about this one, miss?" the lad asked her, holding up a plain black valise.

For a moment she thought it was her own, but just as quickly realized who owned that bag. Mr. Hotchkin.

It was on the tip of her tongue to direct it into the pile that Mingo was overseeing, but just as quickly, she stopped.

"I'll take that one," she said, hefting it with one hand, while she juggled the small hatbox Lady Essex had consigned into her care and hurried after Miss Murray, who had already gone up to her room.

With very little time before her, Harriet went into the small closet of a room off Miss Murray's grand suite and closed the door. Placing Lady Essex's hatbox carefully on the side table, she hefted the valise onto the narrow bed under the window. Taking a deep breath and shooting a guilty glance at the closed door, she shook off any feelings that tinged on guilt.

If no one would tell her what was going on, then she'd discover the truth herself.

Still, her fingers shook a little as she fumbled with the latch and then opened the bag up.

While this sort of espionage might be familiar territory for her brother Chaunce, Harriet found it rather exhilarating. That is until she quickly sifted through the contents — which turned out to be rather ordinary. Socks. Drawers. A comb and brush. Two changes of shirts and a nightshirt.

Harriet stepped back, utterly flummoxed. Why, there wasn't anything of interest inside Mr. Hotchkin's valise. No clues. No grand plan.

She frowned at the black leather bag and considered the inventory she'd made. What was missing?

Then it dawned on her. There were no papers — at least not the leather-bound packet that she had seen him with the night before. What had happened to his reports, the notes he'd been reading?

Then she took another look at the valise and recalled how it was far heavier than it should be for such ordinary belongings.

So she made a closer examination. Running her fingers around the upper edge, she realized that the top seam felt rather wide, and as she felt around some more, she realized it wasn't just a seam, but a flap. And when she burrowed her fingers beneath it, she discovered a hidden pocket.

What might look like a sloppy bit of workmanship was actually a clever way to conceal a hiding spot — one her fingers now dove deeper into and struck gold.

Or rather paper.

She plucked out the mysterious packet Mr. Hotchkin had been guarding so carefully and for a moment considered what she was holding.

Most likely Home Office reports. Confidential government documents. Her brother would probably add that what she was doing, by all accounts, was treason.

Oh, certainly she could make the case that Mr. Hotchkin's valise bore a startling resemblance to her own. But she would be hard-pressed to explain why, after opening the bag and realizing her mistake, she'd continued burrowing through the man's belongings like a common thief.

Or spy.

Yes, well, this might be her only chance to get the answers she sought, so with a sense of practical resolve, she flipped open the portfolio cover.

In for the penny, in for a pound.

At first, the report seemed to have nothing to do with the current state of things — an account of a twenty-some-year-old card game in France, references to Marie Antoinette and her lost diamonds, several mentions of a Comte de la Motte and a list of his contacts in London. While it all went on and on for several pages — with a long account of a trial in Paris and a specific list of suspects — Harriet quickly pieced the entire story together, from the elaborate scheme to swindle the gems to when the diamonds had been brought to London.

But not all of the priceless stones had been accounted for. Some had gone missing. Harriet frowned at the papers she held.

A case that was more than a quarter of a century old?

This hardly seemed a matter for the Home Office.

She leafed back to one of the first pages, the account of a card game in a shady inn in Calais — but the names of the players were faded and the account vague.

Harriet shook her head and knew she should just close up the portfolio and forget what she had seen. She was delving into an investigation that was well beyond an ailing uncle in Bath.

Then her eyes fell on the one line that

stopped her cold.

The deaths of Lord Roxley and his wife were no accident, but murder.

"Miss Hathaway! Miss Hathaway!" The door to the closet rattled sharply. "Are you in there? I need your assistance. Immediately."

Miss Murray. Harriet wrenched her gaze up from the pages. "Um, yes, I'll be right out."

There was a moment of silence from the gel, then she began to rattle the door latch again. "Whatever are you doing in there?"

Harriet hastily stuffed the papers back into the hidden pocket. "I was trying to unpack some things, but the lad brought up the wrong bag."

Once everything was stowed, she flipped open the door and there was Miss Murray, eyeing her suspiciously. "Whatever are you doing? You look flushed?"

"I thought this bag was mine," she said, holding up Mr. Hotchkin's bag. "I fear I wasn't paying attention as I unpacked it and saw the gentleman's unmentionables." She shivered a bit and then held the bag out a bit from her.

"I would think a lady with five brothers would be immune to such sights," Miss Murray commented.

Harriet hoped she didn't have to answer that, because Miss Murray was correct. But luckily no response was necessary, for her employer had far greater problems at hand.

Miss Murray marched over to her open trunk, hands waving over it. "I cannot find my spare handkerchiefs." Miss Murray's accusing gaze pointed at Harriet. "Wherever did you pack them this morning?"

"I . . . I . . ." Harriet's thoughts were still riveted on what she'd just read.

Murder.

"Miss Hathaway!" the heiress demanded with a flounce that nearly got her stuffed inside the oversized trunk. "Do you hear me? I need my handkerchiefs!"

Personally, Harriet had come to believe that Miss Murray's previous companion had toppled off that curb on purpose.

The heiress went to the door. "I'm going downstairs to take tea with Roxley and I want my handkerchief brought down immediately." She sneezed for good effect, and then left muttering something about the horrid state of country air.

Harriet had her own sort of muttering as she began to sift through the contents of Miss Murray's trunk. "Spoiled . . . simpering . . . wretched . . . aha!" She found the ridiculously delicate bit of embroidered lacy linen that Miss Murray desired and was about to shut the lid of the other girl's trunk with a decided thud, when she spied something.

A flap in the seam of the trunk lid.

"What the devil —" Harriet whispered as she slipped her hand inside and pried the false top away.

And what she found there stopped her as cold as the line from Hotchkin's report.

A pistol, along with lead, powder and everything Miss Murray might need to hold off an assault by an entire regiment of highwaymen.

Or to simply commit a murder.

Harriet slanted a glance at the door, a cold thought chilling her blood. "Who are you?"

Lady Eleanor Marshom's residence sat on Brock Street between the Royal Crescent and the Circus.

Roxley had done his best to avoid Harriet for the three days it had taken them to reach Bath.

But avoiding Harriet wasn't just a simple matter of riding outside the carriage, and taking great pains to lavish his attention on Miss Murray at all the stops.

Harriet was everywhere — there at the table, two steps behind Miss Murray at every turn.

And if he was being honest — it graveled him to see her reduced so — not that he could fault Miss Murray's treatment of her new companion, but for God's sakes, Harriet Hathaway was a gentleman's daughter.

A Hathaway. That might not mean much to Miss Murray and her ilk, but to him, to those in the *ton* who had held their noble titles for generations, it was a name that carried respect.

And how little of that — respect, that is — he'd shown her. Every time she looked in his direction he had to wonder if she still cared for him, or if she was simply biding her time before exacting her full revenge.

With a Hathaway, it was such a narrow path between the two. Love and revenge.

Roxley climbed down from his horse and went over to the carriage to assist Miss Murray, glancing furtively over his shoulder at Harriet.

"An excellent address, my lord," Miss Murray said, taking his arm possessively.

Roxley had the sense of being measured and fitted. Worse, he could feel Harriet's gaze boring into his back. He moved out of Miss Murray's leash and said, "My great-grandfather won the house in a card game. It had just been built and Lord Tarvis was about to move in — when he played one too many hands of loo."

The merchant's daughter shook her head in dismay. "To gamble a house away — what foolishness."

"It isn't truly the house, Miss Murray," he hurried to explain. He didn't like the calculating look in her eyes. "Merely the lease."

"The lease?" she asked, glancing once again at the handsome stone residence.

"Yes, as long as there is a Marshom in residence, we hold the lease. I believe Lord Tarvis thought my family in danger of dying out and at worst the wager would be an inconvenience for a few years." He grinned as he bounded up the steps. "That was forty-six years ago."

He had barely rung the bell, when the door was hastily answered.

"Yes?" the fellow intoned, but hardly with the authority of a London butler. He was too young and quite possibly newly hired.

Most likely, indeed. Aunt Eleanor's butlers were always newly hired.

Which meant Roxley didn't recognize the man, but that wasn't unusual. His aunt might be well entrenched in the house, but keeping butlers was another matter.

"I am Roxley, please tell my aunt —"

He got no further before the man's eyes

widened with fright and he began to slam the door shut.

Not so unexpected either.

And as such, Roxley had his boot wedged into the door jamb before the fellow could get it shut.

"Some welcome," he could hear Mingo muttering behind him.

"Is there a problem?" Miss Murray called out, where she stood on the sidewalk looking decidedly put out at being made to wait.

"Open the door before you ruin my boots," Roxley told the man.

"Her Ladyship's orders are —"

"To hell with her orders, open the demmed —"

From somewhere inside came his aunt's voice. "Thortle, is that my dearest darling come to call?"

"Tell her yes," he told the butler.

But the fellow had a better understanding of his position than Roxley had wagered.

"It's the young lord, my lady. The one you told me to never let in."

"Roxley? He's here? Whatever is he —"

Using the distraction his aunt offered, Roxley put his shoulder into the door and gave it a great shove, getting the door open far enough for Mingo to follow him in — his valet bringing with him one of the bags and a valise. Thus armed, they both took up their places as if staking a claim.

Which in a sense they were.

Roxley shot the butler an apologetic glance as his aunt arrived with an expression that bordered on murderous.

Ah, poor fellow, Roxley mused. She'd turn him out for this. But no matter, he had more important matters to attend to.

Besides, given this was Bath, there was always employment for a handsome young man in one of the many households up and down the street.

"Aunt Eleanor, so delightful to see you!" Roxley said, rushing up to his aunt, meaning to give her an affectionate peck on the cheek. His aunt was having none of his warm greeting and glared back at him, standing stonily, with her arms crossed over her narrow chest.

Roxley stepped back and said, "How well you look, Auntie E."

And she did — for while she and Lady Essex were identical twins, there was nothing identical about the way they dressed and comported themselves. In comparison, Aunt Eleanor looked more like a young widow in her trim black gown and her hair done up just so.

Aunt Eleanor always cut a dash.

But right now the only thing that appeared about to be cut was his head — from his neck.

"Get out," she replied, pointing toward the door.

She also had the good fortune to make this statement just as Miss Murray was making her grand entrance, the one where she was introduced and then universally adored.

"Pardon me," the heiress said loftily, nose in the air and hardly the reticent miss that she'd appeared in London.

However, Aunt Eleanor hadn't noticed this grand display of temper for she was busy trying to push the traveling trunk that Mingo was now dragging in back out the door.

"Oh, no, you don't, you vagrant! No trunks. No bags." She wheeled on Roxley. "I told you not to return to Bath, to my house, unless you were ready to muster. And now this? This parade?" She glanced at Miss Murray and then at Harriet, who had managed to breach the portal as well and now stood sentry beside one of the bags.

The lady's small foyer was now overflowing with company.

Unwanted company. Not that Roxley was put off.

"But I have, Aunt Eleanor. I have brought my intended for mustering." He bowed slightly and waved a hand toward Miss Murray.

The lady barely spared a glance at Miss Murray and turned instead to Harriet. "You look like you have too many wits about you to marry into this family, so I'll assume you are not the woman in question."

"You are correct, my lady," she told her. "I am Miss Harriet Hathaway, Miss Murray's companion." She nodded toward Miss Murray and the girl once again struck a very Bath pose.

But Aunt Eleanor hadn't noticed this elegant display for she was still examining Harriet. "Hathaway, you said? You wouldn't be Sir George's daughter, would you? Sir George Hathaway?"

Harriet grinned. "Yes, ma'am. He's my father."

Roxley's aunt shifted, a sort of catlike stretch. "Oh, he was a handsome fellow. A rakish devil if ever there was one. You take after him. The hair and the eyes, that is. No wonder you look so familiar."

"We all do," Harriet replied.

"All?"

"I have five brothers, my lady."

This brought a new sparkle to Aunt Eleanor's eyes. "Five, you say? All as handsome and daring as your father?"

"Worse, according to my mother," Harriet confided.

"Excellent! I will love to meet them at the wedding," she said, turning for a moment and smiling at Roxley, but before he could correct her yet again and explain that Harriet wasn't his bride — something he discovered he was in no hurry to do — his aunt's demeanor changed altogether.

"Oh, bother. That also means you are from Kempton. Born there?"

"Yes, my lady," Harriet replied.

"Dreadful village, dreary really. How Essex can stand being abandoned out there, I will never understand." She glanced over at Harriet again, her nose wrinkling. "As such, you will not do." Now she turned to Roxley. "Good heavens, my dear boy, a Kempton bride? Are you mad? Return her to London immediately, bring back a chit who won't bury a fire iron in your chest on your wedding night," she told him, clearly familiar with Kempton's most notorious, though aptly named bride, Agnes Stakes.

It wasn't Roxley who corrected her, but Harriet herself, who rushed to say, "No, ma'am, I am not the earl's intended. I'm Miss Murray's companion for the trip."

Aunt Eleanor looked over Harriet, there in her new traveling gown, and shook her head. "Truly? The companion? How odd."

Roxley rose to her defense. "Auntie, when Miss Murray's regular companion was injured, Miss Hathaway kindly volunteered her services to assist. It was most generous."

He knew he hardly sounded grateful, a point that Aunt Eleanor did not miss, but wisely chose not to comment upon.

At least not yet.

"Who is this Miss Murray you keep going on about?" she demanded, looking around the foyer.

But before the girl could answer, Aunt Eleanor was once again diverted.

"And who is this?" The lady nodded at the door where Hotchkin stood hovering about as if he didn't know whether to breach the gates.

"That is Hotchkin." Roxley stepped in front of the man like a shield.

"Hotchkin?" Aunt Eleanor moved Roxley aside with the strength of a stevedore. "Excuse my nephew's lapse of manners, Mr. Hotchkin. However are you today?" She held out her hand for him.

"Ah, eh, uh," the poor boy stammered as he looked down at her elegant fingers.

"Oh, he'll do, Roxley," his aunt said over her shoulder, as if he'd brought her a box of comfits.

Roxley reached out and caught his aunt by the elbow and steered her back to the middle of the foyer. Aunt Eleanor would eat such an innocent fellow as Hotchkin alive — as if he were indeed a box of sweets. "He's come along to keep everything in order. Regular fellow — no one you will find interesting."

Not easily swayed, especially when it came to handsome young men, his aunt shrugged, a motion that said she'd get her chance eventually.

This left the lady nothing else to do but turn her attention to Miss Murray. "Miss Murray, I believe?" Her lips pressed together in a solid, definitive line as if testing a theory.

Apparently she was. Ah, leave it to Auntie E to make a younger woman feel welcome.

As Miss Murray curtsied deeply, his aunt continued. "Are you part of the Bagton Murrays?"

"No, ma'am —" the girl began.

"Hmm. The Exeter Murrays?"

"No, my father —"

"Was he from the North then? Don't tell me you are Scottish!" She turned to Roxley.

"Scottish? Really?"

"Miss Murray is from London. Her father is well-known there." Roxley raised a brow and nodded for his aunt to understand.

Well-known for the fortune he possesses.

His aunt's lips brightened only slightly. It would take a tremendously large fortune for her to truly smile.

While Miss Murray did her best to introduce herself, her education here in Bath — at Mrs. Plumley's, a name that brought a slight nod of approval from Aunt Eleanor — Roxley began to direct Mingo as to where the bags needed to go, but his aunt was immediately in his path. "Miss Murray and Miss Hathaway can stay, but not you, Roxley. Out." She pointed toward the door.

"Out?"

"Yes, decidedly. Out."

The two Marshoms, so very much alike, stood toe to toe.

"You may have command of Foxgrove, the Cottage and the house on Hill Street, but not here. This is my abode, and is not yours to command. My father granted me residence here and here I stay."

While she was correct in that regard, it was his money that supported the house and her living, but this seemed hardly the time to point that out.

"But dearest Auntie E, you have plenty of room —"

She was completely unmoved by his charm. "*Harrumph!* Not for a proper distance between the boudoirs. I will not have any suggestion of impropriety under my roof."

There was a slight cough from Thortle, probably sensing that his days were numbered and discretion was no longer needed.

But luckily for him, most everyone ignored his implied contradiction.

Roxley wondered if that included whoever Lady Eleanor had meant the butler to open the door for, notably her "dearest darling."

"I will meet this Miss Hathaway of yours —" Aunt Eleanor continued.

"Miss Murray —" he corrected with an apologetic glance at the heiress, who now wore a murderous expression.

Roxley could almost see the seething letter that would be sent back to London demanding her father cast Roxley and his relations into the deepest, darkest pit that debtor's prison might afford.

"Yes, yes, Miss Murray," his aunt huffed. "But you and your Mr. Hotchkin can take rooms at the King's Cross." When Roxley looked ready to protest, she leveled her best threat. "Press me on this, Tiberius, and I will move out. Leave Bath. Make Lord Tarvis's great-grandson delirious with joy to have the use of his house back. Then where will I go? With you on Hill Street? I've always fancied one last Season in London before I die."

Given the lady's obvious good health and luster, Roxley knew that it would probably be a good twenty Seasons before Aunt Eleanor stuck her fork in the wall.

"Then so be it," Roxley acquiesced. "Mingo, take my bags and Mr. Hotchkin's back to the carriage. We are taking rooms down the hill."

"Of course we are," muttered the ever-aggrieved Mingo.

Still, Roxley deplored letting any of his aunts bully him. "This isn't the end of the matter, Aunt Eleanor. Once I am settled, I will return."

"We won't be here," the lady told him most tartly.

But this time Roxley had her. "Ah, yes, the theater. I nearly forgot. I saw Lady Bindon as we were riding into Bath. She mentioned her, rather *your* plans, and was only too generous to include all of us in her and Lord Bindon's box tonight. *All of us.*"

Lady Eleanor looked anything but pleased. But then her gaze flitted over toward Mr.

Hotchkin.

"Not him," Roxley told her firmly.

"You said 'all of us.' "

"Hotchkin has business to attend to," Roxley told her. "Shall I call before seven?"

"No," she told him, pushing him out the door. "We will meet you at the theater."

And this time, Thortle managed to get the door shut.

Lady Eleanor turned and took only a scant measure of Miss Murray before she turned her discerning gaze on Harriet. "A mustering. Of all the ill-timed ventures." Then she started for the stairs, but whirled around as if in an afterthought. "Whatever do you have there, Miss Hathaway?"

Harriet glanced down and realized she was still holding the hatbox from Lady Essex. "Your sister, ma'am, Lady Essex sent it with her regards."

Slowly, Lady Eleanor came down the steps and took the box from Harriet. She tugged the string around it loose and then, with a hand that slightly trembled, she tipped the lip so she could look inside, and just as quickly closed it. "Whyever did she send this with you?" Her words sounded a bit strangled.

"I don't know, my lady," Harriet replied.

"But she said for me to tell you, 'It is your turn to decide.' "

"Inconvenient mess, that is what this is," she muttered before she rang for the housekeeper, the box cradled to her breast.

After seeing to Miss Murray and helping her decide what would be the best dress for the evening — a trial that took nearly an hour — Harriet wished, and not for the first time, she'd listened to Daphne more often when her friend was on one of her tirades about "good fashion" and "the right touches."

Notions that utterly baffled poor Harriet.

Luckily for her, the job of a companion was not so much to decide whether pearls or a cameo were the better choice, but merely to nod and say in a convincing voice that everything was "perfectly enchanting."

Even when one didn't mean it.

But still, she would have liked to have had Daphne at hand, for when Harriet was free to complete her own toilet, she stood before the array of gowns that her friends had packed up for her and was at a loss as to what to do.

As luck would have it, the housekeeper, Mrs. Nevitt, and one of the maids arrived to see if there was anything else that was needed.

"Is it true the young lord is here?" the maid asked from behind Mrs. Nevitt.

Harriet could tell her impertinent question annoyed the older woman, but even so they were both keen to hear the answer.

"Yes, Roxley's here," she told them. "That's why we are all here . . . for . . . for a mustering." She couldn't keep the wistful note out of her voice and to her dismay, the sharp-eyed housekeeper didn't miss it. She paused and gave Harriet an assessing glance.

Not unlike the one the mistress of the house had shot at her earlier.

Rather than explain herself, Harriet hurried over to her bed and held up one of Daphne's remade gowns. As Daphne had said, since none of her new gowns would fit her in the coming months, it only made sense that someone should be wearing them.

"Lor! That is something," the maid exclaimed, which earned her a dark glance from the housekeeper.

"Is that what Miss Murray will be wearing tonight?" Mrs. Nevitt asked, as she came up to look at the beautiful green silk.

Harriet shook her head. "Oh, no, this is mine."

"Yours, miss?" the maid exclaimed with a

hint of envy.

The housekeeper blinked, taking in both the dress and the "hired" companion before her, and given her expression, Harriet rushed to explain. "I'm not usually a hired companion. The lady who accompanies Miss Murray fell last week in London and twisted both ankles. When it appeared Miss Murray would not be able to travel, I volunteered to come along." When the maid and the housekeeper continued to look at her with expressions of doubt and curiosity, she added, "Lady Essex was in agreement that my coming along was the perfect solution."

Mrs. Nevitt's gaze moved from Harriet to the silk and back to Harriet. "And Lady Essex thought that you might help the young lord?"

Help Roxley? Certainly, that was one way of putting it.

Harriet bit her lip. "Lady Essex thought I could lend some sensibility to the situation." That was about as diplomatic as she could put it.

"Hmm," Mrs. Nevitt mused. "Well, I never! And at a time like this." The woman huffed a sigh and turned back to the gown lying on the bed. "No wonder herself is in such a state."

"Is something wrong?" Harriet asked. "Perhaps I can help." When the older woman appeared doubtful, she added, "Lady Essex is a dear friend of mine and I know she would want me to be of assistance to her sister in any way possible."

The woman gave Harriet another measuring glance. "Oh, I'm certain Lady Essex would have a thing or two to say to her sister. Starting with the company she keeps. Making a fool of herself. Ruinous it is. Ruinous."

"She's in trouble?" Harriet asked.

"We all are, miss," the maid said with a solemn shake of her head.

CHAPTER 8

A muster is also a flock of peacocks, which
at this moment explains much.
   Lady Overton to Miss Darby as they
   watched Colonel Darby assemble his
   regiment on the parade grounds
   from Miss Darby's Perilous Journey

Coming out of his hotel sometime later,
Roxley stood on the sidewalk and considered the quickest route to the theater. He
was already late, which would have his aunt
in a fine fettle. Hence, it might be best if he
waited a few moments so there was no
doubt the lights would be dimming as he
arrived.

Less time for the old girl to get a regular
scold in.

And knowing Aunt Eleanor, by intermission she would have forgotten his transgres-
sion entirely.

"My lord?"

Roxley glanced over his shoulder and found Mr. Hotchkin standing patiently at his elbow.

How long the man had been waiting there, the earl didn't know, but he always had the suspicion that Mr. Hotchkin's true strength was in his ability to observe and catalogue.

And to arrive when one least expected him.

"Good God, Hotchkin! Where did you come from?"

The serious fellow blinked. "Why from inside the hotel, my lord." As if such an answer should be obvious to anyone.

"Yes, yes, I know that," Roxley said, wondering how it was that Chaunce Hathaway hadn't drowned his young, overly serious assistant long before this. "But I thought you had tasks to see to." There had been a large packet of dispatches waiting for Mr. Hotchkin at the hotel when they'd arrived.

Obviously the man had made short work of the stack, for he lowered his voice and said in all earnestness, "My lord, I've some news."

Hopefully something good.

"Grave news," Hotchkin continued, dashing Roxley's fleeting bit of optimism.

Yes, so much for that throw of the dice.

"Miss Murray is not whom we thought,"

the man told him.

Roxley heard the words, but they hardly made sense. "What? She's not an heiress?" He laughed a bit. "Would demmed well seem my fate of late. Find a rich bride only to have her father lose her dowry on the 'Change."

"It isn't that, my lord," Hotchkin was saying, looking up and down the block, and when there was a break in the hustle of people hurrying past, he added, "She never had a fortune."

"Never had a fortune? How can that be?" Roxley shook his head. He'd had Mingo nose into Mr. Murray's dealings and had been assured the man was what he appeared to be: a reputable businessman.

However, he soon discovered there was one very important thing that had been overlooked that the tenacious Mr. Hotchkin had discovered.

"It isn't a matter of the money, sir, rather that there is no Miss Murray."

"No Miss Murray? Whatever are you going on about? I'm about to meet the chit at the theater." He tipped his chin in that direction.

Mr. Hotchkin shook his head. "You might be meeting a lady at the theater, but she is not Miss Murray. For we missed something

258

very important."

Roxley was at the point where he was starting to wonder if the River Avon was deep enough to give Mr. Hotchkin a good soaking. "Out with it, Mr. Hotchkin. What have you learned?"

"Miss Murray is not who we think she is. For you see, I have it on the most excellent authority that Mr. Murray has no daughter. Never has."

Roxley took a step back. Not Murray's daughter? "Then who the devil is that woman?"

Hotchkin shrugged. "That's what we must find out."

Find out? Oh, Mr. Hotchkin. Always so spot on. *Find out?* He'd do more than that.

For months he'd felt as if he were caught in a web of deceit.

Only to discover the spider had crawled into his grasp.

Harriet had thought it wisest to wear her full-length pelisse so as not to call attention to her new gown.

As Miss Murray's hired companion, she didn't want to cause a stir — at least not until it was too late and she had Roxley's entire attention.

If she felt a frisson of guilt over this business, she had only to recall what Tabitha had said in passing, quoting the most authoritative source on the subject they knew, *Miss Darby and the Counterfeit Bride.*

A man should marry the woman he loves, or else he is twice cursed.

Wise words from Prince Sanjit, indeed. And as Tabitha had pressed further, "Would you wish such a marriage for Roxley?"

Not that Harriet thought Miss Murray was a counterfeit bride, but there was certainly something not quite right about the heiress — starting with why Miss Murray had a pistol hidden in her trunk.

Not that it would do the girl much good now, since Harriet had taken the firing pins and tucked them safely away in her own small jewelry case.

Still, why did a Bath-educated miss carry about a concealed pistol? A question she would ask Roxley the moment she could gain his attention.

She had high hopes that her gown might manage to catch his eye and give her just such an opportunity.

That is, if Lady Eleanor didn't send her packing back to the house on Brock Street.

Tentatively, Harriet slipped off her pelisse, and to her relief, no one paid her much heed.

Lady Bindon was still marveling at the news that Roxley had brought a young lady for mustering — not even blinking an eye at this odd Marshom custom — and going on and on how "wasn't it just yesterday that dearest and beloved Tristan had come to Bath with Lady Davinia for his mustering?" referring to Roxley's ill-fated parents.

"Oh, weren't they a scandalous pair," Lady Eleanor was saying with some pride. "I was so pleased that Tristan had found such a clever girl —"

"Clever?" Lady Bindon shook her head. "Pretty, you mean. Prettiest gel out that year. That's why he found her."

"I remember the gown she wore," Lord Bindon said with a laugh. "As immodest as Roxley's bit there." He nodded at Harriet.

Lady Eleanor and Lady Bindon both shot him scandalized glances.

"Bindon!" his wife complained. "Whatever are you going on about? Miss Murray's gown is the height of good sense and fashion." She pointed at the pale silk Miss Murray had chosen.

Lord Bindon glanced at the heiress and shook his head. "Not that one. The pretty chit Roxley means to have. The one in green."

All three ladies turned around and one by

one their mouths opened in shock.

"Yes, that *one,*" Lord Bindon chuckled.

Harriet shifted. Daphne had warned her that the emerald silk might be a bit daring for Bath. And so it seemed her friend had been right. Even Harriet had known it was scandalous at best — hardly the gown of a hired companion. Or even the daughter of a knight.

Lady Eleanor's maid, having fallen into a fit of envy over the gown, had outdone herself with the rest of Harriet's toilet — having piled her dark hair up into a long column of curls that fell down in an ebony cascade, only emphasizing Harriet's height. The girl had even begged a rope of pearls from Lady Eleanor's maid, which glowed with a regal luster against the dark background of Harriet's ebony tresses.

The rich, deep emerald silk made Harriet's green eyes stand out all that much more — like the lustrous pearls winking in her dark hair.

Lord Bindon chuckled. "Oh, that young devil! He has his father's eye for daring young ladies." He winked at Harriet and chuckled again.

He was rewarded with a swat from his wife's fan. *Thwack.*

"You old fool! That's Miss Hathaway. The

hired companion." Then she pointed at Miss Murray, "Here is Miss Murray, the perfectly suited young lady Roxley has brought to be presented to his aunt."

He looked from Miss Murray then back at Harriet and snorted. "Find out where the gel hired that one" — he pointed at Harriet — "and next time you need some chit to traipse after you, use the same agency. This one's a far sight better than the sloe-eyed drabs you usually engage." He grinned at Harriet. "What did you say your name was, gel?"

"Miss Hathaway, my lord."

"Knew a Sir George Hathaway in my day."

Harriet brightened. "My father, my lord."

"You don't say! Well, now that you do, I see quite clearly that you have the look of a Hathaway about you."

Harriet touched her hair without thinking.

"Yes, by golly, that's it." Lord Bindon winked again. "And you have his air of mischief about you, I daresay."

"Oh, no," Harriet rushed to protest.

"Your father is a gentleman?" Lady Bindon asked, taking a closer look at Harriet.

"A gentleman? Sir George? Now there's a lark," Lord Bindon repeated with a bark of a laugh. "The best demmed fellow at finding the most willing bits of —"

"Bindon!" his wife exclaimed. *Thwack.* "Remember yourself."

"Oh, yes, quite right. Fine fellow, your father, Miss Hathaway. Decent chap. Bit wild in his salad days. Well before he met your mother. But weren't we all?"

"Yes, so you were," his wife said before returning to the subject that interested her. "However is it you ended up being in service, Miss Hathaway?" Lady Bindon asked, again glancing at the gown with an expression that said hired companion or not, gentleman's daughter or not, the emerald silk Harriet wore told a story that must include a disgraceful past.

But to Harriet's amazement it was Miss Murray who came to her rescue.

"Lady Bindon, Harriet is the dearest soul. When my own Miss Watson was injured, Miss Hathaway volunteered to accompany me so that there would be no delay in my . . . my . . . future happiness," she said ever so diplomatically. "Giving up her Season to help me, a near perfect stranger." Miss Murray smiled her approval for one and all. "As for her dress — why, it was a gift from her friends, the Duchess of Preston and Lady Henry Seldon. How could she not wear such a rich and beautiful gown?"

"Why not, indeed!" Lord Bindon enthused.

Thwack!

"Miss Murray, you are as kind and thoughtful of others as you are mannerly," Lady Bindon said, tossing an approving glance over at Lady Eleanor. She made no further comment on Harriet's choice of gown.

But then again, her dour glance said it all.

"Well, Miss Hathaway, it seems you have more than one admirer." Lord Bindon nodded across the theater, where in the box directly across from theirs, a man stood waving his arms, and having caught Harriet's attention, grinned and bowed.

"What the devil?" Harriet said without thinking, earning herself more speculative glances from Lady Eleanor and Lady Bindon. "I meant to say, 'Oh, my.' "

That was the problem with having five brothers, one picked up the worst turn of phrases and in times like these, Harriet forgot herself. Now she wished she could forget who was standing across the theater making a spectacle of himself and in turn, her.

"Who is that roguish fellow?" Lady Eleanor asked. But her voice was hardly filled with censure this time.

If Harriet didn't know better . . .

Then she remembered what the house-keeper had confided about Lady Eleanor's latest scandal.

"He's not like her regular cicisbeos," the housekeeper had complained. "Caught him snooping in the drawers in the library I did. Looking at the undersides of the statues like he was appraising them." The housekeeper had shaken her head. "And what does my lady say? 'Let him look in my drawers,' she says. Look in her drawers, indeed! Have you ever?"

With that confidence in hand, Harriet had promised to share the housekeeper's concerns about this Lord Galton, this snooping beau, with Roxley, knowing full well he would find it of interest, since she now knew — well, at the very least suspected — this entire trip, this mustering, might be nothing more than a smokescreen to recover the diamonds from the Queen's Necklace.

Meanwhile, Lady Eleanor's affection for her most recent beau seemed to have been diverted. "Such a well-turned-out gentle-man." She glanced back at Harriet. "Do you truly know this man?"

"Yes, my lady," Harriet said, pursing her

lips together, rather unhappy to have to admit it.

This pleased Roxley's aunt to no end. "Then you must introduce me!"

"Lady E!" Lady Bindon scolded, though with a smile on her lips. "He's too young for you. Leave that one be. He'll give Galton apoplexy and have the baron calling that pup out." She shook her head and then turned to Harriet as well. "But you must tell us who that is."

"Viscount Fieldgate," she replied.

"I didn't know he was coming to Bath." Miss Murray's brow furrowed as if this unexpected event was not to her liking. Definitely not. "Whyever would he follow us?"

"I can guess," Lord Bindon supplied.

Thwack.

Harriet couldn't offer an answer.

Wasn't there an heiress or some other lady about London with good connections and a decent purse to catch his eye? Everyone in Town said he was quite rolled up, so for the life of Harriet, she couldn't imagine why he was so set on courting *her.*

Even now, the handsome viscount was giving her that smoldering glance that had left more than one lady in ruined straits — or so the gossips avowed — but it only left

267

Harriet with the urge to yawn.

To her, Fieldgate, once he got done gossiping and comparing himself favorably to all the other gentlemen around, was a dead bore. A blundering paperskull, if she was being kind.

Speaking of paperskulls, Harriet glanced back at the door. Where the devil was Roxley?

"How like my nephew," Lady Eleanor announced — echoing Harriet's unspoken sentiment — even as the play was about to begin and the one seat left in their box remained unfilled.

"Mark my words, he'll be along," Lord Bindon replied. "With such a pretty intended, why wouldn't he?" The fellow winked at Harriet.

The baron's wife blanched. "That is Miss Hathaway, you old fool. Miss Murray," she advised, nodding toward the heiress, "is Roxley's chosen *parti.*" She huffed a sigh of exasperation at her husband's continued faux pas.

"Ah, yes, of course. I knew that," he said, nodding with restrained dignity at the future Countess of Roxley. But that was after he slanted a glance at Harriet that said he truly wondered as to Roxley's acumen.

"I wouldn't blame you in the least if you

threw my nephew over, Miss Murray," Lady Eleanor was saying. "He's a veritable rogue."

"Hardly that," Miss Murray demurred. "He has his charms, my lady."

Harriet was of the same opinion as Roxley's aunt. He was a rogue. And a devil. And a rake.

All of which she'd been counting on when she'd asked the modiste (out of Daphne's sharp hearing) to lower the bodice of this particular gown a bit more, until it competed with the Cleopatra costume she'd worn to the masquerade at Owle Park.

As she'd put it on tonight, she'd had a delicious moment remembering that night — when he'd quite literally swept her off her feet and carried her into the shadows.

I promised your brothers I'd keep an eye on you.

Then close your eyes.

And to her delight, he had, and she had risen up on her tiptoes and kissed him. And then he'd kissed her back.

If he were to do so again . . . She blushed a bit to even be considering it. Not that she hadn't nearly every day since. And yet, if he were to . . . would it be as wondrous as it had been that magical night?

She suspected it would be even more so

— a breathless sense of anticipation filling her limbs, bringing a deeper blush to her face . . . and to other parts.

"Lady Eleanor, do you see who just came in?" Lady Bindon whispered loudly, ruining Harriet's scandalous reverie.

When they all looked over at the baroness, she pointed her fan subtly in the direction of the floor, and all eyes moved in that direction.

Much to Harriet's disappointment it wasn't Roxley, but a hooded woman who seemed to catch the attention of everyone in the theater.

"Is that —" Lady Eleanor began.

"Yes, indeed, I believe so —" her friend replied. And when the lady in question drew back her hood, the baroness nodded enthusiastically. "It is *her.*"

"Who?" Lord Bindon ventured, squinting down at the main floor.

Lady Eleanor and Lady Bindon turned and gaped at him.

"Who is she? My lord, that is Madame Sybille, the famed occultist," Lady Eleanor explained.

"She can see into the future," Lady Bindon said with a decided note of conviction.

"And find lost things," Lady Eleanor added.

"Perhaps she can discover where Roxley is," Lord Bindon said, adding his own ringing note of bluster to the entire introduction.

His wife and Lady Eleanor ignored him.

For her part, Harriet glanced down at the lady who apparently not only held all of London in her thrall, but Bath as well, and found the woman looking directly up at her, her uncanny gaze bearing into their box.

"Oh, do attend, Lady E," Lady Bindon whispered. "Might it be that Madame Sybille is sensing something about one of us?" Her fan fluttered right beneath her chin.

"Whyever would we be of interest to her?" Harriet asked, earning a nod of approval from Lord Bindon.

His wife rushed to explain. "My dear girl, they say she's inhabited by spirits. She only returned to Bath a few days ago and already she's in great demand."

"For what?" Harriet found the woman quite unnerving, what with her penetrating stare. Lady Essex always said that staring was the height of bad manners.

"Why to speak to the dead of course." Lady Eleanor practically glowed with a spirit of her own, smiling down at the occultist, hoping to catch her eye.

"But who is she?" Harriet was too practical to believe any of this.

"She is French. Of noble birth, or so it is said. Why, Lady Allen told Miss Smythe that Madame Sybille was with the French queen just before she died. In fact she followed that poor lady's tumbrel all the way through Paris and watched as they cut off her head." These last words were said with great effect and a touch of horror.

"Perhaps she should have warned poor Marie Antoinette about the impending loss of her head," Lord Bindon muttered.

At which, Harriet laughed, garnering two disapproving scowls from the older ladies and a wink from the baron.

Miss Murray, who had taken only the slightest glance at the lady before sitting back in her seat, shook her head. "French? Truly?" She sniffed, making a moue that suggested she found the prospect of such an association well beneath her. "Such trumpery. She looks like one of those dreadful Colonials."

"Oh, my, Lady Eleanor, do you think she is receiving a message about one of us?" Lady Bindon whispered.

Whatever the message was, Harriet couldn't shake the sense that it wasn't good.

Just then, the lamplighters began to dim the lights, and in perfect unison, the door to the box opened and Roxley entered.

Harriet would have wagered every bit of her pin money that his timing had been deliberate, and her own disapproving gaze — added to those of the rest of the ladies in the party — buried itself into his back as he settled into the seat next to Miss Murray.

Harriet was about to look away, but something about his greeting to Miss Murray stopped her. Oh, he was polite, but there was a tautness to his shoulders that she'd never seen before.

Except when she danced with Fieldgate.

Something had happened, and Harriet's curiosity began to churn.

Perhaps it was just her own wishful thinking that had her seeing things, but when she glanced again, she knew down to her slippers that something had come between Roxley and his heiress.

"Sorry I was delayed. A business matter," he confided to his aunt, who sat on his other side.

Lady Eleanor's gaze rolled upward and she shook her head, dismissing his excuse. *Business, indeed.*

He glanced down at the stage and then around the box. "Whatever are we seeing tonight?"

Miss Murray shrugged, for it hadn't occurred to her to even bother discovering what the night's entertainment might be.

But Harriet knew and leaned forward, all too happy to tell him.

"The Tragedy of Antony and Cleopatra," she whispered. "Familiar with it?"

Was Roxley familiar with it?

Cleopatra? Every demmed, delicious inch of her.

In an instant he was back at Owle Park, to last summer, on that fateful night when one moment he was teasing Harry about her outrageous costume and before his startled gaze she'd transformed into a seductress worthy of the legendary name.

It had been utter madness. Chasing after her — knowing that every step he took drew him closer to being shot by not one, but all five of her brothers.

But he couldn't resist. He'd realized all too clearly in that moment, he'd loved Harriet since the moment he'd met her.

It was as simple as closing his eyes and letting his heart guide him.

Owle Park, 1810
Close your eyes.

And Roxley did as she asked, against his better judgment, against every bit of honor he possessed.

He'd closed his eyes but he hadn't for a moment forgotten exactly who he was holding — Harry.

His Kitten.

The moment her lips brushed against his, tentative and tantalizing all at once, he gave in to the desires that had been haunting him all night.

Her mouth opened as he slid his tongue inside, and found her as eager to tempt and tease as he was.

A soft moan rose from her. "Ah, Roxley. Whatever took you so long?"

He would have reminded her that this was entirely improper, as he caught her by the waist and turned her, so her back was against the trunk of the tree.

His cock, which had been restless all night, hardened as he pressed his body to hers. He had been waiting since that night in London to do this.

Dreamed of it.

Rich, lurid dreams of his hands cradling her breasts — which he did, cupping them as he continued to press into her, his fingers teasing her nipples.

He rocked against her, and she caught hold of him, her arms winding around his neck, pulling him closer, so he could kiss her deeply, his tongue exploring her moist, plump mouth as other parts of him wanted to make a similar conquest.

To plunge himself inside her, to stroke this madness from his veins, to hear her cry out his name as her release rocked her body.

He tore his lips from her mouth and began to explore her, the nape of her neck, the column of her throat, one of her breasts that he'd slipped free from her gossamer costume.

The ruby tip came to life in his mouth, budding tightly, and again she made that sound — a purring rumble in her chest — a sound of pleasure that ran down his spine.

He paused for a second and it was just enough for Harriet to slip from his trap — she moved from his grasp and went racing across the lawn, her teasing laughter a lure he couldn't resist.

"Roxley, follow me," she called softly from a small copse of trees, and then she was off again, running like a young deer through the woods. "Follow me."

He had no idea where she was leading him, but he couldn't do anything but follow.

Then suddenly he was in a small meadow and he paused, for he did know where they were, the spot the entire house party had come for a picnic earlier in the day.

He looked around until he found Harriet stepping out from behind one of the trees, one of the thick picnic blankets in hand.

Her hair was tumbled down from its former glory and her gown had slipped from her shoulder, leaving one breast nearly exposed.

No more the queen, she was Diana of the hunt, come from her woodland haunts to entice him.

Without a word, she spread the blanket on the ground, and standing beside it, she smiled wistfully at him.

Just before she slipped off her gown and stood naked before him.

Given the expression on Roxley's face, a mixture of shock and longing, Harriet wasn't too sure if she'd just made a mistake.

Certainly she felt a bit foolish, standing here, naked, before him, but that doubt, that whisper of fear was lost and forgotten as he stalked forward, shrugging off the various pieces of his costume, so he met her wearing only his skin-tight breeches and a simple linen shirt open down to his waist.

That, and a dangerous hunger in his eyes.

Roxley said not a word, but caught her by the arm and tugged her to his chest.

For a breathless moment, he stared at her — tucking the unruly strands of her hair out of her face and studying her as if he'd never seen her before.

As if he'd just come out of the woods and found her here.

"If we —" he began, his hands warm against the curve of her back.

"When we —" she corrected, pressing herself closer to his warmth.

"You will be mine —"

"I'd demmed well hope so," she shot back.

"Are you sure?"

"Would I have gone to all this trouble, if I wasn't?"

He glanced down at the blanket. "So you did plan all this."

It wasn't a question.

She nodded.

"For how long?"

"Since you kissed me in London. Since that night I've been unable to sleep —"

"Nor I —"

"I don't want to sleep, Roxley," she confessed.

"Neither do I, Kitten." And so he showed her what he wanted, nay, desired.

His lips began tentatively teasing hers, whispering kisses over hers, playful and full of longing. Again he was touching her —

wherever he wanted to — his hands pulling her bottom toward him, so her cleft rubbed against the front of his breeches, against his rock-hard cock beneath.

Harriet had read all the euphemisms for what was in a man's breeches, but she wasn't about to spend her night with a bunch of flowery phrases meant to shield a lady from the rigid, solid manhood that right now clamored to be freed.

Harriet wanted to touch him.

But first she'd need to free him. She ran her hands — both hands — up his thighs, solid hard thighs, where first she cupped his balls and then slowly ran her fingers up his entire length.

Roxley's breath rattled from his chest. "God, Harriet, what are you doing?"

"What I've dreamed of all these months," she told him as she opened his breeches, and then slid them down his hips.

As his breeches continued their descent, Harriet followed, her lips and tongue trailing over the crisp triangle of hair on his chest, down over the muscled planes of his belly.

She tasted, kissed, let her breath leave a tantalizing trail, as she continued to push his pants off.

He groaned as she went, deep, ragged

breaths that told her she was on the right course.

And as she tasted him, licked him, her senses were filled with the masculine scent of him — Roxley.

Her Roxley.

And then she was kneeling before him and the breeches were gone, tossed over her shoulder to land among the rest of his discarded clothes.

His cock thrust out from the dark patch of hair. Thick and waiting for her, and Harriet feeling bold and brazen, caught hold of him and ran her fingers up and down the entire length of him.

A small bead purled on the very tip and she leaned forward and licked it off, and when her tongue touched him, he shuddered.

"Oh, Harriet, what is this?"

"This," she told him, glancing up as she stroked him, his eyes half closed with pleasure and madness, "is what happens when your aunt gives me the freedom to read in her library *unattended.*"

His eyes opened wide.

So, she'd read from the top shelf as well. Which was good, because she had a number of matters she wanted to explore, starting with this one.

She ran her tongue from the base of his cock all the way up to the tip, where he was slick and throbbing.

She continued to explore him, taking him in her mouth and sucking him, much as he had suckled at her breasts, pulling from him the same sort of pleasures.

Desires.

When he started to groan, a growl really, he stepped back and out of her reach, his breath shuddering for control. Then as his hooded glance landed upon her, he smiled and came stalking forward like a lion.

Desire, hot and irresistible, ran through her as he approached.

He pressed her down atop the blanket, their mouths finding each other, joining again in a dizzy, hot and wet dance.

And now it was his turn.

His hand found her — that delicious spot between her legs — and began to tease it, rubbing against it, exploring the folds that kept it hidden and then going further, until again he was inside her, stretching her, sliding over her.

It was torment, demmed torment, for she was throbbing, her hips rising to meet him, chasing after something that couldn't be seen, couldn't quite be touched.

And yet, how she wanted him to find it.

"Kitten, I need you," he whispered, as he shifted, and now it was no longer his hand pressing into her, but his manhood, as hard and reckless as his fingers had been, but so much more demanding.

So much larger.

"I've always been yours," she told him, opening her legs, her body, her heart to him.

And Roxley filled her. Thrust himself into her and filled her.

Harriet gasped at this urgent, sudden entry. He'd been there and now he was inside her, and she was full, stretched, and breathless.

At least she thought she was until he moved.

Slowly, carefully, he pulled back and then moved inside her again, deeper, thrusting into her, and suddenly it wasn't so much that he was filling her, but that he was teasing her.

Stroking it slowly out and then thrusting against her. The rhythm hard and soft, tease and push.

Her heels dug into the blanket as her hips rose to meet him, to feel his length slide against her nub as he rode back and forth, cantering over her senses.

His mouth caught hold of hers and he kissed her anew, his tongue matching his thrusts, lapping at hers, teasing hers so it was impossible to tell where his touch began and ended.

Roxley was everywhere — inside her, stroking her, bringing her to the edge of madness.

"Roxley," she gasped as the first wave hit her, and hearing her cry, he thrust inside her harder, casting her over the edge, harder and faster and over and over.

Harriet heard him say her name, a ragged cry that caught up with hers, as his thrusts became more wild, more determined, and then he too was shuddering, quick, short thrusts as he came, breathless and hot and wet.

Tangled and entwined, their limbs, their hearts, bound all together in this vast abyss.

One might have fallen and found oneself alone in such a vast ocean.

But Harriet had Roxley, and he clung to her as if he would never let her go . . .

Bath, 1811

Yes, Roxley remembered every moment of that night. How could he not? It had stolen his heart.

She'd stolen his heart. *Harriet.*

Oh, if you asked any one of Roxley's friends and his acquaintances in the *ton,* they would laugh at the notion that the earl knew anything about love, but one of his few memories of his parents was from the night they left for that last ill-fated trip to the Continent — and it had taught him everything about that precious tangle.

Even now he could see his mother kneeling beside his bed, a glaze of tears in her eyes as she leaned forward to kiss his forehead.

Her hand had been soft and warm as it had brushed his hair back so she could look into his eyes.

Then his father had sat on the edge of his bed, murmured something about him being a gentleman for his aunts, to be the man of the house for his Aunt Oriel and Aunt Ophelia.

And as the two of them had risen — together — all Roxley could remember was how their hands reached for each other, their fingers twining, as if pulled together like a seam that had come loose and was once again stitched together.

That was always how he remembered them. Together. Bound so.

And even as a child, he'd known what it was that held them so — love.

And as he'd grown up, he'd discovered how rare that spark, that binding emotion was in a marriage.

It was probably why he'd helped Harriet in her designs to see Preston win Tabitha's hand. And why he'd teased her about Lord Henry and Miss Dale's elopement.

For Harriet was probably the only other person he knew who understood that those marriages were far more than brilliant matches, deeper than a passing fancy.

Then again, what other sort of marriage did Harriet know? Her parents' union had been a terrible scandal and even now, all these years later, Sir George and his bride were as passionately in love as they had been thirty-five years earlier.

Harriet's parents were like a beacon to him now. A light he wanted to emulate, carry on, with their equally passionate daughter.

He was of half a mind to catch up Harry's hand and haul her off to the wilds of Scotland . . . his aunts and those bloody diamonds be damned.

But it was his aunts who stopped him. He'd spent most of his adult life complaining about them — their endless chiding letters, unannounced visits (well, on Essex's part at least) and their scandalous eccentricities.

But after his parents' deaths, nay *murders,*

he corrected, his aunts had circled around him and seen to it that he'd been raised with love and a steady home.

He owed them much — and their care and well-being, their very safety, was his duty now.

It wasn't that there was a debt that had to be repaid — it couldn't have been, not in a century — but his obligation ran far deeper.

The Marshoms, for all their rapscallion ways, never shirked family.

Never.

And that sense of responsibility held him in place. Kept him from turning around and declaring his heart.

But for the first time in weeks, months, there was a spark of hope inside him, that Marshom resolve rekindled, a ridiculous belief that the next hand would be the one that restores all.

If he could find the diamonds . . . discover who this faux Miss Murray might be . . . stop whoever was behind all this . . .

If . . . If . . . If . . .

It was such a Marshom gamble to take. But how could he not?

For Harry.

"My goddess, my Cleopatra," came a man's voice from behind them, even as the curtain was drawn for intermission.

Roxley turned and found a grandly dressed old roué making his way into the box.

"Lord Galton," Lady Eleanor fluttered back. "I had thought you were away from Bath."

"Nothing can keep me very long from your side, my lady. You are the light of my twilight years." The fellow caught hold of her hand and kissed it with a great show of manners and overly familiar affection.

Before, Roxley might have just shook his head at the entrance of yet another aging roué into his aunt's life — she'd always collected admirers in spades — but now he needed to determine which one might mean her harm.

"Come, my dear. I long for a turn about the hall with you." Lord Galton held out his hand with all the gallantry of a Marc Antony — albeit one who'd managed to live past his prime.

Lady Eleanor's chin notched up in royal delight as she followed, yet when she was about halfway out the box, she paused. "I trust you can behave yourself, Roxley?"

"On my best behavior, Auntie E," he assured her, though he wondered if that meant he could dangle Miss Murray over the railing by her ankles and shake the truth out of her.

Probably not.

"Oh, my goodness, is that Mrs. Plumley?" Miss Murray exclaimed as the lights began to brighten. She leaned over the railing, her eyes gleaming.

I will not push her, I will not push her, Roxley mused. Though a glance over his shoulder revealed that Harriet seemed to be plotting much the same thing — her eyes sparkled with mischief. When she caught him watching her, he winked.

She tucked her nose up in the air as if she was still furious with him, but Roxley knew differently.

Besides, she was also blushing quite prettily, having been caught making her own dastardly plans.

"Yes, it is Mrs. Plumley! How delightful," Miss Murray said, turning back to the others.

"You were a student of hers?" Lady Bindon asked, glancing down at the main floor.

"I was, my lady," she replied.

"Of course you were," Lady Bindon said approvingly. "You have the air of one of her better students. Come along with me and we shall greet her."

Harriet rose as Miss Murray did, but this only made Lady Bindon frown. "Perhaps,

288

Miss Hathaway, you should remain in the box. To keep an eye on the wraps." A point she made by glancing at Harriet with a pinched, disapproving expression.

Good God, what had Harry done to Lady Bindon to have her in such a pickle?

"Would you like me to accompany you, Miss Murray?" Roxley asked, rising to his feet, and then made the mistake of glancing down at Harry, and forgot every bit of his manners.

Who the devil was sitting in Harry's spot?

He'd merely glanced at her before, but now that he was standing he could take in the entirety of her.

This breathtaking vision. This elegant woman.

This was Harry? His scamp. His Kitten. The minx who'd stolen his heart?

And it was more than just the gown — the dramatic cascade of raven curls falling over her shoulders lured him to reach out and run his fingers through them.

And if he wasn't mistaken, those were his aunt's pearls wound through the braid that crowned her head.

What he wouldn't give to be the one who unwound that strand, pearl by pearl, letting loose the coal black strands beneath.

Roxley shivered a bit and realized she was

watching him — and he suspected she knew exactly what he was thinking.

Harry was like that. As astute as a cat — with those clear green eyes that peered so easily into his soul.

"Ahem," Lady Bindon coughed. "My lord? Perhaps you should join us." Her brows arched with disapproval.

"Oh, no, that won't be necessary," Miss Murray told her. "I fear the entire exchange would bore the earl endlessly."

"Doesn't look bored in the least," Lord Bindon added, before he was shooed from the box by his wife. Miss Murray followed her, and suddenly Harriet and Roxley were all alone.

"What the devil were you thinking, Harry? Wearing that dress! And in Bath no less." Roxley threw up his hands.

But Harriet didn't rise to his baiting. She sat down, smoothed at her skirt, and then looked up at him with a level, intelligent gaze. "Miss Murray didn't want to introduce you to her teacher."

"So?" Roxley was still a bit mesmerized by the vision she presented to let her words sink in.

"Didn't you find that odd?"

He stole a glance at the door.

"Not in the least," he blustered, crossing

his arms over his chest, for he knew all too well that Harriet *was* spot on. There was something odd about the entire thing.

Nor was Harriet about to let up.

"I mean, aren't most of these Bath schools designed to teach young ladies how to marry up and beyond their station?" she pressed. "And here's Miss Murray reaching quite up to the top shelf and she doesn't want to parade her success before her teacher?" Harriet shrugged. "I find that rather curious."

Roxley paused and then looked back over the railing where the girl was greeting her former teacher like an old friend. As if cementing her position as the real Miss Murray.

But if Murray didn't have a daughter, then who was this imposter?

"Why do you think she didn't want you to go?" Harriet continued like one of the Home Office's best agents. If Old Iron Drawers could hear her, he'd have recruited her on the spot.

Put her in the thick of it, as the man liked to say. What was more perfect than someone so very smart, so very close to Miss Murray to report her every move.

Neck and jowl with the enemy, Howers would declare.

Roxley shivered. No. Suddenly it was even more imperative to get Harriet away from all this.

No matter how much she could help him . . .

No, he wouldn't even consider the notion.

Harriet had continued on with her speculations. "Perhaps she is embarrassed of you, Roxley. Not lofty enough." She'd said it with the same teasing air that harkened back to when they'd been children and the Hathaways would bow and scrape before him, with a chorus of "my lord" and "His Lordship," all done to get a rise out of him.

Of course, it worked still. "Not lofty —" Roxley lurched forward and then turned around to face her.

Of course that was an utter mistake.

For one brief moment he considered hauling her into his arms so he could kiss that smug expression off her lips, but then he realized she'd puzzled out the enigma of Miss Murray all on her own, putting his own skills to shame.

And it struck him like a blow to the chest that he needed her. Terribly.

And worst of all? Harriet knew it. Believed it.

And he wasn't so toplofty that he was unwilling to admit the truth — even if it took being blindsided by it.

But still, it took every bit of nerve he possessed to say those three words.

"Harry, I need you."

Immediately he regretted his moment of weakness. For by saying them, asking her for help, he knew he was putting her in the firing line.

To Harriet, Roxley's request was music to her ears.

He needed her.

Of course he did.

Oh, and how she needed him. She bit her lower lip and resisted the urge to lean forward and offer him anything his heart desired. Hadn't she already done that once, and look at where that had left them.

He'd abandoned her and she'd been left ruined.

He loves you not . . .

For if he did . . .

Harriet's temper began to rise, now after all these months of anxious waiting and worried doubts. If he'd just claimed her last summer as he ought to have, none of this would be happening.

Not Miss Murray. Not his troubles. None of this.

But she knew this wasn't true. She'd read

293

the report, after all.

"I hardly think whatever you have to say is going to be proper," she told him, shooting him the most missish expression she could muster.

"Of course it isn't going to be proper, that's why I'm asking you," he huffed. "Proper! You barged your way into my affairs —"

"Barged?" Now it was Harriet's turn to be a bit outraged.

"Barged!" he confirmed.

"Harrumph." She crossed her arms over her chest. "I merely volunteered." Why couldn't he see she just wanted to help?

What if he truly doesn't want your help? Or your love?

Much to her chagrin, the earl used her own words to his advantage. "And why was that, Kitten?"

Her eyes fluttered open. *Kitten.* Dear God, when he called her that, she melted all over. Blast his bloody hide.

"Kitten?"

"Yes," he shot back. "Kitten." It hardly came out as an endearment this time. Nor was Roxley done. "You say you care not what I do, so why would you offer to help Miss Murray — and in turn, me?" He leaned closer. "That is, why on earth would you come along at all if you don't —"

He stopped short of saying the words that had gone unsaid between them all this time.

. . . if you don't love me.

Instead he paused, looked at her and said, "— if you don't want to do something improper."

She bristled a bit — was that what he was asking?

Why, it was like when her brothers would choose her last for cricket. She was as good a batsman as any of them but none of them liked openly admitting that they really wanted her for their side.

Roxley wanted her, but not to marry.

"Roxley, you wretched, horrible —" She began to rise from her seat, caught between the unfamiliar heat of tears rising in her eyes, and the sheer mortification of how she could have mistaken him so.

"Good heavens, Harry, sit down," he pleaded. "I'm making a muddle of this. I simply need you to let me into my aunt's house tonight — all you have to do is leave the study window unlatched. Then once everyone has gone to bed, I can slip inside."

Simply. Let. Him. In.

She'd point out the last time she'd "simply let him in" it had ended rather badly for both of them.

Well, mostly for her.

"Don't be ridiculous," she told him. "If I am caught, I'll be ruined." She let that sink in a bit. "Besides, your aunt can't keep you out of her house forever. You can call tomorrow and she will have no reason but to let you in."

It was the sensible and proper reply, but in Harriet's mind she saw herself in the shadows of the parlor with Roxley bounding through the opened window like a knight coming to claim her.

Whisk her away.

Ravish her.

Well, a girl could dream.

"Harry —" he continued, barging into her fantasy, "I can't do what I need to do during the day with everyone about."

"If by that you mean hunt around for the lost diamonds, I'll have you know I've already —"

Well, perhaps she shouldn't have sounded quite so smug, for the earl nearly exploded. "You nosy little termagant!" Roxley blustered. "How the devil did you —"

Then he paused and the answer came tumbling out as if the memories now gave him a different perspective. "Hotchkin! His valise. You little thief —"

So he had noticed when she'd returned

the man's bag at the inn.

She sat up a little straighter and smiled at him. "It was hardly theft," she explained, "when one bag looks entirely identical to another."

Roxley's expression darkened. "Don't think you can make excuses for stealing —"

"It isn't stealing, as you so eloquently put it, when one is under the assumption that the bag is theirs." Which was partially the truth. She had thought it was hers. For about two seconds. Happily those two seconds lent a scant bit of truth to her statement.

Not that Roxley was going to concede, even an iota. "Harriet Hathaway, you lying little minx. You knew that bag wasn't yours and directed the lad to take it up to your room on purpose."

"I didn't direct anyone. I carried it myself." When he continued to glare at her, she changed course and launched into a heartfelt defense, "If you had been a bit more forthcoming I wouldn't have been forced —"

"Forced?" he shot back, raking his hand through his hair. "The only one doing the forcing is you, Harry. Why you reckless, foolish —"

But his warning was interrupted by a tall

figure who filled the doorway of the box.

"My heart is reclaimed by the very sight of you, my dearest, my perfect Miss Hathaway!" The man made his way in and caught up Harriet's hand, drawing her fingertips to his lips.

Harriet winced. *Fieldgate.* Oh, bother. She'd forgotten all about him.

Meanwhile, Roxley glowered at this unwanted interruption. "Fieldgate, what a surprise." And not a happy one, given the sour note to the earl's greeting.

"I don't see why," the viscount replied. "When you stole my fair Miss Hathaway away, there was nothing I could do but follow." The two men glared at each other, and Harriet was in no mood for either of them.

"Roxley hardly stole me," Harriet told the viscount, plucking her fingers free from his cloying grasp. "I volunteered. To come as Miss Murray's companion. Nothing more." She shot a challenging glance at Roxley.

"Volunteered to come to Bath? As Miss Murray's companion? You are ever a surprise with your eccentricities, Miss Hathaway." Fieldgate's roguish charm was enough to illuminate the box.

"Harry? She's full of eccentric surprises," Roxley advised him.

"Who is eccentric?" Lady Eleanor's question pulled all eyes to the door. There Roxley's aunt stood, posed like a queen and smiling at the viscount with a wicked light in her eyes.

After a few moments, Lady Eleanor cocked a brow and stared at Roxley, silently reminding him to do the proper thing. Introduce her.

But given Roxley's mood, Harriet imagined the only thing the earl wanted to introduce Fieldgate to was a hasty exit over the railing. Much like the one she'd considered for Miss Murray.

"You'll have to excuse my nephew," Lady Eleanor said, coming down the steps into the box with Lady Bindon and Miss Murray close behind. "I do believe he left his manners in London."

"And I have left my wits there as well," Fieldgate told her coming forward to meet her halfway, "for I cannot believe you are Roxley's aunt. His sister perhaps . . . but aunt? Never!"

Behind her, Harriet could hear Roxley muttering, "Great-aunt, you pandering ape."

Harriet laughed, and then covered her mouth.

And Lady Eleanor, true to her reputation for collecting cicisbeos, blushed and smiled.

"You, sir, should never have left London."

"Not left London?" Fieldgate sounded aghast. "Whyever not, dear lady?"

"I can hear the hearts breaking from here," Lady Eleanor replied, her fan fluttering, while Fieldgate laughed merrily at her jest.

"There is only one lady whose heart matters, and now she is back within my reach," he said, sending a smoldering glance at Harriet.

Not if I push you over the rail first, she thought. She glanced over her shoulder at Roxley and found him grinning at her, as if he knew exactly what she'd been considering.

Make him leave, she mouthed.

"Why should I?" he countered quietly. "He's your beau."

She shuddered at the very thought. "I don't want him."

And the words that should have followed, *I want you,* had to go unsaid.

They both paused for a moment, and for the first time in days, nay months, it was as if they were together again, entwined on that blanket in the meadow. Nothing but their hearts beating together and the stars lighting the way.

Oh, all around them people were retaking

their seats, Lady Eleanor was giving Field-gate her directions and inviting him to some sort of gathering in honor of Miss Murray, but to Harriet, the world around them blurred.

He was her Roxley, and she, his Kitten.

"If you find the diamonds —" she whispered.

This brought his gaze up to meet hers. "I can only hope to find them."

"Hope is something," she offered.

"Hope is that when I come to the window, it will be unlatched."

"That isn't hope," she told him.

"It isn't?"

She shook her head. "No. That's a certainty."

CHAPTER 9

I vow, upon my honor, my heart was never
engaged by that woman.
            Lt. Throckmorten to Miss Darby
from Miss Darby and the Counterfeit Bride

Not long after midnight, Roxley found the
window unlatched just as Harriet had promised.

"Good girl, Harry," he whispered under
his breath as he climbed into his aunt's
house.

"About demmed time you showed up,"
came the unwanted response. Rising from a
chair in the shadows was Harriet wearing
only a wrapper.

God, he hoped she had on a night-rail
beneath it. As if that would make all this
any less scandalous.

"What the devil are you doing here?"
Roxley had to wonder how it was he was
always finding himself alone with her — half

dressed.

Demmed fine luck, that, a wry voice nudged.

"What am I doing? Opening the window," she replied, obviously unaware of the effect she was having on his senses. "As you asked me to." She slanted a glance up at him through half-shuttered lashes.

No, make that perfectly aware of her effect.

He held up the glym — the lamp one of the London housebreakers had left behind — letting its light cast a narrow beam toward his unwanted assistant. Willowy and lithe, she stood before him, her hair now undone, falling in a long thick braid over one shoulder, looking all too ready for bed. *His bed.*

Demmit, he had to stop thinking like that. Yes, he needed her help, but only so far as her assistance kept her out of harm's way.

Which, he supposed, included himself.

Closing the window behind him, and then the curtain, he chided her. "Harry, you know demmed well that is not what I wanted. I merely asked you to leave that window unlatched."

"And just let any thief into your aunt's house? I think not." She returned to her chair and sat down.

He wagged a finger at her. "Oh, no, you don't. You've accomplished all you are going to, and now you can go." Then he pointed toward the door.

"No." If it was possible, she sank deeper into the chair.

"No?"

"No. As in decidedly not." She crossed her arms over her chest. If he wanted her gone, he'd have to carry her out of the room.

Which would involve him having to put his arms around her.

Apparently this was a perfectly acceptable solution to Harriet. But not to him. For to touch her, to hold her . . . That was far more dangerous than mere housebreaking.

"Harry, leave." He stood his ground.

So did she. Most stubbornly. "You cannot ask for my help and then tell me to leave. That just isn't done, Roxley."

He was quickly losing his patience. "I merely asked you to unlatch the window."

She shook her head. "No. You said, and I quote, 'Harry, I need your help.' " She smiled rather smugly. "Truer words, Roxley. Truer words. Though I do wish you'd leave off calling me Harry. I'm a lady now."

"Not that much of one," he shot back. "And as long as you continue to behave like an incorrigible brat, I shall call you Harry."

She tipped her head slightly and let her lashes flutter in that utterly distracting way of hers. "I think you rather like that I'm incorrigible."

"What I would like is for you to leave."

"Not until you find the diamonds."

He let out a deep huff of a breath. "Then you'd best get comfortable living in my aunt's parlor, because I don't even believe there are diamonds to be found." He raked his hand through his hair and glanced about the shadowed room, feeling as if he were seeing it for the first time.

"Roxley, you are a terrible liar," she whispered.

He glanced over at her. "I beg to differ. I am a Marshom. We are marvelous liars." He opened a drawer in his aunt's desk and sorted through the contents. He certainly didn't think his aunt would keep a treasure trove of diamonds in her desk drawer, but he did hope Harry would grow bored and leave.

After a few moments, he found her watching him with that smug expression that said, *What now?*

"You need to return to your bed," he repeated.

"Can't."

"Whyever not?"

"Who would latch the window behind you?" she pointed out. "I couldn't sleep knowing that the window wasn't secured — why, any passing villain could climb in and murder us all in our beds."

"You've been spending too much time with my Aunt Essex," he pointed out.

She preened a bit. "Glad you finally noticed."

"It wasn't a compliment."

She didn't appear to care. "Where do we start?"

"*We* do not." Roxley looked over her and saw so much. The fire in her eyes — the sort of light that left a person believing they were impervious to treachery.

Agents died under that misbegotten impression.

Roxley, on the other hand, had always been rather sensible of his own mortality, given that he'd learned very early in life how fragile one's existence might be. "Harriet, these diamonds are dangerous. People have died — likely been murdered — for these demmed stones. You know that much — at least you should since you snooped through Hotchkin's reports." He heaved a sigh and nodded toward the door. "No, Harry, I won't have you entangled in their curse."

"Rather too late for that," she said. "Besides, wouldn't you admit that I'm uniquely qualified to deal with curses?"

"You?" Of all the utter rot. Roxley went back to searching the bookshelves. Of all his aunts, Eleanor was the most likely one to have custody of the diamonds — despite her penchant for aging Corinthians and card sharks, she was enough of a sharpster herself that no one would ever pull the wool over her eyes.

Not easily.

Meanwhile, Harriet was reciting her qualifications. "I was born and raised in Kempton, therefore I am cursed, and *further* —"

Of course, this was Harry. She would have a "further."

"Further," she repeated having most likely spotted the annoyance in his eyes, "my favorite book is *Miss Darby and the Curse of the Pharaoh's Diamond*."

Roxley closed his eyes and counted to ten.

Meanwhile, Harriet continued. "And despite the diamond being cursed, the story ended most happily." She paused and bit her lip as if considering the matter. "Yes, well, if one doesn't count the demise of Dr. Pierpont, Miss Agatha Bosworth, and the entire French legion tasked with guarding the pharaoh's diamond, but otherwise, Miss Darby managed to persevere through it rather well."

"Of all the foolish, most ridiculous notions —"

"Roxley, do stop blustering," she told him. "You'll wake the house."

"I wouldn't be blustering if you weren't down here with your nobcock romance novel notions of danger."

She rose and faced him. Harriet was tall, rising a good head taller than most other ladies. In only a plain white dressing gown, her hair simply done, she looked like an Amazon, and she spoke like one, in a voice laced with surety and conviction. "You cannot deny that I am made of rather stern stuff."

"Well, yes," he conceded, though he hated to. In the rough-and-tumble world of the Hathaways, Harriet had always held her own.

Much to her brothers' chagrin and now his.

"Must I also remind you that I'm a demmed good shot."

"Unfortunately," he offered, wondering if the day would come when she realized she hardly needed her brothers to avenge her honor.

Harriet could handle the matter quite well on her own.

Then she added her last sally. Which, of course, was more piercing than a round from a pistol. "And then there is the fact that you ruined me —"

That was the last thing he'd expected her to cast up against him.

Still that didn't mean he was above protesting. "I was hardly alone in that venture." He arched his brows, challenging her to dispute the facts.

Follow me, Roxley. Follow me . . .

A deep blush rose on her cheeks. "Oh, of all the impudent, arrogant —"

As she blustered on, Roxley couldn't help smiling.

They'd both been reckless that night, but honestly the fault was entirely his. He'd known better. At least he should have. But the moment her lips had touched his, her hands had cradled his face, her eyes had looked at him with such passionate abandon, he'd known — known from a place in his heart that he'd always thought lost — that she would be his from that day forth.

His. His beloved. His countess. His Kitten. So whatever he'd "ruined" that night, it was only what he desired to hold for the rest of his — nay — their lives.

And then he'd failed her.

When he glanced up at her, he found she

was winding down her tirade.

". . . is this all because Miss Murray has a pistol hidden in a secret compartment in her trunk or because you love me and fear that you might lose me?"

Well, demmit, of course I'm terrified of losing you . . .

Then the rest of what she'd said stopped him cold. "A what?"

"A pistol. Miss Murray has a pistol hidden in a secret compartment in her trunk." She stared at him and he knew she was challenging him to complain about her meddling ways now.

And he wasn't going to even bother to ask how she'd discovered Miss Murray's secret.

This was Harriet after all.

"She's more dangerous than I thought," he said, more to himself than to her as he added this to Hotchkin's revelation earlier in the evening.

Murray never had a daughter.

So, who the devil was this chit?

"Hardly dangerous now," Harriet said confidently. Too much so.

"Harry, you can't cross her — we have no idea who she is," Roxley warned. At least not yet.

"Well, she's hardly going to shoot anyone now. I removed the flint — it shan't spark."

She shook her head. "Really, an upstart mushroom with a pistol! And after having to endure hours of her going on and on about a proper Bath education. *Harrumph!* Roxley, this is exactly what happens when you start involving yourself with *cit*s and their daughters."

"She's not a *cit,*" he told her.

"Not a *cit?* Well, I could have guessed that. Some fishwife's leftover mackerel —"

"No, Harry, you mistake the matter. She's not Miss Murray."

Harriet took a step back and eyed him. "Not Miss Murray? Whatever do you mean? Who else would she be?"

"I don't know." Roxley took a deep breath and plunged in. "Murray has no daughter. Never has."

"No daughter? But if he hasn't a daughter —" Harriet's expression widened.

"Yes, exactly." He could see her adding this to all the information she'd already purloined.

Truly, she nearly put the ingenuous Mr. Hotchkin to shame.

Harriet grinned. "Oh, that is excellent news. Now I don't feel the least bit of guilt tampering with her pistol."

Pistols . . . What other tricks did his faux betrothed have up her well-appointed

311

sleeve? And whatever was she willing to do to play her part in this charade?

He looked at Harriet and suddenly his world tilted. No, not Harriet.

Demmit! The vision of her lost left his chest in knots, his very breath trapped, strangled upon a broken heart.

And here was Harriet blithely tampering with pistols! That was exactly why she shouldn't be involved in any of this.

Roxley wagged a finger at her once again. "You see now why you cannot help me and why you are returning to London in the morning. We have no idea who she is or how dangerous she might be."

If he thought such a sensible notion would work on Harriet, he was sadly mistaken.

"Return to London?" She shook her head. "Poppycock! Roxley, I am uniquely qualified to help. I am her companion. This allows me to stand right beside her and determine everything you need to know about her." She smiled at him. "Rather like in *Miss Darby's Daring Dilemma* when she had to uncover the secrets of Miss Overton's nefarious guardian."

Roxley cursed the day Miss Darby's creator had ever been born.

"Demmit, Harry," he sputtered, and caught her by the elbow and hauled her close. Only problem being, he brought her up right against him, so her hands splayed across his chest and she was pressed against him, ever so intimately.

Everything he wanted to avoid. And worse, everything he desired.

"Yes, Roxley?" she whispered, looking up at him with those glorious green eyes.

"Why are you always so vexatious?" he managed as his body came alive in rapturous recognition — his heated reaction as impossible to ignore as the lady he held.

Harriet tried to breathe, tried to argue, but it was impossible. His words, the heat of his breath rustled against her ear, sending tendrils of desire uncoiling in her limbs.

Beneath her fingers, his heart beat with a steady thud — hard and strong.

She finally gathered together the courage to tip her head up and found him staring down at her, a mixture of dismay and if she wasn't mistaken, longing.

The same sense of dangerous desire that had haunted her for months.

"Vexatious?" she whispered. "What utter nonsense. I am nothing of the sort."

He made a rather inelegant snort, even as he reached up and caught hold of a loose tendril of her hair, twining it around his fingers, letting the dark strand slide through his grasp like silk.

It was an intimate, dangerous moment. Wasn't this how it had all started at Owle Park? One moment they stood just so, perilously close, and the next they'd been kissing.

That was just fine with Harriet, for now all the barriers that had been holding them at arm's length — most notably, Miss Murray — were no longer there.

If she wasn't an heiress, not even a *cit*'s daughter, then Roxley was free to be hers.

Well, nearly.

Still, doubts bubbled beneath the surface of her desires. He wanted her, didn't he?

And then much to her dismay, he unwittingly answered her uncertainties. For instead of catching hold of this spark between them, whispering words of encouragement and promise on it, letting it rekindle and catch anew, Roxley abruptly set her out of reach.

"Vexatious, I say," he repeated, glowering from his solitary post.

"Vexatious, indeed!" she shot back, crossing her arms over her chest and holding back the shivers of regret threatening to rattle her out of her slippers. *Now who was being vexatious?* "I prefer helpful. Useful.

Remarkably resourceful."

Roxley laughed quietly. "Excellent traits in a hunting hound, but in a lady, I would point out that such characteristics are usually described with one word: meddling."

"You know me so well, Roxley." Too well, she realized, recognizing this dance — the one where he put this cold, horrid distance between them.

Like the wall around a convent.

Save Harriet wasn't the convent sort, and had been climbing walls since she was old enough to toddle.

"Harry, I'm doing all this for you. You've got to see that."

See what? She was still furious with him — for leaving her vacillating between hope and despair all these months. And, well, for just leaving! Of all the rotten, ruinous, horrible —

And then she glanced at him. For all his lofty ways, for all the times he'd been rakishly charming, right now the only word that came to her was vulnerable. She'd never seen him look so cast off — as if the entire world rested on his resolve, his wits.

Bother, Roxley! When was he going to see that this was their burden, not his alone? *Theirs.*

Worse, it was nigh on impossible to remain

righteously angry with the man when he was in the same room. He quite tore at her heart standing there, looking like a lost highwayman in his dark clothes and dull boots.

So she did what she could to revive him.

"You got yourself attached to Miss Murray for my benefit?" she teased. "Roxley, you have an odd way of showing a lady you care."

"Harriet, stop being difficult. Leave this all to me."

She threw up her hands. "You can bluster and complain and scold all you want, but I am going to help you. We both know how well you've done with all this on your own."

His features darkened. "I don't want your help, Harry."

"What you want and what you so obviously need —"

"I can manage all this on my own —"

Now it was her turn to snort.

His gaze narrowed. "What does that mean?"

"Have you thought of just asking your aunts where the diamonds might be?"

He laughed. "They are already convinced I'm a complete jinglebrains; whyever would they turn over a fortune in diamonds to me? Besides, I've already done that, *Miss Darby,* and Aunt Essex nearly fell over in a fit of laughter at the suggestion."

She blushed a little bit at his teasing. Still, she held her ground. "Why not tell them the truth?"

Roxley went back to his perusal of the shelves. "What? That some madman believes my father won a fortune that has remained hidden all these years."

"You know exactly what I mean." She nodded her head as if to nudge him. "About your qualifications for such a venture. That they should trust you as the Crown does."

Resorting to his usual London manner, he tipped his nose in the air and said, "Miss Hathaway, I have no idea what you are implying."

"Oh, good God, Roxley! Really? Are we going to play this game now? If I must spell it out, then I know very well that you work as a secret courier for the Home Office. That this" — she waved her hands at him — "this ridiculous character you play about Town and for your aunts' benefit —"

"You must agree it does have its advantages," he interjected.

"Do not change the subject." Once again, she stood firm. "You work for the Home Office."

She said it as one might comment about a man's tailor. Plainly and to the point.

He crossed the room and took her by the elbow, guiding her over to a chair and setting her down in it. "Demmit, Harry! Is there no end to your meddling? No one is supposed to know. Especially not you."

"Well, of all the insulting —" She glared at him. "I can help."

"Which is exactly why I didn't want you to know. You'd insist on meddling."

He had her there. She crossed her arms over her chest and looked up at him. "I still say you should tell your aunts about your heroics."

"What? And give them the slightest excuse to be excessively proud of me? Not to mention the inherent interference that would follow. Why, they'd never leave me alone." He shrugged and went back to his aunt's desk, rifling through another drawer. "Besides, I don't do that much."

This time it was Harriet's turn to scoff. *"Harrumph."*

He looked over his shoulder at him. "You know nothing of what I do, Kitten."

Harriet tipped her head and smiled. "Several years ago, you came to Kempton with Chaunce for Christmas. I overheard the two of you trying to come up with an excuse to go down to the village to take some papers to a Lord Mereworth who was to meet you at the John Stakes. Not that you needed an excuse. Maman was quite used to Papa venturing over to that disreputable place for a 'moment's peace.' "

Roxley closed his open mouth. But only for a second. "You misheard —"

"Hardly," she scoffed. "And not long after you debated your reasons for seeking the public house, Chaunce warned you not to stray too close to the mistletoe hung in the foyer, or else I'd demand a kiss —"

He blanched a bit as if the memory had suddenly come back to him. Still, he wasn't above making a joke. "Sounds like you — still looking, if your refusal to leave tonight is any evidence."

She ignored the jibe and continued on. "And after Chaunce warned you, you said . . . you told him —"

"I'd rather kiss a monkey," he finished for her. "And I meant it. Back then you rather favored the one Lady Bindon used to keep."

Pushing up and out of the chair, Harriet sauntered over to him. "Would you say that now?"

"Yes."

Oh, bother the man.

"Roxley —" She hoped the warning note in her voice reminded him of the last time he naysayed her.

"Well, a very fetching monkey," he admitted. "Besides, I'm better off thinking of you as that monkey-faced, eavesdropping minx than as —"

"As what?"

He backed away. "Harry, don't —"

"Don't what?"

"Tempt me."

"But, Roxley, I must."

"The only thing you are tempting me to do is wring your neck."

She turned from him and wandered back to her chair. "That wouldn't help matters."

"Depends on your point of view."

Harriet shifted her plan of attack. She needed to show him that she was essential to his work.

Essential to *him*.

"As I see it," she began, "you need to find the diamonds —"

"If there are any to be found."

"Determine who Miss Murray really is —"

"Pistol and all," he reminded her.

She ignored him. "And determine who it is that has been behind this from the beginning." She paused and looked over him. "You're certain there is someone behind your misfortunes of late?"

Her implication was clear — *that you didn't manage to muddle this up all on your own.*

Leave it to Harriet not to dance around the issue.

"Not even my luck is that bad," he told her.

"If you say so —"

"I do," he insisted.

Harriet nodded. "Then we must simply find whoever it is who has orchestrated all this mischief and stop them."

There it was. Three simple steps to their happily-ever-after.

Roxley, however, was quite determined to make it difficult. "Harriet, all your sunny, Miss Darby–inspired optimism has no place in my work. You are going back to London on the early morning coach."

Now it was Harriet's turn to lose her temper. "Oh, no, I won't. Not after you abandoned me last summer —" She closed the space between them in a thrice and put her hands on his chest and gave him a shove. "How dare you suggest such a thing."

He opened his mouth to protest and then very wisely closed it.

This wasn't an argument he was going to win.

"Did you ever once consider asking me what I wanted?" She didn't give him a chance to answer. There was no need. They both knew the answer. *No.* "Did you think to come to Kempton and make this my choice?"

"Harry, I couldn't let you take the risk —"

"Risk what? That I'd say yes, or that I'd refuse you?"

There was a bit of truth in both versions, but it was the very vision of what could befall her that had kept him far from her, far from Kempton.

Not that it had been enough. She'd come to London, she'd followed her heart, his heart, and now was embroiled, entangled . . .

The vision returned.

Harriet still and pale, the light gone from her glorious green eyes. Like spring suddenly doused in a late frost.

This was a price he couldn't, wouldn't pay. Not when he, of all people, knew the tally so well.

He caught her by the shoulders and rattled her a bit. "Demmit, Harry! I don't want you to end up dead on the side of some road like my parents did."

There it was. The real truth behind his reticence. His deepest, most earnest fear.

Her eyes widened, as if she saw the agony ripping through his chest in his heartbroken expression — the long-simmering pain, the tormenting grief to keep her well out of the fray, his desolation, so raw and tenable. She moved closer until she was standing right in front of him.

It was, after all, where she belonged.

She was right about that. But oh, no, he couldn't have her if it meant risking losing her.

He couldn't.

And then she did what she did best. Oh, not the vexing part, but the part where she stole away his reason, his fears, his hesitation. She cupped his face in her hands and guided him toward her.

No, he couldn't resist.

Nor should he have.

Roxley's frustrations gave way as Harriet slid against him.

He didn't know what was worse, admitting he wanted her so badly or that there was never a demmed bed around when he had her in his arms.

Not that they had needed one before.

Her fingers curled into the lapels of his jacket and she tugged him closer, teasing him with her kiss, the tip of her tongue enticing him to open up to her.

Determined puss. She was resolved to drive him mad.

Roxley shifted and caught hold of her rounded bottom — his hands cradling her, drawing her right up against him — for he was already hard. Hard and ready.

So it seemed was she.

Ready, that is.

Demmit, she hadn't anything on beneath her night-rail and dressing gown.

Nothing.

Which suited him perfectly.

He caught hold of her and carried her over to his aunt's desk, still kissing her, their lips fused, exploring each other, tasting each other.

He set her atop the desk — hitching up her night-rail as he did so she was bare to him.

Madness, utter madness.

And Harriet, madcap, determined Harriet, seemed to know exactly what he planned.

She caught hold of the front of his breeches and opened them, freeing his cock and smiling as she stroked it.

Nor could he stop. He wanted her. He wanted to be inside her, easing this madness inside him.

And so he did, catching up her leg, hitching it around his hip, and then with little ceremony entered her.

Hard and fast.

Her pink depths were wet and ready for him, and she gasped as he filled her, a moan brimming with desire and frustration and need that he didn't stand on ceremony.

He buried himself inside her, again and again, silencing her cries with a deep kiss that matched his thrusts, letting himself slide into a passionate delirium from which there was only one path to freedom.

From the moment Roxley's lips slammed into hers, Harriet knew she'd unleashed a demon — his frustrations and fears washing over her, mingled with a heated desire.

This wasn't just a kiss, it was need.

And that Harriet understood.

She'd longed for months to be back in his arms and from the moment she brushed up against him, from the second their bodies had touched, her hips against his, she'd been breathless for him.

To have him inside her again.

There was no need for soft touches, teasing kisses — Harriet wanted to be joined to this man.

Wanted him so deeply that she didn't care if he took her up against the wall and dallied with her like some upstairs maid.

She wanted to feel Roxley. To claim him.

He wanted her, and that was all that mattered.

That, and relieving this deep, restless itch of longing that had tossed and turned inside her for months.

He loves me. He loves me not.

All she wanted right this dizzy moment of madness was to be loved.

Furiously so.

And when he picked her up, cradling her backside, and hauled her over to his aunt's desk, she wanted to cry out in triumph.

Her body was already taut and ready, wet to the core and tangled up with need.

Love me, Roxley. Unleash this madness.

He caught up her leg, and before she could draw a breath, he answered her silent plea.

He entered her — hard and fast and it was shocking and exciting all at once.

She began to cry out and found herself silenced by his kiss.

Whatever she'd been going to say — *Roxley! Oh, good heavens! Oh, please yes!* — she couldn't remember because already she was on that dancing precipice and Roxley was pumping himself into her, stroking her, sending her careening toward the heavens.

With each stroke, with each movement of

his rock-hard manhood, she was tossed upward.

And it was a path she willingly climbed, clinging to his shoulders, searching for steady ground as he filled her.

Then his movements began to rush forward, hard, short thrusts, and she could hear the deep rumble rising in his chest as he began to find his way over the edge.

For one frantic moment, she thought he was going over alone, but with a deep final thrust, one that left her gasping, she tumbled headlong after him into oblivion.

After a few moments, Roxley opened his eyes and looked down at the tumbled mess he'd made of things — Harriet's hair fell in a riot of curls down around her shoulders. Her gown was only half on and her head lolled back, her breath coming in labored gasps.

"Oh, God, Harriet!" he whispered. "What have I done to you? God, I'm such an ass." He went to pull himself out of her but she caught hold of him and pulled him closer.

Her hooded gaze studied him before she made a *tsk, tsk* sound. "Roxley, if you start apologizing for your boorish behavior, I swear I will march upstairs and put Miss Murray's flint back in her pistol."

And then use it myself.

"So do us both a favor and be a bit more of an ass, will you?" she teased, nibbling at his ear and whispering just exactly how she'd like him to ruin her again.

Right here on his aunt's desk.

CHAPTER 10

Your heart was not what I was worried about.

Miss Darby to Lt. Throckmorten
from Miss Darby and the Counterfeit Bride

Mr. Hotchkin arrived late to the mews behind Lady Eleanor's house. He muttered a mild curse (the only one he could claim in good conscience) and realized he might have made a mess of things.

But in his defense, he'd been following up on a lead on Moss, one of the Calais gamblers, and so intent had he been on finding the man, he'd lost track of the time.

Taking up a position in the shadows, he watched the house and wondered what the devil he was supposed to do next.

Lord Roxley had promised to meet him here just after midnight, and yet now it was half past and there was no sign of the earl.

This was his first field assignment and

since Mr. Hathaway had recommended him for the task, the last thing he wanted to do was let down his mentor.

Well, he supposed he could wait a few minutes and see if there was any sign of the earl.

Mr. Hathaway had warned him that since Roxley wasn't a career agent, he could be inconveniently unpredictable.

Unpredictable. Such a distasteful notion, Hotchkin mused.

Taking a deep breath, he did as he had so many times since the first time he'd stumbled across the dusty files on the Queen's Necklace: he ran through the facts that could be verified.

The diamonds had been part of a necklace that was to be a gift to Marie Antoinette from Cardinal de Rohan.

The intermediary, Madame de la Motte, had instead broken up the necklace and given the diamonds to her husband, a self-proclaimed comte, to bring to London to be sold.

He paused, for everything after that was all conjecture and rumor.

Hotchkin shuddered.

He found assumptions abhorrent, preferring facts.

Then there was the notion that the stones

themselves were cursed.

Cursed. The word echoed in his thoughts and for no rational reason, he moved deeper into the shadows and scanned the mews and gardens around him.

There wasn't a bit of movement in the small garden behind Lady Eleanor's house, nor in the mews that ran behind the houses on Brock Street.

And yet . . . Hotchkin stilled. There was someone close at hand. He could feel it.

And even as he scolded himself for such an irrational notion, there in the corner of his eye he sensed movement.

Someone was there. Watching Lady Eleanor's house, much as he was.

'Tis Lord Roxley, he told himself, and was about to step out and make himself known to the earl, when a stern lecture from Mr. Hathaway echoed in his thoughts.

Think twice, Hotchkin, his mentor always said. *And look once again before you leap.*

So Hotchkin paused and looked again, realizing almost immediately that the cloaked figure edging down the alley wasn't near as tall as the earl.

Hotchkin's hand slid slowly and quietly into the pocket of his jacket and he drew out his pistol, his heart hammering.

For there was one line in all these reports

that had woken him up more than one night of late.

Someone wants these diamonds more than the French. And the evidence is clear they are most willing to kill for them.

And then he nearly found out how true those words were, when he was struck from behind.

A sharp retort of a pistol tore Harriet and Roxley apart.

For a second, both of them stood there, half dazed, still lost in that breathless frenzy they'd just shared.

A crash and a shout wrenched them farther apart.

The world — and its inherent dangers — had come calling.

When Harriet looked about to say something, Roxley's hand shot up, covering her mouth, shaking his head at her even as he did so.

He cocked his head and listened. Already upstairs, he could hear his aunt's cries and the shuffle of feet on the stairs above them. But it was the tramp of feet below that held his attention.

Someone was trying to get into the house.

Or had already breached it.

Roxley whirled around, cursing as he

turned and hastily straightening out his clothing. Then he moved Harriet behind him, shielding her with his body.

For a moment, he listened a bit more, and then turned to Harriet. "Stay here. Close the door behind me and don't let anyone in."

"I think not," she said, following him as he opened the door.

Nor was there time to argue the matter as there was another large crash and a flurry of shouts from downstairs.

"Demmit," Roxley said, dashing out into the hallway. All through the house, there were the echoes of feet hitting the floor, doors opening.

Going down the back stairs toward the ground floor behind the house, he met Thortle coming up from his room in the cellar, a candle in one hand and a fire poker in the other.

"My lord!" he cried out.

"Roxley! Good heavens! What is the meaning of this?" Aunt Eleanor cried out from the top of the stairs.

"My lady," Thortle said. "Stay where you are! There are housebreakers afoot."

The intrepid lady came boldly down the stairs anyway. "The only thief I see is my nephew. Roxley! Again, I ask you what is the meaning of this?" At the sound of a creak on the stairs, they all turned to find Harriet standing there. "And Miss Hathaway. My, my, you are most fleet of foot — why you've made it downstairs before any of us. I am all astonishment," she said, her brows rising as she sent a scorching glance at her nephew.

Harriet slid back a bit and did her best to appear as unobtrusive as possible. Which given her height was rather impossible.

"Aunt Eleanor, please go back upstairs and take Harriet with you," Roxley told her, moving out of the stairwell and down the narrow hall toward the breakfast room where there was still a bit of a clatter.

"I will remind you, I am a Marshom," she replied hotly, following him, with Harriet right on her heels.

" 'Tis hard to forget," Roxley muttered as he approached the double doors to the room.

Aunt Eleanor caught up with him just then. "Whatever are you doing?"

"I'm going to investigate," he told her. "Now, please stay back."

"And have you killed in my house? Hardly," she replied. "Essex would never forgive me if you were murdered and we were left to the mercies of Cousin Neville."

Roxley glanced over his shoulder and wondered if he should remind her that Cousin Neville had passed away over a decade ago and he, Tiberius Marshom, was all that stood between them and the title being lost.

Probably not.

But it wasn't like he could hold her back either, for they had reached the open door and inside lay a figure sprawled out on the floor before them.

"Who are you?" Roxley demanded, pointing his pistol at the man.

Aunt Eleanor shoved his arm aside, the pistol firing and sending an errant shot into the wall. Undeterred, she hurried forward. "Good heavens, Roxley! What have you done? You've gone and killed my dear Lord Galton."

"It is nothing, Lady E, nothing," Lord Galton said for the twentieth time, as the lady fussed over the bruise on the back of his head. "I'm quite certain I sent those ruffians away with far worse."

Roxley shot a glance at the ceiling and sent up a little prayer for patience. "Tell us again, Lord Galton, what you were doing lurking about the back of my aunt's house?"

"One might ask the same of you," Aunt

Eleanor pointed out, sending a censorious glance over at Harriet.

Roxley had a reply at the ready. "I was returning from a late meeting —"

His aunt's eyes widened with horror. "Oh, heavens, Roxley, don't tell me you've gone and joined that noisy bunch of Methodists up the street?"

"Not that sort of meeting," he told her. "But as I was saying, I was passing on Brock Street and noticed a light on in the study —"

"I fear it was me, my lady," Harriet interjected. "I . . . I . . . I couldn't sleep, so I came down to the library."

"Yes, well, when I peered in the window, I nearly scared Miss Hathaway out of her wits —"

"And then when I realized it was Lord Roxley, I allowed him in —"

Lady Eleanor looked from one to the other. "Yes, I daresay that's how it happened," she replied dryly. "Yet none of that explains why someone would want to break into my house." Again, those hawkish features bored into Roxley.

"You are known to be a lady of quality," he offered.

Aunt Eleanor wasn't a Marshom for nothing. "Balderdash!" she told him, further dismissing his bluff with a wave of her hand. "I think you've made this all up to gain an invitation to stay under my roof, not to mention the bullet hole you've put in the wall. The entire room is spoiled — it will need to be repapered, an expense I will not bear."

Of course, any excuse to start redecorating the house, Roxley realized. Even in all the excitement, his aunt was quick to claim an advantage. "I hardly came over tonight to shoot up your breakfast room."

"Then why are you here, Roxley —" Her voice ended, but her gaze was pinned on Harriet.

A very tumbled-looking Harriet, who backed into the hallway and out of sight.

"Don't be too hard on your nephew, Lady E," Lord Galton said, intervening. "He has the right of it. There was someone in the house. It was demmed lucky your nephew came by when he did. I had just arrived when I saw them — two figures going into the breakfast room doors —"

Roxley pushed off the wall and studied the man. "You just arrived? Isn't it rather late for a social call, my lord?" Now it was his turn to pin a glance on his aunt, who had the dignity to blush and then turn to study the hole in the wall.

Before she could start casting forth some exorbitant amount to repair the damage, a figure came staggering through the open doors which led to the garden.

Roxley swung his pistol up, unloaded as it was, but nonetheless took a deadly stance. "Who goes there?"

Thortle held his candle aloft, and it cast a weak light on Mr. Hotchkin, bloodstained and wavering, a pistol held loosely in one hand — not that he was in any condition to wield it.

Roxley rushed to the younger man's aid, with Harriet close behind.

"Oh, Mr. Hotchkin!" she exclaimed, helping Roxley guide the man to a chair. "What has happened to you?"

"I was in the mews, and it turns out, I wasn't alone —"

Lord Galton sniffed when all eyes turned on him.

Though in Roxley's estimation, it could well have been Lord Galton who orchestrated all this.

Mr. Hotchkin continued on, "— whoever it was, had help. Someone came up from behind and struck me over the head."

"There's more than one of these villains?" Aunt Eleanor was all aghast.

The young man nodded.

"So you can stop listing Galton as one of your suspects, Roxley," his aunt told him. "He always arrives alone."

Roxley thought it the better part of valor not to point out that this wasn't evidence in her favor, so instead he turned to Hotchkin. "Where were you standing?"

"Near the arch in the garden," he replied.

Roxley and Galton shared a glance, and the earl guessed they were both thinking the same thing — whoever had knocked out Hotchkin had come from inside the house. For the only way someone could have crept up behind him was if they'd come from the house.

Someone who could move quietly, efficiently and with near deadly aim.

Glancing up at the ceiling, Roxley had to wonder where his faux betrothed was at the moment. Then he spied Harriet.

She mouthed exactly what he needed to know. "Still in her bed."

So that's where she'd disappeared to. To discover where Miss Murray might be.

"I fear I've failed you, my lord," Hotchkin was saying, his misery apparent in every word.

"*Tsk, tsk.*" Roxley waved aside the man's apology. "You most likely slowed them down and saved the day, Mr. Hotchkin.

More importantly, I believe you will need a surgeon to see to that head of yours. It will require a few stitches."

"I can do it," Harriet announced.

"Oh, Miss Hathaway, no," Mr. Hotchkin exclaimed. "It wouldn't be proper."

"I've stitched up most of my brothers one time or another, I daresay your head isn't any harder."

There was a sniff from Lady Eleanor, but whether it was in approval or quite the opposite, it was impossible to discern. Not that the lady was giving any further clues for she was already nudging at the mud that had been tracked into her once immaculate breakfast room, lips pursed and expression guarded.

Oh, there'd be a new carpet out of all this as well.

Meanwhile, Harriet directed her attention to Thortle. "Is there hot water in the kitchen?"

"Always, miss."

"Fetch a large basin and a clean rag. Then I'll need a good sewing needle and plain silk thread." She paused and glanced at her patient, who was once again wavering in his seat. "And a bottle of something. Strong, I think."

"The bottle of whiskey, Thortle," Lord

Galton added. "The one Her Ladyship keeps on the top shelf of the library."

Lady Eleanor looked askance at all this, but whether she was grim over the prospect of adding bloodstains to her already ruined breakfast room or her best whiskey being used for medicinal purposes, who knew. She was too busy scolding her nephew. "You have brought this folly from London with you, Roxley. I blame you entirely."

"Don't be ridiculous, Aunt Eleanor," he replied. "I directed Mingo personally on what to pack, and housebreakers were not on the list." He grinned at her. "They take up too much room."

"I cannot believe I missed all the excitement last night," Miss Murray declared as she was finishing up her breakfast the next morning.

"Yes, your absence was most unfortunate," Lady Eleanor remarked as she glanced up from a letter she was reading and shot a pinning glance at Harriet — which she had no desire to interpret.

While Lady Essex was so easy to read — her mercurial shifts of mood revealed in her expression like a barometer, her twin, Lady Eleanor, was such a mystery.

At least, so Harriet thought.

"Miss Hathaway, is it be true you stitched up Lord Roxley's friend?" Miss Murray asked.

Harriet tried to follow Lady Eleanor's example and kept her face as bland as possible, even when her every instinct was to march to the end of the table, pin this impostor to the floor and beat her with the silver salver until she talked.

Well, perhaps nothing that drastic, but she certainly didn't like having to keep her promise to Roxley.

He'd pulled her aside the previous night, after she'd finished closing the wound on the back of Mr. Hotchkin's head.

Harry, you mustn't do anything to risk your life. You stay well clear of Miss Murray until I can determine who she is. Promise me.

Then the wretched man had leaned over and stolen another kiss from her lips — a slow, tantalizing brush of his lips, followed by a heated glance full of reminders of what had transpired between them.

And of delights to come.

So like a fool, she'd nodded in agreement.

When he kissed her like that, she was incapable of thinking straight.

Still, Harriet thought the salver would make short work of all this madness.

Then, as if sensing the imminent danger

she was in, Miss Murray abruptly got up from the table. "My! Look at the time. The morning has quite gotten away from me! And I promised Mrs. Plumley I would drop by first thing so we could have a decent coze."

Harriet rose, as a good companion ought, but Miss Murray shook her head and waved her off. "Oh, Harriet, but you've only just gotten to your breakfast. I wouldn't dream of making you accompany me on such a dull visit, and so early. I can manage quite well on my own."

"Yes, but you shouldn't go alone," Harriet told her. She wasn't about to let this gel out of her sights. "What would Mrs. Plumley say?"

"How right you are, Miss Hathaway," Lady Eleanor agreed. "But Miss Murray is also correct — you must finish your breakfast. You need your nourishment after the night you've had, or you'll faint dead away before tea." Harriet was about to point out that she'd never fainted in her life, but Lady Eleanor continued, "You can take Nan with you, Miss Murray. She's a silly little flibbertigibbet — not an intelligent thought in her head, but she does know her way around Bath."

"She sounds perfect," Miss Murray said,

smiling graciously, before she left the room, all elegance and poise.

"Yes, she is," Lady Eleanor muttered under her breath as the last of Miss Murray's skirts turned the corner.

Harriet moved to follow her, but was stopped by a quiet command. "Sit, Miss Hathaway."

"But I —"

"Sit and finish your breakfast."

Harriet did so, most reluctantly. She could hardly tell Her Ladyship why exactly it was pure folly to let Miss Murray out of the house unsupervised, but then she discovered that she didn't need to.

Even so, she hurried along to consume her toast and bacon and the lovely dish of fruit compote Lady Eleanor instructed the footman to fetch her, all the while listening to the voices and footsteps overhead that indicated Miss Murray, accompanied by the aforementioned Nan, was leaving.

Slipping away, as it were.

When the firm thud of the front door closing behind her, Harriet let out a sigh of exasperation.

"There is no need to worry, Miss Hathaway," Lady Eleanor declared, putting down the letter she'd been calmly reading. "While Nan might appear to be the stupidest girl alive, she also gossips like a fishwife. She'll relate everything Miss Murray has done, gone and seen when they return."

Harriet gaped.

"Truly, do you think I believe a word that comes out of that gel's mouth? Heiress, indeed! She might have gone to Mrs. Plumley's, but anyone of consequence goes to Miss Emery's School. Not Mrs. Plumley's School for the by-blows."

Her mouth fell open further.

Lady Eleanor made a *tut-tut,* and continued to tidy up her place setting and the letters she'd been reading. "Does Roxley know?"

"Know what, ma'am?"

"That his Miss Murray is most likely some fiend's natural child?"

Harriet drew a deep breath and chose her words carefully. "He isn't sure who she is."

"Well, that's a relief," she replied. "I was starting to think he was as useless as most men."

"How did you know?" Harriet posed, her natural curiosity winning out over any practical thoughts.

Lady Eleanor smiled. "It is obvious she isn't of a good birth, nor has she any true English breeding. That, and she tries too hard. If I were to venture a guess, I'd say she is French. Or half French, which isn't any better."

Sitting back in her seat, Harriet shook her head. "That's it. She's French."

"Yes, makes sense, doesn't it," Lady Eleanor agreed, pinning another one of those looks on Harriet that suggested she expected something in return for this offering.

But Harriet had another question if she was to connect the threads of this mystery. "Lady Eleanor, may I ask you a question?"

The lady nodded.

"What is in the box?" Harriet ventured. She'd spent the remainder of the night puzzling out where the diamonds might be. Well, that and remembering Roxley.

And as it was in the wee hours of the night, she'd spent a good deal of time worrying.

For not once had Roxley said he'd loved her. That he'd marry her. That he wanted her properly.

Oh, good heavens, had she once again tried in the entirely wrong way to jump the fence that separated her from Roxley?

What was it her brother George had once said about the earl? Oh, yes, that he was different from them.

Toplofty, where we are just . . . well, us.

Harriet had tossed and turned on that notion. The earl being so above her, he could take whatever his heart fancied — and didn't know anything different. That was what came of being born above nearly everyone else.

He doesn't need to love you . . . that errant voice of doubt had whispered.

But he does, she wanted to shout, reveling in the memories of being in his arms just a few hours earlier.

I want you, and only you, he'd whispered as he'd entered her. Taken her. Possessed her. It had been so breathless, so ruinous. So very wonderful.

It left her a little breathless even now.

"The box?" Lady Eleanor was saying, nudging Harriet from her woolgathering.

She blushed a little under the lady's piercing gaze and went back to the subject at hand, lest she discover Lady Eleanor possessed Madame Sybille's alleged skills and could read minds. "Um, yes. The one your sister sent to you."

Lady Eleanor's brow quirked upward, much like Lady Essex's often did when she was both amused and chagrined. "You didn't look?"

Harriet shook her head. It wasn't her place. She'd been entrusted by Lady Essex to carry it to Bath and she'd done so.

But that didn't mean she wasn't immensely curious.

Lady Eleanor picked up her napkin and dabbed her lips. "Not the diamonds, if that is what you are asking."

"You know?"

"Of course I know," she said, making a *tsk, tsk,* as if she'd never heard such a foolish question. "Wretched things, diamonds. As cursed as Kempton."

"No more," Harriet told her.

"No more what?"

"Kempton. It isn't cursed any longer. There have been two marriages of late. Miss Timmons married the Duke of Preston —"

Lady Eleanor snorted at this, as most people did, for Preston had a terrible reputation as an unrepentant rake.

"— and Miss Dale. She married Lord Henry Seldon."

"A Seldon and a Dale? Married? I'm surprised the Tower of London hasn't toppled over." Lady Eleanor once again waved her hands at Harriet. "Still, if neither groom has turned up with an inconvenient fire iron in his chest, I suppose any number of things is possible."

"And the box?" Harriet nudged.

"Ah, yes," she said, and rose, Harriet rising as well.

Lady Eleanor nodded for her to wait and left. A little while later, she returned, box in hand. This time, she took the seat next to Harriet, and Harriet could see the lady had a misty look to her eyes.

Gone was the lofty daughter of an earl.

And for a moment, Harriet almost regretted asking such an obviously personal thing — for she could see quite clearly this was a difficult thing for the lady.

With trembling fingers, Lady Eleanor undid the sturdy string that tied it shut and went to remove the top, but she stopped and had to dash away a tear.

Harriet put her hand over Lady Eleanor's. "If you don't want to —"

She brushed her effort aside. "Yes, well, I think this is best."

Setting aside the lid, she slowly withdrew a small leather portrait case, which, once she carefully opened it, revealed a miniature.

"Why that's Roxley," Harriet exclaimed as she looked down at the very familiar face.

Lady Eleanor shook her head. "It is, but that isn't Tiberius. 'Tis his father, the sixth earl. Dear, dear Tristan." She drew her finger around the pearl-studded oval frame. And then glanced away.

"They look so much alike," Harriet said softly.

"Yes," Lady Eleanor agreed, "but they are much different in temperament."

She said this in a way that Harriet suspected meant she was relieved that Roxley, her Roxley, hadn't taken after his father, no matter how much Lady Eleanor had loved him.

She reached inside the box and withdrew another leather case, identical to the first one. Once opened and set up next to the first, it showed a small boy, with brown curly hair and a mischievous smile.

"That," Lady Eleanor said, with her own impish smile, "is your Roxley. Terrible scamp that he was. Still is. We had high hopes he would outgrow that, but alas." She hardly sounded as if she regretted such a state.

Harriet smiled, for she'd met Roxley when he was nearly eleven and he'd seemed grown up then — especially to her younger, seven-year-old self.

Meanwhile, Lady Eleanor had reached in and pulled out the last of the treasures in the box. A twist of honey blonde hair in a memorial locket. A string of pretty beads. A tiny painting of a bridge over a canal. A stub of a candle. A tiny silver button. A scrap of red silk. And finally . . .

"Pug," Harriet said as the familiar dog

made its appearance.

"Yes, so you two have met," Lady Eleanor said, setting the ugly figurine down in the middle of the collection, where it towered over the other bits and bobs. "Davinia adored that ugly thing. She got it from an aged cousin of her mother's when she was young and took it everywhere with her." She shook her head and arranged the belongings with the candle in the middle. "There, that is how she liked to have them arranged." The lady leaned back and studied the collection of lost treasures. "They — Tristan and Davinia — lived such a gypsy life, but she always said as long as she had her shrine close at hand, she was always home."

"What a lovely idea," Harriet said, wondering what claim each of the mementoes held in the lost countess's heart.

"Rather papist, I always thought," Lady Eleanor said, "but Davinia had her own way of doing things." She let out a sigh and re-arranged the pieces once again, like a gambler shuffling the deck one more time for luck. "My sisters and I have honored her memory by keeping her shrine with us. We loved her like a daughter. And she gave us our dear Tiberius —" She reached out and touched the little boy's curls as if she could smooth them down. "Though I can hardly forgive her that name. Tiberius! Whatever were those two thinking?" She shook her head, a sad smile playing on her lips. "Dear Davinia. She never complained, not once; whatever folly came into Tristan's head, she was at his side."

Harriet had been looking at the first miniature. "I imagine Roxley has her eyes, doesn't he?"

This took Lady Eleanor aback and she looked away, silent for a few moments before she turned the tables. Her firm, quiet question bowled Harriet over. "You love him, don't you?"

There was nothing she could do but answer honestly. From her heart. "Ever so much."

Lady Eleanor nodded and began to pack Davinia's treasures back into the plain box from which they'd come. Once she was satisfied they were all nestled in as they ought, she closed it up and tied the string tight.

Then she handed it to Harriet. "I entrust you to take this to my sister Oriel —"

"— but, my lady, we aren't leaving for —"

The older woman shook her head. "I am sending you along tomorrow. I'd send you along today if I could, but I promised to bring you to the assembly tonight and there would be talk if you and Miss Murray didn't attend. Then again, this is Bath and there is always talk, even when there is nothing to natter on about."

She smiled at Harriet, a bit of twinkle in her eyes, and rose, as did Harriet, the box clutched to her bosom. "Go with my blessing, Miss Hathaway. Oriel will help you find what you are looking for." Then she left, with Harriet gaping after her.

And it was only after a few minutes that Harriet realized the lady had quite nimbly sidestepped her questions about the diamonds. It was an opportunity lost, she thought with some regret, but suspected that no matter how she was pressed, Lady Eleanor would not reveal what she knew.

And was sending Harriet and Roxley on a course that she believed to be fated.

Yet what if all this mystery around the Queen's Necklace was for naught? Or worse, she and Roxley ended up sharing his parents' tragic fate?

CHAPTER 11

A proposal of matrimony must be carefully scrutinized, examined and endorsed by all who know you best, my dear. And then as quickly as you can, say yes, before the man changes his mind.

Lady Lowthorpe to Miss Darby
from Miss Darby and the Counterfeit Bride

"I will not wait around upon her demands," the man complained. "This is foolhardy of her. She'll ruin everything."

Sybille did her best to curb her impatience with him. He had grown peevish of late, desperate to gain the diamonds. Including last night's debacle. The closer they got to the stones, the more irrational he became.

And worse, dangerous.

More so than usual.

"It must be something of great importance, milord, for her to have contacted me."

"We shall see," he muttered, staring moodily into the darkness.

She studied him for a few moments, furtively, because she was of the opinion the man could see behind him without turning around. This wasn't the worst place he'd probably had to cool his heels, but it was probably not the most comfortable for a man. The back room of a milliner's shop. But the owner was an old friend and wise enough not to ask questions when the use of her storeroom was requested.

One day, Sybille would repay her. But not quite yet.

"What is the time?" he demanded.

"Half past eleven, milord."

He didn't thank her, or acknowledge her answer, as if her immediate attention to his needs was a given. As if it was his due.

Milord. She didn't even know his name. Oh, he'd given her a common, ordinary name once long ago, but it wasn't his real one. Of that she was certain. For she knew an *aristo* when she met one.

Nor was she so foolish not to realize that he was someone with deep connections.

Deadly ones.

Not that she wasn't without her own resources, but better he still considered her nothing but a necessary step in his unrelenting madness to gain the Queen's Necklace.

Or what was left of it.

That was a desire Sybille knew all too well, and she would have followed this English devil to the very gates of Hell to gain the stones that were hers by right.

And so she waited. As did he. Because after so many years, this was the closest they had come.

When the door opened, a slight figure slipped inside the back room. "I have but a few moments."

"Shouldn't be here to begin with," milord complained.

Both women ignored him.

"He won't marry me," Miss Murray told them. "He won't. Not as long as there is a possibility that he might have *her*."

"What do you care if he will marry you or not?" the man complained, rising from his chair — the only chair in the room — and coming to stand before the girl.

Not one to be cowed, even by this fierce man before her, Miss Murray stabbed his chest with her finger. "You said the aunts would give up the stones when he became engaged — but if he takes her over me — then they are lost."

"Bah. He must marry you. He is all but ruined."

"He loves her," Miss Murray shot back as

if that was answer enough.

Not to this man who had clearly never loved anything or anyone.

"Missish nonsense," he declared. "If Lady Eleanor hasn't turned them over to her nephew, then you must see to it that you continue on to Marshom Court without delay."

Miss Murray, who hadn't Sybille's patience, turned to her and said in rapid French, "She is dangerous enough to uncover the truth."

"Then she must be dealt with," Sybille said, trying to soothe the younger woman's concerns.

That wasn't good enough for Miss Murray. She whirled back to milord, taking out her dismay on him. "Boarding school, lies, promises, and for what? Bah!" She waved him off, her frustration filling the crowded room.

Of the three of them, her part had been the most demanding, the one that had taken years to orchestrate. But she was young and impatient, and couldn't see the great gains before them. The years of reward about to become theirs.

"What is this?" he demanded in English.

Always demanding. Sybille tamped down the fire banked in her chest.

357

For he wasn't speaking to Miss Murray, but to her. And though she knew he spoke French perfectly, knew exactly what had been said, he had to be in command of everything.

"Miss Hathaway is proving problematic," Sybille said, switching back to English.

"Then we shall have to —"

Whatever he thought to do to Miss Hathaway was lost as there was a commotion going on out in the shop.

"But I saw her come in here. Miss Murray. You cannot have missed her," a deep male voice insisted.

"I am sorry, monsieur," the shop owner was saying. "You must be mistaken. Perhaps it was the shop next door that she entered —"

"I know what I saw —" he continued in that arrogant English way.

"Fieldgate," Miss Murray supplied, glancing over at the door. "Wretched fellow —"

"Isn't he the one who has followed you, rather, followed Miss Hathaway here to Bath?" Sybille whispered.

"Yes," Miss Murray complained. "A fortune hunter chasing after a penniless girl of no consequence. Beef-witted fool!"

Sybille cringed at the contemptuous tones the girl used. She'd picked up this highborn attitude at the finishing school to which milord had insisted upon sending her. But Sybille would deal with that problem later.

Out in the shop, the viscount continued pressing his case. "She was wearing a blue bonnet and a matching pelisse. Quite fetching lady. You can't have missed her." His steps echoed around the small shop as if he were inspecting all the corners.

"Fieldgate?" The man beside her eyed the door warily. "Troublesome fellow. Too bad he hasn't listened to what they are all saying at White's and carried that gel off."

Sybille had been about to ignore his complaints, but then she paused. "Carried her off?"

The man made a distracted wave of his hand. "Eloped with that Hathaway chit."

Sybille smiled at this and glanced over to find Miss Murray smiling as well.

"Why should we risk getting rid of Harriet Hathaway ourselves when we have just the fool to do it for us?" Sybille mused aloud.

And then she whispered her instructions to Miss Murray and sent the lady on her way.

Poised and ready, Miss Murray slipped out the door of the storeroom and made a loud exclamation of surprise. "La! Is that you, Lord Fieldgate? However did you find me out? I was hoping to gain a new bonnet without anyone noticing —"

"How could the world not notice you, Miss Murray!" the viscount said, all charm and wit.

Sybille nodded at milord with her own form of charm. *All is well now.*

In the shop, Miss Murray's voice was all enchantment. "You are exactly as Miss Hathaway claimed — the most charming man alive. What a terrible shame Miss Hathaway isn't with me this morning — she was ever so thrilled last night that you had come to Bath. Why you are all she talks about. Lord Fieldgate this . . . My dear Fieldgate that . . ."

"Truly?"

"Lord Fieldgate," Miss Murray said in all confidence, "whyever would I lie to you?"

"Roxley! What the devil are you doing here?"

The earl looked up and found Harriet standing at the garden gate. The afternoon shadows had lengthened and before long it would be dark.

"Watching the house," he said, holding fast to his spot in the mews. He didn't dare come closer — for here she was. His Harriet. Her dark hair done loosely in a knot, a plain muslin gown and a look of determination on her face. He didn't dare take that step that would bring them together and put him right back on temptation's path.

As it had last night. How had that happened — one moment he'd been ordering her back to London and the next . . . dear God, what had possessed him?

Harriet, that was what.

He glanced up and found her studying him. "Yes?"

"Yes, yourself," she shot back.

"Well, nothing," he told her, feeling a bit mulish, knowing he should apologize but also remembering her threat to go get Miss Murray's pistols if he dared. "What are you doing out here?"

"Escaping!" she said with a long sigh.

"My aunt, yes," Roxley replied.

"Oh, good heavens, not your aunt. She's delightful," Harriet enthused.

Auntie E? Delightful? Roxley considered calling a surgeon.

Harriet continued on with her story. "That demmed impostor of yours brought *him* home."

"Him?"

"Fieldgate," she shuddered out. "He's in there still, fawning over your aunt and winking at me every time she looks away. So when I told them I wasn't feeling well and needed to be excused, it was truly no lie. I thought I was going to cast up my accounts if he called me 'his fairest girl' one more time."

Roxley laughed.

"It's not funny. I should be in there with my hands around Miss Murray's neck rattling the truth out of her," she shot back. "It works, you know. I did it once to Benjamin when he claimed I'd eaten all the jam tarts."

He had to imagine she would, and that was his worst fear. "Harriet, something will trip Miss Murray up and it won't be you."

She pressed her lips together as if stopping the words that looked ready to come spilling out.

But that was the way it had to be. He had no idea how dangerous Miss Murray could be and as it was he'd already entangled Harriet deeper into this mire than he cared.

But I'm already entangled.

Her words from last night echoed forth as if she'd said them again.

And it wasn't just a statement, but a declaration. She was entangled because she chose to be.

She was entangled because she loved him.

Just as he loved her.

Roxley looked at her, remembered how he felt with her, and found himself drawn toward her yet again.

Like turning onto the long drive at the Cottage.

This is home, his heart told him, with all the conviction of one of Mr. Hotchkin's reports.

It *was* exactly as she'd said.

Separate they were just that — apart. Incomplete. At odds.

Together . . . Well, he knew what that meant. And beyond the words that immediately came to mind — passionate, combustible, aflame — there was also the one word that trumped them all: unstoppable.

Together they were unstoppable.

"I've been thinking," he began, tentatively testing this notion.

Together they were unstoppable.

"Yes —" she answered just as hesitantly.

"That all this, this —"

"Problem?"

"Quandary," he decided, "is a long game."

"A what?"

"A long game," he repeated. "At least that is what Chaunce and Mereworth always call them. A long game. When a plan has been

363

in the works for years. Planting an informant. Gaining a confidence."

Harriet nodded, and he could see her quick and agile mind working over the implications to the situation at hand. "Miss Murray."

"Exactly." Roxley smiled. "Someone put her into all this years ago — if only to gain her an identity, a past."

"Your aunt thinks she's French," Harriet told him. "Not completely. Perhaps a by-blow."

"Good heavens, my aunt shouldn't be discussing such things with you."

She made a bit of a snort, and shook her head. "As if I don't know what one is. Really, Roxley. Theodosia Walding back in Kempton is the natural daughter of some-one — who, no one knows — but I'm not so sheltered that I don't know what that means. Especially after last summer — I can see how such things might happen."

Roxley blanched at bit, for her jibe hit the mark. "Be that as it may," he said, moving the subject along, "I've been standing here considering why someone who has waited all these years to discover where my parents hid the diamonds —"

"Would suddenly decide the time was perfect to ruin your life?"

"Yes, quite," he said. "Why now?"

"More to the point, what changed?" Harriet asked, all practical miss once again. And it was just the question that put an exclamation point onto why Roxley needed her.

For Harriet was spot on. What had changed?

And when he looked up at the woman before him, he had his answer. "You."

"Me?"

"Yes, you. Everything changed the moment I decided to marry you."

"Marry me?" Harriet's mouth fell open a bit. "You mean to marry me?"

"Of course, Kitten. Why else would I be in Bath and trotting about the countryside with a faux betrothed if I didn't want to marry you."

"When you say it that way —" she huffed, arms crossing over her chest.

"Oh, bother, you aren't the type for a flowery proposal, and you demmed well knew I was going to marry you and all."

"And how was I supposed to know that?" she shot back, her Hathaway temper rising to the forefront.

"Well you know it now," he told her.

"I know nothing." The set of her jaw was positively murderous.

Now who was being mulish?

"Demmit, Harriet Hathaway, will you marry me?"

Her chin notched up a bit. "I'm undecided on the matter."

Definitely mulish.

"When you decide, will you let me know?"

She nodded.

Well, with that taken care of, he started back into the business at hand. "Everything went wrong just after I decided to marry you —"

"A fact which you withheld from me, but obviously told someone," she said, sounding most missish.

Roxley suspected he would never live that one down, but at the moment, he realized why he was better with her help. She made a very good point.

"Who did you tell, Roxley?" she pressed.

Memories of last summer flitted through his thoughts. After the night at Owle Park, he'd ridden pell-mell for London with the intention of getting a Special License and then going on to Kempton to gain her father's permission. But on the way, he'd stopped at an inn and run into an old friend . . .

An old friend . . .

But that couldn't be . . . and yet . . .

He glanced up at her, the shock evident

366

on his face.

"Who? Who did you tell?" she repeated, this time quietly and warily.

He moved forward and caught her in his arms, pulling her close — well, as close as one could with a garden gate between them, and kissed her. His lips taking hers, with a thoroughness that spoke what his heart feared.

You are mine. You always will be. You must be.

He set her back down and kissed her once more on the tip of her nose. "Mind this: you must keep well clear of all this. Do not do anything that will bring you to the forefront. Please, Harriet. I would be lost without you."

The implication was clear. *You are in terrible danger.*

And for better or for worse, Harriet was no fool. She took him at his word and with her lips pressed together, she nodded in silent agreement.

"What are you going to do?" she said. Well called after him, for he was already off and half running down the mews.

"Never mind," he said over his shoulder, forgetting every notion of working together, for this entire venture had taken a most dangerous turn. "Just be ever so careful.

And don't do anything foolish."

There was a great huff from her, but he didn't look back. He couldn't. He had too much to do.

His first stop would be to call on the one person in Bath who could confirm all this for him. The one person who was connected to both Miss Murray and her sponsor, her protector. Her employer.

And the most deadly enemy he could think of.

Demmit, Harriet Hathaway, will you marry me?

Well, it wasn't exactly a proposal out of Miss Darby, *but it was still a proposal,* Harriet mused later that evening as she stood in the Bath assembly rooms.

All around her, the fine society of Bath was gathered for the Thursday evening ball, and she found herself chafing at the promise Roxley had wrenched from her.

For he had pulled it from her. His face, the expression, the very wariness in his eyes had told her that whatever it was he suspected, whoever he suspected, the answer was not good.

And that much should have warned her off, but in her heart she knew Roxley needed her.

As surely as she had wanted to say yes to

his proposal. Should have jumped at it. But she'd still been in a bit of pique at having spent the afternoon in the company of Fieldgate.

What she wanted was to marry Roxley and get on with their lives. *Together.*

Then he'd gone and kissed her, and that had probably startled her more than his expression. For there in his kiss was such longing, and more to the point, something akin to a fear that it may be their last moment together.

Harriet shook her head slightly, tossing that thought aside, her hand going to her lips, as if she could keep hold only of the memories that made her heart sing — not the ones that left her cold with dread.

What if this was all as dire as she suspected? As the look of pure fear in Roxley's expression had said so clearly?

She glanced over at Miss Murray, who was listening politely and patiently — like the perfect London heiress — to Lady Bindon's gossip about some recent *on dit* of little import. To anyone looking at her, she would appear quite what she seemed to be, but all Harriet saw was the roadblock to all her dreams, her wishes.

This is a long game, Roxley had said. *Patience. We must watch and wait.*

Wait. That was not a word that came easily to Harriet.

"Miss Murray! Oh, yoo-hoo! Dearest Miss Murray, there you are."

Harriet froze. Oh, good heavens no. *Not her.* Before she could even say anything, she found herself being nudged aside as a lady in a grand silk gown and a towering arrangement of feathers pushed herself between Harriet and her charge.

"Miss Murray! My dearest friend!"

Oh, yes. It was Lady Kipps. Glancing up, Harriet spied the lady's unfortunate husband trailing a few steps behind his wife.

While the assembly ball was a terrible crush, the arrival of the beloved earl and his recent bride — to Bath, no less — caused a great stir.

Harriet glanced over at the newly arrived pair, remembering Roxley's assurance. *Something will trip her up.*

If there was anything or anyone that could throw a good horse lame, it was the former Miss Edith Nashe.

"Lady Kipps," Miss Murray stammered out.

"I have surprised you," the countess said. "I am delighted. See, Kipps, I told you how Miss Murray would be overcome by our arrival. See how she gapes." Lady Kipps leaned forward, fan fluttering and speaking loud enough for all to hear — for she loved being the center of attention. "I couldn't abide you leaving London. And me not knowing how you were faring with this medieval mustering the Marshoms have demanded. Medieval, I say!"

"Harrumph," Lady Eleanor glanced down her nose at this interloper and dismissed her at once.

Countess or not, a mushroom would always be mushroom in Lady Eleanor's estimation.

Harriet suppressed a smile.

"How is your new hired companion?" Lady Kipps asked, looking left and right as if she hadn't the faintest idea where Harriet was. "Wherever is *poor* Miss Hathaway?" With those ringing tones, she made sure one and all knew Harriet's status.

Daughter of a baronet she might be, but reduced to hiring out as a companion. *Poor, poor, Harriet.*

She turned again, and this time spied Harriet nearly at her elbow. "Oh, there you are, Miss Hathaway. Lurking about in the shadows. How I missed you, I'll never understand, for you stand out like a Maypole, and oh, my —" That was the moment Lady Kipps actually looked at Harriet and spied the gown she was wearing.

If the silk Harriet had worn to the theater had been scandalous, this one, a red creation, was cut too daring — sleeves that weren't really much more than an afterthought, leaving her shoulders bare, and a neckline that plunged far too deep.

It would be dramatic on any lady, but on Harriet, with her dark hair and striking height, it commanded the attention of one and all, including the imperious Lady Kipps, who appeared downright dowdy in her choice of a puce silk that hadn't the hint of style and dash that Harriet's gown showed in every detail.

And better still, Lady Kipps knew it.

"Yes, well, there you are," the countess finished, sounding very put out.

"Don't see how you missed her," Lord Bindon interjected.

Thwack.

Taking a breath, Lady Kipps returned her full attention to Miss Murray and did her best not to draw any further notice to Harriet. "Now you must tell me everything, my dear Miss Murray! Though I can see quite clearly you are so overcome with joy that you don't know what to say!"

"Yes, something like that," Miss Murray said, a smile forced to her lips.

"But, dear me," Lady Kipps declared, fan aflutter and looking around again, "where is Roxley? I would think he would be right by your side, if only to ensure no other gentleman would steal you away. Especially since you look so lovely tonight — so divinely innocent." Then seconds later shot a disapproving glance at Harriet that said clearly she thought her appearance was quite the opposite.

Harriet smiled as if she hadn't the least suspicion that she'd been insulted. She only hoped that one day she could be the one to tell Lady Kipps that her "dearest friend" was an impostor. A nobody. A trespasser into society.

Oh, yes, that would be worth a raft of her insults and insinuations.

Then before Harriet could continue her plotting — something to do with Mr. Muggins and his entire litter of feather hating progeny, Roxley came up and turned her attention elsewhere.

Roxley.

It was nearly impossible not to step forward and into his arms. Claim him as she longed to do. Instead, she stepped back and looked down at his boots, taking as demure a stance as she might — if only to hide the love that was surely shining in her eyes.

Demmit, Harriet Hathaway, will you marry me?

Yes, Roxley, I will, she would gladly shout right this moment. *I will.*

"Lady Kipps?" he managed, then recovering quickly, he nearly grinned from ear to ear. "Why yes it is! Dear Lady Kipps! Such an advantageous surprise! Wouldn't you agree, Miss Murray?"

The best the girl could manage was a tightly set smile.

"You've completely done her in," Roxley told the countess.

"As I intended, Roxley. As I intended. Dear Kipps and I came down to see how you two lovebirds were doing and to help you charm your aunt into agreeing to your marriage as quickly as possible so Miss Murray can return to the very bosom of society, right where she belongs."

"She belongs beside me," Roxley declared, stepping closer to his quarry.

Harriet bit her lips together to keep from correcting him. *Where she belongs is in the bosom of hell.*

"Kipps," Roxley said with a slight nod to the young earl, who stood just a few steps away from his own bride.

"Yes, well, hello there, Roxley." The young earl's reply sounded more like an apology.

"Lady Kipps wanted a bit of a belated wedding trip. Didn't want to impose, but she was worried about her friend."

"Worried? More like frantic!" his wife declared, winding her arm into the crook of Miss Murray's.

"No need, she is in good hands," Roxley told her, extracting the girl from the countess's clutches and steering her toward the dance floor. "I was promised this dance, was I not, Miss Murray?"

"Yes, indeed," she said, fleeing with Roxley.

Once again, Harriet found herself contemplating Miss Murray's demise, if only because now she was left alone with her second least favorite person in the world.

And Lady Kipps, finding herself so quickly abandoned, turned her smiling countenance on Harriet.

Not that Harriet was deceived by the friendly overture. The former Miss Edith Nashe had the cold, calculating heart of a merchant, no matter what title she dressed herself up in.

"Miss Hathaway! Always a delight," she said, moving closer.

Harriet knew exactly how a fox felt when it heard the hounds begin to bay.

"How are you finding your employment?"

the lady asked.

"It isn't actually employment if one isn't being paid," Harriet explained.

"Good practice for your future, I daresay. And Miss Murray has such a kind heart — she will be hard-pressed not to give you anything but a glowing reference no matter how things turn out." Before Harriet could open her mouth, the lady went on, "Perhaps you can provide the same service to Kipps's sisters." Her fan snapped shut and for a moment her smile waned, her eyes narrowing. "His mother is being most insistent that they be brought out. All four of them! Can you imagine, me having to bring out those ungainly girls? La! As if I have the time."

Harriet glanced over at Lady Eleanor, expecting the lady to rise to her defense, as she was used to Lady Essex rushing in where angels feared to tread, but not so with her sister. The particular Marshom stood by, a droll expression on her face, apparently waiting to see how this duel of sorts played out.

"After all," Lady Kipps continued, "your services won't be needed much longer, not when Miss Murray and Lord Roxley make the most excellent couple. Rather like me and my Kipps. Yes, she will do quite nicely for him, won't she, Lady Eleanor?"

Both Harriet and Lady Kipps turned toward the regal spinster and waited for her reply.

But all Lady Kipps got for her interference and inferences was the condescending look of an earl's daughter whose place in society hadn't been purchased, but borne of generations. Lady Eleanor was not one to suffer fools, and the rise of her brows, the slight tilt of her mouth said she found the entire subject just that: foolish, and more to the point, tiresome.

Lady Bindon, who by some miracle had been silent through all this, spoke up, if only to fill in the uncomfortable silence. "It is delightful to see Roxley finally taking interest in starting his nursery."

It was probably the most diplomatic and sensible thing the baroness had ever said, however Lord Bindon made a loud *harrumph* and stalked off, muttering something about "a touch of whisky somewhere."

And before Lady Kipps could launch into another one of her prattling opinions, they were interrupted by the arrival of a most notorious figure, entirely clad in black, her presence stopping the flow of chatter in an instant.

"Oh, dear me, if it isn't Madame Sybille," Lady Bindon whispered. Though this being

Lady Bindon, it was more a loud declaration.

"Madame Sybille?" Lady Kipps replied, her eyes widening. "She is all the rage in London! Whyever has she come to Bath? And in the middle of the Season, of all times."

As the mysterious woman approached them an odd twinge ran down Harriet's spine. The countess was right — it was curious that Madame Sybille would leave London so abruptly, when her services were so much in demand.

The sense of foreboding only continued when the infamous woman stopped right in front of her. "Miss Hathaway, is it not?"

She nodded and curtsied.

Not to be outshone, Lady Kipps all but moved Harriet aside to make her own curtsy. "Madame Sybille, what a delight and honor to meet you here in Bath. Perhaps you don't recall being introduced" — and then realizing she was talking to an occultist, she laughed — "oh, but of course you do, you see everything, don't you? But as I was saying —"

Madame Sybille waved her off with a dismissive air. "I came to speak to Miss Hathaway. To warn her —"

"Warn Miss Hathaway?" Lady Kipps

pressed forward, determined, her pushy mushroom roots showing. "How droll. But as I was saying, you might recall —"

"Miss Hathaway is in grave danger," the woman continued, again casting a warning wave of her hand over Harriet.

"In danger?" Lady Bindon squawked. "Are you certain?"

Madame Sybille nodded, her grim expression focused on Harriet.

"In danger? How ridiculous," Lady Kipps declared. "The only danger facing Miss Hathaway is the very certainty that she'll remain a spinster the rest of her days."

But since no one was really listening to her now, her mean-spirited jest went unnoticed.

"Warn me?" Harriet managed. "I don't see why —"

Madame Sybille caught her by the hand and turned her fingers palm up. "I can see it more clearly now. You are in terrible danger."

Of course, these dramatics caught the attention of everyone nearby and it wasn't but a few moments before half the room was watching the scene unfolding before their eyes.

"Your life," Madame Sybille continued

ominously, "is at a very dangerous cross-roads."

"So she needn't cross the road," Lady Eleanor said, but not even her dry wit was heard.

"Miss Hathaway, I implore you, return to London immediately. Or better yet — to your home. To Kempton, is it not?"

This left Lady Bindon goggle-eyed. Even Lady Kipps seemed taken aback, her thin lips gaping open.

Whispers hurried around the room, sharing Madame Sybille's latest proclamation as if it gave more credence to her unearthly powers, for she knew where Harriet came from. Or rather, where she should go.

Anywhere but here. Which given the rumblings around the room, Harriet suspected by morning the general population would be clamoring on Lady Eleanor's doorstep demanding she leave Bath immediately.

"Please heed me, my dear girl! I see danger all around you." Dropping Harriet's hand as if it were suddenly poison, Madame Sybille backed away and then left in much the same theatrical manner in which she'd arrived.

It was all too much for the usually staid assembly crowd of Bath, and fans everywhere began to flutter nervously. One silly old widow, known for her flighty ways, gave in to a case of vapors and collapsed onto her poor hired companion.

"Oh, my," Lady Bindon declared, taking two steps back from Harriet.

Indeed, most everyone around them cautiously eased away, and those who didn't stared at her with equal measures of dismay and fear.

Oh, bother. This was hardly what Roxley had in mind when he'd admonished her to be unobtrusive. Harriet drew a deep breath and put on what she hoped was a brave expression.

For it wasn't Madame Sybille's declaration that she was in danger — good heavens, Harriet already knew that — but that the woman knew so much about her and had chosen now, of all times, to come warn her.

"Well, that was rather unsettling and most odd," Lady Kipps said loudly. "More to the point, I find her ever so intrusive — just inviting herself into our party and ruining the evening." She shook out her skirts and once again took command of the conversation, by scanning the room for something else to discuss.

Unfortunately for Harriet it was something worse than Madame Sybille's lurid predications.

"Yes, well, isn't that Lord Fieldgate coming across the room?" Lady Kipps announced. It wasn't as if she was looking for an answer, rather that she wanted to continue where she'd left off bedeviling Harriet. "I do hope you are avoiding that rogue, Miss Hathaway. He is bad *ton.*"

Lady Eleanor made a rather inelegant snort, and if Harriet had been a wagering sort, she would have laid down her last guinea that the older woman's sentiments could be translated as follows: *takes one to know one.*

"You haven't continued to show him your favor, have you?" Lady Kipps pressed. "Not that I understand in the least why he bothers with you, when everyone knows he is under the hatches. He needs an heiress, which you are not." With that point made, she smiled, until suddenly her expression widened. "Ooooh, perhaps he is the danger that dreadful woman was nattering on about. And here he comes — and looking determined. Shall I ward him off?"

If ever there was a moment that Harriet regretted in her life, it was this one. She should have put her pique aside and allowed the countess to send the rakish fellow packing, for it was what she truly wanted.

But Lady Kipps had gotten under her skin, leaving her itching to be contrary. Her pride, pricked and prodded, got the better of her.

"My dear Miss Hathaway," Lord Fieldgate enthused, catching up Harriet's fingers and bringing them to his lips. "Such a dire scene. I came immediately to offer my assistance."

"Dear Fieldgate!" Harriet replied with an equal measure of enthusiasm, copying Lady Kipps' grand, overblown manners. Not that the woman noticed. "There you are. I thought you'd never come rescue me. I have been subjected to the most dreadful and uncouth company."

Words to regret, for certain, but at that moment they made Lady Kipps look as if her fan had been stuffed somewhere rather unpleasant.

In Roxley's estimation, an assembly at Bath was the last step before one descended into Dante's circles of hell.

Oh, the place might have been fashionable forty years earlier, but now, the city was filled with mushrooms, poor gentry, invalids, and those who claimed infirmities which were more imaginative than substantive. Then there were the ladies like his aunt, who could hold a place of rank in the smaller world of Bath, whereas in the London milieu, she'd be shuffled to one side as a spinster of good birth, but sadly of no consequence.

He'd dodged teetering old ladies and creaky swains as he'd danced with Miss Murray. But his trip to the punch bowl had taken forever as he worked his way through a milling tide of aging Corinthians and be-wigged widows. Steering a course past anxious mamas and their gaggles of ungainly daughters, relations and wards who had been sent to Bath in hopes of an advantageous match that would be difficult at best among the glittering Originals and Diamonds of London.

And speaking of anxious relations, Aunt Eleanor descended upon him in a whirlwind when he returned, nearly overturning the punch cups he was carrying.

"Gracious heavens, Roxley! Where is Miss Hathaway?"

The question appeared to loft past Miss Murray like the music from the alcove. She glanced over at Roxley, smiled and accepted one of the cups of punch.

He scanned the room but saw no sign of Harry, which seemed unusual since she was impossible to miss in that outrageous red gown.

"Where the devil has she gone to?" he muttered aloud before he realized it.

"She's dancing," Miss Murray supplied. "Yet again."

"Oh, I'll take that," Lady Bindon exclaimed, catching up the other cup of punch.

Roxley hadn't noticed her standing there next to his aunt.

Lady Bindon sent a glowering glance at the dance floor. "My, my, Miss Murray, your Miss Hathaway is cutting quite the swath tonight." It wasn't a statement of approval.

Nor was Roxley in an approving mood. So it had been all night — with every man in the room seeking an introduction to the divine lady in red.

Red. Harriet should not be allowed to wear such a gown. It was more scandalous than that seductive silk she'd worn to the theater the previous night.

And hardly, he wanted to point out, contributing to her promise to remain unobtrusive.

Miss Murray, meanwhile, had gulped down her punch and was even now setting the empty glass on the tray of a passing server. "Really, Roxley, you should mind yourself. The way you are carrying on, one would think you have a *tendré* for Miss Hathaway." She looked at him, once again with that businesslike assessment, while much to his chagrin, behind her, his aunt was making much the same inspection.

Well, do you? her quizzical expression said.

He hoped his said in return, *None of your demmed business.*

"You missed all the excitement, my lord," Lady Bindon said. "Madame Sybille paid us a visit. And such terrible news she bore."

Yet the baroness sounded ever so delighted to share the grave tidings.

"Madame Sybille?" That charlatan from London?

"You must have heard of her! She's an occultist. She sees things," Lady Bindon whispered too loudly for it truly to be a whisper.

"I would hope she sees things," Roxley told the lady. "Otherwise she'd be bumping into everything. Most inconvenient."

Thwack. Lady Bindon struck him in the arm with her ever-present fan. "Roxley, you are as droll as they say."

"And bruised," he replied, rubbing his arm.

"Do attend, Roxley! Madame Sybille,"

Lady Bindon continued, "had terrible news to impart on Miss Hathaway." She paused and drew closer, again whispering in that terrible stage voice of hers. "Our Miss Hathaway is in grave danger." She nodded twice, as if to punctuate the true magnitude of the situation, and then stepped back, fan at the ready.

"She did sound quite convincing that Harriet is in grave danger," Miss Murray added.

Only from you. Roxley put no stock in the fortune tellers who plied their trade amongst the bored members of the *ton.*

So whatever was the lady doing here in Bath? And why was she warning Harriet?

A shiver of foreboding ran down his spine and he glanced quickly, frantically about the room — where to his dismay he still couldn't spy that outrageous red gown. "Where is she?"

"With Lord Fieldgate," Lady Bindon supplied.

Fieldgate? Roxley ground his teeth together.

"I so adore how the viscount looks at Miss Hathaway. How a man looks at a young lady says so much. Why I remember when I was young. Bindon looked at me like that and I knew, I just knew he was . . ." The baroness sighed. "I got shivers when he claimed Miss

387

Hathaway's hand for yet another dance — their second dance — especially when he declared her the most perfect lady in the room. So besotted."

Lady Eleanor joined in. "Yes, he was quite effusive. I believe he called her gown 'divine.' "

"Perfectly divine," Miss Murray amended.

"Perfectly divine?" Roxley managed. Perfectly irritating, perhaps. For it was cut too low and it skimmed her lush, tall figure, giving her the appearance of a goddess come to tempt mortal men.

Himself included.

And so it seemed, Fieldgate as well.

What the devil was he up to? The man was farther up the River Tick than Roxley was, so his pursuit of Harriet made no sense.

Unless it was, as Lady Bindon had all but suggested, a case of love.

"Harriet is very fond of him," Miss Murray confided to the older ladies. "She is always going on and on about the viscount."

Roxley blinked and then glanced over at the lady beside him. "Pardon?"

"Lord Fieldgate and Harriet. Didn't you know?" She smiled serenely as if the match was as secure as hers to him.

"Was he an officer, Roxley?" Lady Bindon

was asking.

"A wha-a-a-t?"

"Fieldgate — was he an officer?" she pressed. "I only ask because of his bearing — so elegant and commanding."

He knew it was rude, but he was gaping. "Have you known many officers, Lady Bindon?"

She swatted him with her fan again and laughed. "Of course not! Oh, how you tease, Roxley. How you tease."

"Perhaps Fieldgate is the danger Madame Sybille spoke of," Lady Eleanor suggested with a pointed glance at her nephew. Her glance said so much more. *I don't like this. Any of this.*

Neither do I, he would have told her. But he was demmed sure going to get to the bottom of it. He looked around the assembly rooms but couldn't catch any sight of the pair.

Lady Eleanor must have been following his line of vision as well. She rose up on her tiptoes and glanced around the room. "Good heavens, they've gone."

"Gone?" Roxley went cold.

"Oh, I'm certain I just saw them over there," Miss Murray said, nodding toward the punch bowl on the far side of the room. It was the fact that she sounded both practical and confident that jangled his every nerve.

"Perhaps they've eloped!" Lady Bindon enthused, sounding utterly delighted by the idea. "Or they are sharing a rare moment of longing."

"A what?" Roxley asked, pulling his attention away from his frantic search of the room.

"A rare moment of longing," the baroness repeated. The she paused, lips pursed, fan tapping at them. "My lord, haven't you read the Miss Darby novels? Perhaps Miss Hathaway is indulging in a rare moment of longing — like dear Miss Darby and her beloved Lt. Throckmorten do." The lady's eyes twinkled wickedly. "You do you know what one is, don't you?"

Roxley nodded. "Yes, Lady Bindon, I do. I'm having one right now."

The longing to murder a certain viscount.

"Finally, a moment alone, Miss Hathaway," Viscount Fieldgate said as he led Harriet out onto the dance floor.

Here she'd hoped to avoid the viscount altogether, but with all eyes on her she could hardly have snubbed the man without being an object of gossip.

More than she was already.

"Now we can continue our discussion about our understanding," he said, smiling at her.

"Our wha-a-at?" she managed.

He leaned down, close to her ear. "Our understanding." His words purred over her.

But they hardly served to lull her into whatever spell he hoped to weave. Rather they incited a ration of panic.

He didn't mean . . . ? She glanced over at him. The viscount shot her a smoldering gaze full of smoky promises.

Oh, dear heavens, he did! He wanted to marry her.

Was he mad?

She stole another glance and found him preening with self-confidence. Yes, most decidedly mad.

"Perhaps you would prefer somewhere more private to discuss our future," he suggested, sensing her hesitancy.

Private? That might be better. She hardly wanted to throw the man over in front of every gossip in Bath. Bad enough all eyes were on them.

"Yes, that would be perfect," Harriet enthused, and probably a little too much, for he mistook her intent entirely, a rather lascivious light illuminating his eyes, so she rushed to add, "But Lady Eleanor . . . and my obligations to Miss Murray . . ."

"Leave this to me, my dearest Miss Hathaway," he said, catching hold of her arm and smoothly moving them from the dance floor into the crowd and then cutting a quick path toward the open doors which let out to the street.

Outside there were a number of people milling about — late arrivals, and a few aging Corinthians who, by the way they weaved and wobbled toward the door, had spent the better part of the early evening with a brandy bottle. There was also the usual collection of drivers and lads who tended to the waiting carriages, along with the cheeky fellows who plied the streets of Bath with salon chairs.

Not wasting any time, Fieldgate dropped to one knee before her, holding her hand right up to his lips. "Miss Hathaway, my dearest lady, will you do me the honor of —"

"Oh, no!" Harriet gasped, trying desperately to tug her hand free. When that failed, she did her best to try and tug the fool up from the ground before anyone noticed.

Unfortunately, a proposal of this order was not something anyone missed. All eyes now turned in their direction.

"But Miss Hathaway! Hear me out —"

Fieldgate said, rising to his feet.

"I won't, my lord. You've made a mistake," she shot back. "A grievous one —"

"But we have an understanding —" he said loudly.

Too loudly for Harriet's liking.

"We have nothing of the sort!" she shot back, trying to keep her voice level and steady, despite the panic racing down her limbs. "Lord Fieldgate, you are most mistaken."

"There is no mistake, Miss Hathaway. You have led me on a merry dance all these months — being coy and flirtatious — but now I will gain my due." He caught hold of her hand and tugged her toward a waiting carriage.

The driver hopped down from his perch like a hawk swooping down on a mouse, and got the door open, as if this — kidnapping innocent ladies — was all in a day's employment.

"I will get my due," the viscount continued to clamor.

"Your due?" Something dangerous ruffled down her spine and Harriet drew up to her full height. She nearly matched the viscount nose to nose, and a smarter man, a wiser man would have known that it was time to let go of the lady and beat a hasty retreat.

Fieldgate was neither wise nor smart.

"Exactly. My due," he informed her. "A man doesn't dance attendance on a lady all these months without getting his reward. And mine is your hand in marriage." With that he pulled her close. "One way or another."

For better or worse, Harriet had inherited the Hathaway temper. It served her brothers well — lending them daring and dash — but in a lady, it was rather inexcusable.

Though in some instances, one might say it came in rather handy.

This was one of those.

"My lord, I'm warning you," she said, digging in her heels. Her brothers knew that tone and always heeded it.

Even Roxley, at the tender age of eleven, had learned not to overly vex Harriet Hathaway, and only if you were willing to suffer the consequences and the years of humiliating torment from her brothers that followed when she delivered one of her infamous facers.

But Fieldgate was determined and to Harriet's horror, his head began to dip down in an attempt to steal a very public kiss that would be her ruin.

As she reeled back, her hand fisting into a tight, lethal ball, there came a deadly challenge from the doorway.

"Let her go, Fieldgate and I might let you live."

Roxley!

Harriet's head twisted to see him standing there, his face ablaze with fury. No capering Corinthian, no fancy gallant. Here was an earl with every ounce of noble blood afire.

So much for keeping their feelings for each other hidden away.

Yet in his blazing anger, Harriet could see one thing most clearly.

He loves me.

With all his heart, and it distracted her from the problem at hand just long enough to give the viscount time for one last rally.

"Harriet, my love!" Fieldgate declared for all to hear and then went to steal that kiss. The one that could seal them together.

Forever.

His plans, however, met an untimely hitch. For all that Fieldgate claimed he knew Harriet, knew her heart, in truth he knew absolutely nothing about the woman he sought to ruin.

If he had, he wouldn't have dared.

Her Hathaway temper was now an inferno — for he stood in the way of Harriet's heart, her only wish — and so she let fly with a facer that would have made Gentleman Jim weep with envy. There were gasps up and down the street, which said all too clearly this was going to be an *on dit* of infinite proportions.

A tale that became Bath legend.

Especially to every gentleman, driver and scruffy fellow who witnessed it (save Fieldgate).

And to a man, every single of them wished two things:

One, that they had such a bang-up chop;

And two, that they'd had a wager on its outcome.

The viscount teetered for about two seconds, disbelief widening his eyes, before he crumpled to the ground with a crash.

"My nose! My nose!" he wailed, his hands covering his hawkish beak.

Harriet glanced down at him and sniffed with dismay. "What a paperskull."

Then she turned around, sweeping her hands over her red silk skirts, as if to remove every trace of the man, save when she looked up she realized the depth of what she had just done.

For not only was Roxley in the doorway, but also Miss Murray, Lady Eleanor, Lord and Lady Bindon, and worst of all, Lord and Lady Kipps.

Oh, yes, she'd just dispatched Fieldgate,

but she'd also consigned her reputation to the flames.

Ruined beyond redemption if the malevolent look of delight in Lady Kipps's eyes was any indication.

No matter if Roxley found his diamonds, discovered a way to extract himself from the ruinous entanglements around him, she was no longer fit to be a countess in the eyes of society.

Her lofty dream, her grand wish, was as lost as the remains of the Queen's Necklace.

Roxley's gut twisted at the scene before him. This was all his fault.

Harriet's shattered expression tore at him. He should have sent her back to London, nay, Kempton, from the beginning and now . . .

He marched forward and got between her and the still-fallen Fieldgate. He'd never trusted the man, and now he had even less reason.

"Stay down," Roxley ordered as the viscount began to struggle to his feet.

"Good advice," came a voice at his side. Roxley turned to find Lord Galton at his elbow. "My carriage is at your service, sir," the old Corinthian said. "I'll have the ladies home in a thrice." He nodded toward Lady

Eleanor, who now had Miss Murray on one side and Harriet on the other.

Roxley nodded his consent to the cool-headed gentleman, who then gathered his charges together and began to escort them across the street and well away from the growing crowd.

Save Harriet, who pulled herself out of the protective circle and turned to him. "Roxley, I —"

"Not a word out of you, Harry. Not one word," he told her, far more severely than he intended. But good God, she'd scared him near to death.

Going off with a bounder like Fieldgate.

Oh, Harry! Whyever did I let you into this mess?

But all too quickly, Aunt Eleanor had her in hand once again and led her away. A veteran of her own scandals, the spinster knew what needed to be done better than most.

When Roxley turned around, he found the viscount scurrying along the ground like a rat. He stepped in front of him, blocking his escape. "I should kill you for this — and you'd be glad for the favor. Believe me, if I don't, her brothers will. I promise, you won't like their idea of making things even. Not in the least."

"What do you care what I do? You have your own heiress," Fieldgate shot back, finally finding his feet and rising up, wiping at the claret running from his nose with the back of his hand. "Leave me to mine. You can't have them both, Roxley."

"Heiress? Don't be a fool. Besides, I believe the lady refused you," Roxley pointed out. "Quite thoroughly."

"Refused me?" Fieldgate said. "She'll have to marry me if she doesn't want to spend the rest of her days ruined."

The earl moved quickly, catching the other man by the throat and hauling him up so he nearly dangled at his boot tips. "Over your dead body." Which given Roxley's current frame of mind could mean sooner rather than later.

Fieldgate twisted and clawed to get free. "Oh, I'll marry her," he gasped. "And get her dowry. Payment enough for all these months she'd led me on."

Dowry?

Roxley let him go and took a step back. What the devil was the man nattering on about?

"Harry has no dowry," he told him.

Fieldgate laughed. "Harry? My, aren't you on friendly terms. But when she's my wife, I'll have none of that. And while you might be cozy with her, I know better than you. I know for a fact that the man who marries Harriet Hathaway will be well compensated."

Roxley gaped at him. How hard had Harry hit this fool?

"Fieldgate, you're mistaken," he said slowly, so each word could sink in. "Miss Hathaway has no dowry."

"You would say that," the viscount sneered. "What? Are you angry because I've beaten you to the sort of prize you Marshoms are so famous for? I've stolen a better heiress right out from under your nose, so there it is."

Roxley flinched at those words, for he could almost hear half the audience muttering exactly what Fieldgate was implying.

A Marshom marries well and cheats often.

Still there was one problem with all this. "What makes you think Miss Hathaway is an heiress?"

"I am privy to the closely held fact," Fieldgate replied, "that her father has extensive holdings in the West Indies. A sugar fortune."

At this, Roxley laughed, thinking of the Pottage back in Kempton. "You corkbrained fool! Would her brothers be serving in the navy and the army if their family was as rich as you say? Her brother Chaunce is attached to the Home Office. Do you see him prancing about White's in a new jacket every week?"

Fieldgate took a step back, as if Roxley's words were a blow with the same force as Harriet's well-aimed fist. For they sank into his thick skull as he examined the notion. But still he clung to his madcap theory. "It is naught but one of her family's many eccentricities. I have it on good authority that Miss Hathaway is an heiress. And I'll have my due."

Roxley groaned. This man and his due. The only thing due him was a good piece of lead in the chest. "What do you mean, 'good authority'?"

"Kipps!" he declared, pointing at the young earl who was even now backing behind his own heiress, the one he'd married not a year ago. "Kipps told me last summer Miss Harriet Hathaway was an heiress. He claimed her dowry surpassed that of Miss Nashe's. We diced for them and . . ."

"You diced for me?!" Lady Kipps exploded, whirling around on her husband.

"I only did so to keep him away from you, dearest," Kipps rushed to explain, but the deep blush on his fair features told the real truth. He'd led Fieldgate astray to gain the advantage.

"You lied to me?" Fieldgate erupted, in much the same hot manner as Lady Kipps. "You dishonorable, wretched little cheat —"

"Yes, well, caught in your own folly," Roxley told him. "For Miss Hathaway is no heiress."

The man staggered a bit. "Not an heiress?" He shook his head. "But . . . but . . . the sugar fortune . . ." He glanced again at Kipps. "He said . . ."

"No, you fool," Roxley told him. "How many times must you be told? Harriet has no money."

"No money?" This came out like a sad whimper.

"Not a farthing," Lord Bindon told him. "Great fellow, Sir George, but the Hathaways have never been all that plump in the pockets. Rare tempers, deadly shots, but not a farthing to spare. Seems the only one who's ruined is you, Fieldgate. 'Specially when the Hathaways discover what you've done." He gave a great shudder. "Deadly shots, did I mention that?"

Ruined. That word sparked the life back into Fieldgate. For the man knew exactly what that meant. He'd ruined her and now he would have to marry her.

"Egads," he gasped, before turning tail and running for his waiting carriage. "Go! Go!" he shouted at his driver.

"What the devil?" Roxley gasped and was about to light after him, when Lord Bindon caught him by the arm.

"He'll be to the Continent before you stop him. And do you truly want to catch him?" the baron asked, shaking his head.

The earl paused. If he caught Fieldgate, other than the personal satisfaction of beating him to a pulp, then what? There would be no other answer than seeing Harriet married to the man.

No. Never that.

The conviction behind his unspoken words struck him raw and deep.

"Yes, well," Lord Kipps began, "I'm certain that's the last we'll see of him. Demmed fool." He smiled as if it all had been a grand lark.

But neither Lady Kipps nor Roxley saw it as such, and so Roxley took out his anger and frustration on the true cause of Harriet's misfortune.

He leveled the facer he'd wanted to slam into Fieldgate's smug face into Kipps and sent the man flying backward.

"Yes, now that was well done," Lord Bindon said, stepping over the fallen earl and slapping Roxley on the back.

CHAPTER 12

Traitors come in all forms, Miss Darby. Do not be deceived by the meekest of enemies or the strongest of allies, not when there is a fortune to be had.

Prince Sanjit to Miss Darby
from Miss Darby's Reckless Bargain

Damn Fieldgate to hell for not being able to carry out something as simple as an elopement, Miss Murray fumed as they made the shameful walk to Lord Galton's carriage.

More so, who would have thought that Miss Hathaway could lay a man low with a single punch? She watched Harriet quickly clamber up into the carriage. Unnatural, wretched girl.

Though obviously she'd underestimated Miss Hathaway's ambitions. A viscount wasn't good enough for her — she wanted a countess's coronet in her jewel case.

Like all the rest of her sort.

Miss Murray took her seat and turned her head to look out the window. Not far away was Madame Sybille standing in the shadows.

The lady nodded once at her and disappeared into the night. Finally, they were to do this themselves. It had taken her sister far too long to come to the realization that milord was no friend to either of them. If only she'd listened years ago.

For Miss Murray was many things. But a fool was not one of them. And she knew, even before they got to Brock Street, that her time as the daughter of a well-heeled London merchant was over.

Thank God, she thought as she was hustled inside Lady Eleanor's house much like she remembered being carried by her sister into La Conciergerie when she was but a small child. Certainly this house was no prison, but yes, the suspicions were all there — from Lady Eleanor's tight demeanor, to Lord Galton's speculative glances — none of which were directed at Miss Hathaway as they ought — but at her.

She wasn't sure how — for it couldn't have been that scatterbrained maid from this morning, the one she'd sent back to the ribbon shop to fetch her reticule which she had deliberately left behind — but somehow, some way, they had discovered she wasn't who she was supposed to be.

So much for milord's assurances that no one would ever uncover the truth.

The earl knew, for she'd felt the chill in his demeanor since the moment he'd arrived in the theater. Oh, he was still polite, but there was an edge to his manners that masked a deep-seated distrust and wrath.

Yet even in his discovery of her, she'd come to her own realization about him.

There was one bit of leverage left that would most certainly force the earl into giving up his portion of the diamonds.

"I think I shall retire for the evening," Miss Murray said as they came inside the house.

Lady Eleanor nodded tightly and directed Miss Hathaway toward the library — probably for a good scold — which would give her just enough time . . .

For as she stole a glance down the stairs at Miss Hathaway, she knew for a fact that the lady was as valuable to the Earl of Roxley as any treasure trove.

That he'd do anything to keep Harriet safe.

How unfortunate for Miss Hathaway . . . and the earl, she supposed, as she gained her room and retrieved her pistol.

Harriet watched Miss Murray go up the stairs and wished she could follow — but that was not to be, for here was Lady Eleanor pointing her toward the library and there was nothing Harriet could do to escape.

But the real shock came when Lady Eleanor closed the door behind them, leaving Lord Galton in the foyer. Thus closeted away, the lady began her lecture. "My dear Miss Hathaway, if you hold any hope of becoming my nephew's countess, that was certainly not the way to achieve it."

The lady couldn't have said anything that shocked Harriet more. *Become Roxley's countess . . .* Had she heard her correctly?

Meanwhile Lady Eleanor paced before the fireplace. "Essex avowed you were a perfect candidate for mustering, but I can only assume my sister has developed rats in her rafters."

Mustering? Harriet's eyes widened. "Me, my lady?"

"What sort of mustering is this when my sister sends along a gel foolish enough to go outside with an obvious ne'er-do-well? Good heavens, I've known the man less than two days and I knew he wasn't to be trusted."

"I never thought he'd . . ." Harriet paused, for certainly this was not the conversation she'd been expecting.

"What? Try to take advantage of you?" The lady waved a hand at her. "Believe me, bounder or vicar, rake or gentleman, taking advantage of a lady is all they think about."

Did that include her nephew? Harriet didn't dare ask. Instead, she raised a slight defense. "I believe Lord Fieldgate was more interested in my fortune."

That brought Lady Eleanor's attention right up. "Your fortune? You have a fortune?"

Harriet hated to prick her apparent hopes and shook her head sadly. "No, I fear not. Someone must have led him to believe I was an heiress. Then . . . well, you know the rest."

"Men! What they will do!" Then, to Harriet's surprise, she barked a laugh. "Poor fellow. Felled by a lady in front of half of Bath society, and by now he's sure to have discovered his heiress is penniless. He's probably halfway to the Continent for fear he will be made to marry you."

Harriet gasped — for that thought hadn't occurred to her. "I won't marry him!"

Lady Eleanor nodded her approval. "Good

girl. Smartest thing I've heard you say since you got here." She pointed at the chair. "Now sit and tell me how you intend to gain Roxley's hand."

Harriet sat, but only because her knees gave out. Had she heard the lady correctly? Gain Roxley's hand?

Nor was Lady Eleanor done. "You came all this way to undo this wretched entanglement of Roxley's, didn't you?"

Harriet didn't know what to say. She'd only admitted as much to Tabitha and Daphne. But to Lady Eleanor?

The older woman threw up her hands and sighed. "How am I to help you if you cannot even admit the truth?"

And then Harriet saw it. How much Lady Eleanor was like her sister, and was about to confess everything when there was a heavy thud and then the sound of someone falling in the foyer.

"Moss," the lady gasped, and flew to the door. When she yanked it open, there was Miss Murray setting aside the silver salver and Lord Galton lying on the floor.

"Whatever happened?" Lady Eleanor demanded as she knelt by his side, cradling his head.

But Harriet knew immediately. For there on the stair was Miss Murray's smaller traveling valise.

And in her hand, a pistol.

Not to mention the salver on the stand.

"Yes, I hit him with it," Miss Murray said, having followed the direction of Harriet's gaze and her line of thought.

"Whatever for?" Lady Eleanor demanded.

"I don't need him," she said plainly. "But I do need the two of you." She pointed the pistol at Harriet.

Lady Eleanor's eyes widened in horror.

Harriet sighed and began to step forward. "That pistol will be of no use. I removed the flint."

Miss Murray's eyes flickered for a second, glancing at the pistol in her hand and then back up at Harriet. "But I have two pistols, Miss Hathaway. Did you remove both flints?"

Harriet paused. It was a bluff. It must be.

Then Miss Murray turned the pistol on Lady Eleanor. "You might risk your own life, Miss Hathaway, but are you willing to risk hers?"

That was enough to stay Harriet's advance.

"Yes, I thought as much," Miss Murray agreed. "Now up, Lady Eleanor. He'll be well enough in the morning."

As Harriet helped a reluctant Lady Elea-

411

nor to her feet, Miss Murray propped a folded piece of paper atop the salver, where it sat next to Pug's box, exactly where Lady Eleanor had left it earlier.

"What is that?" Harriet demanded.

"A note for Roxley," the girl told her. "I'm changing the terms of our betrothal. Now, shall we?" She wagged the gun toward the door.

"What do you think you are doing?" Lady Eleanor stood her ground. "I won't go anywhere with you, you impudent girl!"

"We are taking a small trip to Marshom Court, where I am certain Roxley will come to fetch you." She pointed to the door again.

"I am not leaving my house!" Lady Eleanor announced. "If I leave town, I will have abandoned my lease. Lord Tarvis —"

None of which was of any concern to Miss Murray. She raised the pistol so it was aimed at the lady's head. "Choose: lose your lease or your life." Again, Lady Eleanor stood firm, so Miss Murray moved the pistol so it pointed at Harriet. "I do believe, my lady, your nephew would be most put out if you were to let his beloved Harry be lost. Now shall we?"

A reluctant Lady Eleanor came, but not before she gathered Pug's box in her arms, and went out the front door, her back ramrod straight, and only looking back over her shoulder once, with a gaze of great longing, but whether it was for her beloved home or the still form of Lord Galton, Harriet wasn't too sure.

Then again as Harriet glanced back, she longed for something else. The silver salver atop the stand. She should have ignored Roxley's admonition to keep well away from Miss Murray and knocked the girl out cold with it when she'd had the chance earlier in the day.

Had that only been this morning? Harriet shivered and caught hold of Lady Eleanor's hand, tucking it into the crook of her arm to steady Her Ladyship as they went down the steps.

The old girl shot her a grateful smile.

In the street a carriage awaited, and Miss Murray prodded them inside, where they found yet another surprise.

Madame Sybille.

The famed occultist smiled. "As I said earlier, Miss Hathaway, you are in very grave danger. You should have heeded my warning with more care."

With Fieldgate on the run, Roxley turned his heavy heart toward Brock Street. He needed to see Harriet.

Apologize to her. Beg her forgiveness.

He'd led her down this path. The fault was his. He should have dispatched the viscount and his unwanted attentions a year ago.

But even as he set out for his aunt's house, here was Hotchkin, once again making one of his unlikely and untimely appearances.

"My lord, there you are," the man said, falling into step beside him.

"Not now," Roxley told him.

"But I've had reports come in from London. About Mr. Murray," Hotchkin came to a stop. "And something else — about the lady you visited earlier in the day."

There was a hitch to the man's voice. Roxley stopped and glared over his shoulder at the younger man. "What is it?"

Hotchkin shook his head. "Not here."

Roxley knew enough about Chaunce's overly cautious assistant to know that the man would never spill what he knew in the open, with just anyone and everyone wandering by. So Roxley pointed him to the nearest public house, tossing a coin to the man and steering Hotchkin to a back parlor. "Talk."

And he did.

By the time Roxley had heard all the reports and weighed the information against

414

what he'd learned on his visit to Mrs. Plumley's School, he knew it was time to act. And quickly.

He held a terrible suspicion who was behind all this . . . but still, he must be wrong. It couldn't be . . .

Yet, if he was correct . . .

Roxley quickened his pace until the two men were jogging up the hill to Brock Street.

"Have you a pistol?" he asked Mr. Hotchkin as they neared Lady Eleanor's door.

"Yes, but —"

"Good man. Wouldn't be honorable if I shot my nearly betrothed," Roxley told him. "I'll leave that task to you."

Hotchkin's mouth fell open. "But my lord . . . I don't think I can shoot a —"

Roxley chuckled. "It was a joke, Hotchkin. Really, I am going to have to speak to Chaunce about your education."

"Yes, my lord," the man grumbled as they got to the door.

But almost immediately, Roxley was on edge.

The door stood slightly open, and there was no sign of Thortle. Inside a meager bit of light shone.

"We might have to test your resolve," Roxley told him, drawing out his own pistol and going forward into the house.

There in the foyer, a figure lay on the floor, groaning and struggling to get up.

"Lord Galton?" Roxley said, coming to the man's aid. He didn't need to look or ask to know that the house was empty.

He could feel it. "Where is my aunt?"

"Lady E? She's not here?" Galton asked, as he rose into a sitting position, leaning against the stand. He rubbed the back of his head, his eyes closed. "Oooh."

Roxley put his hand there and could feel a sizeable lump. "You've been hit." He rose, shouting as went, "Aunt Eleanor? Harriet?" When that produced no response, he continued, "Thortle? Mrs. Nevitt?" They all stilled and then, from deep within the house, they could hear pounding.

He nodded for Hotchkin to go investigate and the young man hurried down the back stairs.

But Roxley found his answers a moment later, when he spied the note on the salver. He caught it up and opened it, walking into the library where a single candle still burned.

Bring the diamonds to Marshom Court, or else.

He cursed thoroughly.

Galton staggered in and sank almost immediately into a chair. Roxley handed him the note, and after the man read it, he shook his head. "That girl has a decided lack of originality. *Or else!*" he scoffed. "What utter poppycock."

Hotchkin returned moments later. "The butler, housekeeper and maid were locked in the cellar. Miss Murray forced them inside at gunpoint."

"How long ago?"

"An hour, maybe two," Hotchkin told him.

Roxley cursed again. "Wretched demmed diamonds. I wish my father had never —"

"You wouldn't say that if you could have seen them that night," the older man admonished. "The most dazzling pile of gems one could imagine."

Roxley froze. *"Who are you?"*

"Galton," the man said, as if they were being introduced for the first time. "My friends call me Moss."

Lord Galton glanced at the two men before him and sighed.

It was time.

"You were there," the younger man gasped.

He nodded to the fellow. Hotchkin, he thought his name was. Something to do with the Home Office. An honest enough looking chap. Good. They'd need him in short order. "Yes, I was there."

Roxley took a step back. "I don't believe this."

"I rather don't care either way. But you must listen to me if you are to get my Eleanor back. And your Miss Hathaway."

The earl sank into a chair, his eyes narrow and wary.

As they should be, but Galton was in no mood to spin a gambler's tale, it was time for the truth. "You know about the card game?"

Roxley gave him a tight nod.

Hotchkin, on the other hand, was rather like an overly excited puppy, giving an enthusiastic bob of his head.

"Yes, well, your father won that night — fair and square," he told the earl before he smiled at the memory. "He was all but rolled up, like all of us were that night, but when that Frenchie started adding those stones to the pot, well, after that, the earl couldn't lose. He kept winning. And winning, and the comte continued to wager — recklessly, cursing his luck and tossing more and more diamonds into the pot — desperate to get his treasures back." The man grinned. "But to no avail."

"So Lord Roxley did win the Queen's Necklace," Hotchkin said, as if in vindication.

Moss nodded. "Well, half of the stones as well as we can figure."

"We?" Roxley quickly asked.

Galton smiled. And Lady E was always going on about what a flighty, ruinous mess her nephew was. Nothing could be further from the truth.

"Yes, *we*," he said. "My fellow gamblers and I. The next morning, your parents had left in the company of the one man who hadn't played that night."

"The Englishman," Hotchkin said a low voice.

Moss shot a quick glance at him. "Yes."

"Do you know who he was?" the younger man asked, once again all eagerness.

But it was to Roxley that he replied. "No, but I believe you do know."

Not even a flicker passed over the earl's expression.

Just like his father . . . not a tell to be had.

Moss rubbed his aching head. "Yes, well, I imagine we'll find him at the end of Miss Murray's lead." He looked again over at Roxley, studying him for a moment. "You look like your father, but you have your mother's sharpness about you. I remember

419

her the most. A stunning beauty, Lady Roxley. The memory of her chestnut hair and glorious eyes has long buoyed my resolve to aid you."

Roxley shook his head slightly. "Help me?"

The old gambler nodded. "After your parents left in the company of that dastardly fellow, we knew they were in danger."

"You mean to say, you, Corney and Batty," Hotchkin nudged, hoping to get more information.

Moss shot the fellow another glance, but this time there was a bit of a twinkle in his eye that said he appreciated a sharp mind. "Yes, they've been my compatriots for years. A league of sorts. Even back then, young as we were, between the three of us, we'd seen enough of the world to know someone who couldn't be trusted — who should be feared. Knew the moment that fellow settled into that chair by the fire that he was one to keep an eye on."

He paused for a moment, lost in the memory. To Moss it seemed like yesterday. The sour smell of Berti's. The delight of playing. That sound the cards made as they were shuffled.

Pfffft.

"Why didn't you warn my parents before it was too late?" Roxley asked, prodding at his reverie.

He looked up slowly. "Because they sailed out before dawn. And since your father had lightened our purses as well, it took us the rest of the day to scare up the necessary blunt to pay for our crossing." Moss sighed, his head bent. "By then it was too late."

"How can you be certain it was this Englishman from the game who killed Lord and Lady Roxley?" Hotchkin pressed.

"He wore a very distinctive beryl stone ring," he said, once again looking to see if Roxley gave any indication he knew their adversary. And to Moss's chagrin the man gave nothing away. "Moreover," he continued, "when we got to Dover we discovered Lord Roxley had hired a barouche and was seen in the company of his wife and a man who fit the description of the Englishman they'd left Calais with. The man who had watched the earl win that fortune. They left Dover together — the three of them."

"And yet when my parents were found —" Roxley couldn't manage the rest of the words.

"Exactly, my good man," Moss acknowledged. "Your parents and the driver were found shot to death, but there was no sign of the stranger."

Roxley had been pacing for some time,

but at this he stopped. "You were there."

Moss nodded. For this was a memory that haunted him. "We were too late. We followed on horseback, but by the time we arrived, all was lost." He looked over at the earl. "I'm ever so sorry."

"It was not your doing."

The words were truly meant, but they hardly erased the guilt. If he or Batty or Corney had won, it would have been one of them dead on the side of that road.

Lady Luck. Always so demmed fickle.

As if reading from a report, Hotchkin argued the point. "A posting lad was first upon the scene."

Moss shook his head. "No, we were. But then we left since we feared being accused of the deed."

Hotchkin persisted. "The lad said it looked as if someone had spent some time tearing apart everything in the carriage — everything — and yet stole nothing."

"Yes, indeed," Moss said. "They had searched everything. The only thing that wasn't slashed open or smashed was that ridiculous china figurine — I found it next to your mother, half hidden by her skirt."

"Pug," Roxley whispered.

"Yes, so I learned later. And all her treasures dumped beside her . . ." His voice caught, for the sight of Lady Roxley, only days before so vivid and lovely, now lost, had torn his heart out. "She was still wearing her wedding ring and earbobs. So we knew it was him. He'd gotten the diamonds and fled. Or so we believed."

"Did you search for the stranger?" Hotchkin prompted.

Galton nodded wearily. "But he had, like the diamonds, disappeared."

Roxley's chest contracted. "So the diamonds *are* lost."

"That is what we thought — at first. Then we returned to London — imagine our shock when we discovered the true origins of those stones, just who exactly our comte was and who that necklace had been intended for." He shuddered. "Marie Antoinette! They might have hung us!"

Quiet for a moment, he was prodded into continuing by Hotchkin. "But only half the diamonds were sold —"

"Yes, yes, right you are. And so they were. Corney was able to learn that from a London dealer — that the comte had only possessed half the stones."

"And the other half? The half Roxley's father won?" Hotchkin asked.

"Never seen again." Moss waved his hand like a magician making a coin disappear.

"We knew if those gems had gone the way we supposed — that the stranger had killed your parents and made off with your father's winnings — the diamonds would start making their appearance in London. It is the only place to sell gems of that quality."

"Why not take them to the Continent?" Roxley posed.

Galton shook his head. "If he had, they would have been spotted and identified immediately."

"Why not sell them outside of London? In York or Edinburgh?" Hotchkin posed.

Again Galton waved them off. "Even if you sell them in the country, they will eventually find their way to London. And since these were quality stones — the sort a trader would never forget — we left word that we would pay handsomely for any hint of their reappearance."

"But they didn't —" Roxley looked as if he'd just walked through the ruin of his parents' murder himself.

"No. They never showed up," Moss said.

"Yet, you never reported any of this," Hotchkin pressed. More like chided.

Galton smiled at the eager young man. "And how were we to do that? We knew it was him who had shot them, but we didn't know his name. And we could hardly go to

Bow Street and claim an unknown fellow had killed the Earl and Countess of Roxley, without revealing all we knew." He shrugged, for certainly there was no changing the past. But the present . . . He glanced up at Roxley. "Then something came to me . . . about your mother. She had a way about her — she could move a coin through her fingers like a pickpocket — no offense meant, my lord."

Roxley nodded, smiling for a second, as if he too held the same memory.

"She struck me as a bit of a conjurer. At the time I was relieved to be playing against your father and not her — even if your father held all the luck that night. But still, I began to wonder if she might have hidden them where they wouldn't be easily found, disguised them as well as she did her own abilities." Moss straightened. "We knew if we hadn't forgotten, if we suspected as much — that she'd hidden them somewhere no one would discover easily — so would he. And that he'd keep looking. Keep waiting. So we swore a vow to find them first — for you, and your aunts — an obligation we failed when it came to your parents."

He got to his feet shakily. "And now the time has arrived to lure that devil out into the open."

■ ■ ■ ■

"This is madness, my lord," Hotchkin argued an hour later, as Roxley and Galton stood waiting for the baron's carriage with the new set of horses they'd ordered. "Madness."

That was the seventh time he'd protested thusly.

Roxley shrugged, as he had each and every time. Part of him agreed. It was madness to trust Galton when he barely knew the man, but . . . "Sometimes it isn't about superior planning, Mr. Hotchkin, or great cunning, but a bit of demmed luck."

Hotchkin blanched at the word.

Luck. It was far too fickle and mercurial a thing to trust one's life to it.

Especially when those lives included Lady Eleanor and Miss Hathaway.

But on this Roxley was certain, going up against who they were, *luck* was their best chance.

The carriage came shuddering around the corner. It wasn't the fanciest conveyance, but the horses looked fast, just as Galton had promised.

It seemed one of the hostelers in Bath owed the old gambler a bit of blunt and they had managed to work a trade.

"Off to London with you," Roxley told Hotchkin, nodding at the extra horse the posting lad led. "Don't give that report to anyone but Chaunce."

Hotchkin looked ready to make one more protest, but it was at that moment the carriage door opened and a well-appointed man in a bright waistcoat and an overabundance of lace climbed down.

"Moss, you pontificating fool!" he called out in greeting. "Whatever have you dragged me out of bed at this outrageous hour for?" The man blinked a few times in the lamplight and then his gaze focused on Roxley. "Oh, my. 'Tis you."

Lord Galton smiled. "Batty, we must act. Did you bring them?"

"Aye, I've got them," he said, digging into his coat and pulling out a large pouch that jingled with the sound of stones. "Thought you were larking about when your man said to bring these."

"I never lark," Galton replied with his usual dignity.

"This won't do," Hotchkin muttered as he climbed onto his horse, turning toward the London road.

Roxley could only hope that for once, the

usually bang-on and unerring Mr. Hotchkin could be proven wrong.

CHAPTER 13

A life of deceit and lies can only end in the same manner.

Prince Sanjit to Miss Darby
from Miss Darby's Terrible Temptation

The pace set by Miss Murray and Madame Sybille was unrelenting. They drove through the night and into the morning, stopping only to change the horses.

Miss Murray had admonished both Harriet and Lady Eleanor that if either of them called out or caused a commotion, the other would die.

So Harriet thought it best to let this entire scenario play out.

And wait for her chance to act.

What had Roxley called it? A long game.

She'd play as long as she must to keep Lady Eleanor safe and ensure the Queen's Necklace stayed out of Miss Murray's greedy grasp.

Roxley, I need you, she'd whispered more than once into the passing countryside, hoping her words were like breadcrumbs and would guide him to her side.

With all her heart she knew he would follow. Hell-bent and furious, she imagined, just as he'd looked when he'd come upon her and Fieldgate.

Murderous.

She only hoped he was sensible enough to send Mr. Hotchkin for help and not bring the young man along.

He was a smart enough fellow, but had no instincts for fieldwork, something she would inform her brother Chaunce at the first opportunity.

If I get the chance, she mused as she glanced up and found Miss Murray watching her like a feral cat.

Sometime late the next afternoon, they arrived at Marshom Court, the sight of which brought a smile to Harriet's face.

She'd heard Roxley describe it in many terms — the interminable pile of stones, the Cottage, that wretched tumble.

It was none of those things and all of them.

The Marshoms, as it turned out, loved their family seat deeply — one could see it in the three wings that made up the house — wings built when they were flush with money, and cared for as best as they could when they weren't.

It reminded her of the Pottage — though on a much grander scale.

Lady Eleanor glanced out the window and for a second there was a flicker in her eyes — a light of recognition, a sense of place. But she was too regal to be overly sentimental for too long.

They pulled up the drive and to the front of the house, and the carriage stopped.

For a moment, they all waited — for a footman to come hurrying down the steps, for the butler to come forth — someone, anyone to open the grand doors, but no one did.

"Oriel must be home at present," Lady Eleanor remarked. "She isn't overly fond of company."

"She will make an exception for us," Madame Sybille declared, nodding for Harriet to get out.

As she began to alight, Miss Murray wagged the pistol at her. "One false move and she dies."

Harriet shook her head slightly. "Yes, yes, I heard you the first time and every time since. I do anything, she dies. Yes, I am quite clear on this."

Lady Eleanor pinched her lips together, for she looked about to laugh at Harriet's disgruntled outburst.

"Get out," Miss Murray ordered.

Harriet did so, and then turned and helped Lady Eleanor down.

"Something is wrong," the lady whispered as she glanced up at the house. "Terribly wrong."

"Stay close," Harriet replied softly before she was prodded in the back by Miss Murray.

Up the stairs they went, and Harriet paused before the closed doors.

"Go ahead, open them," Miss Murray prompted.

And so Harriet did, going inside slowly, where a large open foyer greeted them. To the right led into the heavy stone portion of the house that had once been a keep, with the usual decorations of ancient armor and pikes and shields upon the walls, while the left side gave way to a classical wing that had been built in the last two hundred years, with its graceful statues and art that spoke of former continental tours.

All four of them stood in the grand foyer and Lady Eleanor huffed a large sigh of aggravation as she looked around. "Wherever is Shingleton? He should be here. At the very least, where is my sister?"

And then like an ethereal sort of sprite, Lady Oriel arrived, coming out of the classical wing, wearing little more than a wrapper over a diaphanous gown that made her look like a Greek statue come to life. Her gray hair fell in a simple loosely bound braid down one shoulder, a few strands curling loose from the pale blue ribbon that had been woven in along with her hair.

"Eleanor?" the woman exclaimed, her expression all puzzlement. "Is that truly you?"

"Oriel," Lady Eleanor replied in greeting. "Dear sister."

Lady Oriel floated down the trio of steps that separated them and held out her hands for Eleanor. "Whatever are you doing here? Has some evil befallen Bath?" She paused and glanced at the others, then dismissed them in a blink. She leaned forward. "You didn't let Lord Tarvis lure you into some tawdry card game for the lease, did you?"

"Nothing like that, my dear," Lady Eleanor assured her. She glanced uneasily over her shoulder at Miss Murray and Madame Sybille and continued, choosing her words carefully. "I have some distressing news —"

"It isn't Tiberius, is it?" Lady Oriel paled

and then as quickly recovered. "But it couldn't be — why he's sent an artist to paint me — the boy is ever so thoughtful." She smiled at the others. "Eleanor, do you think we could entice Essex to return and then we could be painted together as before — the Three Graces — once again." She smiled over her shoulder at a grand painting in the alcove beyond that indeed did depict the Three Graces, all of them nude, dancing in a circle.

Harriet blinked and looked again. "Good heavens!" she gasped, unable to stop herself. The one on the right couldn't be . . . "Lady Essex?"

"Yes, that is Essex. She's Grace, and the one on the left is me, Beauty." Lady Oriel preened a bit. For her part, Lady Eleanor put her back to the painting and looked as if she wished it had never existed.

"Yes, yes, this is all wonderful," Miss Murray said, "But I want the diamonds. And I shall have them now."

Lady Oriel blinked at the girl several times, then turned back to her sister. "Whoever is this, Eleanor?"

"I'll explain later, dearest," Lady Eleanor told her, and then carefully placed herself between Miss Murray and her younger sibling.

"She is as unpleasant as the artist Tiberius sent to paint me," Lady Oriel whispered loudly. "He's been ever-so-difficult since he arrived this morning."

"Who else is here in the house?" Madame Sybille demanded.

"Just me," came a deep voice, and obviously a familiar one to their captors, for they jumped at the first sound.

"Milord!" Madame Sybille gasped. "Whatever are you doing here?"

There was a hiss of recognition from Lady Eleanor. "You! Lord Mereworth!" The lady appeared shocked and furious at the same time. As if she'd just discovered a snake in the house.

He spared a shocked glance over at Roxley's aunt, but his attention and sharp focus returned in a snap back to Madame Sybille and Miss Murray.

Mereworth? Harriet watched this looming man come down the steps. So this was Roxley and Chaunce's mentor, the one of whom she'd heard so much about over the years?

And if he was here — she looked around — Roxley couldn't be too far away. Lady Eleanor should look relieved. Harriet was. He was here to help.

But when she looked at Lady Eleanor's

435

fearful expression, she wasn't as certain.

"Mereworth, is it?" Miss Murray said, stalking forward, pistol in hand. "Now that we know who you are, we'll know where to send your body."

Her hand came up, the pistol at the ready, but Mereworth was faster.

How, Harriet didn't know, but his arm shot out and a pistol blazed to life.

One shot, the report like a canon inside the marble foyer, echoing and jarring them all.

And what followed was just as piercing — the wild keening shriek of Madame Sybille as she rushed to Miss Murray, who was even now slumping to the floor, a look of shock on her face.

Harriet tried to breathe — for she couldn't quite believe what she was seeing. The girl's eyes widened and then it was as if her spirit, that bit of fluttering life inside everyone, lifted off like a butterfly and flitted away.

This moment of great violence, and then a sudden quiet, a stillness that was death.

Harriet reached out and caught Lady Eleanor's arm — knowing not if she steadied the lady or herself.

Madame Sybille knelt beside her fallen partner for a moment, a sound so guttural bubbling up from inside her. "You —" she breathed out, the fire of vengeance ablaze. "You bastard —"

Mereworth strolled forward, his face coolly composed. Reaching down, he picked up the pistol that had fallen from Miss Murray's grasp and pointed it anew. "Didn't see that one coming, did you, dear, dear Madame Sybille?"

Sybille stilled.

"Yes, well, you are much wiser than your sister. And I will have need of you." He turned and smiled with the same cool malice at Harriet and the Marshom sisters. "All of you."

"Eleanor," Lady Oriel whispered, as they followed his directions. "I don't believe this fellow is an artist at all."

Mereworth herded them down into the wine cellar, where they found the rest of the small household staff huddled in one corner. The large cavern was lit by a few candles, and all around them were casks and bottles of wine, filling the air with a dry, musky odor.

Harriet thought this might have been a dungeon once, and then converted in more peaceful times for wines rather than prisoners.

"Shingleton, there you are!" Lady Oriel scolded. "I will write Tiberius and tell him

you are neglecting your duties — woefully."
She sat down on a cask with a huff.

"Yes, my lady," the butler agreed, then his
weary gaze alighted on the rest of them.
"Lady Eleanor?"

"Yes, Shingles, 'tis me." Lady Eleanor held
out her hands to the elderly man and he
took them, smiling.

"I am heartily restored to see you here,
my lady," the butler told her. Then he
lowered his voice. "But I fear the situation
is grievous. That fellow is mad."

There was another huff from Lady Oriel.

"Indeed, Shingles, he is that and more,"
Lady Eleanor agreed.

Shingleton continued. "He arrived early
this morning with some story about being
an artist sent by His Lordship. Then he
began locking us all away until it was only
him and Lady Oriel above stairs. I've been
half out of my mind with worry."

"Yes, well, Tiberius will be here soon,"
Lady Eleanor assured him. "All will be
well."

At this, Madame Sybille who sat off to
one side by herself, lost in her grief, made a
grand *harrumph,* and then began a long,
loud soliloquy in French, ranting and raging for some time, before she even realized
she was speaking French.

"My goodness, I don't believe we were taught half of those words, Eleanor," Lady Oriel remarked. "Whatever is all this fuss about?"

"The diamonds, Oriel," Lady Eleanor told her, a note of resignation in her voice.

"The diamonds?" Oriel shook her head. "I told that horrible fellow that the Three Graces would never be painted in diamonds. Would ruin the pastoral theme of the painting." She huffed again and went back to staring off into space.

"Those diamonds are mine," Madame Sybille hissed. "Mine."

"Yours?" Lady Eleanor inquired with all the imperious airs of a queen. "How is that?"

And so Madame Sybille told them.

Roxley had ridden much as Harriet and her party had, hard and fast for Marshom Court, with Moss and Batty clinging to their seats across from him.

Oh, Harry, I should never have let you come along. He'd never forgive himself if anything happened to her. He hadn't even had a chance to apologize to her for not rescuing her earlier from Fieldgate — and then he'd all but exploded at her, sent her off in fury.

Only because he'd been mad at himself

and how close he'd come to losing her.

To distract himself, he began to explain the layout of the house, but Galton's boon companion, Batty, waved him off. "I know Marshom Court well. My dear boy, I've been watching over it and your aunt nigh on twenty years now. Ever since you went off to Eton."

Roxley paused and all of a sudden made the connection that had been eluding him since Poggs had cornered him at Lady Knolles's soirée.

Sir Bartholomew Keswick. Aunt Oriel's suitor.

"Batty," he whispered. "I know who you are." *Now.*

"Yes, at your service," he said with a flamboyant wave of his hand and tip of his hat.

It seemed Roxley owed his Aunt Oriel an apology. "I thought my aunt had made you up." All these years he'd just assumed her Sir Bartholomew was nothing more than a figment of her very fertile imagination, like so many of the fabrications of her fractured sensibilities.

"No, no, I am real," he advised. "Oriel's Sir Bartholomew, and Ophelia's dear Batty. Magnificent ladies, your aunts. Both of them."

Roxley had heard Aunt Oriel called many things, most often "mad," "cursed," and "nicked in the nob," but magnificent in her madness was not one of them.

For there it was, she wasn't quite right. And it had happened when she'd trusted the wrong man in her youth. Rather than discard her as many families would have when her young life was shattered, his great-grandfather had brought her home to Marshom Court and given her free rein over the grand house, to live her life. As Oriel when she wanted, or as Ophelia, the personality she had created to hide behind when the memories of what had happened or what she had lost became too difficult to bear.

Roxley knew her no other way. The two of them, Oriel and Ophelia, had been there all his life, and most of his father's, so to Roxley they were two people.

Yet her dual existence had given new credence to the expression "mad as a Marshom."

A designation he would most likely claim if this insane plan failed.

The carriage turned and as it did, Roxley didn't even need to look. *Home.* He could feel it the moment the wheels crunched down upon the long drive.

Harry, I'm almost there. Be patient.

But this was Harry he was talking about.

The carriage pulled to a stop, and the three of them got out. "He won't know the difference," Batty assured Roxley, handing over the pouch. "He'd need a jeweler to know these stones aren't the real ones. And where the devil would he find one out here?"

"My father was Monsieur Bassanges." Madame Sybille paused for a moment and looked around as if this alone should give her some sort of standing, but when no one seemed to recognize the name, she huffed a bit and continued. "He was one of the jewelers who created the Queen's Necklace. When it was lost, he and his partner were ruined. We all were."

Harriet exchanged a wary glance with Lady Eleanor. Now they realized just how Madame Sybille was connected to all this.

And how much she had invested. How much she had lost. And what she hoped to gain.

"When the revolution came, it didn't matter that we were living in ruin, my father had been the queen's jeweler and that was all it took for them to arrest us. Flore was so small, I had to carry her into the prison." Her eyes closed as if she were fighting back an entire legion of grief, but when her lashes fluttered open, there was nothing but raw fury in her eyes. "Then *he* came."

"Mereworth," Harriet supplied.

She nodded. "Yes, but I did not know that was his true name until today." After a few moments, she continued, "He arrived not long after that murderous rabble cut the queen's head off. They had already taken my mother and father, but they had left us. Me and Flore. He bribed our way out —"

Harriet glanced over at Lady Eleanor and the lady shrugged slightly.

"— he promised much. Claimed he knew who had half the necklace. Half was better than nothing, he said. I knew the stones — I had helped my father select their placement." She glanced down at her hands. "He said I had a talent for the work."

"Then you would know the stones better than anyone," Harriet muttered aloud, seeing what Mereworth had.

"Of course I would," Sybille snapped back. "I can still see them. They were the most perfect diamonds my father had ever procured. A necklace fit for a queen." Her chin arched up as if she were to carry their weight around her neck.

"So what did Mereworth expect you to do?" Lady Eleanor said, lending a sensible, commanding air to the woman's rising tenor.

"For a time he let us be. We had a small house outside of Bath and we lived a quiet, private life. But then he returned and made his demands. He wanted Flore."

"Miss Murray," Lady Eleanor prompted.

"Yes." This came spitting out. "*Miss Murray.* He transformed her. She was trained, sculpted, and arranged at that horrid school to be the perfect bait. A lure. And in the process, he destroyed her."

Harriet couldn't argue with that. Not that she'd ever been all that impressed with a Bath education.

"He promised to restore us. With the diamonds, we could start a new life wherever we wanted. All Flore had to do was entice Roxley to find them." Her gaze drifted off and then suddenly snapped back to clarity, focusing on Harriet. "And it all would have worked if it weren't for you —"

"Me?" Harriet edged back, for the woman was starting to frighten her.

"Yes, you," Sybille said, her voice rising once again. "You turned his head. Lured him away."

Whatever was it about these diamonds that had everyone associated with them going short a sheet? Harriet slanted a glance

444

over at Lady Eleanor and the woman was looking not at Madame Sybille but just over the woman's shoulder — where a large silver salver sat. The sort a butler might use to carry up wine bottles. Then the old girl shot a poignant glance at Harriet.

And the plan behind Lady Eleanor's steady gaze lay out before her. There would be no escape with this madwoman at their heels.

So they needed to silence her.

For the time being.

"— he promised us the diamonds," Sybille was once again ranting. "We were to have a new beginning."

"And you believed him?" Lady Eleanor said, adding a bit of a *tsk, tsk,* as if she'd never heard anything so foolish.

"Of course, I didn't," Sybille told her, her focus now on the lady and not Harriet.

Taking the opportunity afforded her, Harriet moved around a shelf and along the wall, sliding her slippered feet across the stone floor.

"Then whyever would you agree to any of this?" Lady Eleanor persisted, holding the woman's rabid attention.

"Because he was useful," Sybille spat out. "And when the diamonds were discovered, he would no longer be so." Her sneer suggested she wasn't too far above the rabble that had killed the poor queen.

"Whatever would you have done then?" Lady Eleanor inquired.

"You might return to France, I imagine," Lady Oriel offered. "It is lovely this time of year. Do you remember, sister, when Papa took us? It was in April, wasn't it?"

"France! Never," Sybille told them with such vehemence that the housemaid crossed herself and began to weep.

"Then where?" Lady Eleanor asked, catching the woman's attention again, while Harriet continued to ease her way around the wine cellar, until she was right behind Madame Sybille.

"Spain, perhaps. Copenhagen," the woman was saying, giving a very Gallic sort of shrug. "Anywhere I could be a jeweler again. Flore would work in the front for she has a way about her." Then she caught herself. "Flore," she sobbed. But her grief lasted only a moment. "I will have what is mine by right. He promised. He promised me." Once again her gaze was unfocused and far away.

"Men make many promises they have no intentions of keeping, my dear," Lady Oriel told her sadly.

"The diamonds were never paid for. They

were stolen from my father. And when I get out of here —" She rose up, a towering, raging bull of a woman, her madness swirling around her like a grand court dress. In her hand was a knife — the sort used to cut the wax off a wine bottle.

When she'd picked it up, Harriet had no idea. Not that it mattered. It was a knife nonetheless.

"I will kill him. I'll kill you all for what you have done. I will make you all —"

Harriet had heard enough. She caught up the salver and with all her might brought it down on the woman's head.

Clunk.

Madame Sybille wavered, her unfocused gaze searching for something, someone to lash out at, and then she collapsed, a puppet lost without its strings.

"Horrible story," Lady Eleanor said, getting up and brushing off her skirts.

"I rather liked it," Lady Oriel told her. "So very tragic."

Harriet was already on her way to the door, pulling one of the pins left over from last night's arrangement of her hair.

One down. One to go.

"Sir," she said to the butler. "Is there an extra key?"

"No, miss. Just the one he took." He being Mereworth.

"Good. Then he thinks we're trapped." Harriet knelt down before the door and studied the lock for a moment.

"I take it we aren't?" Lady Eleanor asked.

"Not if I have any say in the matter," Harriet told her as she quickly and effectively opened the door, just as she had once before when Sir Mauris had locked her and Daphne and Tabitha inside their room in London.

And countless times when she wanted to annoy her brothers.

Besides, on the other side of that door — somewhere, somehow — was Roxley. And the very thought made her heart beat that much faster.

Roxley walked alone up the steps and into Marshom Court.

The stillness of the house had his every nerve on edge. Nor did it do his heart any good that his first sight was that of a woman's body crumpled in a corner.

Harriet! The air rushed from his lungs as he rushed to her side, pulling her over.

But it wasn't Harry. Relief flooded through him, but still, the sight of the girl's wide blue eyes stared vacantly at the ceiling was haunting.

"Miss Murray," he gasped. Then after a moment, he reached out and closed her eyes.

Whatever she'd done, whatever secrets had led her to this place, Roxley would be hard-pressed to believe she deserved such a fate. Justice perhaps at the hands of a magistrate. Lawful justice.

He looked up and around the foyer, searching for clues, but he knew what he was looking at.

This was nothing less than murder.

Murder. His chest tightened again, and he was all the much more frantic to find Harriet and his aunts.

He rose, and even as he did he heard the voice he'd been expecting.

"Roxley, you've made good time."

Mereworth. So he hadn't been mistaken.

He'd suspected as much since he'd gone to question Mrs. Plumley. The schoolmistress had been less than forthcoming in her answers, but when Roxley had threatened to bring in the Home Office for a complete investigation, she'd been a bit more helpful. She'd described "Mr. Murray" in detail, save the man she'd painted hadn't been the brutish figure of Aloysius Murray, but of another.

And then there had been Moss's mention

of a beryl ring.

Like the blood red stone that winked on Mereworth's hand even now.

"You aren't surprised," he commented as he confidently strolled forward.

"No," Roxley told him, shaking his head slightly and turning around to face his former mentor.

"Good. I would have been a bit disappointed if you hadn't figured it out. I trained you after all." Mereworth nodded at the bag in Roxley's hand. "You've brought them, I assume."

"Yes." Roxley's gaze swept the room for any other signs of violence, but there were none. Save Miss Murray.

At least not that he could see.

"They're safe," Mereworth assured him. "For the time being. Now let's discuss the diamonds."

"We need a diversion," Harriet whispered over her shoulder as she peered around the corner into the foyer, where Roxley faced Lord Mereworth.

"Like in *Miss Darby's Daring Dilemma,*" Lady Oriel suggested.

Harriet perked up. "You read Miss Darby?"

Lady Oriel nodded. "But of course! Who

wouldn't?"

Lady Eleanor nodded in agreement, but hers was more of a nod of guilty pleasure than her sister's blatant enthusiasm. "That particular diversion would never work. We haven't a legion of fusiliers."

Lady Oriel looked overly crestfallen at this, and then brightened as if she might have one handy and then frowned again.

Once Harriet had gotten the door to the wine cellar opened, Lady Eleanor had dispatched one of the maids, a fleet young girl from the nearby village, to run for help, while keeping Shingleton and the footmen to assist them. The rest of the staff she'd sent on to safety.

Lady Oriel had refused to be shuttled off, her eyes bright with the excitement of an adventure. "Wait until Ophelia discovers what I've done." The lady quivered with joy.

Lady Eleanor shook her head. "I doubt she will be amused," she pointed out, as she took a peek at the situation before them. "As long as he has that pistol pointed at Tiberius, there is naught we can do."

Harriet stilled. "Which pistol?"

"Miss Murray's. Don't you recall — he picked it up after she fell."

Miss Murray's pistol.

That gave her an idea. "This is exactly like

Miss Darby's Daring Dilemma."

Lady Oriel preened at having her suggestion vindicated. "Yes, but dear girl, whoever you are, we can't allow that terrible artist to shoot Tiberius. That just wouldn't do."

"No one is going to get shot," Harriet said, as she looked as closely as she could at the pistol Mereworth held.

It had to be the one she'd disarmed. There had been only one pistol hidden in the trunk.

Miss Murray must have been lying about having two pistols.

Just as she'd lied about everything else.

Harriet drew a deep breath. There was only one way to find out. For Mereworth could shoot only one person and then he'd be disarmed. And more importantly, stopped.

And while she hadn't an entire regiment of fusiliers behind her, the more targets that Mereworth must choose between, the more unlikely he was to win.

She went to walk out into the foyer, but Lady Eleanor caught hold of her. "Are you mad?"

"Indeed, I do believe so," she said, gently removing Lady Eleanor's grasp and walking boldly out into the fray.

"I rather like her," Lady Oriel told her

sister. "Who is she again?"

Eleanor's brow furrowed deeply. "If she lives, she'll be Tiberius's countess."

Oriel shook her head. "Only if she passes muster."

"I think she's about to," Lady Eleanor said, following Harriet as bold as brass.

Roxley's heart tripped at the sight of Harriet. *She was alive.*

Then he realized exactly what she was doing. And most likely why she was doing it.

Oh, good heavens, he was going to kill her. What the devil was she doing walking into Mereworth's path as bold as a London strumpet?

"Ho, there, Roxley!" she called out, as calmly as if he'd just arrived for a social call.

Mereworth whirled around. "Miss Hathaway! How did you —"

Again, the polite smile. "Truly? You have to ask, my lord?" Harriet shook her head. "Apparently you were under the impression that Chaunce was the only Hathaway capable of picking a lock." She took up a position in a corner opposite Roxley's. "Who do you think taught him?"

"What are you doing?" Roxley demanded.

"Saving you," she replied.

"Ah, there you are, my dear Tiberius!" Lady Eleanor came down the steps and into the foyer, taking up a post in another corner. "Shall I ring Shingleton for tea?"

Before anyone could say anything, Lady Oriel made her entrance. "No bother, I've already done so." She spared a glance at Mereworth. "You, sir, are an imposter!" She continued to walk across the foyer, taking the sole remaining corner. "Tiberius, this man is no artist. Why, he blushed when I posed for him. One might think he'd never seen the female form before." She went to slip off her dressing gown, but suddenly all the players were in accordance.

"No!" came the cry in unison.

Lady Oriel shrugged. "No one appreciates art these days."

Mereworth, now surrounded, circled like a tiger, watching all of them and ready to lash out at the least provocation. "What is this?"

Miss Darby's Daring Dilemma," Harriet replied. When the baron made no reply, she smiled. "No? Haven't read it? How unfortunate. For then you would see that you are defeated and that it would be best for you to put down that pistol."

"I have come for the diamonds," he told her, pistol extended toward her. "And I will have them."

"Dear me," Lady Oriel protested. Mereworth moved to face her. "But I don't recall that there were diamonds in that book. I think you have this confused with *Miss Darby and the Curse of the Pharaoh's Diamond.*"

Harriet edged forward, as did Lady Eleanor.

Mereworth's eyes narrowed and Roxley didn't think he'd ever seen a man look so desperate. As if he were willing to do anything.

And what that might be, Roxley didn't want to know. So he stepped forward as well into whatever mad plan Harriet had up her sleeve.

As if in answer, two of the footmen appeared at stairs, another from the old wing and a third at the new wing. Then, despite their promises to stay well out of this business, Batty and Moss came through the front door.

Harriet smiled in triumph. "Terrible dilemma, Lord Mereworth. Surrounded on all sides." She stepped forward.

"Yes, my dear, so it seems," he said. "But I have the advantage. I have the pistol."

Roxley didn't like this, not in the least. He could see it all unfolding before his eyes.

There was one shot in Mereworth's pistol, and after that, he was outnumbered.

But it was the devil's own choice — if he shot, who would he choose?

"You are still ruined, Roxley. Ruined beyond repair." Mereworth chuckled. "But give me what I want, and I will see what I can do."

Taking a furtive glance at Miss Murray's example, Roxley had no desire to see anyone else die over a bag full of diamonds. He took another step forward. "Then take these and leave," he told the man, holding them out.

"But dear Tiberius, what are you thinking?" Lady Oriel protested. "You cannot mean to —" A sharp glance from all the rest of the parties stopped her words. Especially when Lord Mereworth pointed the gun at her.

"You have something to say, Lady Oriel?" he demanded.

The lady looked at the pistol and shook her head slightly. "Just what I said earlier: Beauty would never be painted wearing diamonds," she told him. "So very gauche." She sniffed and tucked her dainty nose in the air.

"Give them to me," Mereworth said, moving the pistol to point at Harriet. "Give them to me now or I shall shoot her."

Harriet looked at him, and Roxley could hear her as clearly as if she had spoken. *Trust me, Roxley. Trust me.*

And she was right. Mereworth had only one way out, and that was with a loaded pistol. The moment he fired, he'd be overtaken. Even as mad as the fellow was, Roxley had no doubt that like a rat off a sinking frigate, Mereworth knew his escape depended on his having a loaded pistol.

Roxley smiled and then overturned the bag. As the last bit of sun peeked through the second story windows above, the light hit the diamonds as they tumbled free, illuminating their brilliance before they scattered across the floor.

Mereworth's face turned to rage as he scrambled to gather up his long-sought treasure. "Stay back," he threatened. "Stay back."

Then came a chilling voice at the top of the stairs. "Bah! You are such a fool. Can you not hear them?"

Madame Sybille stood framed in the door, disheveled and angry. Her scornful gaze swept over the glittering array and she scoffed. "Paste," she repeated. "They have tricked you with worthless bits of glass. They rattle like trash."

Mereworth looked at the handful he held

and then back up at Roxley. "Paste?"

"Afraid so, my good man," Roxley told him, and he gave a nod to the footmen and they began to rush forward.

Mereworth roared as he rose, his arm lashing out, the pistol aimed at Harriet. Roxley had only a second to react, so he threw himself in front of her.

But where there should have been a retort and anguished cries, there was naught but a click of the hammer as it struck the plate.

The plate missing its flint.

"I knew it!" Harriet cried out triumphantly, even as Roxley looked down at his chest, still half expecting to find a hole in his waistcoat.

But not even Miss Darby could have foretold what happened next.

"*Batârd!*" Sybille cried. "Lying, ruinous fiend. You took everything from me." She wrenched one of the pikes off the wall and came rushing forward with it.

And didn't stop until it was buried in Mereworth's chest.

CHAPTER 14

But a life of love and happiness? That is worth all manner of struggles and effort to discover. Of this, I am certain.

Prince Sanjit to Miss Darby
from Miss Darby's Terrible Temptation

The next day

As twilight drew upon the surrounding countryside, Harriet wandered across the wide lawn of Marshom Court toward the lake that could be seen from what the Marshoms referred to as the "new wing."

New being a relative term in the long history of Marshom Court.

The past twenty-four hours had been almost too much to bear. After Madame Sybille had vented her revenge on Lord Mereworth, she'd been subdued and locked away. The magistrate had arrived with reinforcements, brought by the maid who'd been sent for help.

A messenger had been sent to Lord Howers, and Harriet knew that Mr. Hotchkin and Chaunce were due in the morning. All that was missing were Lady Essex and Miss Manx, and Harriet wouldn't put it past the intrepid spinster to arrive, if only so she didn't have to hear all the reports from Lord Poggs via his gossipy *maman.*

But it was Roxley who concerned Harriet the most. The murder of Miss Murray and the death of Lord Mereworth had left him shaken. While he'd handled all the particulars, his haunted expression tore at Harriet's heart. Especially when Miss Murray's body was taken away.

"I wouldn't have wished that on her," he'd said to no one in particular as the coroner carried the still form out amid her sister's mad cries of grief as the magistrate escorted her to her own fate.

Harriet agreed. She had wished a thousand things heaped down on Miss Murray, but killed in spite? No, never that.

Lady Eleanor had taken over shortly after, seeing to it that everyone was given rooms and that suppers were sent up.

Even today, it hadn't been until tea that nearly everyone had gathered. The conversations had been strained and carefully polite.

Worst of all, Roxley had been missing.

Awash in her own anguish and tired of sitting in her room, Harriet had fled the house, the calm waters of the lake offering a solace in contrast to the unanswered questions that plagued her.

Did Roxley still love her?

As she got down to the water's edge, she tossed a stone out as far as she could throw it, and watched the ripples spread out in wide circles.

"On occasion, our lake does grant wishes," came a soft whisper.

Harriet whirled around. "Lady Oriel, I didn't see you there."

The woman sitting on the bench nearby shook her head. "No, no, dear, I'm Lady Ophelia. Have we been introduced?"

"Um. Well. Yes. I'm Harriet Hathaway."

"Are you related to Sir George?" But before Harriet could reply, the lady smiled. "But of course you are. You have the look of a Hathaway. Such a lovely family. So very lively."

Harriet nodded in agreement. She was quite certain this Lady Ophelia was wearing the exact same gown Lady Oriel had been wearing at tea not two hours earlier — right down to the earbobs and scuffed-up slippers. "I thought Lady Ophelia was away," she said, glancing up at the house to see if there was a carriage or perhaps luggage waiting to be carried inside.

The lady smiled wanly. "I was in a sense. They tell people that I'm away to spare my feelings." The woman smoothed her skirts and sighed. "I know I am not quite right, and that Tiberius and Essex and Eleanor have kept me here for my own good, but oh, how I long to travel. Oriel has her arts, but when it is my turn, I imagine myself in London again. Mayhap even Paris." She looked up at the house as well. "Thank goodness my dear Batty comes to call often. His stories do renew me."

Harriet nodded at this, finally understanding what Lady Eleanor and Sir Bartholomew had been avoiding at tea when she'd asked about Lady Ophelia. And why Lady Essex always spoke of her younger sister in such guarded tones.

She'd just assumed Ophelia and Oriel were twins like Lady Essex and Eleanor, but now she saw the truth. They were one and the same. She glanced again at the lady and smiled.

"Ah, so you do understand," Lady Ophelia said warmly. "And you don't mind?"

Harriet shook her head. Who was she to judge? The Hathaways were often looked upon a bit askance for their own eccentrici-

462

ties. Good heavens, her parents' infamous courtship should have put them beyond the bounds of proper society for several generations.

Had, in some circles.

"Tell me of London, my dear," Lady Ophelia asked, inviting her to sit down on the bench beside her. "You were there for the Season, weren't you?"

Harriet nodded, and proceeded to tell the lady all about Tabitha and Daphne's romances, of the various bits of gossip that she thought Lady Ophelia might enjoy, and of the sights that she loved most — the marbles at the British Museum, the Tower — as well as the house party at Owle Park.

"Every house party should have a decent scandal," the lady observed as Harriet related the tale of Daphne's runaway marriage.

"Indeed," Harriet agreed, avoiding any mention of her own improprieties. Truly, was it a scandal if no one knew about it? She stole a glance at the house, where the sun was setting behind it, illuminating the butter-colored stone in cozy light.

Yet, someone else did know about that night. And he was ever so close, and yet, he seemed so very far away.

She couldn't help feeling in her heart of

hearts that something was still wrong. Was it her mistake with Fieldgate? Would the scandal of that night be too much for Roxley to overcome? Not to mention the melee of gossip that would come out of not one, but two murders . . .

"Whatever is it, child?" Lady Ophelia asked, reaching over and laying her hand atop Harriet's. "What troubles you?"

"I . . . that is . . ."

"Ah, Tiberius," she said with a knowing smile. "Troublesome scamp."

Troublesome rake would be more like it, Harriet mused, stealing another glance at the house.

"Miss Hathaway —" Lady Ophelia began.

"Yes, my lady?"

"Whatever did that awful man mean when he said that Tiberius is ruined?"

"You heard that?"

"Yes, I fear so." She glanced up at Harriet. "I know Oriel is most distressed."

Harriet pursed her lips. Whatever was she to say? It hardly seemed her place.

"Oh, come now, you can tell me, since he was threatening us all."

"Roxley is all but ruined — apparently at Lord Mereworth's hand."

The lady's eyes narrowed. "Ruined?" She shook her head. "Why that is ridiculous. A

Marshom is never ruined. Oh, a bit extended, perhaps, but ruined? No."

Harriet hesitated, in the face of the lady's conviction, but she was too practical to lie to her. "I fear it is true — there were some investments gone wrong, then Mr. Ludwick, Roxley's man of business, stole a large sum of the earl's money and has disappeared."

She left off the part about the debts and vowels Mr. Murray held. Perhaps they were as fictional as his daughter.

At least Harriet hoped so.

"You must help him, my dear," Lady Ophelia said, getting up.

Harriet rose as well. "I'm not sure I can," she admitted. "I haven't any —"

The lady stopped her with an imperious wave of her hand. "You love him — I can see that — and that will suffice." She leaned over and picked up two stones, handing one to Harriet, nodding at her to follow suit as she tossed hers into the lake. "You have everything you need to save Roxley," she assured Harriet as they watched the ripples spread and collide. "Go to him."

"Your sisters have said much the same thing," Harriet replied. "But I can't see how it is true. I'm no heiress —"

Lady Ophelia perked up at the word, but then having taken in all that Harriet had said, the lady's hopes flagged a bit. "Pity that," she remarked, then she straightened. "When you arrived, you had Pug, did you not?"

"Pug?" Harriet could hardly see how a battered ceramic dog could save the day.

"Yes. I swear you had his traveling box. The one with Davinia's shrine. You were carrying it when you came into the house. I remember that distinctly, for it is always wonderful to have Pug home. Where he belongs, mind you, but don't tell Essex I said that."

"No, my lady," Harriet told her. "And yes, we did bring Pug and his box. Lady Eleanor insisted."

The lady looped her arm with Harriet's. "Excellent. It is time Tiberius gained his true inheritance. And all you must do is to keep Pug close. He'll guide the way."

"Keep Pug close," Harriet muttered to herself as she made her way down a long corridor. What utter nonsense, she mused as she looked down at the box with its battered figurine and some old bits and bobs and a pair of beloved miniatures.

Beloved.

Harriet paused. The word lodged in her heart. *Beloved.* That, she understood. All too well. As impractical and foolish as it was to cling to, she supposed it was all she had.

Her love for Roxley.

She looked up and realized she was at the turn Lady Ophelia had described: *Take a left at the gallery and continue to the end of the hall. You'll find Roxley in the large chamber on the left.*

Yet all the rooms she passed appeared to be bedchambers.

Lady Ophelia hadn't sent her up to Roxley's . . .

Harriet came to an abrupt halt before an open door and looked in.

Why, yes, she had.

"Harry!" Roxley called out, bounding up from a chair near a fireplace. "What are you doing —" He caught her by the arm and tugged her into the room.

His room. His bedchamber, to be exact. The large, ornately carved bed gave it away rather quickly.

That wicked old girl had sent Harriet to the earl's bedchamber!

Harriet didn't know whether to chide Lady Ophelia like Lady Essex might, or hug her.

For here she was finally and truly alone with Roxley.

"What are you doing?" he asked as he closed the door. "My aunts would be horrified if they found you . . . us . . ."

"It was your aunt who sent me," Harriet confessed, standing in the middle of the room and doing her best not to look at the bed. "Your Aunt Ophelia."

"Ophelia?" Roxley took a step back. "Ah, so you've met Ophelia."

"I did indeed," she chided. "Good heavens, Roxley, you could have told me about them. Oriel and Ophelia."

"I thought you'd ride for Scotland once you realized —"

"Just how mad your family is?" She laughed. "You obviously haven't met my Cousin Verbena. Besides, after all the time you've spent at the Pottage, you think a little thing like your aunt's . . . aunt's . . ."

"Eccentricities?" he suggested.

"Good heavens, Roxley," Harriet exclaimed, moving farther into the room and setting Pug's box down on the chair. "So, she's a bit mad."

"A bit?"

She turned around and laughed. "So she's wrong in the upper story, but you've met my family."

"I rather like your family." His quietly said words tugged at her.

"And I adore yours," she said, feeling a bit stubborn for no reason whatsoever. "Your Aunt Essex is a dear. Lady Eleanor, a surprising delight. And your Aunt Oriel or Ophelia, or whoever she desires to be, is a treasure."

Roxley barked a laugh. "Truly, you adore Aunt Essex?"

Harriet nodded. "Ever since the day she informed me that proper ladies do not play with suits of armor."

"Her scolding endured her to you?" His stance was one of disbelief.

Harriet's eyes misted a bit. "Yes," she said ever so passionately. "She was the first person I ever met who thought I might be a proper lady."

And there it was. Being a Hathaway had always meant being able to run the fastest, shoot the straightest, ride over the hedges like the devil was nipping at your heels.

But no one had ever thought of Harriet as proper. Or possibly proper.

Until Lady Essex.

And then, ever so many years later, there was Roxley. He'd looked at her one day with a glance that said, *I know,* and he'd stolen her heart.

But right now, the way he was looking at her, as if she was tearing him in half, didn't bode well. "Roxley, what is it?"

"Harry, I'm all rolled up."

She shrugged. "Yes, I know that."

"But it's over — there is nothing I can do. With Mereworth dead, there is nothing left to be done. Whatever he's managed can't be undone, not now." Roxley shook his head. "You must see what that means."

"But certainly Mr. Murray can be made to understand —"

"Murray is dead as well, Harry."

Dead? Her face must have shown the shock of the news. "How?"

"Murdered."

A terrible thought came into her head. "They don't think you —"

"No, no, nothing like that. Besides, we were in Bath —"

"Mereworth?"

He nodded. "Likely. He had something over Murray. Something terrible. But now there will be no way of proving it. Not that it matters. His estate will demand the debts be paid immediately." He walked over to a small table beside his chair and picked up his drink, taking a swallow.

She went over and took the glass from his hands and set it down. "Roxley, I can help."

He shook his head. "I can't ask you to be part of this. I'm . . . I'm releasing you,

Harry. It's probably best if you go. For your own sake."

Harriet blinked. What the devil was he suggesting? Go? Leave him? Was he mad? After all they'd been through?

They. Not him, but they. Together. Good heavens, when would he ever learn?

She caught him by the lapels of his jacket and gave him a shake. "Release me? How dare you!"

He managed to look affronted. "I'm being honorable here."

"Honorable? Were you honorable at Owle Park? Or in your aunt's library? Bah, I say. Bah and humbug to your demmed honor!"

"Harry, you'd be living in thin straits for the rest of your life. With my aunts. I repeat: With. My. Aunts." He raked his hand through his hair. "I don't even know how to tell them."

"Roxley, we've already established that I love your aunts. As for the rest of it —" Harriet sighed. "I've lived in 'thin straits' all my life. You've seen how my family makes do. And none of that has ever mattered. Not when you have a family around you. Your aunts love you. Desperately so. And they know none of this was your making."

"Yes, that might be, but it was mine to fix. And I've failed them." He shook his head and pulled away from her. "As I've failed you."

"Oh, what utter rot." Again, Harriet tugged him back so he faced her. "Can't you see how it works with us? That when we are apart, it all falls to pieces, but when we are together, how right it is. How grand. We fit, you and I. We work together. Only together. And if you could just believe for one more night, that we deserve, nay, that we must be together —"

"But Harry —"

She shook her head and covered his mouth. "No, Roxley, you will listen to me. It is just this one night we must work together. And then tomorrow, we'll do it again. And then the next. That is how love works. That faith, that staying together. Whatever would you want to accomplish without me at your side?"

He drew back a bit as her words finally pierced that stubborn hide of his. "Nothing," he said softly. "There is nothing I want more, but —"

"No, you can't argue this. I won't hear of it. You love me. I love you. You asked me to marry you and I am saying yes." She worked her way right up against him, placing his arms around her and settling in against his chest, her head atop his heart. "Yes, Roxley.

There it is."

"You didn't say yes before," he pointed out.

"I think that my saying yes now when you haven't a feather to fly with would show you the depth of my affections."

He laughed a little, the sound rumbling up from his chest. "One could argue it shows the depths of your madness." With one hand, he brushed away the errant strands of her hair that were falling loose around her face.

His touch was like grace itself. A promise and vow all in one. "Together, Harry. But I daresay, you'll change your mind in the morning."

"We'll see come morning." She tipped her chin up so he could see what she desired most between now and then. "But if you make this night unforgettable, you'll never be rid of me."

Roxley knew this was madness. He hadn't a rag to his name. He should be setting her aside. Letting Harriet go so she could find someone worthy of her.

But the moment her lips touched his, a sense, an understanding of what she'd been trying to tell him, ignited inside him.

For when he was with her, his life did

make sense. It always had with her close at hand. From the first time they'd met, when she'd twined her chubby fingers around his hand and led him outside into a world he'd only imagined.

Harry. With her unforgiving temper. With her practical sensibilities. With her ridiculous romance novels and Miss Darby quotations. She was a bundle of contradictions and light.

His light. And as he drew her closer, he saw the truth of it. Felt it in the warmth of her body, the steady rhythm of her heart. Harriet Hathaway. His heart and his only desire.

His one and only wish.

He sealed a silent vow, to love her always, to the end of his days, with a deep, passionate kiss.

Harriet sensed the change in him almost immediately. His kiss deepened, his tongue easing past her lips and tantalizing her with promises of what was to come.

For the rest of their lives.

Her hands slid beneath his jacket, sliding the wool from his shoulders, marveling at the muscles beneath, letting her fingers trail over them, knowing only too well what they would feel like naked. The hard strength, the crisp triangle of hair on his chest, the muscled ripples of his stomach.

Her lips sought his out, because she had to taste him, have part of him inside her, even if it was just his lip, his tongue, which she suckled, even as she tugged at his shirt.

Madness. It erupted inside her as he kissed her. Yes, this was madness. But she longed for him. Was incomplete without him.

Touch me, Roxley. Touch me, she wanted to shout.

But she didn't need to, for his hand was on her gown, pulling it up, the hem rising quickly exposing her legs, her bottom, his fingers trailing over her exposed skin, leaving fire in their path.

Their mouths joined in a deep kiss, tongues sliding over one another in a manic, welcoming frenzy. Quickly, her gown slipped off, her petticoat and shift quickly following.

Then in quick succession, Roxley's shirt and breeches were added to the pile.

In a tumble, they fell naked onto the mattress.

A bed, Harriet marveled. *They were in a bed.*

Roxley laughed. "Yes, this is far more comfortable than my aunt's desk."

"I believe I still have a bruise from the inkwell," she teased back.

"Allow me to inspect your injuries," he replied, rolling her over on her stomach and kissing his way down her back, a wet, heated path that left her shivering. "Ah, yes. A most grievous inkwell injury," he told her, running his tongue over the spot.

Harriet giggled. It was all so ridiculous, so deliciously wicked. So very Roxley.

Having examined her, he flipped her again, so he looked up at her, his mouth set in that sardonic smile that teased at her heart, his hooded glance full of promises.

His next kiss was a whisper. "Open for me." It blew over her, teasing at the soft pink folds of her apex, wet and hot all at once. "Open for me, Kitten," he teased, even as his finger drew a line from the top of her curls slowly and tantalizing down to the very opening, brushing against that taut nub that left her quivering, and ever so willing.

She couldn't do anything but give in to him. Whyever wouldn't she?

He growled softly and then came closer, his lips tracing the path that his finger had made. Harriet sucked in a deep breath as his tongue touched her. There. Drawing a slow, lazy circle around her. And then again, laving over her, kissing her, probing her, lapping at her, until she was rising up, the sheets wound into her fisted hands and she was trying to breathe even as the pleasure began to wash over her, rushed at her from all directions.

"Roxley, I'm —" And then she came, hard and fast, lost in a world of pleasure.

He looked up at her again, this time the smile was a grin. "Yes, I suppose you did."

"Hmm," she purred, and reached for him, drawing him up, so she could kiss him, feel him atop her, his cock hard against her thighs. "More," she managed.

And that, Roxley happily gave her.

Keep Pug close.

Harriet awoke sometime later, thinking that someone had called out those very words. Yet the room was empty — save for her and Roxley — the only bit of light, the glow of the coals in the fireplace.

Beside her, Roxley stirred slightly and she smiled as his toes stroked her bare calf. It was intimate and silly and perfect all at once.

Keep Pug close.

The words nudged at her.

Whatever had Lady Ophelia meant by that?

And for that matter, where the devil was the wretched figurine?

She slipped from the bed and looked around, finding the box sitting precariously on the edge of the grand chair by the fireplace.

"There you are," she whispered. "You are worse than Mr. Muggins."

She went to catch up the box and it slipped, and for a second, she thought it was going to crash to the floor, but in the last moment, she caught it, saving Pug from a smashing end.

"Dear heavens," Harriet managed as she peeked inside the box to see if the china dog had survived. "Lady Essex would have my hide if anything happened to you."

Pug's crooked eyes stared back up at her, accusingly.

Harriet shook her head and carried the box over to the bed, settling back in beside Roxley and arranging the contents on the nightstand.

Pug, the miniatures of Roxley and his father. Harriet smiled at the resemblance between the earl and his father. No wonder Davinia had been wildly in love with him — her Roxley had been a handsome devil as well.

The shell, the bit of ribbon, the stub of

candle, the little trinkets all went on display, and Harriet smiled as she got it all arranged just as Lady Eleanor had done.

"Whatever are you doing over there," Roxley murmured sleepily as he rolled over, catching Harriet as he came around and pulling her beneath him.

She was rather certain he was about to make love to her again — well, he certainly was ready — but then his gaze lifted to the nightstand and he stilled.

"Good God! Where did that come from?"

Harriet craned her head to look at the display. "What, this? That was why I got up in the first place." She smiled. "Not that you gave me any time to explain."

He grinned at her and then reached out to touch the miniature of his father. "That is exactly as I remember him."

"Do you know what the other pieces signify?"

He shook his head. "I asked my mother once, but she said that love has its own secrets. And these were hers. They meant the world to her. And here all these years, I thought this lost."

Harriet reached up and brushed a strand of his hair back from his face. "Your aunts have kept this part of her with them — in a hidden compartment in Pug's traveling box."

"Pug!" he snorted with nothing less than disdain. "I have loathed that dog for years and now I find he's been keeping secrets from me." He spoke directly to the figurine, wagging a finger at him. "Don't think this improves my opinion of you!"

Harriet giggled. "It is just a china dog."

"You wouldn't think so by the way my aunts squabble so over him." Then he glanced down at Harriet, and his gaze turned more wicked by the moment.

"Whatever am I doing arguing over that bad piece of china when I have the most beautiful woman in the world in my bed?"

"Most beautiful —" she scoffed back, playfully struggling to get out of his arms. "You are mad."

Roxley caught hold of her and the game was on, both of them wrestling back and forth, kissing each other to distract the other, a touch here, a stroke there, until Roxley caught her around the waist and flipped her around, Harriet landing with a thud into the deep mattress, her arm flying akimbo and sweeping across the nightstand — sending the little shrine scattering to the floor.

Including Pug.

The moment the back of her hand hit the dog, she knew what was about to happen. Roxley was already busy nuzzling her neck and all Harriet could do was cry out, "Oh, no! No!"

Roxley looked up, for it was hardly the reaction he'd been expecting, but at the sound of the crash, the crack and tinkle of china being shattered, they both stilled.

"Oh, no, indeed," he said, looking at the empty nightstand. "I think you've broken Pug."

Harriet whirled around. "No! No! No!"

Roxley leaned over the edge of the bed. "Oh, yes, he's good and smashed. Well done."

His relief only lent to Harriet's panic.

"This is a bad omen," she told him.

"A bad omen?" He laughed. "Now you sound like Aunt Oriel."

"It must be a bad omen," she told him. "Your aunts have guarded Pug ever since your mother died."

And then they both paused.

Ever since your mother died.

In unison, they leaned farther over the side of the bed and peered down at the mess of broken china.

"Perhaps not the omen you thought,"

Roxley said, picking carefully through the shards.

"Not?"

Roxley's fingers brushed against a velvet pouch and he caught hold of it by the strings and drew it up out of the ruins. When he gave it a heft, it made a distinctive rustle, the sound of stones nestling together.

They both looked at each other in amazement. Could it be?

Roxley opened the bag and, without any hesitation, upended the contents onto the tousled sheets.

And out came a shower of diamonds.

EPILOGUE

Have you ever wondered why a star falls from the sky, Miss Darby? I believe it is envy — for it looks down from the heavens, sees us together and realizes that such love is only found between two perfectly suited souls. It is envy that entices them to leave the heavens. Envy of us.

Lt. Throckmorten to Miss Darby,
on the occasion of their wedding night
*from Miss Darby and the Curse of the
Pharaoh's Diamond*

London, three months later

"There," Roxley said, as they got out of their carriage in front of the house on Hill Street. "That business is concluded."

"I am ever so glad," Lady Roxley replied, smiling up at him.

"That" being the sale of the diamonds. Mr. Eliason, London's premier diamond merchant had been more than happy to buy the entire lot, which Roxley and Harriet had agreed was for the best.

"You don't regret not keeping one of them?" he asked.

Harriet shook her head. Vehemently. Neither of them wanted a single one of the stones in their possession, and had ignored Aunt Essex's badgering that a solitary diamond necklace wasn't too much to set aside.

Hadn't these diamonds done enough already?

"Well, I fear the money won't be ours for long," he told her as he tucked her hand into the crook of his arm and led her up the steps. "Mr. Murray's attorney will be waiting for us and the diamonds will barely cover what I owe."

"But we'll have Foxgrove and Marshom Court," Harriet reminded him.

"Aunt Essex has Foxgrove, as she will remind you," Roxley teased. "And luckily for us, Aunt Eleanor made it back to Bath in time."

Mrs. Nevitt had been most resourceful at keeping Lord Tarvis at bay for the few days Lady Eleanor had been missing. Even going so far as to call one of the less reputable doctors in town and bribing the man to give

the pushy lord dire reports of Lady Eleanor's condition.

It had been to Lord Tarvis's great dismay
when Lady Eleanor had turned back up in
Bath social circles in the pink of health and
looking like she'd live to be a hundred.

"My lord," Fiske intoned, opening the
door for them. "There is a certain person to
see you."

Fiske regarded anyone not in the nobility
as not truly worth His Lordship's notice,
but there were times . . .

"Yes, yes," Roxley told him. "The lawyer."
He turned to Harriet. "Shall we?"

"You want me there?"

He nodded. "Together. Just as we promised at our wedding."

And wedding night, Harriet mused.

Mr. Murray's lawyer did not appear
amused to have been kept waiting, but even
less so to find that Lady Roxley would be
present for the meeting. "Most unusual, my
lord," he complained as he pulled out the
papers from his valise.

"Yes, well, I am an eccentric," Roxley told
him, winking at Harriet.

She did her best not to laugh.

"Hmm. If you say so, my lord. Allow me
to conclude our business. I was instructed
to give you this." The man handed Roxley a

folded piece of paper that was sealed with a thick piece of wax.

Roxley, uncertain what to do, looked back at the attorney, who nodded for him to open it.

"Mr. Murray ordered me to give that to you, and you alone, in the event of his untimely demise." The attorney's brow furrowed, for it was apparent he found the entire situation distasteful.

Besides, one of his best clients had been murdered. It was bad business all around.

Roxley broke the seal and began to read. As he did his eyes widened and then his mouth opened. When he finished, he gaped at the note for a moment more before handing it to Harriet.

Harriet took the thick paper in her hands and before long, she too was gaping.

Dear Lord Roxley,

My life has been spent in the solitary pursuit of profit. And now, as I know my end is near, I realize it has gained me nothing but misery.

Sometime ago, Mereworth — our mutual acquaintance — discovered some matters of which I am not proud. I will be honest: I lied and cheated at times to gain advantages. He used his knowledge of these dealings to force my presence into your life. I should have refused.

I should have been more like you.

Your deep and noble desire to right the wrongs around you has haunted me these past weeks. I was not strong enough to stop him. I pray you have.

In return for your forbearance, your noble example, I forgive all the debts I hold in your name. All of them. I expect no repayment. Since I have no heirs to speak of and my ill-gotten gains are mine to dispense, I am free in this to do as I desire. And so I forgive you your obligations, if you can forgive me.

Your obedient servant,
Aloysius Murray

"Is this true?" Roxley asked the lawyer.

The fellow was already gathering up his papers. "Yes." He sounded neither happy nor thrilled by this turn of events. Then he handed over the rest of the papers. All Roxley's debts — satisfied. He bowed and left.

"Poor fellow," Roxley said after the door closed behind him.

"Why is that?" Harriet asked.

"I suppose he was hoping for a long and expensive legal struggle. This tidy and neatly handled matter must be a bitter pill."

Harriet laughed, and then got up and wound her arms around Roxley, giving him a kiss. "We are saved!"

He caught up Harriet and carried her toward his desk. "I beg to differ."

"You do?" Her eyes alight.

"Yes," he told her most gravely. "I am saved, but you, my dearest, darling Harry, are not."

"I'm not?" Her arms wound tighter around him.

"No. You," he whispered, "I fear, are about to suffer another very grievous inkwell injury." And with that, he deposited her on his desk.

And the injury was most grievous.

Indeed.

AUTHOR'S NOTE

The Affair of the Queen's Necklace is an infamous chapter in French history that some claim was the beginning of the end for Marie Antoinette. The theft of the spectacular diamond necklace was conceived by Jeanne de la Motte, a con artist and court hanger-on, who convinced the Cardinal de Rohan to purchase the necklace as a way to curry the queen's favor. When the diamond necklace was given to Jeanne to take to Her Majesty, she and her husband instead broke up the necklace and the comte headed to London, where the diamonds were sold.

When the Paris jewelers began to demand payment and the cardinal realized he'd been swindled, the entire scheme came tumbling down upon Jeanne de la Motte, who was tried, convicted and horsewhipped. She later escaped from prison and joined her husband in London. She died under mysterious circumstances after a "fall" from a window.

After researching the actual historical event, I knew I had to use it as the plot device for Roxley and Harriet's story, adding the infamous card game in Calais. Who's to say that the comte didn't gamble a bit on his way to London. And who's to say Jeanne de la Motte's accidental fall wasn't an encounter with Lord Mereworth?

On another matter, you may find the references to the Miss Darby novels familiar; this is because the author, Rebecca Tate, was the heroine of one of my earlier novels. I so adored creating the fictional Darby series that I hated not to use them again. As I began to write the Rhymes with Love series, I saw a chance to make them Harriet's favorite novels and therefore have liberally quoted from them herein.

You can find Rebecca's story, and read more excerpts from Miss Darby, in *It Takes a Hero.*

All my best to you. I hope you have enjoyed Roxley and Harriet's story.

Best wishes,
Elizabeth

P.S. If you are wondering who is the mysterious lady Crispin, Viscount Dale married, as mentioned early in this story, please read my e-novella, *Have You Any Rogues?*

The employees of Thorndike Press hope you have enjoyed this Large Print book. All our Thorndike, Wheeler, and Kennebec Large Print titles are designed for easy reading, and all our books are made to last. Other Thorndike Press Large Print books are available at your library, through selected bookstores, or directly from us.

For information about titles, please call:
  (800) 223-1244

or visit our Web site at:
  http://gale.cengage.com/thorndike

To share your comments, please write:
Publisher
Thorndike Press
10 Water St., Suite 310
Waterville, ME 04901